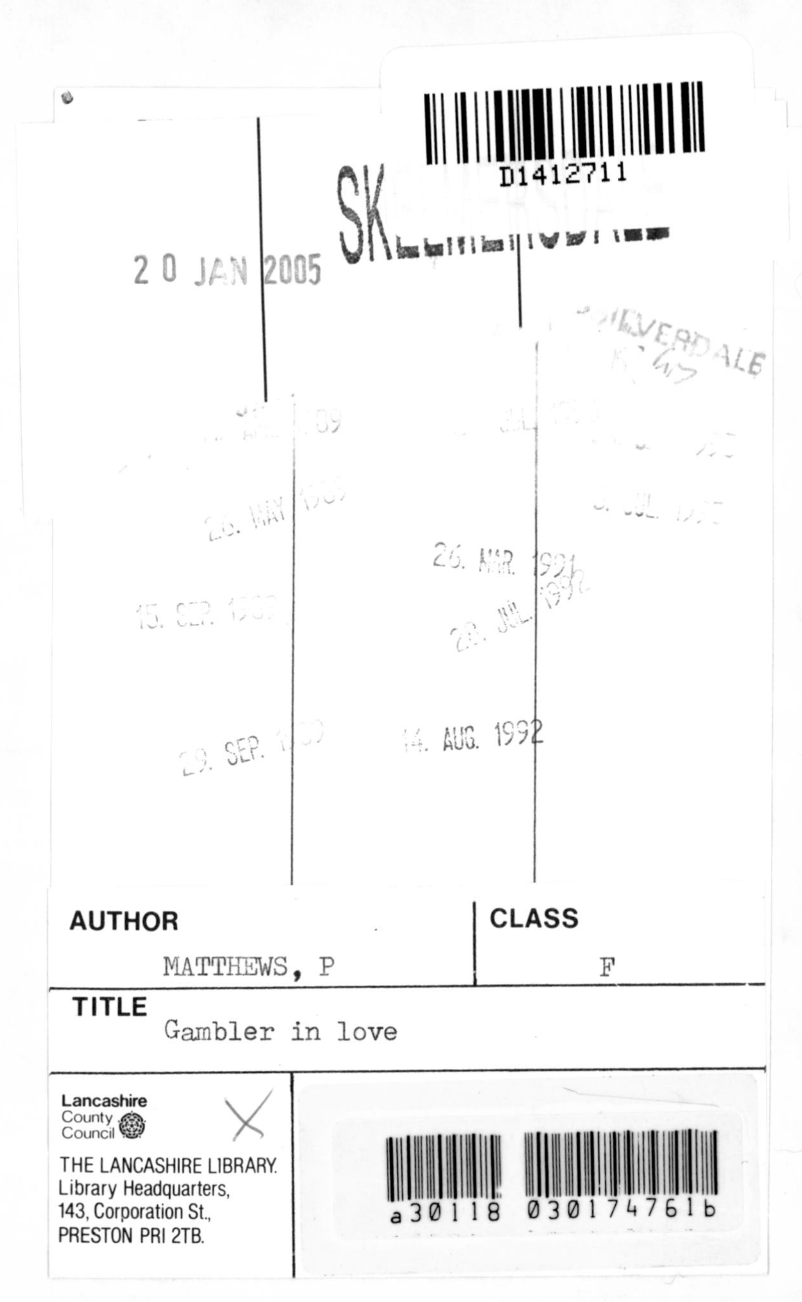

Gambler in Love

By the same author

FLAMES OF GLORY
LOVE'S BOLD JOURNEY
LOVE'S SWEET AGONY
DANCER OF DREAMS
EMPIRE (with Clayton Matthews)

Gambler in Love

Patricia Matthews

C

CENTURY PUBLISHING
LONDON

First published in Great Britain in 1985 by
Corgi Books
This hardcover edition published in 1985 by
Century Publishing Co. Ltd, Portland House,
12–13 Greek Street, London W1V 5LE

ISBN 0 7126 0875 3

Published by arrangement with Bantam Books, Inc.

Reprinted in Great Britain by
Photobooks (Bristol) Ltd

To my favorite hero, my husband,
Clayton Matthews

AUTHOR'S NOTE: Men and women who worked on the many canals in the United States were known as canallers, but there was a special breed on the Erie Canal who called themselves canawlers. They were Irish, they were vagabonds, a breed apart, hard drinking, hard fighting, and hard working, with a contempt for the land-bound, living out their lives like gypsies on their canal boats, having as little as possible to do with people other than their own. They were, in the main, canal freighters, and to them other canal people were simply canallers. Thus, the two different spellings in this book: canallers and canawlers.

The Henry Wells mentioned in Chapter 22 was, a number of years later, cofounder of the famous Wells Fargo Company.

Chapter One

THE air rising from the turgid waters of the Erie Canal was cold and damp, and Catherine Carnahan shivered and hunched her shoulders inside her worn, plaid mackinaw.

The fog had begun creeping in with the dusk, and now it surrounded the canal boat like a thick wall of gray cotton batting, so that she could barely see her hand upon the tiller. The towpath was completely obscured, and only the muffled clop of the mules' hooves on the hard, beaten earth and the movement of *Carnahan's Cat* let her know that they, and Timmie Watkins, the hoggee, were there up ahead doing their job.

The lanterns in the bow were not visible from where she manned the tiller. Canal boats were not supposed to move at night in a fog as thick as this; but it would be foolhardy to moor here, in the Side-Cut, for this area was an infamous caldron of crime, violence, and debauchery. Within an area the size of two city blocks there were twenty-nine saloons, frequented by criminals of every degree of depravity. People said of the Cut that it witnessed several hundred fights a day, and a body a week in the canal; and although the hard cases usually left the canawlers alone, occasionally one was drunk enough, or crazy enough, to attack one of the slow-moving canal boats.

Cat muttered an oath under her breath. But for Mick,

they would have been through the Cut in the daylight hours, and now would be safely moored much nearer Albany, having a hot meal. She should have kept a closer watch on her father, should have noticed that he was getting that jumpy, nervous look that always preceded a drinking bout.

However, she had not noticed, and Mick had simply disappeared from the dock while she and Timmie were getting the *Cat* ready to embark, and had not appeared again until this morning, mindless with drink. If the times had not been so hard, it would not have been so bad; but as it was the lost hours had to be made up, and that was why they dared not stop for the night. They had a delivery date for their cargo of flour; and if that date was missed, they would have to pay a forfeit—so much off their haulage fee for every day they were late.

For a moment Cat thought bitterly of her father, Mick Carnahan, snoring drunkenly in his bunk below; but then, not being given to crying over spilled milk, she turned her attention back to trying to penetrate the fog. After all, she was not having it as bad as poor Timmie, who was having to walk all these miles behind the slow-moving mules; at least she could ride in relative comfort. There were times when a hoggee could ride one of the mules, but not on a night such as this, when he had no visible contact with the *Cat*.

Faintly, through the muffling curtain of fog, Cat heard the sound of a tinny piano and the braying of raucous, drunken laughter. The sounds caused her to shiver again. If any of the seedy denizens of the Cut knew that *Carnahan's Cat* was passing the Cut, and that it was manned only by a girl of twenty-two, with a boy of nineteen behind the mules, the temptation of easy pickings might be too much to resist.

Of course, those unfamiliar with the *Cat* might not realize that it was a girl at the tiller of the canal boat, for Cat was wearing a man's trousers, boots, and mackinaw, and her long, straight brown hair was tucked up under a man's wool cap.

Only a close inspection in good light would reveal the delicate features of the woman she was. Her face was rather narrow, with lively blue eyes, a small nose, and a generous mouth. Still, from a distance the illusion was protective enough, for Cat was a tall, rather broad-shouldered girl, with a rangy look about her that, in men's clothing, gave the illusion of boyish awkwardness.

The other canawlers, many of whom had known her since her birth, of course knew her sex, but they were a close-mouthed lot who seldom spoke to the landsmen unless necessary; and even if they had, they would not have thought to mention Cat, for they were, as a rule, people who admired a certain amount of unconventionality and accepted it as natural.

Despite the damp cold and her apprehension, Cat felt herself beginning to doze. It seemed to her that she could not remember the last time she had slept, and her body cried out for rest.

And then she heard a sound that jerked her fully awake. Lifting her head, she heard it again—the grunt of a man's voice, and the sound of scuffling. She strained her eyes against the fog, but could see nothing.

Tensing with apprehension, she called softly, "Timmie?" There was no reply. Had something happened to him? Had he been attacked? It had been known to happen along the Cut, although it was common knowledge that a hoggee had nothing of value to steal.

She called again, a bit louder, "Timmie?"

The movement of the boat had slackened slightly, and in a moment the drifting boat nudged the bank; and Timmie, a short, stocky youth with a mop of fiery red hair, emerged suddenly out of the fog.

"Some'un is being attacked by thugs, I think, Miss Catherine. All I could see was that there was a bit of a melee going on. Looks like three fellers beating on a fourth!"

Cat hesitated, torn between conflicting emotions. She felt sympathy for the victim, but on the other hand there were many victims of violence every night along this stretch of the canal. It was foolish of the man, whoever he was, to place himself in this predicament, and it would be equally foolish of her to come to his rescue. She could easily come to harm herself; sympathy could be expensive in the Side-Cut.

With a sigh she reached for the Colt in the holster fastened to the stern beside the tiller. She hated guns, but she had doggedly forced herself to learn how to use one, for most of the ruffians along the canal understood nothing but force.

"Stop the mules, Timmie," she said softly.

As the mules were drawn to a full stop, and the boat nudged against the bank, she clambered over the side and onto the footpath.

Timmie gaped at the Colt. "Miss Catherine, you're not going to . . ."

"Foolish of me, I know, but I can't bring myself to let some poor soul be beaten to death without at least trying to help him."

"Then I'll come with you. . . ."

"No!" she said firmly. "You stay with the mules. Someone might steal them, if left alone. You know mules are valuable. I'll be all right." She hefted the Colt. "I know how to use this."

Cocking the gun, she advanced in the direction of the sounds, and heard a groan of pain. Abruptly, a puff of wind from behind her blew a rent in the fog, and she saw four figures. One was on the ground, and three other men were bent over him. One of the assailants had a short club in his hands; and even as Cat watched, he brought it down on the prone figure with a sickening crunch.

Gripping the Colt tightly in both hands, Cat raised it. "Hold it right there, gents!" she said, pointing the gun at the nearest man.

The three men, dirty, tattered, and reeling from strong drink, froze in their tracks.

Cat motioned with the gun. "Now, I suggest that you three back off real slow, and then git. That is, unless one of you craves to have a new belly button!"

The men stared at her with blurred faces, uncertain how to cope with this new development. Then one of them said with a sneer, "Hell, mates, it's only a lad." He took a step forward.

Cat snapped, "I meant what I said, gents! I know how to use this gun, and I have no qualms about using it on water rats like you. Now go on, git! Git!" To add emphasis to her threat, she fired a bullet into the ground at their feet.

The three derelicts began to back away, until the fog hid their forms; and then Cat heard the pounding of their feet fading away toward the Cut.

She waited for a moment to be certain they were gone, then slowly advanced toward the figure on the ground, finally leaning down over him. The man was youngish, apparently in his early thirties, but his face was too beaten and bloody for her to be certain.

However, he was well dressed, and Cat shook her head. Foolish, plain foolish. Everyone knew that folks of means did not go poking around the Side-Cut at night. What could he have been thinking of?

She whirled quickly as she heard footsteps behind her, but it was only Timmie, his face pale. "I couldn't wait any longer, Miss Catherine. I thought you might be . . ." He broke off to gaze down at the man at their feet. "Lordy, Miss Catherine! That poor feller 'pears to be in sorry shape."

She said urgently, "Help me get him onto the *Cat* before someone comes along."

"But, Miss Catherine," he said dubiously, "do you think that's wise? Maybe we should ask Cap first. . . ."

"My father's too liquored up to be asked about anything," she snapped. "Now help me."

The man on the ground was tall and large, but they managed finally to get him on board the boat, by half-dragging and half-carrying him, with Timmie carrying him under the shoulders and Cat lifting his feet.

When they had him stretched out on the deck by the tiller, Cat turned to Timmie. "Go back to the mules, Timmie, and get us under way. We have to hurry and get out of here before I can look to his hurts."

The term *hurry* was something of a misnomer, since the best speed a canal boat could make was two to four miles per hour. But a half-hour later, Cat estimated that they were far enough from the Cut to risk mooring up against the bank, so she could look to the stranger's wounds.

When they were tied up, Cat and Timmie hauled the man below and stretched him out on the spare bunk in her father's cabin. Mick Carnahan, on his own bunk, snored lustily through it all. When the stranger was settled in, Cat sent Timmie topside with a warning to keep a sharp eye out.

"You think it safe to leave you alone with him, Miss Catherine?"

"For God's sake, Timmie," she said tartly, "in his condition he couldn't harm a kitten. Now above with you, you lummox."

Cat went into the galley, stirred up the fire in the wood stove, and heated some water. With a pan of hot water and a washcloth, she returned to the stranger and gently washed the blood from his battered face. There was a large, pulpy lump on the back of his head; and as she sponged it, the man on the bunk groaned, stirring, but did not rouse.

When his face was cleansed, Cat saw that he was handsome in a rugged way. He had high cheekbones, a prominent nose, and a wide, well-shaped mouth. She ascertained that no teeth had been knocked loose. There were several cuts on his face, but none too deep or severe, although there was a bruise turning purple at the corner of his right eye. She hesitated about removing his clothes to look for further wounds; not from shyness, but to save him embarrassment if he became conscious and discovered she had undressed him. There would be time enough for that when he came to. She did remove his boots, not without some difficulty.

She went to the medicine chest in the galley, took out a bottle of medication, and returned to dab at the cuts on his face. The sting of the medication finally brought him back to consciousness. His eyes, a deep brown, fluttered open and focused on her dazedly.

He muttered, "Wha-at? Who are you, sir?"

With one motion she removed the cap, releasing a fall of fine, straight brown hair.

Surprise flickered in his eyes. "A girl! I'll be damned. My apologies, ma'am." He tried to raise his head to look around. "Where am I?"

"You are on the *Cat*, sir, a canal boat belonging to my father and I. Don't you remember what happened to you?"

He frowned, then winced, his hand coming up to feel the bump on his head. "I can't . . . seem to remember anything."

"I can't say I'm surprised. You have a nasty lump there. Three ruffians were attacking you, off the towpath. One had a cudgel. I think you're all right, except for cuts and bruises. I could find a doctor for you, but the nearest one is miles down the canal. My name is Catherine Carnahan, by the way."

"I am . . ." He frowned again, a look of bewilderment sweeping his face. "I don't know *who* I am! I can't even remember my name."

She nodded in sympathy. "A stout blow will do that. I'm sure you'll be all right tomorrow. Right now, the best thing for you to do is rest and sleep. Do you think you can get undressed by yourself, or should I help you?"

"Oh, I'm sure I can manage that all right," he said hastily.

"Fine, then. I'll be just outside the cabin. If you do need help, call out."

Cat left the cabin and stood by the rail just outside, within hearing distance. She should be getting under way again as soon as possible. All this foolishness had caused more time lost. Curse Mick anyway! If it were not for his drinking, all this would not have happened. It was hard to love him at times like this, hard to remember how he had been in the old days, before the tragedy. For years now she had been operating the canal boat almost by herself.

His heavy drinking had begun after her mother died. Cat had been only twelve when it happened, and it was hard to remember too much about the woman who had been her mother, just a few faint memories of a soft, pretty face, and gentle, loving arms. Her death had been a shattering tragedy; she had fallen into the canal and drowned. Mick Carnahan had been drunk at the time, and he had always blamed himself for her death. But guilt, instead of causing him to stop drinking, had only made him drink more; nowadays he was scorned by most of the canawlers; but Cat's stubborn pride always made her bristle in his defense. It was only when she was alone with him that she scolded him.

She sighed heavily. His failing had not been so bad in other years; in the daytime at least he was usually sober enough to help on the boat; and if they occasionally had to tie up for a day or a night, until he sobered up, it was no great catastrophe. But this year, 1832, was different. The country was in the grip of the first great depression it had ever suffered. Prior to the depression, the canal boats had been busy day and night, with all the business they could handle. Now a lost day *was* a disaster, and Cat could not afford to hire another man to help on the boat. . . .

She stirred, remembering the man in the cabin. She had been gone for some time; he should be undressed and settled down into the bunk by now.

As she turned toward the cabin again, Cat saw Timmie on the towpath and called to him, "Bed the mules down,

Timmie, and bed down yourself. We won't travel any farther tonight, but get an early start in the morning."

In the cabin she found her father still snoring, and the stranger was also asleep under a blanket. She hung the man's clothes neatly on hooks beside the bunk, and looked at them until her curiosity got the better of her. Quickly she went through the coat, trousers, and vest, but the only thing she found was a gold watch, with a long chain in the vest pocket. There was no wallet, no coins in the pockets, and no papers of identification. Evidently his pockets had been rifled before she had come to his rescue, but the ruffians had missed the watch.

Rubbing her fingers idly over the watch case, she felt a series of indentations on the back. Turning away from the bunk, she struck a match and quickly read the letters engraved on the back of the watch: MORGAN KANE.

She had to consider the fact that the man on the bunk was a thief, that he had stolen the watch. Anyone abroad at night in the Side-Cut had to be either a fool or a criminal.

She returned the watch to his vest, then made her way forward to her own tiny cabin. She was bone weary, having been at the tiller of the *Cat* since dawn of the day before.

Despite her weariness, Cat did not go to sleep at once. The face of Morgan Kane, if that was his name, swam behind her closed eyelids. She had never paid much attention to boys, or men, for she had all she could do to keep the canal boat operating; and besides, most of the unmarried men along the Erie were rowdies, or worse, and held no attraction for her.

But thinking of the stranger in her father's cabin quickened her pulse, and she realized that she was attracted to him, and that would never do. For all she knew, he was some kind of criminal, like the rest of the inhabitants of the Cut. Besides, she did not have time to be interested in men in a romantic way.

Angry at herself, she tossed and turned for a time before she finally drifted off to sleep.

She was awakened by a knock on her cabin door and Timmie's voice: "Miss Catherine, are you all right? It's time we were under way."

She sat up with a start and saw that the sun was shining in through the tiny window. It was long after her usual getting-up time. She called out, "I'm all right, Timmie. Hook up the mules, and I'll be right up."

She jumped out of the bunk and quickly threw on her clothes. By the time she reached the deck, Timmie had the mules harnessed and on the towpath. Taking her place at the tiller, Cat gave the order to get under way. The animals strained in the traces, and the *Cat* began to move.

It was a spring morning, and there was a chill in the air. Patches of last night's fog still hovered in the lowlands, but soon it began to burn off.

Cat gazed around the boat; she was proud of the *Cat*, from the tow mast in the bow, set four feet high above the deck, high enough to keep the towlines from fouling, yet not high enough to snag under a low bridge, all the way back to the sweep in the stern. The *Cat* was seventy-two feet long by fourteen feet wide, and could easily carry sixty tons of cargo in the holds. Cat was especially proud of the fact that the *Cat* was a decked boat, with the cargo hold in the stern, and the smaller living quarters and stable for the mules in the bow. Many cargo boats had open holds, fitted with deck cloths for foul weather. The living quarters and the cargo hold rose two feet above the main deck, with narrow windows providing light and ventilation below.

Stretching, Cat felt content. She loved life on the canal. It gave her a sense of freedom she could never feel on land, and she never tired of the ever-changing panorama of the Erie. No matter how many times she traveled the canal—and she had been born on the *Cat*—every trip was different: the changing seasons painted different colors along the canal banks, and the canal boats they met were always different; here another cargo boat, riding low in the water with a full load; there, a passenger boat, with people riding on top of the cabins, waving and calling to her as they drew abreast. . . .

A husky voice growled behind her, "What's that feller doing in my cabin, daughter?"

Cat turned about to face her father. Mick Carnahan was about fifty-five, but the drink had added years to his appearance—hair a dirty white; blurry gray eyes shot with red; capillaries broken and purple across his big nose and cheeks; body bloated and soft. Cat could remember when he had stood tall and proud, when he could do the work of two men, when he could work from dawn until dusk and take her mother dancing that night.

"He was attacked by thugs as we were passing through the Cut."

"That doesn't explain how he got into my cabin."

"I went to his aid, ran the thugs off with my pistol."

He gaped at her in astonishment. "Saints save us! Are you out of your mind, girl? How many times have I warned you against going ashore in the Cut, most especially at night?"

She shrugged. "If I hadn't gone to his aid, he would likely be dead now. As it is, the poor man can't remember his own name."

"That's all well and good, Catherine, but it wasn't your place to do it." He shook her shoulder roughly. "You could have come to great harm."

"Who else was to do it? You?" she said caustically. "You were dead to the world, Mick."

He flushed, his glance dropping away. "It's sorry I am for that, but that doesn't excuse you taking such a great risk, and for a stranger at that."

"You wouldn't have left the man to die," she said in a gentler voice. "You know you wouldn't. Now, why don't you go below and make us all some breakfast?"

He nodded dumbly and started to turn away. "Catherine . . ." He faced around again. "I know I'm a sorry excuse for a father, but I do love you. You're all I have left in this world."

"I know you do, Papa," she said softly, "and I love you, too. Now go below."

As she watched her father shuffle below, Cat blinked back tears. She did love him. Most of the time he was a gentle, loving man; and even when drunk, he was not a mean person, just ineffectual and useless.

That was not quite true, she thought with a slight smile. Unless he was too drunk to function, he was a good cook, and he made their meals with a great deal of grumbling about its being "women's work."

Cat was an indifferent cook, and would much rather be at the tiller of the *Cat* than in the tiny galley below. Her father often scolded her for that. "How will you ever snag a husband, girl, if you don't know how to cook?"

"If a man won't marry me because I can't cook, I don't want him for a husband."

She turned back to the tiller as two more canal boats came toward the *Cat*. Both were larger than was the custom, with high sides, and were painted in bright colors. Many canal-boat owners never bothered to paint their craft at all.

As the oncoming boats drew abreast, Cat saw the reason for the bright colors—they were circus boats. A banner stretched across the top of the cabin of the lead boat: BLANTON BROTHERS CIRCUS!

Why would anyone want to leave the canal, except to transact business? Everything needed in life could be found here—showboats, medicine shows, dentists and doctors, saloons and dancers, dining boats, even church services.

A hesitant cough sounded behind Cat. "Good morning, miss."

Cat turned to look at the stranger. He was pale and wan, the bandages she had used on his head stained with blood.

"Are you the young lady who rescued me? I seem to

remember some angel of mercy hovering over me last night, but I'm not sure it wasn't just a dream." He smiled with an obvious effort.

Cat smiled. "I'm the one. How do you feel this morning, Mr. Kane?"

"I'm not sure yet, Miss . . ." He frowned. "I seem to remember you introduced yourself last night, but I . . ."

"Catherine Carnahan, but everybody calls me Cat."

"Well, about your question: I'm not sure just how I feel. I'm sore all over, and my head . . ." He gingerly touched the bump on his head, and winced.

"So far as I know there isn't a doctor in the Cut, but I certainly wasn't going to look for one there last night, at any rate. We'll be coming into a town a few miles farther along. Maybe you should see a doctor there. I did the best I could for you, yet I know little about doctoring."

"We'll see how I feel then." He gave her a puzzled look. "You called me Mr. Kane. How did you know my name? I didn't even know it myself last night."

Cat felt herself flushing with embarrassment. "Since you didn't seem to recall anything, I went through your pockets, looking for identification. All I found was a watch, but it had your name engraved on it. That *is* your watch, and your name, isn't it?"

He hesitated for a moment, looking off, before saying slowly, "To be truthful, I'm not sure. But I suppose it must be, don't you?"

"If you don't know, how should I, sir?" she said with a shrug.

He started to speak, then broke off as his attention was caught by something across the canal. Cat turned to look and saw another canal boat coming toward them, almost abreast.

It was a dingy-looking craft. The original paint had long ago flaked away, and it had not been painted since. Two men stood in the stern. The man at the tiller was big and bulky, well over six feet, with long black hair and a full beard; he was dressed in work clothes. The man standing beside him was quite well dressed; in fact, he struck Cat as something of a dandy.

The man at the tiller was shaking his fist and shouting abuse at his hoggee on the towpath. His voice carried across the way: "Shake those damned mules up, you lazy lout! I want to get there sometime before Christmas!"

Now the big man turned his head and saw Cat staring at him. He bared his teeth and shook his fist at her as well. "What are you staring at, you damned female! Tend to your own affairs, and I'll tend to mine!"

Cat did not bother to answer, but neither did she look away. They locked stares across the narrow stretch of water between them, until the well-dressed man prodded the big man in the ribs and spoke urgently to him. The man at the tiller snapped his head back around, and saw that, in his inattention, his boat was veering away. With a foul curse he threw himself against the tiller in a desperate effort to correct his error.

Cat laughed in glee, letting her laughter carry. Then the two boats were moving apart, yet not so fast that the big man's string of curses could not still be heard.

Morgan Kane said, "Who *is* that?"

"That, Mr. Kane, is the scourge of the Erie," Cat said in a dry voice. "At least he thinks he is, and in some ways he's right. His name is Simon Maphis. Canawlers are a rough lot, but he is about as unscrupulous as they come. He is capable of any underhanded shenanigans to get what he wants. As I'm sure you know, we're in the middle of a depression right now. Business is very bad along the canal, and we all have to scratch for business. Simon Maphis underbids everybody for cargo, and he tromps over anybody competing with him. It has been rumored that he has killed canawlers, and that he has, more than once, scuttled other boats so he could fulfill their contracts."

Morgan looked at her curiously. "Isn't there any law along the canal?"

"Very little, as long as we don't cause trouble with

landsmen. They pretty much leave us alone, and whatever we do among ourselves is our responsibility."

"It strikes me as a strange life for a woman."

She said seriously, "It's not so bad. Most canawlers are not like Maphis. Some of the men may fight among themselves, drink and carouse, but in the main we're hard working, and we leave each other alone. Unfortunately, there are exceptions." She sighed. "Like Simon Maphis."

"He seems to know you. I somehow got the impression that he doesn't like you at all."

She laughed curtly. "You may say that. He found me alone on the *Cat* once, and . . ." She hesitated, feeling her face flush, and did not finish the sentence. "I managed to defend myself. The word got around, and he became the laughingstock of the Erie. He doesn't take well to being laughed at."

The unpleasant incident was vivid in Cat's memory, and probably always would be.

It had taken place eighteen months ago, two weeks short of her twenty-first birthday. They had just unloaded a cargo of grain, and were tied up to the canal bank for a few days of deserved rest. Cat was alone on the boat; her father had gone to the nearest tavern, and Timmie was visiting an uncle in the town.

Cat welcomed the chance to be alone for a bit. She was bent on giving her tiny cabin a fresh coat of paint. She had spent the morning scraping the old paint off onto an old blanket spread on the floor. The cabin, even with the door and small windows open, was sweltering. To seek some relief, Cat wore a pair of man's trousers, cut off at mid-thigh, a man's shirt with the tails out, with only two buttons fastened across her unfettered breasts, and she was in her bare feet. Since they were moored in a deserted side-cut off the main canal, she thought nothing of going on deck to empty the old blanket of paint scrapings in her skimpy costume.

She was just beginning to paint the cabin bulkhead

when she felt the boat quiver a little, then heard the tread of heavy footsteps overhead. She paused, listening, hoping that Timmie had not somehow decided to return early. It would hardly do for him to see her dressed like this—she had known for some time that he was mooning over her. But the footsteps were too heavy to be Timmie's; it had to be her father. Reassured, she continued to paint.

Cat loved to paint; there was something rhythmic, almost mindless in the strokes of the brush. Once she got involved in it, her concentration on it was total, freeing her mind temporarily from all worries. She seized every opportunity to paint the *Cat,* often enlisting Timmie's help in doing the exterior. In contrast to many canal boats along the Erie, the *Cat* was always spick-and-span; and her father, naturally, received compliments on its appearance, when in fact he had not held a paintbrush in years.

Consequently, she gave a great start, and whirled about with a cry of alarm, when a strange voice spoke from the doorway of the cabin: "Cat, ain't it? Ain't that what they call you?"

The man in the doorway was huge, filling it completely. His heavy black beard, black greasy hair, leering smile, and cold black eyes lent him a sinister appearance.

He advanced a step into the cabin. "Saw you out on the deck, girlie. Always before you been all bundled up in them men's clothes. Didn't realize how pretty you was. It's a shame, covering up them pretty limbs and all like that, now ain't it?"

His gaze was hot on her half-exposed breasts. Involuntarily, Cat brought up one arm in an attempt to hide her breasts. She knew suddenly what was in his mind, and her thoughts searched frantically for a means of escape. She could not run past him out the door, and the cabin was much too small to allow her much room to maneuver; and she knew it would be useless to scream for help.

The man looked somewhat familiar, but Cat could not put a name to him. To stall for time, trying to keep her voice steady, she said, "You have the advantage of me, sir. You know my name, but I do not know yours."

"I'm Simon Maphis, owner of the *King*. That's me, King of the Erie." He grinned wolfishly and took two steps into the cabin, swaggering. "And if you're thinking that knowing my name will save you, forget it. Who's to do anything? That drunken sot of a father of yours? That snot-nose hoggee?"

She assumed a puzzled expression. "Save me? Save me from what, sir?"

Simon Maphis laughed harshly. "You're not stupid, girl. You know what I'm after, and I'm not leaving until I get it. Simon Maphis always gets what he wants." He took another step. "You can take it easy or you can take it rough, whichever way you see fit. Me, I like my women either way. From what I hear, you're a fiery little bitch. It's about time you were tamed, and Simon Maphis is the feller who can do it."

He moved slowly, warily, and then he was so close that she could smell his body odor—the rank smell of an animal long caged and unwashed. She still had the paint bucket in her left hand, the brush in her right. She did not flinch one inch from where she stood, and neither did she scream.

This lack of fear evidently surprised Maphis a little, for he stopped, within arm's reach, and then he started to grin. "The easy way then? That's smart, girlie. Shows you got sense."

He took another short step toward her, and Cat brought up the paint bucket with all her strength, smashing it into his groin. Maphis yowled with agony. As he started to bend over, clutching at himself, she swiped the paintbrush once across his face, then again the other way, leaving two broad, yellow stripes.

Maphis half-turned, moaning; bent over, still clutching at himself, he moved like a wounded animal toward the cabin door. Cat followed, right on his heels. She kept dipping the brush into the pail, swabbing paint over him with every step.

When they finally reached the deck, she was still behind him, still splashing paint over him.

And then, to make Maphis's humiliation complete, two canawlers chose that moment to stroll along the towpath. They stopped, mouths agape, at the sight. One of them suddenly guffawed, nudging the other. "You know who that is, Ned? By God, that's Simon Maphis, the King of the Erie himself!" He raised his voice. "What happened, Cat? You tryin' to paint the King in his true colors?"

Maphis did his best to ignore them. Still in great pain, he climbed over the edge of the *Cat* and onto the towpath.

Cat called up to the two men, "The bastard tried to rape me!"

The men's laughter died, and they stared at Maphis in stern judgment. "That's a foul thing to do, Maphis," one of them said. "You know that Cat is one of us. Why don't you save that kind of behavior for the girls in the Cut?"

Maphis still ignored them. Straightening up with a grimace of pain, he glared down at Cat malevolently. "You'll live to rue this day, girl. Nobody makes a fool out of Simon Maphis."

One of the men laughed again. "Seems to me she just *did*, Maphis. You'd better get along with you, before she decides to use the rest of the paint on you."

Maphis swung his glare on the men, and they fell silent, shifting their feet nervously. Maphis turned on his heel and walked away up the towpath, taking each step with care.

"Are you all right, Miss Catherine?" one man asked. "Did he harm you?"

Staring after Maphis, she said tightly, "I'm all right. Thank you for your concern, sir."

"That's a mean thing to do," the other man said. "Simon oughtn't to be allowed to get away with it. Should we scout up a constable?"

"No!" she said sharply, whirling on them. "We canawlers

take care of our own, isn't that the way of it? Besides, raising a fuss would only make it worse. Sooner 'tis forgotten, the better."

"Only one thing wrong with that. Simon Maphis is a mean'un, a grudge-bearing man. Like he said, he ain't likely to forget it easily."

"I can take care of myself," she said firmly. "As you've just seen."

She turned away to reenter her cabin, and heard them begin to laugh again, as one said, "Did you see that paint on Simon's face? By God, if this ain't a grand tale for telling! Simon Maphis bested by a slip of a girl, and painted yellow for his trouble. Oh, my!"

Cat knew that it was indeed a tale that would spread along the Erie as fast as a raging flood; Simon Maphis would be the butt of jokes for a long time to come. She wished fervently that the incident had been unobserved. Worst of all, she knew that she would have to tell Mick. He was bound to hear about it sooner or later, and there was no telling what foolishness he might try if he got enough drink in him.

She had just enough paint left in the can to finish the cabin, and was cleaned up by the time Mick and Timmie returned. Her father was stumbling drunk. She decided to wait until the next morning to tell him about it.

His face grew red with outrage as she related what had happened; and when she had concluded, he was up and pacing the deck. Big fists doubled, he roared, "By all the saints above, I'll beat the sculpin into a bloody pulp!"

"You'll do no such thing," she said sharply. "It would accomplish nothing, only make it worse. And you're no match for Simon Maphis, Mick. He'd tear you into little pieces and throw the pieces into the canal."

He gaped at her. "You mean I'm to do nothing? The villain tries to despoil me only daughter, and I'm to do nothing?"

"That's just what I do mean. He didn't despoil me, he only tried."

"But, Catherine, at least I should get the law on him. I agree that I'm no match for him," he said in a more subdued voice. "Not the pitiable excuse for a man I am nowadays."

"The law! They would do nothing," she said scornfully. "You know their opinion of canal folk. They would probably think I deserved anything that happened to me!"

"And maybe they would be right," he muttered, looking away.

"What did you say?"

He looked her full in the face. "A girl like you shouldn't be working the canal. You should be living in a fine home, wearing decent clothes, not my castoffs. You should be married to some upstanding boyo, having my grandchildren."

She sighed in exasperation. "Mick, we've thrashed this out I don't know how many times. I don't want a fine home or decent clothes, or to be married to some 'upstanding boyo.' I'm happy right where I am, doing what I am, and I intend to stay here." She took on a firmer tone. "Now that's the end of it. I wanted you to hear it from me first. We'll talk no more of it."

And that had been the end of it, except for the rare times when the *Cat* crossed Maphis's path and she received the benefit of his baleful glare. The story of her encounter with him had gone up and down the Erie, and Maphis had been a laughingstock for a time; but like all such tales it had eventually been forgotten, just as her father had conveniently forgotten the episode, as though it had never happened.

However, Cat knew that Simon Maphis had not forgotten it; and she had vowed to herself that she would never be caught alone with him.

She told none of this to Morgan Kane, of course. She simply said, "We carefully avoid each other. The only times we see each other are passing along the canal, like today."

"Are there many other girls like you, working the canal boats, I mean?"

"Not too many, I suppose. Most canawlers are men who live on their boats, sometimes with wives and children." She stared at him curiously. "Tell me something, Mr. Kane. . . . A moment ago you said you weren't sure that was your name. Are you saying you still remember nothing, who you are, why you were wandering around in the Cut last night, or even why you were attacked?"

"From what you told me about this place called the Side-Cut, the answer to the last is obvious, I should think. The object of the attack was robbery. As for the rest . . ." He hesitated, looking off, and then said slowly, "I'm afraid the answer is no, Miss Carnahan. I remember nothing of my past. I do not even know for sure who I am."

Chapter Two

MICK Carnahan, busy in the galley, was unhappy. In the first place, he was badly hung over. He had a blinding headache, his mouth tasted foul, and he was assailed by waves of dizziness from time to time, as the odors of frying ham and eggs wafted up to his nostrils. His stomach rebelled at the odor of the food; the last thing he wanted right now was to eat; he would have given his soul—if he had one left, he thought sourly—for a drink. But he well knew that there was no liquor on board the *Cat*.

His daughter had set her foot down about that. "There will be no liquor on board the boat, Mick. I can't stop you from drinking while on land, but I absolutely forbid it on the *Cat*. Anytime I find any, it goes over the side."

Mick knew he would have to wait until they tied up for the night, would have to suffer through the long day; but that was not the real source of his unhappiness; he was accustomed to that.

The main reason for his bad mood was the presence of the stranger Cat had taken on board last night, and from the Side-Cut, no less! Maybe he was the victim of an attack by thugs, and again maybe he was not. His injury could just as well have come about through a falling-out among thieves. True, he wore clothes several cuts above those worn by the majority of the inhabitants of the Cut;

on the other hand, he could have stolen the clothing. Cat had more gumption than was good for her.

Mick had many regrets about his misspent life, especially the years since the untimely death of Katey; but his daughter was not one of them. She was the only thing he loved in this life, and he was damned proud of her. He would rather have seen her living like the lady she should be; yet he was secretly proud of the way she had taken hold of the canal boat, although he bickered with her about it from time to time. She ran it better than most men could have. Lord knew they were fortunate enough that *somebody* could, or they would have long since floundered. These last years he simply had not been capable.

Mick was well aware of his many failings, but despite his numerous resolutions to straighten out his life, in his heart of hearts he knew that he never would. He was too weak. Once, he had been a proud man, proud of the three loves of his life—*Carnahan's Cat;* his wife, Katey; and his daughter, Catherine.

He had come to the Erie relatively late, and by a strange route. A good portion of the canawlers were Irish, and many of them had originally helped to construct the Erie Canal; but Mick had not been a common laborer; in fact, he had been a gentleman of sorts, a schoolteacher by trade. However, there was a streak of the fiddlefoot in him, and the life of a schoolteacher had begun to pall on him after Catherine was born. Mick had a little money saved, and he had heard there was more to be made along the Erie. If a man had a sound boat and a stout pair of mules, he could make his fortune.

He had put the question to Katey, from whom Catherine had gotten much of her spirit and love of adventure; and she had been willing to take a chance. The early years had been good. Mick drank very little then, and he had been more than able to hold his own with the hard-working, free-wheeling canawlers. They had been doing well, and then tragedy had struck; Katey had come to an unpleasant death, a death for which Mick held himself at least partially responsible. He had been off helling around some tavern, and Katey, foolish Katey, had never learned how to swim. Hanging wash on the line that stretched across the cabin, she had lost her footing and fallen. Catherine had been up the canal, visiting, and the only witness had been an old woman on an adjoining boat.

It was a terrible shock to Mick, one from which he never fully recovered. In his more sober moments he knew that it must have been an awful shock to Catherine as well, yet she had managed to survive and grow up into a sweet, levelheaded girl. For those first few years after Katey's death, Mick swore to himself again and again that he would sell the boat and return to the land—at that time he could have gotten a job teaching again—but the drink and sheer inertia had stayed his hand; and now it was far too late.

There was one thing he could be grateful for. With his background as a schoolmaster, he had the ability to instruct Catherine, and that much he had insisted on. Under his tutelage she was as well schooled, if not better than, most girls her age. It was true that she sometimes spoke as crudely and sounded as illiterate as any canawler, but that was her own choosing, not from upbringing. . . .

The breakfasts were cooked. Mick piled plates of ham and eggs and toasted bread high on two wooden trays, and carried them outside—it was their custom to eat on deck in fair weather while the *Cat* was in motion. He set one tray down before Cat at the tiller and the stranger by her side, then motioned to Timmie up ahead. Timmie dropped back to take the tray, letting the mules tend themselves for a few minutes as he gulped a mug of coffee and made a thick sandwich of ham and hard-fried eggs. Mick noticed that the lad shot many a curious glance at the stranger, and guessed that Timmie was worried about Catherine's feelings for the man. The stranger was a good-looking chap, that much Mick had to admit; and it had been obvious for some time that the young hoggee had yearnings of his own concerning Catherine.

And then Timmie was gone, back to the mules; and Mick leaned against the cabin, while Cat and the stranger began to eat. All Mick had was a mug of thick, black coffee.

"Aren't you having any breakfast, Mick?" Cat asked.

Shuddering inwardly, he lied, "I had a bite while fixing yours, daughter."

Cat indicated the stranger. "This is Morgan Kane, Mick. This is my father, Mick Carnahan, Mr. Kane."

"How do you do, sir?"

Morgan Kane extended his hand, and Mick shook it, somewhat unwillingly.

Cat said, "Mick, Mr. Kane still hasn't regained his memory after the beating last night. He doesn't remember a thing of his past."

"It's sorry I am to hear that, Mr. Kane. We'll be going through the locks along the canal a ways. There's a doctor there. I'm after thinking you'd better have him look you over."

"He has no money, Mick, and no memory of what he does for a living. We can't just leave him there."

Mick said warily, "What did you have in mind, girl?"

"I thought maybe he could travel along with us for a spell, until he regains his memory. We were just talking about that before you came up. He'd be willing to work for his room and board."

"Would he now? His idea, is it?" Mick said acidly.

"No, as a matter of fact it was mine. We need another man. We need a poler, you know that, and a man for the loading and unloading. You've been handling those chores yourself, and you know that your . . . uh, health isn't always up to it." Her glance dared him to disagree.

Mick felt heat rush to his face. "But do you think that's a good idea, Catherine? You said he doesn't even know what his trade is, if any."

She motioned scornfully. "What's to know about canalling? All that's needed is a strong back for loading and unloading, and sense enough to pole the *Cat* away from the bank, if it gets too close. No offense, Mr. Kane."

"None taken," he said in a dry voice.

"Catherine . . ." Mick said. "Can we talk in private for a minute?"

"No, we can't!" she said sharply. "You're not going to talk me out of it. We need another hand on the boat. I can't handle the tiller and a pole at the same time. It's a wonder we haven't wrecked the *Cat* already."

Mick said desperately, "But he's a complete stranger. We don't know a thing about the lad."

Morgan said, "Maybe you should talk it over."

"No, you sit still!" Cat snapped, without looking at him, her gaze intent on her father. "Mick, I've made up my mind. Aside from the fact that we need somebody, and God knows he's offering to work cheap enough, it wouldn't be humane to let him go his own way in his condition, not even knowing who or what he is."

"It's me boat," Mick muttered.

"And I run it," she said defiantly. "That may sound cruel, Mick, but you know it's true. We would have gone out of business long ago but for me. Can you deny that?"

Mick's ire was up, and he longed to strike her. But she was right and he knew it. With an angry shake of his head, he turned on his heel, moved across the cabin, and jumped onto the bank to join Timmie and the mules.

With a feeling of sadness, Cat watched her father walk away. She rarely talked to him in such a manner; but he was especially irritating this morning. She was also somewhat mystified at her own behavior, coming to the defense of a man she knew absolutely nothing about.

As if divining the direction of her thoughts, Morgan said, "I'm sorry if I've caused a row between you and your father. Maybe it would be best if I just left when we reach the next town."

Her annoyance increased, and she said crossly, "And do

what? It's been decided. You'll stay with us until your memory returns, until you're able to manage on your own. As for Mick . . ." She waved her hand holding the fork. "It's nothing new. We're at odds most of the time. And just so you'll know, not that you wouldn't find out sooner or later, Mick drinks. To put it bluntly, he's a sot. I love him dearly, but I'm not blind to his faults. I can never depend on him. He won't stay angry long, anyway; he never does. Generally, Mick is sweet-natured, and so . . . so damned likable." She choked up for a moment, close to tears. "That's what's so blasted infuriating, how nice he can be when he wants to be!"

They fell silent for a moment, finishing their breakfasts. Then Morgan chuckled softly. Cat shot him an irritated glance. "What do you find so humorous, sir?"

"Oh . . . I just remembered an old Chinese proverb. It goes something like this: If you save a man's life, you're forever after responsible for that person."

"Well, you can be damned sure that I'm not going to be forever responsible for you. When you're well enough, you can be on your way, and good riddance!"

"Then I'll have to get well soon, won't I?" He began to smile, his look suddenly bold. "On the other hand, I can't see all the hurry."

She was flustered by his scrutiny. "Just what does that mean?"

He continued to look at her, head cocked to one side. "You know, Cat, you'd be real pretty, take you out of those clothes, clean you up a bit, and put you in a dress. But then, do you even *own* a dress?"

"That, sir, is none of your affair!"

"You're right, it isn't. My apologies, Miss Carnahan."

There was an impudent twist to his full lips, and a roguish twinkle in his eyes, that gave the lie to his words of apology.

At a loss for words, Cat turned her face resolutely forward. She called out angrily, "Timmie, snap the whip at those mules! We'll never get anywhere at this rate!"

In a moment her answer was the pistollike crack of Timmie's whip, followed by a second, and their speed increased fractionally.

Her anger appeased, Cat said, "There's one thing clear about you, Mr. Kane."

"And what is that, Miss Carnahan?"

"You're a man of education—your cultured manner of speaking, and quoting Chinese proverbs."

Morgan laughed softly. "I'm not sure whether I should take that as a compliment or not. From my rather short acquaintance with them, it strikes me that canal folk have little regard for education."

Cat rounded on him. "That's not true! Mick was a schoolmaster before he came on the canal."

"That does surprise me a bit. But I did notice that you can speak well when you choose to do so."

Somewhat mollified, she said, "Mick taught me himself before he . . . Well, I have as good an education as most, perhaps better than many landsmen."

"What did you start to say? Before he became a toper?"

She flushed, started a hot retort, then changed her mind. For some reason she found herself telling Morgan about the death of her mother, and how her father blamed himself.

Morgan nodded soberly. "I can see how that might change a man. But it seems to me that it makes it rather rough on you."

She shrugged. "I don't mind, most of the time. I like life on the Erie. It's the best life there is, in my opinion."

"I can see how it might have its attractions. But I also have a feeling that you are an exception. I mean, I'm sure that an educated person is a rarity along the canals."

"That is true," she admitted reluctantly. "An education isn't necessary on the Erie. You don't need to read or write. An ability to do your sums is a help, but most canawlers are little educated."

"Canawler? What kind of word is that, pray?"

"A canawler is an Erie canaller, a special breed. Most of us call ourselves canawlers, at any rate."

"But why not just canaller? Why the *w* in there?"

"I don't really know." Cat had never given much thought to the origin of the word. "It's peculiar to the Erie. On all other canals, they are called only canallers. But, as I said, most of us here consider ourselves a breed apart. We're clannish, distrustful of the land-bound. Canawlers on the Erie are a rough lot." She laughed suddenly. "I do recall an explanation I heard once, I don't know who said it. Probably someone who doesn't like us. Whoever it was said that the word came from canal brawlers. It could be true, I suppose. . . ."

"Hello, the boat!"

Cat looked up at the towpath. A man and a woman were striding along, trying to keep pace with the *Cat*. The man was tall, with a stern, forbidding countenance, and was dressed all in black. He looked to be in his fifties, and further study revealed to Cat that the woman was a girl really, younger than she. She was pretty, with blond hair in ringlets under a bonnet; she wore a long gray dress and held the skirt up out of the dirt with one hand, while the other held a parasol over her head to shield her face from the sun.

The man spoke again: "Gentlemen, do you happen to know the whereabouts of a canal boat called the *Saving Grace*? I am the Reverend Luther Pryor, and this is my daughter, Lotte."

Cat said, "The *Grace* is tied up back down the canal. I passed her yesterday, on the other side of the Cut."

The Reverend Mr. Pryor squinted down at her, scowling in a puzzled manner. "Is that the notorious Side-Cut?"

"That's the place, Reverend Pryor."

"Inhabited by harlots, drunkards, and sinners," he intoned.

"Among others," she said dryly.

The reverend drew himself up. "A place where Satan

dwells," he said in pulpit tones. "I have received the call to come among them to save souls."

"You'll not be the first," she muttered.

"I beg your pardon, sir?"

She raised her voice. "I wish you good luck, sir. Many others have come and failed." On a mischievous impulse she tugged off her cap, letting her hair fall free.

The Reverend Mr. Pryor recoiled with a gasp. "A woman, running a canal boat! Living and working among the sinners. God would not approve, young lady."

"Perhaps that is so, Reverend Pryor," she said coolly. "But I'll wager that my morals are as uncorrupted as any lady's on land."

"Come along, my dear," the reverend said, turning his daughter about, and they proceeded back the other way. But not before Lotte Pryor had time to send a shy glance at Morgan Kane by Cat's side.

Cat was laughing as her boat moved on along the canal.

Morgan was smiling also, but he said reprovingly, "I think you shocked the reverend, Cat."

"Perhaps he needed shocking. He's going to receive several shocks if he tries to convert the people of the Cut. It's been tried time and again, without success. And I noticed"—she gave him a glance out of mischievous eyes—"that you seemed to catch his daughter's eye, Mr. Kane."

He waved a hand and said airily, "Oh, I expect that's because the bandage on my head caught her attention."

"Oh, I don't know. You're handsome enough to catch a lady's eye." Now why on earth had she blurted out such a statement? She was appalled, and knew that she was blushing furiously.

He said amusedly, "Do you really think so, Miss Carnahan?"

"It doesn't matter what I think," she said curtly. "If you intend to work on the *Cat*, it's time you made yourself useful. We're coming into the locks. The waterway narrows here until we're through the locks, so you'll have to keep a watchful eye out, and pole us away from the banks if we get too close."

"You'd ask that of a man in my condition?" he said mockingly.

"Oh! I'm sorry, I forgot," she said in some confusion. "I just didn't think . . ."

Her father's voice cut in: "I'll do it, Catherine. Mr. Kane is right, we shouldn't be after asking something that strenuous of him just yet." Mick was standing above them on the cabin top.

Without looking at either of them she said crossly, "Just so one of you does it, I don't care who."

As his boat left the *Cat* astern, Simon Maphis twisted his head about and stared balefully after it. His gorge always rose when he heard the name Cat Carnahan or happened to catch a glimpse of her. He would never forget the humiliation he had suffered at her hands that day eighteen months ago; no slip of a girl could best Simon Maphis without living to regret it!

Unfortunately, the right opportunity to avenge himself had not yet presented itself, and he dared not make the opportunity. Those two gawkers on the towpath that day had heard his threat; and if anything happened to Cat Carnahan, and there was the slightest chance that Simon Maphis had anything to do with it, they would come haring after him. The canawlers might not be too law-abiding, but they were quick to retaliate when one of their own was treated in a manner they deemed unfair.

But someday, Maphis swore to himself, his big hands tightening on the sweep handle, I will get even with the bitch. The thought brought a lascivious grin to his lips as he imagined the scene of his revenge.

"Mr. Maphis?"

Maphis started, looking at the man by his side. "Sorry, Mr. Brawley. Reckon I was woolgathering there."

Tate Brawley grinned unpleasantly, his glance going back to the *Cat*, now dwindling in the distance. "The fellow on the boat we just passed . . . Strikes me you don't like him very well, and it appears that the feeling is mutual."

Maphis grunted and spat over the side. "That's no fellow, that's a damned female wearing men's clothing. A shameless hussy," he said righteously. "The likes of her should be chased off the Erie."

"A woman?" Brawley said in astonishment. "Running a canal boat?"

"Yeah. A hell of a thing, if you ask me."

Brawley was a tall, slender man of about forty, wearing expensive clothing, including a stovepipe hat. He had muttonchop whiskers, and a nervous habit of combing the right side with his fingertips. He was affable enough, but no smile ever seemed to reach his watchful gray eyes.

Maphis was no fool; he knew a slicker when he saw one, and this gent was slicker than most. But that did not bother Maphis; he had done business with slickers before, and none had gotten the best of him yet.

Brawley had ridden up to the *King* at the last town, riding a fine horse, introduced himself, and asked permission to board the boat. "I have a business proposition for you, sir."

Maphis's eyes had brightened. "Any profit in it for me?"

"A goodly profit, Mr. Maphis."

"Then hop aboard and ride a spell with me."

Now Brawley was speaking. "This proposition I mentioned . . . A new canal is being proposed over in Pennsylvania. A lottery has been organized to raise funds. . . ."

"If you're selling lottery tickets," Maphis grumbled, "you can get off my boat right now. Simon Maphis ain't fool enough to risk hard-earned money on lottery tickets! Besides, lottery-ticket salesmen all along the Erie are thick as fleas on a dog."

"Oh, my dear fellow, I'm not a lottery-ticket salesman," Brawley said in his slickest manner. "I'm running the lottery, and I am recruiting salesmen. That is why I approached you. Who would make a better salesman than a man spending his life on the Erie? And who better to know the value of a canal lottery ticket than a canaller? You will earn twenty-five percent commission on every ticket you sell."

Maphis squinted at him shrewdly. "You say you're running the lottery?"

Brawley nodded. "That is correct, Mr. Maphis. I have been empowered by the sovereign state of Pennsylvania to conduct the lottery outside the state."

"You know that the state of New York has made the sale of canal lottery tickets against the law?"

Brawley shrugged. "That need not concern us, now should it? The canal is to be constructed in Pennsylvania, not New York."

"Just where in Pennsylvania? And what is the name of this planned canal?"

"The Lower Allegheny Canal," Brawley said quickly, too quickly.

Maphis grinned over at him. "There ain't any such canal, is there, friend? There is none proposed, nor is there ever likely to be. This Lower Allegheny Canal project is all right in your head, now ain't it?"

Brawley hesitated for just a moment, then smiled slowly. "Right, Mr. Maphis. Is it a deal?"

He held out his hand, and Maphis said, "Forty percent instead of twenty-five?"

Brawley laughed outright. "Forty it is. You're a man after my own heart, Maphis."

"We're in business, Brawley."

Maphis now accepted the outstretched hand, and they laughed together heartily.

Chapter Three

DESPITE the slump in business along the Erie, there were several canal boats lined up at the locks, and *Carnahan's Cat* had to take its place at the end of the line. Passing through the locks was a slow procedure. As they waited, Cat sent Timmie up ahead to pay the lockmaster his fee.

To Morgan she said, "As I told you, Mr. Kane, there's a doctor here. You have time for a quick visit and can still catch us by the time we get through the locks."

"I don't think so," he said. "I'm feeling much better. I imagine I'll be black and blue and sore for a few days, but I'm sure that's the extent of it."

"Suit yourself," she said with a shrug. "I know you haven't any money, but I'll loan you the dollar to pay the doctor for an examination."

His eyes probed hers. "Just when I think you're . . ." He broke off with his slow smile. "No, thanks, Cat, not that I don't appreciate the offer."

Finally, it was their turn through the locks. With Mick fending the boat away from the sides after the first gate was opened, the *Cat* nudged into the narrow space, which was only a few feet wider than the boat. Cat noticed Morgan watching with interest as the gate behind was swung back and locked in place. Then the front gate was opened, and the water level in the lock elevated until it reached the level of the canal on the other side.

The mules strained in their traces, and the *Cat* emerged from the lock and proceeded on its way. Looking back, Morgan murmured, "Interesting. Are there many locks on the Erie?"

"A large number, eighty-two altogether," Cat replied. "As we travel westward, the land raises quite a bit, and the locks are a means of raising us gradually."

"And coming back this way, you're lowered to accommodate lower water levels." At her nod, he added, "Like a series of stairsteps."

"I guess I'd never thought of it in quite that way, but that's pretty much how it works. Don't you know *anything* about canals?"

"It seems that I don't know much about anything," he said. "Of course, I suppose I could even have worked on canals in some capacity, in my former life, so to speak, but I have no way of knowing. However, I doubt it. After all, I know how to do simple things like eating, so if I worked around canals, it should come back to me quite naturally."

"Wearing those clothes, I hardly think you had anything to do with canal life," she said. "I've certainly never seen a canawler dressed like you are."

"I could have stolen these clothes, you know." At her start of surprise, he smiled grimly. "I was sure that thought had passed through your mind."

"They're such a good fit it hardly seems likely that you stole them."

"Oh?" He cocked an eyebrow and smoothed a hand down over his shirtfront. "You really think I look good in them, do you?"

Flushing, she snapped, "I didn't say that! You men are so vain about your clothes."

"I always thought it was the ladies who were vain."

"That's a male canard, foisted off on us by men."

"Touché, Miss Carnahan." He bowed mockingly.

"Catherine?" a voice called.

"Yes, Mick?"

"There's the *Paradise*." Mick, coming back from the bow, motioned forward and to his right. "She's tied up in that cut up ahead. I thought Samuel might be somewhere around here. It'll soon be dark; why don't we spend the night here? I wouldn't mind eating food not my own cooking for a change, and listening to some fiddlin' and singin'."

Cat stared at him hard. "You sure you don't have it in mind to fill your gut with liquor?"

Coloring, he held up his hands. "By my sainted mother, that wasn't on my mind. How about it, daughter, if I promise to stay sober?"

"Hah! Much good your promises are." She sent a glance at the horizon up ahead, to the sun about to set. "All right, it is late, and I was at the tiller most of last night. I could stand a bit of relaxation."

"Dandy, dandy!" Mick clapped his hands. "I'll tell Timmie to tow us into the cut, and help him take the mules in."

Mick watched for his chance and leaped across onto the towpath.

Morgan said, "What is the *Paradise*?"

"It's a sort of floating restaurant, with entertainment and a bar." She made a face. "I can just see Mick staying away from that. But at least it's not a low dive, like most land taverns along the canal. Samuel O'Hara is a giant of a man, but gentle as a pussycat, unless you get him riled up. He keeps things quiet and orderly, but he has a shillelagh behind the bar, and he lays about him with a will when a ruckus starts. The lowlifes know that, and are wary of his place." She glanced at Morgan sidelong, suddenly and strangely shy. "They even have dancing."

He looked surprised. "Dancing? You can . . ." He bit off the words, then said casually, "You're going, I suppose?"

"Of course. They serve very good food. And I have to keep an eye on Mick. He watches himself when I'm along. Most of the places he frequents I wouldn't dare go inside."

"You're going like that?" He motioned to her garb.

Cat flared, "I do have dresses, Mr. Kane! As hard as that may be for you to believe!"

"No insult intended." He bowed his head. "My apologies, ma'am."

Cat refused to speak or to look at him again, devoting her attention to the *Cat*, as her father and Timmie turned the mules down the towpath running along the side-cut until they tied off almost nose to nose with the *Paradise*. Cat noted that several other boats were anchored along the cut—Samuel O'Hara would do a good business this night.

"You're welcome to accompany us this evening, Mr. Kane."

"I have no money, you know that."

"I will pay for your supper," she said crossly. "Nobody who works for the Carnahans starves, sir!"

"Then I accept your kind invitation." He gave her a half-bow.

Cat locked the sweep in place, then went across the top of the cabin and down below.

Morgan looked after her, bemused. She intrigued him mightily—she was half-hoyden and half-woman. She was highly intelligent, no doubt about that, and she also had a blazing temper. She was as prickly as a thorn bush, and half the time he longed to slap her; but the rest of the time he wanted to kiss her, to stop her sharp tongue with his mouth on hers. He had a powerful curiosity to see what she looked like dressed as a woman should be. His feeling was that she would be damned attractive!

He went forward, watching with interest as Mick and Timmie stretched a plank between the *Cat* and the towpath, then herded the mules on board and into a small stable in the bow of the boat.

Astonished, Morgan said to Mick, "You keep the animals on board?"

Mick nodded. "Many canal boats do that, lad. Mules and horses go at a premium along the canals, and we'd have to be keeping guard over them if left on land, to keep some sneaking sculpin from making off with them. Also, there's no graze for them on the towpath. And exercise ain't a problem." He laughed heartily, then sobered, looking at Morgan intently. "How you feeling, laddy buck?"

"Not too bad, Mick, considering. I think I'll survive."

"Decided to stay with us for a spell then, have you?"

"If it's all right with you."

"We need another hand, Catherine's right about that." He coughed, gazing off in some embarrassment. "Catherine's a fine woman, Mr. Kane. Sharp of tongue and suchlike, but she means well. Don't know how I would have managed without her. I ain't . . . uh, been well for some time now. The thing is, she's led a sheltered life, strange as that may strike you, strange to the ways of canawlers as you are. On the canal we don't have much truck with landsmen."

"So she told me, Mick," Morgan said gravely. "Are you trying to warn me about something?"

Mick cleared his throat and coughed. "Maybe. The thing is, the lass knows naught about the ways of men."

Morgan was hard put to suppress a smile. "From what little I know of her, it seems to me that your daughter is quite capable of taking care of herself."

Mick nodded vigorously. "Oh, aye, she is that. But when it comes to . . ." He paused, then blurted, "I don't want the girl hurt! Do you catch my meaning?"

Morgan was now definitely amused, but also touched by the man's concern for his daughter. He said gravely, "I think you have little cause for worry, Mick. I don't even know for sure who I am, man! Any fears you have as to my hurting your daughter, you may put to rest. You have my word on that."

In her cabin Cat was studying the contents of her wardrobe, ruefully remembering her brave words to Morgan Kane. She had exactly two dresses to her name. One was an old garment of her mother's altered to fit her; the second was a dress that Mick had bought her almost a year ago for her birthday. She had worn it once, to please him; that had been the last time she had put on a dress. Left to her own devices, she would have gone to the *Paradise* in her usual garb—men's trousers and shirt. No one would be shocked, for canal people were accustomed to seeing her in men's clothing. In fact, they would be more likely to experience shock at seeing her in a dress!

But Morgan Kane had, in effect, flung down a challenge, she had accepted it, and she would be damned if she would back down!

Opening her clothes chest, Cat took out the dress that her father had given her and shook out the fabric. It was badly creased and wrinkled from the long storage, and the material smelled a bit musty. She would have to hang it out to air, and then press it if she could find where she had stored the sad iron that had belonged to her mother.

Holding the garment in front of her, Cat looked at herself in the cracked and crazed glass of her mirror. The dress was simply and modestly cut, but it was a beautiful color, a rich periwinkle blue, which became her.

She much resented the fact that she must air and press the dress; but she had brought it upon herself, and there was no help for it. Sighing, she began the task.

However, at dusk, when she was finished and stood again before the mirror, she could not deny a flush of pleasure. Occasions for dressing up along the Erie were rare, either for a man or a woman; and she had to admit that she was pleased with what she saw in the glass. Her blue eyes, aglow with candlelight, smiled back at her in the glass; and her brown hair, the tangles taken out with a good brushing, had a lustrous shine. She had twisted it and pinned it into a smooth coil atop her head, leaving a few tendrils in front of her ears; she had curled them with rags so that they made a soft frame for her face.

As a final touch, she took out the small chest that she always thought of as her "treasure chest" and removed the delicate pearl earrings that had once been her mother's. The girl in the glass made her feel shy and awkward, as if she were looking into the eyes of a stranger.

The fitted bodice of her dress showed a narrow waist, which accented the womanly fullness of her breasts, and the full skirt felt strange and somehow exciting against her legs. The fully puffed sleeves, which ended just above her elbows, were trimmed with lace tied with blue ribbon, as was the neckline, disguising her wide shoulders and giving her a look of delicacy.

It did not matter, of course, but she could not keep from wondering what Morgan would think of the new and different Cat. Would he find her pretty?

"Catherine," her father bellowed from above. "Are you going to stay down there all night? Mr. Kane and I are ready to go, and the hour grows late. Sure, and Samuel will have stopped serving supper if we don't go over soon."

"Coming, Mick," she called up.

Cat took a last look at herself, and then, with a deep breath, she climbed the short cabin steps and walked onto the deck. Feeling strangely shy, she stopped just outside the door, bracing herself against the immediate attention of her father and Morgan Kane.

Morgan let his breath go with a sigh. "You, Miss Carnahan, are indeed a beauty!"

Her father was staring, his mouth agape. "Sure, and you are indeed, Catherine," he said in a hushed voice. "I never realized, until just this very minute, how much you resemble my poor, dead Katey, when she was a young girl, all those long, lost years ago."

Morgan said, "Then you are indeed a fortunate man, Mick Carnahan, to have been blessed with two such beautiful ladies in one lifetime."

"I'm after thinking you are right, Mr. Kane."

Feeling her face burn, yet absurdly pleased, Cat said tartly, "Well? Didn't I hear you bellowing at me to hurry up, Mick?"

As if of two minds, the men arranged themselves on each side of her; Cat took their arms, and they went up the plank to the towpath. Her father was dressed in his only suit—at least ten years old. It was funereal black and usually worn to wakes and funerals. The seat and the elbows were shiny, and it hung loosely on his shrunken frame; yet he was dignified and handsome, except for the coarseness of his features, brought about by the drink. Morgan Kane had cleaned and brushed his suit, had shaved until his cheeks were pink, and had removed the bandage on his head. Both men smelled strongly but pleasantly of Mick's bay rum.

Swept by an impulse, Cat said, "I don't think a lady could have two more-handsome escorts." She squeezed their arms.

It was just dusk, a warm evening, and all the boats along the banks of the cut showed yellow lights. The *Paradise* had torches blazing on the bow and at the foot of the gangplank leading up to the deck. Everywhere she looked, Cat saw couples strolling arm in arm toward the boat. There was a festive air about the evening, as the people, dressed in their best, converged on the gaily lighted *Paradise*.

Cat said in a low voice to Morgan, "The *Paradise* is well known along the Erie. It's actually two boats. This one is totally given over to the restaurant. Samuel O'Hara and his wife, and his crew, live on a smaller boat behind. Even the kitchen is situated on the smaller boat. This was once a passenger packet until Samuel bought it, ripped everything out of the inside, and turned it into what it is today."

In the open doorway stood a huge, redheaded man with a jolly face, welcoming all comers. At the sight of Cat he reared back in feigned astonishment. "And who is this beautiful young creature visiting my poor boat? Some famous opera star stranded on the Erie? Or perhaps visiting royalty?" He made an elaborate, sweeping bow. "Welcome to my humble establishment, milady!"

Laughing, Cat said, "Samuel, you make me feel foolish. Now stop it!"

"What?" He peered at her closely. "But it is, it's our own Catherine Carnahan! Cat, I would never have known you."

"Damn you, Samuel O'Hara, that's enough!" Out of the corner of her eye she saw her father smiling, and Morgan laughing soundlessly. "Why such a big to-do about a girl wearing a dress once in a while?"

Immediately contrite, Samuel O'Hara sobered, and took her into his arms. "Welcome Cat. And forgive me for having my bit of fun with you. I wouldn't embarrass you for the world." He motioned grandly to a waiter hovering nearby. "To make amends, you shall have my best table, and the first drinks are on me."

The waiter escorted them inside. The interior was not on a grand scale, seating perhaps fifty people at a time, with room left for a small dancing area; but candle chandeliers dangled from the ceiling, splashing dazzling light over glittering silverware and china. The tablecloths were white, as spotless as everything else in sight. The waiter led them to a table for four situated on the edge of the dance floor.

After Morgan held a chair for Cat, and then sat down himself, he glanced around. "This reminds me of the ballrooms of the riverboat packets on the Mississippi. Not quite as lavish or as splendid, but certainly splendid enough." At Cat's sharp look, he took on a sheepish expression. "I don't remember when or how, but I just know that I have been on a riverboat at one time or another."

The waiter murmured, "What would the lady and the gentlemen like to drink?"

Mick brightened and said quickly, "I'll have a whiskey."

"You promised, Mick," Cat said.

"One whiskey can't hurt a man, Catherine."

"That's what you always say, but it's funny how one

drink leads to two and so on. All right then, one whiskey. And I'll have a glass of port. Mr. Kane?"

"I'll have a whiskey as well."

When the drinks were served, Morgan held up his glass. "May I propose a toast to Miss Catherine Carnahan, my rescuer, however reluctant she may have been."

Mick said, "I'll drink to that," and drank thirstily.

Morgan also drank, but Cat did not raise her glass.

Morgan glanced at it with an arched eyebrow. "It's perfectly proper for the recipient of a toast to drink, Cat."

"That's not the reason," she said sharply. "I think I resent the fact that you used the word *reluctant*."

Mick said reprovingly, "Now, Catherine, that is uncalled for. The lad was joshing, I'm thinking."

Morgan sighed elaborately. "My God, you *are* quick to take offense, Cat. Your father is right, I was being facetious. I know full well the risks that you took for an utter stranger, risks that many men would not have taken. I fully appreciate what you did. Now, shall I rephrase the toast? To Miss Catherine Carnahan, my most lovely rescuer."

"But I can't drink to that," Mick said comically. "My bloody glass is empty!"

Involuntarily, Cat exchanged glances with Morgan, and suddenly they were both laughing helplessly.

"I fail to see anything all that funny," Mick said, offended. "It's come to a poor pass when a grown man has to ask his own daughter for permission for one drink."

"One, Mick?" Cat got her laughter under control. "Order yourself another, for heaven's sake, and stop making it sound like you're so abused. You're far from abused."

"I can get my own, thank you." Mick got to his feet abruptly, scraping back his chair, and stormed off toward the bar at the far end of the room.

Cat opened her mouth to speak, then closed it, staring helplessly at his retreating back.

Morgan said in a low voice, "Shall I try to fetch him back, Cat?"

"No! That's the worst thing you could do. Saying no to Mick only goads him on. I can only pray that he will drink moderately tonight, since he got so drunk last night. He usually only drinks beyond his capacity once a week or so, and for that reason I know he's been suffering horribly all day." She looked at Morgan defensively. "My father is not a hopeless drunkard, I want you to understand that. He just gets these spells now and then when he remembers too much, and he has to drown the memories in drink. Besides . . ." Her laugh had a wry twist. "The Irish are notorious topers, didn't you know that?"

"I don't remember knowing many Irish."

"Then you certainly can't have been around the Erie much. It was built mainly by Irish labor. That's why so many of the canal people today are Irish: they stayed around after the Erie was finished, and became canawlers. You could even be part Irish yourself."

He shook his head. "No, I'm sure not."

"Why not?" she snapped. "You think the Irish are trash, like so many people do? Bogtrotters?"

He looked at her with a slow, amused smile. "I'm not going to debate the point with you. I've learned a bit about you, Catherine Carnahan. You deliberately provoke a man, I do believe, so he'll debate you."

"That's not true!" she said hotly. "You, sir, are a most exasperating man!"

His maddening smile remained in place, but he did not respond, since Mick chose that moment to return with his drink; and the waiter also appeared to take their food orders. The main item on the menu was beefsteak, and they all settled on that.

By now the room was almost two-thirds filled with customers. Out of the corner of her eye Cat noticed that the table on their right was now occupied by a man alone, an immaculately groomed man, nattily dressed, who seemed vaguely familiar. She looked more closely, just as the man glanced over at her. He had muttonchop whiskers and calculating gray eyes. Noting her glance, he smiled insinuatingly, a smile that did not reach his eyes, which remained flat and watchful; and his hand came up, long fingers absently combing his side whiskers. There was something about his manner that made Cat uneasy; she flushed, her glance dropping away.

She deliberately did not look at the man again, devoting her attention to the food. She was pleased to see that her father ate hungrily, which was always a good sign. When he intended to drink heavily, he usually ate very little.

By the time they had finished, two men, with a fiddle and a banjo, had mounted the small platform at the edge of the dancing area and begun tuning up their instruments.

In a few moments they struck up a tune, and the banjo player began to sing a rollicking song:

"Come listen to my story, ye landsmen, one and all,
And I'll sing to you the dangers of the raging Canal;
For I am one of many who expects a watery grave,
For I've been at the mercies of the winds and the waves.

I left Albany harbor about the break of day,
If right, I remember 'twas to second of May;
We trusted to our driver, altho' he was but small,
Yet he knew all the windings of that raging Canal."

After a few such verses Morgan leaned across to Cat and said behind his hand, "How long does this song go on?"

"Depends on how many verses he cares to sing," she replied with a laugh. "There're some fifteen in all."

"Speaking of the Irish, that melody has the sound of an Irish jig."

"Most of the canal songs you'll hear are nothing more than old Irish songs, with new words."

The pair on the platform sang other canal songs: "The E-R-I-E"; "Everybody Down"; and "The Ballad of John Mueller and the Lock Tender's Daughter."

Morgan whispered to Cat again, "John Mueller? That name doesn't sound Irish."

"I know. I didn't say we were *all* Irish, just most of us."

Finally, the fiddler stepped forward, clearing his throat for attention. "For those of you who'd like to dance, we'll now play a jig or two."

Morgan raised an eyebrow. "Sorry, Cat. I'm afraid I've never attempted an Irish jig."

Cat shrugged. "That's all right. I've never been fond of the jig myself."

"Well, the pair of you can sit there like lumps on a log. Me, I'm in the mood for a spot of fun," Mick said.

He got up and crossed down the room as the musicians started up a lively tune; and a moment later Cat saw her father on the floor, with a woman she recognized as the widow Shannon, who lived with her brother on a canal boat. Mary Shannon was about Mick's age, buxom, with red hair lightly sprinkled with gray and a plump, merry face.

Soon, booted feet stomped in rhythm to the lively music, and the boat rocked slightly from the pounding.

After two more jigs, the fiddler raised his voice: "And now a waltz for those of a more sedate nature."

Morgan leaned toward Cat and said gravely, "Will you honor me with this waltz, Miss Carnahan?"

Cat hesitated; she had little experience at dancing, but the prospect was tempting. After a brief hesitation she said, "I accept with pleasure, Mr. Kane, but I must warn you that I am not a very good dancer."

Morgan got up, bowed slightly, pulled back her chair, and held out his arm. Cat accepted it, and they moved onto the floor. There were only a few couples dancing now, since the jig was far more popular with canawlers than the waltz, for which Cat was grateful. She realized at once that Morgan was an excellent dancer, and this knowledge made her nervous, causing her to miss a step or two; but he was equal to the task, guiding her over the stumbles so expertly that Cat was certain that anyone watching them would not have known she had made a misstep.

And then they were gliding across the floor gracefully,

as smoothly as if they were soaring, sailing along a few inches off the floor. She had never enjoyed dancing more; and at the same time she was aware of the man leading her, every sense acute to his nearness—the male smell of him, the lithe grace of his movements, the strength of his hands holding her.

Her heartbeat quickened, her blood seemed to sing through her veins, and she could not remember ever feeling so alive, so much a woman. She was breathless when the music stopped, and her face was flushed and hot.

She whispered, "Thank you, Morgan. I enjoyed that very much indeed."

"Not half as much as I, Cat," he said with a slight dip of his head. "And you do yourself a grave injustice; you are a marvelous dancer."

Flustered, she said, "Not before tonight. So you must accept part of the credit."

"Gladly, ma'am, gladly."

Just before they reached their table, a man intercepted them. It was the well-dressed man Cat had briefly noted before.

Arm across his chest, the man bowed. "May I introduce myself, Miss Carnahan? I am Tate Brawley."

Cat looked at the man with suspicion. "How do you know my name, sir? I am not acquainted with you."

Tate Brawley grinned sardonically. "We have a mutual acquaintance, I believe. Simon Maphis."

"Simon Maphis!" Cat stiffened in anger. "The very sound of that man's name is an obscenity!"

Brawley looked slightly startled. "I knew you weren't the best of friends, but . . ."

"If you will excuse me, sir, I wish to return to my table." Cat started to brush past him.

Again Brawley stepped into her path. "May I have the pleasure of the next dance?"

"You may not! I refuse to dance with a friend of Simon Maphis."

"We are not exactly friends, my dear Miss Carnahan, merely business acquaintances. I still beg you for the next dance."

"And I refuse, sir. I am here with another gentleman, as you can see, and my father."

"I would like to meet your father, after we have our dance. It's possible we could do business together."

Cat looked at him levelly. "Just what business would that be, Mr. Brawley?"

Brawley's smile broadened. "I am the organizer of a new canal lottery, and I am recruiting ticket salesmen along the Erie. It can be a lucrative sideline, I assure you."

"And also a dishonest sideline," she said curtly. "Most canal lotteries are a swindle." Mick had been known to invest money they could not afford on lottery tickets, especially when he was drinking.

Brawley stiffened. "Are you intimating that I am a swindler, Miss Carnahan?"

"I'm not intimating anything, sir, but I would very much appreciate it if you would move aside so that I may join my party."

Morgan, who had been listening quietly, now stepped forward. "You heard what the lady said. I would suggest that you remove yourself, Mr. Brawley."

Brawley glared at him. "And just who are you?"

"Who I am is not important. I am asking you politely to step aside. If a polite request is not sufficient, I am prepared to remove you by force if necessary."

Brawley stared at him in a cold rage, his face reddening. "I am not accustomed to being addressed in such a manner."

"Perhaps if your manners would improve," Morgan said mildly, "it would not be necessary."

Brawley stroked his whiskers with the fingers of his right hand. Then abruptly he shrugged. "I dislike public brawls, so I will step aside. For now. But be assured, sir, that I will not forget this, whoever you are."

As Brawley started to turn away, Morgan called after him, "The name is Morgan Kane, sir, for future reference."

Cat unaccountably shivered. In a low voice she said, "I do not like that man, and I have a feeling that you have just made a mortal enemy, Morgan."

Unruffled, Morgan glanced at her, and for the first time she noticed that his eyes were cold and hard. "You may be right, Cat, but I'm sure that I have made other enemies in the past, and likely will again."

Chapter Four

MORGAN Kane had awakened that morning with full realization of who and what he was; however, he had deemed it prudent to keep this to himself for the time being, in view of the fact that his purpose along the Erie concerned the canal lotteries.

Lotteries had been popular in the United States for many years, and had been used by the clergy, colleges, patriotic societies, and even government administrations as a painless means of raising funds; and during the early years of the nineteenth century, when over fifty canals were constructed, or at least projected, a large number of them were financed in this manner.

Soon, state governments were granting lottery privileges to a great many concerns; Pennsylvania alone gave lottery privileges to fifty companies. Such companies were magnets for swindlers and confidence men, who rushed to them like filings. These swindlers rigged the lotteries and sold worthless stocks; and the most shameless of them simply kept all the money themselves. Millions of dollars were stolen by such men, and the lotteries soon became a national scandal.

One state that had not legalized the lotteries was New York; the Erie Canal and its various branches within the state had been financed by state appropriations. That did not mean, however, that lottery tickets for canals in other states, some legitimate and some not, were not sold along the Erie, for canal workers were a lucrative source for any kind of gambling; and the Erie was the busiest of the nation's canals.

And that was where Morgan Kane came into it. Morgan was uniquely qualified to look into the machinations of gambling enterprises. Born and raised on the Mississippi at Saint Louis, he had become a gambler on the flatboats and the packets of the river, and had made his living in such a manner. After eight years of this life, he had grown restless, left the river, and moved East, trying his hand at running poker games in New York City, and then moving on to Pennsylvania, where he worked as a lottery-ticket broker for a year with the now notorious Union Canal Lottery of Pennsylvania. The Union Canal Lottery Company was undoubtedly the richest and largest lottery concern doing business; it was reputed to have more than twelve hundred ticket brokers spread throughout the states of Pennsylvania, Ohio, New York, and various other eastern states; but Morgan found that he was not suited for the business. The competition was fierce—it was not unusual for him to encounter almost as many lottery-ticket brokers, and from his own company, in a particular town as customers. But it was not the competition he minded, cutthroat though it was; it was the fact that he decided that he was working for a firm of swindlers, and he quit in disgust. He was in Pittsburgh when he arrived at this decision, and by chance he had an uncle in Pittsburgh, his mother's brother, Sherman Morrison.

Morgan had always liked his uncle, who had visited the Morgans in Saint Louis often when Morgan was growing up. Morrison had gone into politics about the time Morgan had left home, and was now serving his fourth term in the Pennsylvania State Legislature.

Morgan had not seen the man during those ten years, but from newspaper stories he knew that Sherman Morrison had become a powerful figure in the state, in the legislature, the chairman of several important committees; and he had been mentioned often as a possible candidate for governor.

As it happened, the legislature was not in session, and his uncle was at home, living rather unpretentiously on the outskirts of Pittsburgh, the house a dingy gray from years of exposure to the smoking mills that often turned day into night.

Despite the fact that Morgan had not kept in touch, the older man appeared happy to see him. His uncle lived alone except for a housekeeper, who admitted Morgan, first to the house and then to his uncle's study.

When Morgan was ushered into his uncle's presence, Morrison got up from behind his desk, a portly, stern-visaged man in his sixties, and peered at his nephew over his spectacles. "Morgan!" He came toward Morgan with long strides. "Great God Almighty, it *is* you!" He threw his arms around his nephew in a fervent embrace, then stepped back to look at him. "I would not have recognized you, after all this time. I must say you've turned into a handsome, strapping lad."

"Hardly a lad, Uncle Sherman," Morgan said dryly. "I'll soon be thirty."

"Well, sit down, sit down! Martha," Morrison bellowed, "bring a bottle of the best sherry."

He stood beaming fondly down at Morgan as his nephew took the big chair before his desk. "When Martha first told me that I had a caller, I thought it might be one of my constituents. If they know I am here, away from the capital, they're liable to barge right in here with their complaints. Martha has instructions not to admit anyone without checking with me first, but she has a soft heart, and if they give her a hard-luck story, she's likely to herd them in here, weeping all the while. When she said your name, I couldn't believe it was you!"

Morgan looked around the book-lined room. "Where's Aunt Agatha?"

"She's passed on, didn't you know?" Morrison said

somberly. He went around his desk and sat down. "She died nigh onto three years ago. The influenza, it was. I'm all alone now. Your cousins, Beth and Henry, have left the nest. Henry is practicing law over in Harrisburg, and Beth is married to a fine man, and has borne me two fine grandchildren."

"I'm sorry about Aunt Agatha; I didn't know."

"How could you, nephew?" Morrison said with some asperity. "You took off from home like a scalded cat, and I've hardly had a word of your whereabouts since."

"I know, Uncle, I realize all that, but you have to understand something. I never did get along with Daddy, and when Mama died suddenly, I simply couldn't stay around home any longer. I just had to leave."

Morrison nodded. "I can understand that. I never did get along too well with Frank Kane myself. I advised sister against marrying him, but she was smitten, and wouldn't listen. I haven't been back to Saint Louis since sister passed on."

Morrison sat up as the housekeeper came in with a tray holding a bottle of sherry and two glasses. When she had left the study, Morrison filled the glasses and handed one to Morgan. "Here's to you, nephew; and I'd be interested to hear where you've been all these years."

Morgan sipped at his drink, a slight smile on his lips. "I'm not sure you would like to hear, Uncle Sherman. Daddy always preached to me that I'd come to no good in the end, and he was probably right."

"Sowed some wild oats, eh? I'm no holier-than-thou, Morgan. I sowed a few myself in my youth."

"Not to put a fine point on it, Uncle, I've been making my living as a professional gambler."

Instead of being shocked, Morrison looked interested. "Any good, are you? I play a pretty fair poker hand myself. Cards are popular with the legislators when things get boring, as they often do."

"I'm good, Uncle Sherman," Morgan said with a grin.

"To make a living as a professional, a man has to be good. It's not a pastime, as it is with you and your friends."

"Content with your life then, are you?"

Morgan's grin faded away, and he sighed. "Not really. I'd like to do something else, but I'm not trained for anything. Still, I've had a good enough life, until recently, that is."

Morrison squinted at him. "What happened recently?"

"Well, you have to understand that I've been an *honest* gambler. That is, I was until last year, when I became a lottery-ticket broker for the Union Canal Lottery Company. It didn't take me long to learn that that operation is *not* honest, and I quit in disgust."

"Lotteries! Bah!" Morrison got up in agitation and began to stride up and down his study. "You don't have to tell me about canal lotteries. There's a stinking scandal about them here in our state. Don't misunderstand me, many of them are honest and aboveboard, and have resulted in needed canals dug that could not have been financed any other way. But many others have gotten out of hand, especially here in Pennsylvania."

"Then why hasn't the state outlawed them? New York State has."

"You think some of us haven't tried? It isn't all that easy, nephew. The lottery companies have powerful lobbies in the capital, and they're popular with the people as well. How else can a poor man hope to strike it rich, to win more money than he'd ever hope to earn in his lifetime? The fact that some companies, like the Union Canal, pay little prize money is not known to the general public."

Morgan said sourly, "I've yet to meet anyone who's won the jackpot."

"Not very many have, but there have been a few, and those are the ones everyone hears about. Although it's a form of gambling, and all gambling is stacked in favor of the house, it isn't so bad, however, if the lottery is honest and aboveboard."

"Well, the Union Canal Lottery Company is a hell of a long way from being honest."

"I'm well aware of that fact. Since they went into business in 1811, the Union Canal Lottery Company has conducted an average of two lotteries a year, and claims to have distributed fifty million in prize money. But a great share of that, I have been told, has been paid to the company itself."

"How did they manage that?"

"By withholding thousands of tickets from sale, and then at a drawing they drop those ticket stubs into the drum, along with the tickets the public bought, so it follows that the company draws a great many prize-winning tickets. A shame, a damned shame!" Struck by a sudden thought, Morrison halted, staring at Morgan intently, flicking his thumbnail against his teeth.

After a little the clicking sound of thumb against teeth began to annoy Morgan, and he said testily, "Uncle Sherman?"

His uncle gave a start. "Oh, I'm sorry, Morgan. I just had what may be a brilliant idea. You're familiar with all aspects of gambling, and you know the workings of the Union Canal Lottery Company."

"And so?" Morgan said warily.

"There is a state legislative committee set up to investigate canal lotteries in Pennsylvania, and I'm the chairman of that committee. Actually, the Union Canal Lottery is our target, but we can't name that company openly, not right now. The committee has been in existence for some time now, with meager results. I might say none at all."

"What has all that to do with me?"

"How would you like to become a special investigator for our committee?"

Morgan stared. "*That* is your brilliant idea?"

"What's wrong with it? Who is more qualified? As chairman I'm empowered to employ investigators, and to pay a decent salary."

Morgan laughed uneasily. "Uncle Sherman, I'm flattered that you think so highly of me, but I've never done anything like that."

"You use a thief to catch a thief. Haven't you ever heard that expression?"

"Thank you very much," Morgan said in a dry voice.

Morrison waved a hand dismissively. "You know what I mean. If I did not think you were honest, I would not consider this, but you know gambling, and you have had some experience with selling lottery tickets."

The idea had some appeal, Morgan had to admit. There was an element of adventure and danger in it that intrigued him. He said thoughtfully, "What exactly would I be expected to find out? Prove that Union Canal is crooked?"

Morrison shook his head. "No, much more than that. We'd like to have evidence that most, if not all, canal lotteries are, if not outright swindles, not good for all concerned. Of course, we'd need strong proof against Union Canal; but if that's all you came up with, that company would scream about taxpayers' money being spent just to discredit them."

"To find evidence of all that would take some time, and a lot of traveling, mingling with people along all the canals, not just those in Pennsylvania."

"Yes, I'm fully aware of that, Morgan, but I'll see to it that you have all the time you need. I'm determined to erase this scandal and corruption from the grand state of Pennsylvania, if it takes the rest of my life." He had struck a pose, his voice rising.

Morgan recognized it as his public-speaking posture, and grinned faintly. "And what if you're not in the legislature that long?"

"Oh, I'll be there." Then Morrison noted Morgan's grin, and he smiled in kind, somewhat sheepishly. "Speechifying, wasn't I? A politician cannot help politicking at times, even in private. But I can stay in the legislature as long as I like. I'm very popular with the voters, if I may be permitted that immodesty. The other side has about given up on beating me. They just throw a token candidate in against me, come election time." His manner grew slightly pompous again. "I could be elected governor like a shot, if I chose to run."

"I've read that in the newspapers. Why don't you?"

"Too much responsibility and too much exposure to the public eye. In the governor's chair, a man might as well have a telescope trained on him, with some galoot selling tickets to watch him, at a penny a look. In my years in the legislature, I've built a base of power, until I'm damned near as powerful as the governor, and no exposure. And you're evading the question, nephew." Morrison planted himself squarely before Morgan. "Will you take on the job?"

Morgan weighed his answer for a moment more, then said, "I guess I'll give it a try. It sounds like it might be interesting. But you'll have to be patient with me until I learn how to operate. I've never done any investigative work before. Will it be public knowledge?"

Morrison was shaking his head. "Only a few people besides us will know about it, and those will all be on my staff, people I would trust with my life."

"All right then, I accept, Uncle Sherman." Morgan rose to his feet.

Beaming, Morrison stepped forward to clasp his hand, and clapped him on the shoulder with his other hand. "Good fortune to you, Morgan. I must warn you to be careful. There are some villains out there who would see your throat cut if they knew what you were about. And from what I have seen of canals, there are many places where cutthroats lie in wait to steal a man's purse."

Two months later, Morgan was to remember his uncle's parting words with a grimace.

By that time he had worked his way along several canals, naturally gravitating to the Erie, the crowning achievement of canal builders. He had ventured into low taverns, into small pockets of sin, venality, and crime, and had come through unscathed. After all, he had seen life at its worst in riverfront dives along the Mississippi and the Tenderloin district in New York, yet he realized later that nowhere had he ever encountered people as vicious and depraved as the inhabitants of what was called the Side-Cut. There, life meant nothing, and thugs would rob and kill a man for the clothes on his back. Morgan knew that he had been stupid to venture into such a place at night; but he had wanted to learn how much of their ill-gotten gains the sots, the criminals, and the whores of the Cut spent on lottery tickets. He had found the Cut teeming with ticket salesmen, all doing a brisk trade. Even the worst drunkards and the pocked, aging whores somehow managed either to buy lottery tickets or to go shares with others. A Union Canal lottery ticket was five dollars; but to make it possible for the poor to participate, tickets could be divided into eights, which meant that a person could buy one share of a ticket for sixty-three cents.

The eternal pot of gold at the end of the rainbow, Morgan had reflected wryly.

Nightfall had caught him still in the Cut, wearing expensive clothes and carrying a satchel. He had been in the Cut all day, having arrived in a canal passenger packet that morning; and he had only now learned that none dared stop at the Cut to pick up passengers after dark. It seemed that he had two choices open to him: he could stay overnight in the Cut, or he could walk out. Choosing what he thought was the lesser of two evils, he chose to walk.

Keeping a wary eye out, and walking briskly, he made it out of the Cut itself and onto the main canal without mishap. Thinking himself out of danger, Morgan allowed himself to relax slightly and slow his pace. He had traveled only a short distance when he was set upon by the thugs, who came out of the thick fog as silently as ghosts. Taken totally unaware, Morgan had gone down fighting under their assault.

Thanks to the timely intervention of Catherine Carnahan,

he had escaped with his life intact, but the satchel was missing; undoubtedly his assailants had stolen it. There was little in the satchel that would be of value to a thief—a change of undergarments and stockings, a razor, shaving mug and brush, et cetera; but the satchel had also contained a journal filled with notes that Morgan had taken concerning the lottery-ticket operations along the canals he had traveled; and Morgan knew that if anyone read the journal and realized what it meant, he would be in danger, for the book had his name in it. If Cat had not found his watch, he could have assumed a false name, but it was too late for that now—it would be sure to arouse her suspicions. He knew quite a bit about canal life and the operation of the boats, so he had to deceive Cat about that as well.

However, he did make up his mind to one thing. As soon as he could, Morgan was going to purchase clothes more befitting a canawler; and never again would he wander through a place like the Side-Cut dressed like a gentleman!

Also, he had decided to stay aboard *Carnahan's Cat* for at least a time. Morgan found himself deeply attracted to Catherine Carnahan, but he told himself that the only basis for his decision was the fact that the canal boat offered him a perfect cover as well as an excellent base for his operation. If a smooth article like Tate Brawley was working a lottery-ticket scheme along the Erie, it must mean that it was fertile ground for lottery brokers; and Morgan decided that he wanted to learn as much about Mr. Brawley as possible.

Cat was both annoyed and pleased that Morgan had helped to extricate her from a potentially embarrassing situation last evening. She brooded over her conflicting feelings as she stood at the tiller of the boat next morning.

It was a brisk morning, and mist still clung to the ground. Morgan and her father were below, preparing breakfast; and Timmie was up ahead with the mules, riding one and leading the other. All she could see was his head bobbing up and down out of the mist.

Again her thoughts returned to Morgan Kane and last night's scene in the *Paradise*.

Although he was a kind and loving father in his sober moments, Mick had never given Cat much direction in her life. While her mother was still alive, he had spared as much time as he could to her, giving her the benefit of his teaching; but he had evidently calculated that his responsibilities ended there; and after her mother drowned, and he began drinking heavily, Mick had found little time for his daughter.

Cat had not resented this, but the end result was that she passed through her adolescence very much on her own. She had learned to rely on her own resources, for rarely did a man, or a woman, along the canal come to her defense; it was not their way. Still she had managed well enough on her own—even in the unpleasant episode with Simon Maphis—and she was fiercely proud of her ability to fend for herself in any situation; it was for this reason that she resented Morgan Kane's interference last night. In her opinion she had handled herself well and succeeded in putting Brawley in his place. Morgan had no business coming to her defense, as if she were some weak, sheltered, plantation belle!

Yet, at the same time, the memory of Morgan's gallantry brought a feeling of warmth to her, and it was a pleasant sensation. She could not help but wonder what it would be like to spend the rest of her life cherished and protected by a forceful man like Morgan.

Cat snorted softly to herself. She would not care for it, of course. She was not a helpless, eye-fluttering female, and she would not be happy in such a life.

She stiffened as she saw Morgan's head emerge from below. He climbed atop the low cabin and made his way back toward her. "Your breakfast is about ready. Why don't you go below, Cat, and eat? I can mind the tiller. I've been watching you. . . ."

She made a scornful sound. "Just because you've been watching me, and for not much more than a day at that, doesn't mean you are ready to man the tiller yet. One mistake, and the *Cat* could be smashed to splinters against the bank. No, we've been making good time. We'll tie up shortly and have our breakfast together."

"Fine with me," he said cheerfully. He cocked an eyebrow at her amusedly. "But I must confess to some surprise."

She gave him a look of suspicion. "And why is that, Mr. Kane?"

"Why, your willingness to waste time eating," he said. "You've struck me as a slave driver, although you drive yourself, as well as others, I'll grant you that."

"That's very generous of you," she said with elaborate sarcasm. "I may be a slave driver, in your view, but in these hard times, it isn't easy to make a canal boat pay, even by working round the clock."

"That was something I was wondering about. Why don't you travel at night?"

"For one thing, the locks are closed at night, by law, from sundown to sunup."

"That doesn't mean that you couldn't travel between locks at night."

"True, and some boats do, but it's risky, because there could be a collision. *I* don't usually do it because we don't have enough people on the *Cat*. And we only have two mules. They need some rest."

"Perhaps if I learn to man the tiller . . . to your satisfaction, of course . . ." He made a half-bow.

"We shall see, Mr. Kane," she said coolly. "Right now, why don't you go forward and tell Timmie to watch for the side-cut and turn the mules?"

"Your wish is my command."

She watched him turn and walk gracefully across the cabin top toward the bow, cupping his hands around his mouth to shout at Timmie. Although the four-mile-an-hour rate of the *Cat* certainly was nothing compared to the rate of a seagoing ship, it usually took a landsman several days to be able to walk surefootedly on the deck of a canal boat in motion. Yet Morgan walked with an easy, sure stride, and the superb grace of a cat; he certainly showed no signs of his injuries.

He was an irritating man, Cat decided. He had been on the canal boat little more than a day, and yet he had arrogantly announced that he could take over her duties at the tiller. What made it even more annoying, she suspected, was the fact that he quite probably could. There was an air of competency about Morgan Kane, a confidence that he could perform any task he undertook, and well.

A half-hour later, they were tied off in the feeder canal, eating breakfast. The three men were eating on deck, but Cat had put her food on a tin plate and walked across to sit in the shade of a tree just off the towpath. The sun had burned away the mist now, and the day was becoming quite warm. After she had eaten, Cat leaned back against the tree trunk and closed her eyes. It was peaceful here, with only the humming of insects in the weeds, the lowing of cows in a distant field, disturbing the quiet. She closed her eyes for just a moment and drowsed.

She thought some sound, some motion, awakened her, but on opening her eyes she saw Morgan's face inches from hers, his eyes soft and musing.

"You are very beautiful, Cat," he said in a hushed voice. "When you are asleep like that, your face is as innocent as a babe's."

Fully awake now, she felt her face burn, and she shrank back against the tree trunk. "How dare you say such things?"

"Dare? *Dare?* Are you so accustomed to canal life that you cannot even receive a compliment gracefully? Surely, some man, sometime, has told you that you are beautiful?"

Thrown into confusion now, she stammered, "What . . . what are you doing here anyway?"

Morgan sighed. "Your father sent me to fetch you. He said it is time we were getting under way again."

"What time is it? How long have I . . . ?"

"How long have you been sleeping?" He grinned. "For a while, for a while." He took out the engraved pocket watch, snapped back the lid, and peered at it. "It is now past ten." He looked at her again. "Mick thought you might be ill."

"Past ten! Good heavens, we should have been under way long since!" She scrambled to her feet, adroitly avoiding the hand he offered to help her up. "Why didn't you wake me?"

"It wasn't my place to do so, and I thought you probably needed the rest."

"I can't afford lost time! At least Mick should have known better."

She stepped around him and started toward the canal boat, her long legs covering the ground quickly.

Morgan stared after her for a moment, a rueful smile on his lips. Christ, she was a difficult female! Insulted just because he had paid her a compliment! Perhaps he was making a mistake remaining on the *Cat;* it seemed to him that any hope he might have for a relationship with Catherine Carnahan was doomed. Yet he had plenty of time, and the Erie was a hotbed of lottery activity.

He noticed with a start that Timmie already had the mules moving, and Cat was at the tiller. The boat was in motion by the time he reached the towpath, and leaped aboard. Cat eyed him balefully, and he gave her a jaunty salute.

The Reverend Luther Pryor was very upset. It had been his hope that John Simmons would welcome him on board his boat, *The Saving Grace*. After all, they had attended Bible school together, and Pryor had always considered Simmons his warm friend; and were they not both shepherds of the Lord's flock? Of course, it had been years since they had seen each other, having gone their separate ways after being ordained. Pryor, afire with missionary zeal, had gone off to Africa to save the heathens, taking to wife, Constance Linden, before he sailed. Unfortunately, the heathens had not responded well to his sermons. After twenty years in Africa, his dear wife died of the fever, and his own health was so impaired that he was strongly advised to return to his homeland, or risk his own death. The Reverend Luther Pryor, a man determined to the point of foolhardiness, might have taken that risk, but there was his nineteen-year-old daughter, Lotte, to consider.

So he came home. As a reward for his years of devoted service, he was given his own church. Within six months he was chafing; he was plain bored. Every member of his church was saved; there were no sinners to convert. The reverend knew that he had to battle Satan on his own ground, where sinners were as plentiful as weeds in a neglected field. As he explained to Lotte, he had to be in that field, plucking the weeds with his own hands, so to speak, and turning them into God's flowers, to be content.

Lotte, long accustomed to her father's missionary fervor, merely acquiesced with eyes downcast to the hands folded in her lap, and asked a simple question: "Where are we going, Papa?"

"I have given the matter much thought and study." He was pacing, hands clasped behind his back. "From all I can gather, the canals of this country are cesspools of sin, the Erie foremost of all. There shall we go!" He waxed eloquent, hands waving. "Men of the cloth are badly needed there. We shall rescue many a poor sinner from the Devil's grip, daughter. I shall write to my old friend, John Simmons, who has a floating house of worship on the Erie. We shall join hands with him and do the Lord's work!"

However, it had not worked out that way; John Simmons had not greeted them with open arms. He had said, "I am happy to see you after all these years, Brother Pryor. But my boat is small, as you can see, and the members of my flock are few."

"But together, our flock will multiply."

"There is no room to expand, and I am old, Brother Pryor, and weary."

"A man never gets too old for the Lord's work!" Pryor had cried, impassioned.

"Speak for yourself, Brother Pryor. I still do the Lord's work, but I must leave it to younger men to carry the larger burden. I am content with what few parishioners I have. If you intend to preach along the Erie, you must get a canal boat of your own."

But without money, Pryor thought, how could he? They had barely enough money to sustain body and soul for more than a few weeks.

If not for Lotte, he would have stood on the streetcorner in the Sodom and Gomorrah that was the Side-Cut, and there preached the gospel to anyone who would listen, sustaining himself on what poor offerings he might garner unto himself; but he had visited the Side-Cut now, and had grasped the depth of its infamy and depravity. To take a maiden of Lotte's beauty into the Side-Cut would be to risk her ravishment, or worse. And when he had told John Simmons that he might preach on the streets there, Simmons had warned against it. "I beg you to reconsider, Brother Pryor. They have no respect for a man of God there, and would willingly cut your throat for even those few coins that might be tossed into your hat."

So here they were, moving along in the buggy, all their worldly goods with them. Pryor was brooding, his thoughts bleak, while Lotte sat idly watching the scenery. The canal was on their right, hidden from view by the high towpath.

"Somehow I must raise enough funds to purchase a canal boat and turn it into a floating church."

"Yes, Papa," Lotte said dutifully.

Pryor scarcely heard her; he was more or less talking to himself. "There has to be a way. The Lord will provide, He always has in the past."

He stopped talking as the road took a sharp turn to the right, and he had to haul back on the reins to slow their horse. The buggy went up a small incline, and they were on the bridge over the canal.

"Oh, Papa!" Lotte exclaimed, putting a hand on his arm. "I've never had such a view of the canal. Stop here for a moment, there's no one else coming."

Pryor obeyed, halting the buggy on the empty bridge. They could see for a long distance in both directions. Pryor vaguely recalled that the stretch of canal along here was called the Long Level, going for many miles in both directions straight and level, without a need for locks. There were canal boats of all sizes and descriptions going both ways—freight boats; the higher, more brightly decorated passenger packets; and there was a boat with a sign on the high cabin: JONAS ROLLINS, DENTIST: TEETH PULLED; FALSE TEETH MADE.

Pryor struck his knee with his fist. "There *must* be a way to raise the funds we need!"

"What funds might that be, sir?"

Pryor gave a start, glancing around to his left. Unheard by him, a horse and rider had stopped alongside the buggy. The rider was wearing the clothing of a gentleman, which allayed Pryor's first feeling of alarm that they were being accosted by a highwayman. Not only was the rider debonair in attire, but he was handsome in a sardonic way.

Now he grinned. "I am indeed sorry, sir, if I startled you, and the lady with you. I was riding abreast of your buggy and overheard your rather intriguing remark. I am Tate Brawley." He doffed his high, beaver hat and looked past Pryor at Lotte. "At your service, ma'am."

"And I am the Reverend Luther Pryor," Pryor said. "And this is my daughter, Lotte."

"I am delighted to make your acquaintance, Miss Pryor." Smiling, Brawley stroked his side whiskers with the fingers of his right hand. "And yours as well, Reverend. Is this your parish, may I ask?"

"Hardly, Mr. Brawley. I am from out of state, having only this week arrived at your Erie Canal." Pryor frowned disapprovingly. "I find it a wicked place, sir, a most wicked place."

Brawley's eyes gleamed. "Ah, that it is, no denying that. But why should a man of the cloth be in dire need of funds, if I may be so bold as to inquire?"

"For that very reason, sir, for that very reason. I came here to preach the gospel to the heathen . . . to the sinners along the canal. But I find that to reach them successfully, I need a boat that I may use as a church."

"I see. And you have no funds for such a church?"

"Regrettably, that is correct, Mr. Brawley."

Brawley's eyes lit up. "Perhaps I could be of some assistance, Reverend."

Pryor gave him a startled glance. "In what way, sir?"

"I have in mind a means by which you might raise money. How do you stand on lotteries?"

"Lotteries, Mr. Brawley?" Pryor said warily. "I believe I have read that many canals were built by money raised from lotteries."

"That is correct, Reverend."

Lotte had been listening with interest, fanning herself. Now she leaned forward to say, "But isn't that a form of gambling, Mr. Brawley?"

Brawley bowed his head in acknowledgment. "Strictly speaking, that is true, Miss Pryor. But many people see nothing wrong in it, when the monies raised are for a good cause. Many churches raise money by raffles or lotteries, for worthy causes."

Pryor experienced a rising excitement. "You're suggesting that is a way for me to raise money for my floating church?"

Brawley nodded gravely. "I am, Reverend."

"But I know nothing of such matters. I have no idea as to how to go about it."

"Oh, I could help you there." Brawley stroked his side whiskers. "As it happens, I am a lottery-ticket broker, and I would be happy to advise and assist you, Reverend." He tipped his hat again. "And you as well, Miss Pryor."

Chapter Five

MORGAN learned quickly and well; Cat was willing to grant him that. By the time they reached Schenectady, where they were to unload their cargo, Morgan could perform every function on the *Cat*, and do them well. Also, he was a hard worker, and he often relieved Timmie on the mules, which most canawlers considered beneath them. At first, Cat was reluctant to turn the tiller over to him; but when finally she could refuse him no longer, she watched him carefully, and could find no flaw in his work.

Since they had been forced to work the *Cat* short-handed for so long, Cat was unaccustomed to leisure, and at times she felt that she was not needed on board. But gradually she adjusted to the new schedule; and by the time they neared Schenectady she was beginning to enjoy the novelty of having time to herself.

In the early days Schenectady had been the eastern terminus of the Erie, before the canal was extended east to flow into the Hudson River; and it was there that all freight and passenger traffic had ended. When the canal was extended, the city lost some trade, for the freight boats usually passed on through to the Hudson; yet the towns along the way that had sprung up since the canal's completion still had need of the products brought by the canal boats, and flour was one of those products.

However, as Cat now explained to Morgan as they neared Schenectady, due to the depressed times there was little prospect of picking up a load for the return trip.

Morgan said, "While your father and Timmie clean up the boat after we unload, why don't I look around and see if *I* can't find something for us to haul?"

She looked at him with a scornful laugh. "You? What do you think *you* could find?"

"I have no idea." He shrugged. "But I won't know until I look, now will I? Besides, what harm could it do?"

"Well, I suppose that's one way of getting out of the dirty work of cleaning up."

He did not take offense. "If you think that, my dear Catherine, then of course I shall remain on board and share the labor."

She looked at him intently. She did not know if he had regained his memory—they had not discussed it recently—but she assumed that he had not; still, a change had come over him in the past few days. For one thing, he had stopped wearing his gentleman's clothing, having exchanged it for a canawler's rough attire and work boots. Also, the hard work he had been doing had quite clearly toughened him, giving him a better muscle tone. His body had been trim and graceful before, yet there had been a certain softness about him, as though he was unaccustomed to physical labor; but the week's work on the *Cat* had eliminated the soft look.

"I see no reason why you shouldn't try, even though I do think it's a waste of time." She added cuttingly, "I would never stand in the way of a man and his ambitions."

"It's hardly *my* ambitions, my dear Cat," he said in a bland voice. "If anyone benefits, it will be you. All I could hope to gain is your esteem, and I've about decided that is a vain hope."

Morgan left the *Cat* in Schenectady after they had finished unloading, and after he had cleaned himself up. He did not return that evening, and still had not returned by noon the next day. By that time the *Cat* was shipshape and had the cargo holds ready for use. Despite herself, Cat experienced a growing dismay at Morgan's continued absence. She was beginning to suspect that he was gone for good. This should have pleased her, yet she knew that she was going to miss him.

Cleaned up, she was sitting on deck, staring up the street, a look of longing on her face, when Mick came up behind her. "I'm thinking he's gone for good, daughter." As she glanced around with a start, he added, "And good riddance, if you ask me."

"You may be right, Mick."

"Then shouldn't we be moving on? There's no money to be made tied up here."

"We'll wait out the night. If Morgan isn't back by morning, we'll head back toward the Hudson."

Mick gave an elaborate stretch, and said without looking at her, "I think I'll stroll up into town for a wee drop or two."

"Mick, please! If Morgan comes back, we might have to leave this afternoon."

"Didn't I tell you, girl? He ain't coming back."

"There, you're wrong." She was looking past him with a pleased smile. "Here he comes now."

Mouth falling open, Mick looked around. Morgan was just getting down from the seat of a wagon. Two more loaded wagons were pulling in behind the first.

With a lithe leap Morgan spanned the space between the towpath and the deck of the boat. "There," he said with a sweep of his hand. "Three wagonloads of cargo for the *Cat*, and I have at least two more after we unload these."

"Morgan!" Cat exclaimed in delight. "How on earth did you manage it?"

"More to the point," Mick said suspiciously, "what *is* it you have there, lad?"

"Bolts of cloth. Mainly, dress goods."

"Dress goods?" Cat said with a frown. "Who are we hauling for? I've never had that kind of cargo before."

"It belongs to Bremerton and Sons, a dress manufacturer here in Schenectady. The bad times have forced them to the edge of bankruptcy, and they . . ."

"If they are bankrupt," Cat interrupted, "how can they afford to pay us?"

"That's not quite the arrangement I've made. I took the goods on consignment."

"On consignment? I don't understand."

"We go west from here, toward Buffalo, selling the cloth along the way."

"Selling!" Mick roared in outrage. "Damn and blast, Morgan! We're canal men, not bloody peddlers!"

Cat said, "He's right, Morgan. Our business is hauling cargo, not selling it. That's for land people."

"I understand that, but it's difficult times right now. We'll earn fifty percent on everything we sell."

"But what if we don't sell *anything*? Then the trip will be for nothing."

"Oh, we'll sell it, every bolt of it. If not before, in Buffalo for sure. Buffalo is the jumping-off point for settlers moving to the West. They'll buy anything they can get their hands on. The move West isn't big yet, but it soon will be. It's inevitable."

"That ain't the bloody point, bucko!" Mick exploded. "We're not peddlers, can't you get that through your skull?"

"You don't have to do the selling, if you feel it's beneath you," Morgan said, his voice burning with contempt. "I'll handle it."

Stung, Cat said, "It's not that we feel it's beneath us."

"By all that's holy, I do," Mick thundered. "I'm a canawler, and I won't stoop to peddling."

"Don't be so high and mighty, Mick," Cat said thoughtfully. "We hardly have room for pride right now. Morgan may be right. At least let's think about it."

"Think about it!" Mick glared, eyes bulging in disbelief. "I can't believe me ears, me own daughter, talking such."

"Oh, don't sound so righteous, Mick," she said wearily. "You know I love canalling, but it's not the only thing in the world."

"To me it is. It's an honorable profession."

"I didn't say it wasn't, but you weren't always a canawler, you were a schoolteacher. Is that less honorable?"

"Better than peddling it was, yes. And I'll not be listening to any more of this. If you're going to side with this slick-tongued sculpin against your own da." He clamped his mouth shut and jumped off the *Cat*.

Cat stood staring after him in dismay. "When he gets angry, or *pretends* to be angry, he talks like the rawest bogtrotter." She sighed. "And now he'll head for the nearest tavern."

"Don't worry, Cat," Morgan said quietly. "I'll see to it that he comes back reasonably sober. If you still want me around, that is."

She swung around to meet his gaze. "If I'll go along with your scheme, is that your meaning?"

"Not necessarily." He shrugged. "But I do think you should consider it."

"Oh, I'll go along with it, since you paint such a pretty picture. But I warn you, Mr. Kane," she said in a harsh voice, "you had better be right. If we travel all the way to Buffalo and don't sell the goods, I'll have no choice but to sell *Carnahan's Cat*, and in these hard times, I might as well give her away."

"It won't come to that. We'll sell every yard of the dress goods. I'd gamble on it."

Morgan worked very hard at it, Cat had to concede. At every town where they moored, he left the boat early, clean-shaven and clothes brushed, a bolt of cloth under his arm. But at their first three stops he did not make a single sale.

Mick grumbled, and Cat frowned, but Morgan remained doggedly optimistic. "I'll sell it, don't worry."

On the fourth stop he came back to the boat early in the afternoon, riding in a cart driven by a stranger. As the cart halted abreast of the *Cat*, Morgan jumped down and came aboard with a light step. Smiling, he gestured to the man in the cart. "This is Mr. Holt, a storekeeper here in town. He wants ten bolts of gingham."

"You did it!" Overjoyed, Cat clapped her hands. She had to fight an overwhelming urge to throw her arms around his neck and kiss him.

"Don't rejoice too much, until you hear the rest," Morgan said somewhat sheepishly. He scrubbed his knuckles across his chin. "Mr. Holt has no . . . uh, cash."

"Not another credit transaction?" Cat cried.

"Not exactly. Mr. Holt has been swapping his goods for things in lieu of cash. He'll swap those things to us for dress goods. He's offering very generous terms."

"What sort of things?" Cat asked suspiciously.

"Oh . . . chickens. The cart holds several crates of chickens. And a pig."

Mick, standing nearby, made a strangling sound. "Chickens? A *pig*?"

"Somewhere along the Erie we'll be able to sell them for cash money, I'm sure." Morgan laughed somewhat defensively. "Failing that, we can always eat them."

"Chickens! Pigs! Saints preserve us, the man is turning the *Cat* into a pigsty!"

Realizing that her father was working himself up into one of his fine rages, Cat gestured impatiently. "All right, Mick, no need to carry on so. Let's hear him out."

"Carry on so! I have the right. If this bucko has his way, I'll walk to Buffalo. I'll not be riding on me boat, because I'll not share it with a pig!"

"Mick, you do share your boat with the mules," Morgan said in a reasonable tone. "You stable them in the bow. I'm sure temporary arrangements can be made for some chickens and a pig."

"Temporary, Mr. Kane?" Cat said with a smile. "You *are* the one for extravagant promises, aren't you? First you load us down with bolts of cloth with promises to sell it easily enough. Now you're trading cloth for animals, which you promise to sell for cash."

"There's nothing wrong with the barter system, Cat. It goes back down through the ages."

He was smiling in turn, and for a moment she felt a spark of annoyance; apparently he had surmised that she would go along, again, with his scheme. He had an irritating habit of reading her thoughts. She said tartly, "And who will be feeding the chickens and the pig during the rest of the journey?"

"I will, of course," he said quietly. "I was raised on a farm, you know."

She stared at him. "No, I didn't know. Has your memory returned and you didn't tell me?"

He looked startled, then puzzled. "No, not really. But somehow it just came to me that I had been raised on a farm, and one of my chores was feeding and otherwise tending the stock."

As Morgan helped Mr. Holt unload the crates of chickens and the pig, he silently cursed himself for his lapse. He had made a slip and almost given himself away. That was the trouble with trying to act out a lie—you had to be on guard constantly. Of course, it probably would do no great harm to reveal that he had regained his memory, that he had really never lost it, but almost a week had passed since the attack on him; and he suspected that Cat, with her quick intelligence, would be suspicious of him if he tried to claim that his memory had suddenly returned; and since he had committed himself to the lie, the time was long past when he could tell her that he had never really lost his memory.

He was certain that she would be angry with him if he revealed his real purpose on the canal, and would undoubtedly insist that he leave the *Cat*. No matter what he might say, she would naturally think that he was spying on the canawlers, and he had already learned that they did not trust the law.

Morgan bade Mr. Holt goodbye after the merchant had been given his cloth, then he returned to the boat to find Cat frowning at him. Both she and her father had disappeared earlier, and Morgan was a little piqued at them for not even offering to help load the chickens and the pig.

Hands on hips, she said, "One thing occurred to me, now that you have stored your livestock on board. . . . What are we going to do with the mules at night?"

"I fail to see why they can't bed down on the bank at night for a few days. I notice that many other canawlers leave their animals out at night. The nights are warm now. If it rains, surely a little water won't do them any great harm."

"And how about thieves?"

"I'll guard them with my life, all right?" He heaved a sigh. "In fact, I'll even spend the night with them, if you like, with your old Colt in my hand."

"Do that and I don't know if I'll allow you to come near the boat," she said with a hint of a smile. "Bedding down with a pair of mules can make a man pretty gamy."

"At least that would give you a good excuse to keep me at a distance, wouldn't it, Miss Carnahan? It strikes me that the presence of a man younger than your father, or older than Timmie, makes you almighty nervous."

She flushed. "And you, *Mister* Kane, can go to the devil! Sleep in the canal, for all I care!"

She turned on her heel and stormed below. Morgan watched her go, and just before her head and shoulders disappeared, he gave a low, taunting laugh, and was gratified to see her shoulders stiffen.

At the next small town where they stopped, Morgan sold half of the chickens, and for a decent price. He had guessed correctly that no matter the hard times, taverns would still be doing a thriving business, and the first tavern he tried bought the chickens. Since he had received a good value in exchange for the cloth goods, he was able to sell the fowl below the going rate and still realize a good profit.

After he had delivered the chickens, he stopped in the taproom for a glass of ale. The barroom was about half-full; and as he sipped his ale, Morgan reflected that it was time he was beginning anew with his investigation. Since all his notes were in the stolen valise, he would have to begin all over again.

Before he was done with his ale, Morgan was able to observe a lottery broker in action, as a man entered the tavern carrying a small black bag. After ordering an ale, the newcomer stood with his back to the bar, and raised his voice.

"Gents, your kind attention, if you please! I have a little business to transact with those of you interested. It is a fine opportunity for you to win some prize money for yourself, and to perform a public service at the same time. I have here a number of lottery tickets. The proceeds from the sale of the tickets are to be used for a worthwhile endeavor, the building of a much-needed canal in the great state of Ohio. The Ohio and Erie Canal, the lottery sponsored by no less than Alfred Kelley himself, of the Board of Canal Commissioners of Ohio! Now, I have only a very few tickets left. They have been selling like wildfire. There will be three guaranteed winners in this lottery. First, second, and third!"

As Morgan listened to the broker's pitch, he was reminded amusedly of medicine showmen hawking snake oil; but the man had a receptive audience, as all the men in the barroom crowded around, vying with one another to purchase the tickets. Morgan saw several pool their coins to buy a single ticket. No matter how dire a man's financial circumstances, Morgan reflected, he always seemed to manage to find money to drink or gamble.

But at least this was a legitimate lottery, not one conducted by the Union Canal Lottery Company; Morgan knew that the Ohio and Erie Canal was being built; it had been under construction for a stretch of years, although work had stopped any number of times for lack of funds; and undoubtedly a few fortunate souls would win prize money in the lottery.

It was ironic, Morgan thought, that although canal lotteries were illegal in the state of New York, here was this broker hawking his tickets as openly as if he were vending fruit on the street. Of course, there was little effort to enforce laws against lottery-ticket sales along the Erie; it was low on the scale of crimes committed, and investing in the lotteries was a highly popular pastime.

As Morgan drained his ale and rose to his feet to leave, he noticed that another man had entered the saloon while the ticket broker had been making his pitch. The newcomer was standing off to one side, listening with an amused smile, a high, beaver hat in one hand, a black bag in the other. Something about the man struck Morgan as familiar. Then he remembered where he had seen him before: he was the ticket broker who had accosted Cat on the *Paradise*. What was his name? Brawley? Yes, Tate Brawley.

Curious as to Brawley's purpose here, Morgan settled back down onto the bar stool. Brawley, his attention on the group around the ticket broker, had yet to see Morgan.

Suddenly Brawley said in a loud, carrying voice, "Gentlemen, your attention, if you please!"

The voices died slowly, and everyone turned to face Brawley. The first ticket broker said angrily, "Who are you, sir, and why are you interfering with my business?"

"I am Tate Brawley, and I spoke up before you have taken all the gentlemen's money. If you wish to purchase lottery tickets, gents, I have some for sale, and for a more worthy cause. Not only is it a worthy cause, but it directly concerns your own Erie Canal."

The first broker gestured contemptuously. "Don't listen to this charlatan, fellows. It is a well-known fact that no lottery exists as concerns the Erie."

"Ah, but there you are wrong, my good man," Brawley said in a soft voice. "My lottery is for the purpose of building a canal boat, not a canal. A boat for a good Christian purpose. The Reverend Luther Pryor is contemplating a floating church on the Erie, and he has authorized me to conduct a lottery for this purpose. The good reverend is a former missionary, engaged for many years in saving the heathen in foreign countries, before being brought down by tropical fevers. He has returned to his native land, and intends to devote his remaining years to bring the word of God to the canallers. For this he needs a church. It will be called God's Floating Tabernacle. So, if you gentlemen wish to contribute to a good cause, and earn a chance at a substantial prize at the same time, buy your lottery tickets from me."

A lottery for a floating church! It was all Morgan could do to keep from laughing aloud. Meanwhile, Brawley had placed his bag on the bar, opened it, and begun taking out lottery tickets. The other broker glared at him venomously, and then they both began their sales pitch at the same time. The men in the saloon, Morgan noticed, seemed about equally divided now, about half purchasing church lottery tickets and the rest buying from the first broker.

Morgan ordered another ale and watched with amused interest. In about a half-hour all those who had decided to buy tickets were finished. The first broker closed his bag with a snap and stalked angrily from the tavern. Brawley, smiling to himself, returned his unsold tickets to his bag, closed it, and motioned the bartender down, ordering a whiskey. Waiting, he stroked a thumb along his side whiskers. His glance met Morgan's, started to move on, and then came back; he frowned, evidently experiencing a flicker of recognition.

Morgan drained his ale and, smiling slightly, moved down the bar to Brawley. As he approached, he saw Brawley's eyes go cold and hard. Morgan said, "I see that you recognize me, Mr. Brawley."

"Morgan Kane, I believe. The man who accosted me on the dinner boat."

"Accosted?" Morgan's eyebrows climbed. "It strikes me that it was the other way around. You accosted Miss Carnahan on the dance floor, and I merely came to her aid."

"You may put it any way you wish, sir, but I perceived it as an affront."

Morgan shrugged. "We all have our little problems, don't we?"

"Do not provoke me, sir!"

Morgan grinned lazily. "Oh, I wouldn't think of it."

"I don't believe we have anything to discuss," Brawley said coldly, and started to turn away to pick up his glass of whiskey.

"But I might wish to purchase one of your church tickets. I must say, Mr. Brawley, this is rather a comedown from selling canal lottery tickets. Wouldn't you agree?"

"No, I would not! It is for a worthy cause, and I am always willing to support a worthy cause."

"I'm sure. You're taking no brokerage fee, then? Doing it out of the goodness of your heart? That seems out of character."

"What do you know of my character, sir? As for character, I would not sell a ticket to a man of your caliber. Such a transaction would sully the good name of Reverend Pryor. Now, if you will excuse me."

Brawley turned his back, and Morgan tensed, his temper rising. Then he realized that the man was being deliberately provocative, and if he, Morgan, pushed it further, he could end up engaged in a barroom brawl; and such a fracas would be far from dignified.

"I resent your implications, Mr. Brawley, but this is hardly the time or the place to settle it. I'm sure we shall meet again. I do hope it will not be to your regret, sir."

"If we settle it, as you say," Brawley said without turning, "it will be to your regret, not mine."

Chapter Six

BRAWLEY kept his back rigid as Morgan Kane, the insolent young pup, left the tavern. Brawley always carried a pistol in his satchel, since he often toted large sums of money; and he had to restrain himself from snatching the gun from his bag and shooting Kane for his damned impertinence.

But that would never do. Always a cautious man, Brawley had taken note of the fact that Kane was unarmed. To gun down an unarmed man, even with provocation, would place him under scrutiny by the law, and that would not be wise. If this had happened in the Side-Cut, he could have killed Kane with impunity, since the authorities seldom investigated a killing in the Cut. Maybe the next time he encountered the man, the circumstances would be different.

Brawley drained his whiskey and curtly motioned to the bartender for another, pushing all thoughts of Morgan Kane from his mind.

That done, his feeling of euphoria returned. This was the first time he had hawked lottery tickets for the reverend's floating tabernacle, and it had gone well, as he had been sure it would. Of course he would take a percentage of every ticket he sold, but his motive in undertaking the project was more complex than just a chance to earn a few extra dollars—he had his eye on Lotte Pryor. The fact that she was a minister's daughter did not deter him in the least. In his experience Brawley had learned that not all minister's daughters were as set against the sins of the flesh as their fathers were; and when one was willing, she was a juicy handful. Although he was reasonably certain that Lotte was still a virgin, he suspected that she was ready to lose that virginity. And who better to lose it to than a presentable man who had given her father a hand when he badly needed one?

He would have to proceed with care, wooing her with caution, but he was confident that in the end he would succeed. Brawley was a womanizer, with a lusty sexual appetite, and his vast experience at the pursuit of the female of the species had made him skillful. He was not accustomed to being spurned, and Catherine Carnahan's snub had angered him. Of course she was not the only fish in the Erie. Still, there was something about her, a quality of intelligence and spirit that set her apart; and he sensed that the boyish garb was, in a way, a disguise behind which she hid her femininity. Because of her private, prickly ways, she offered a challenge that would make a conquest of her all the sweeter; and he would, at some point, manage to catch her alone, but until then . . .

He finished his whiskey, paid his bill, rubbed his hands together briskly, and left the tavern. Thoughts of Lotte Pryor and Cat Carnahan had aroused him, and he went seeking satisfaction. Although he had been working along the Erie for only about six months, he had become acquainted with a number of women, widows mostly. Widows were usually good, easy pickings. Brawley was reluctant to pay for sexual favors; it offended his sense of confidence; but a ripe widow was usually grateful for his skilled attentions. There was such a widow down the pike a way.

Feeling fine, he mounted his horse and rode west out of town, following the towpath alongside the Erie. A short way along he reined in, scowling. *Carnahan's Cat* was moored there, moving gently in the waves created by another passing canal boat. The deck was empty, and there seemed to be no one about. For a moment Brawley was sorely tempted to sneak on board; and if there was no one there, to cause what damage he could.

A glance around helped change his mind. It was still daylight, and there were people about. He could be seen and perhaps identified later. The risk was not worth what damage he could inflict in a short time. Still, he sat his horse, glowering down at the *Cat*, which now housed two people who had crossed him—Morgan Kane and Cat Carnahan.

Brawley finally rode on.

It was full dark when he reined in before a two-story cottage a few miles west of town. A stiff wind had come up, and a sign over the front door swung slightly in the breeze: LUCY CRAWFORD: BED AND BREAKFAST.

Brawley dismounted, tied his horse at the hitching rack, and thumped his fist on the heavy door. Footsteps sounded shortly, and the door opened.

The woman in the doorway was in her late thirties, buxom, with brown hair and blue eyes. A floor-length dress and apron failed to conceal her lush curves. Her face was flushed from kitchen heat. As she recognized Brawley, a huge smile bloomed on her face. "Tate!" she said in a husky voice. "I'm glad to see you, even though I wasn't expecting you."

"Just happened to be in the neighborhood and decided to drop in on my favorite widow." Brawley stroked his side whiskers with his thumb.

Lucy Crawford preened, her flush deepening. "You caught me in the kitchen, cooking. I look a sight."

"Not at all. You're pretty as a queen."

"You do flatter a girl, don't you, Tate?" She stepped back, motioning. "Well, do come in." She brushed a hand across her forehead, leaving a streak of flour. "I was just making sweets for the morning's breakfast, and was about to pop them into the oven."

"That can wait, Lucy," he said roughly. He reached for

her and pulled her against him. "I haven't seen you in a month. That's a long time for a man who likes you as well as I do."

Flustered, she threw back her head, her heavy hair swinging. "But it's hardly decent, Tate, early as 'tis." But already his hands were on her demandingly, and her slow smile was heavy and languorous.

"Early or late, what's it matter?" he growled. He ground his mouth on hers, and he could feel the pout of her hardening nipples through his shirtfront.

After a moment she took away her mouth, and said with a flirtatious roll of her eyes, "Wouldn't you like a bite first?"

"We can eat later. Come along, let's go upstairs." Arm around her waist, Brawley led her toward the narrow staircase just to the right.

Lucy whispered, "Quiet as a mouse now. I have two roomers, and one is in his room this very minute. I wouldn't want him to know what's going on." She giggled. " 'Twouldn't be good for my reputation, now would it?"

Since the stairway would accommodate only one at a time, Lucy went first. Brawley placed a hand familiarly on her ample buttocks and said, "I should think it would enhance your reputation, my dear, not harm it."

She giggled again, and swatted at his hand, without force. There were four bedrooms at the top of the stairs, and Lucy's was the last one on the right.

Once inside, the door closed and bolted, Lucy lost all coyness, and became a wanton, her body plastered against his, her hot mouth seeking his lips. Her fingers worked against his back, as her lower body arched in to cuddle his hardness.

"Ah, ah," she whispered. "Yes, Tate, yes! It's been as long for me as for you, indeed it has."

"Then let's get to it."

Her urgent fingers began to pluck at his clothing. He stood quite still while she loosened buckles and buttons, and soon he stood in just his underdrawers. While he divested himself of those, Lucy stepped back to tear at her own clothes. Her breath left her in a gasp as he stepped out of the last garment, and she saw his erect manhood bold and throbbing.

As he started toward her, she fell across the bed, her arms and body open to him. She welcomed him into her with a glad cry, and immediately began to moan loudly and thrash about on the ancient bed, the springs squeaking in furious counterpoint to their movements.

Apparently she had forgotten about the roomer now, Brawley reflected with amusement; certainly the man would know what was going on, unless he was deaf.

Brawley savaged her roughly, and brought her to a groaning climax twice, before he achieved his own satisfaction.

Afterward, they lay side by side, struggling for breath. In a little while Lucy stroked a plump, white hand down across his hirsute chest, and said in a cooing voice, "You're good for me, Tate, indeed you are! Just think, we could have a high old time for ourselves every day, if'n you'd move in with me. You'd have a good place to stay and good meals. . . ."

"And you'd have a husband," he said harshly. He pushed away her hand. "I've told you more than once, Lucy. I tie myself down to no woman."

"You don't have to marry me, although I'd like that," she said in a subdued voice. "But you could stay in one of the rooms. I wouldn't charge you room and board."

"And what would that make me, your fancy man? I go and come whenever I please, and if that doesn't suit you, tell me, and I won't be bothering you again. You're not the only woman along the Erie."

"No, no!" she said frantically, and threw herself across him. "You can go and come as you please, Tate!" She began to caress and kiss him in an effort to arouse him again.

* * *

Morgan had walked a longer distance than usual from the Erie, having learned of a tavern two miles from the canal, on an inland road, that might be interested in buying the pig. He was growing tired of Mick's sneering remarks about having a pig on board the *Cat*, and Morgan was determined to sell it. Since it was a nice day, and since he would probably have to deliver the pig to the tavern if he made the sale, he did not hire a horse or rig, but walked to the tavern. But at least the trip was profitable—the owner of the Rose & Crown bought the pig sight unseen, and for cash.

So Morgan was content enough as he trudged back toward town. When he had covered about half the distance, he heard hoofbeats behind him. He stepped off the narrow road and turned to see a horse and buggy approaching. As the vehicle drew nearer, he saw that it was occupied by a man and a woman.

Although he had given no sign of wanting a ride, the buggy slowed, then stopped abreast of him. The man with the reins wore a black suit and hat, and something seemed familiar about him. Then, as he leaned out, Morgan saw that it was the Reverend Luther Pryor; and he remembered the scene with Tate Brawley a few days ago back down the Erie.

"If you are going into the village, sir," Pryor said, "we would gladly share our vehicle with you."

"I do appreciate it, Reverend Pryor."

"It only seems the Christian thing to do." Then Pryor's gaze sharpened. "Do I know you, sir?"

Morgan climbed into the buggy, squeezing in alongside the reverend's daughter. He said, "You may not remember me, Reverend, since we weren't really introduced, but you approached a canal boat some weeks back, near Albany. You were inquiring about a church boat, I believe, called the *Saving Grace*. I was on that boat."

Pryor frowned in memory. "Oh, yes, there was a young lady at the tiller."

"That's correct; Catherine Carnahan by name. I am Morgan Kane."

"How do you do, Mr. Kane." The reverend lightly flicked his whip, and the buggy was in motion again. "I cannot say that I approve of women on canal boats."

"The lady in question, and her father, own the boat, *Carnahan's Cat*. It is not uncommon, I understand, for women to live on board canal boats. Wives, daughters, whole families, for that matter."

"Perhaps what you say is true, sir, but this canal is a sinful environment."

Morgan did not comment on Pryor's remark, sensing that any argument to the contrary would only inflame the man. It did not take much acumen to realize that the man was a zealot. Instead, he said, "Did you find the boat you were searching for?"

"I did, but to no avail. I had hoped to combine forces with an old friend, John Simmons, and together we would endeavor to save souls along the Erie. Unfortunately, my friend was not willing to share the Lord's work with me. But that shall not stop me!" Pryor shook a clenched fist. "I shall soon have my own church on this wicked canal!"

"Yes, I know," Morgan said in a dry voice. "I met your . . . uh, benefactor a few days back, selling lottery tickets for your church tabernacle. Tate Brawley is a rather unsavory character for a reverend to associate with, wouldn't you say?"

"In what way is that, Mr. Kane?" Pryor said stiffly.

"Well, he is by profession a lottery-ticket broker. If that alone isn't bad enough, he works for the Union Canal Lottery Company, which is known to be unethical, if not downright crooked."

"I do not know of this Union Canal Company you speak of, Mr. Kane. At any rate, it does not matter. Mr. Brawley was kind enough to offer his services, and when I was in dire need. It is a means to an end, sir, a means to an end. If I can get my church under way through Mr. Brawley's services, the many souls I shall save will be well worth it.

After all, the Lord Himself walked among thieves, harlots, and other, as you called it, unsavory characters."

Privately, Morgan thought that that hardly applied to this particular situation, but prudence kept him mute. They rode along in silence for a few moments, and Morgan began to notice something rather strange. They were naturally cramped for space, three people in a seat made for two, and his thigh had been in contact with Lotte's from the moment he had sat down. But now he noticed that her leg was touching his, and she was slowly increasing the pressure, instead of drawing back. He stole a glance at her face. She was perfectly composed, hands folded primly in her lap, staring straight ahead. As if she felt the impact of his glance, she moved her leg ever so slightly against his again.

Was it wholly inadvertent, or was she engaged in a little mild flirtation? Morgan found it hard to believe that it was inadvertent; and yet, if deliberate, it hardly seemed fitting behavior for a minister's daughter. On the other hand, she was an uncommonly attractive girl, and she could be rebelling against her father's strictures. Morgan could easily understand how difficult it would be living under the wing of a zealot like the Reverend Luther Pryor.

He said casually, "And what is your opinion of Tate Brawley, Miss Pryor?"

The leg was still for a moment, then the pressure eased. She said softly, "Mr. Brawley seems a gentleman, and it is not my place to question my father's church decisions."

"Lotte is her father's daughter, Mr. Kane," Pryor said sternly. "She does not question my decisions. Lotte knows her place in the world and does as she is told. I handle churchly affairs, preach the sermons, and tend to my flock. She keeps my household and leads the choir. She has a fine voice for singing the praises of our Lord."

"I must attend to hear her sing sometime," Morgan said gallantly. Then he added daringly, "May I say that you are a fine figure of a woman, Miss Pryor. Have you any thoughts of marriage?"

"That, sir, is hardly a fitting remark for a gentleman." Pryor's mien became stern and forbidding. "When I deem it is time for my daughter to wed, I shall find her a suitable husband. She is well aware of that."

"My apologies, Reverend, Miss Pryor. I meant no offense," Morgan said, and fell silent. They were well into the small canal town now, and the reverend slowed the buggy.

"Where shall I let you off, Mr. Kane? I am heading west along the towpath, and can drop you at your canal boat, if it is in that direction."

"It is, Reverend, just below Main Street. I would be most grateful."

With a start Morgan realized that the pressure of Lotte's leg was back, more insistent this time. His first impulse was to return it, just to see what would happen, but he finally decided against it. If he made an advance, however clandestine, there was no telling what kind of Pandora's box he would be opening.

He saw the boat up ahead, with Cat standing on deck. He motioned. "There, there is my boat, Reverend."

When the buggy drew to a halt, Morgan climbed down. He said, "I am much obliged, sir. It was most kind of you. I trust we shall see each other again. And I wish you good fortune with your canal tabernacle." Knowing that Cat's gaze was upon them, Morgan was seized by a devilish impulse. He reached back into the buggy and took Lotte's hand. He bowed over it and raised it to his lips. "I also trust I shall be seeing you again, Miss Pryor. It has indeed been a pleasure making your acquaintance."

Cat was indeed watching as the buggy stopped alongside the canal boat. With a start of surprise she recognized Morgan getting out, and then her astonishment mounted as she saw him reach back inside for a hand and hold it to his lips. As he did so, the person in the buggy leaned far out, so that Cat could see that it was a young woman, and a pretty one.

Suddenly she experienced a strange feeling. She was angry and miserable at the same time, and it gave her pause. Was she jealous, jealous of Morgan Kane and this strange girl? To her utter dismay she realized that she was, and it was damned unsettling. Not only was jealousy an unfamiliar emotion to Cat, but it was one she would not have thought herself capable of feeling.

Then Morgan released the girl's hand, the buggy moved away down the towpath, and Morgan came toward the *Cat* with a jaunty step. He leaped lightly on board, and faced her, hands on his hips. He said smugly, "Guess what?"

The grin further infuriated her, and she said icily, "I'm not good at guessing games, Mr. Kane."

"Mr. Kane? Why so formal all of a sudden?" His eyebrows climbed, and then he shrugged, his grin still in place. "I just sold the pig you and your father have been grousing about!"

"Who to? The girl in the buggy?"

"Huh?" He looked disconcerted. "Of course not. I sold it to a tavern owner a ways out of town."

"And the girl's his daughter, I suppose? You were kissing her hand out of gratitude?"

He stared at her, his smile gone. And then, slowly, he began to smile again; and it was apparent to Cat that he was enjoying himself hugely. "Why, Catherine Carnahan, you're jealous! I'm not sure whether I should be flattered or not."

"I am *not* jealous!" she flared. "It just struck me as a little odd that you should be kissing the hand of a strange woman."

"On second thought, I do believe that I am flattered. As for the girl, she's not that much of a stranger. You've met her, too. That was Lotte Pryor and her father, Reverend Pryor. They stopped to make an inquiry of us some time back. Remember?"

"Oh," she said in a small voice.

"The tavern where I sold the pig is a goodly distance

out of town, and they came along in the buggy and were kind enough to give me a ride back. I thought kissing her hand was the least I could do in gratitude."

Mick had come up in time to hear Morgan's last words. "You mean you really sold that bloody pig?"

"I did," Morgan replied. "And for cash, too. Now all I have to do is find some means of delivery."

"I'll give you a hand, Morgan," Mick said. "It's glad I am to be seeing the last of the creature, stinking up my boat. There's a place up the street with a cart and horse for hire. Come along, boyo, and we'll take care of it."

He led Morgan off the boat. Just before stepping off onto the towpath, Morgan glanced back over his shoulder at Cat, and winked.

Furious, Cat swung down below to her cabin. Reluctantly, she was forced to admit to herself that she was made even more angry by the fact that Morgan was right—she *was* jealous. Or had been at the time. Now that she had learned the girl was a minister's daughter, the jealousy was not so severe.

Morgan had disposed of all the chickens and bolts of dress goods by the time they reached Buffalo. At least he was decent enough not to gloat about it, Cat conceded.

And Mick was gracious enough to admit that he had been wrong. Clapping Morgan on the shoulder, he boomed, "I was wrong about the whole thing, me bucko. I guess you saved our bacon." He guffawed. "Which is fitting, considering the bloody pig."

Cat said, "Now if we can get a load back to Albany, everything will be great."

"I'll get us a cargo in Buffalo," Morgan said confidently.

True to his word, he got them a full load of grain to haul to the Hudson River, for shipping on to New York.

Cat was grateful to him, yet she was reluctant to come right out and say so. "I don't really know how we managed all these years without you, Mr. Kane," she said, with more sarcasm than she intended.

"Your gratitude is overwhelming, Miss Carnahan," he said with a mock bow.

"Oh, all right," she said crossly. "I'm grateful. Of course I'm grateful," she said in a softer voice. "It's just that I'm not used to . . . Well, I'm not all that accustomed to people doing things for me."

He looked at her with raised eyebrows. "You mean, you don't like to accept favors from a man?"

Cat felt herself flush. "That's not it at all . . . Well, maybe it is, a little. I'm afraid that I haven't had much experience with men." She was surprised and not a little disconcerted by her sudden burst of candor.

"Then isn't it about time that you did?"

"What do you mean?"

"You can start by having dinner with me tonight, before we leave Buffalo."

Thrown into confusion, she said quickly, "But we're loaded and ready to go. It's only the middle of the afternoon. I figured that we'd be miles down the canal by nightfall."

"Cat," he said gently, "a few hours more or less doesn't matter all that much. I think we both have cause to celebrate. Why not do it together? Nothing dire will happen. We'll have an excellent dinner, and get an early start in the morning."

He took her hand in his. Her first instinct was to snatch it back, but then she let it remain. His hand was warm and gentle, and she discovered that it was a good feeling, having her hand held by Morgan Kane, and being invited out to dinner with him. It meant having to get dressed up, wear a dress, but suddenly she found the prospect quite appealing.

"All right," she said abruptly. "I'll do it!"

Simon Maphis stared at Brawley incredulously. "You're what? You're running a lottery for that sermon-spouting bastard?"

Brawley nodded complacently. "I am. It'll put a few extra dollars in my purse, and it'll do me good to be known along the Erie as a fellow willing to help a fellow Christian."

"Fellow Christian!" Maphis snorted. "You're about as much a Christian as I am. Well, don't expect me to sell any damned church lottery tickets. There're too many Bible thumpers along the Erie now to suit me."

"Oh, I wouldn't expect you to do that, Simon. You just keep moving the canal tickets. How are you doing, by the way?"

"Fine. I've about sold all that batch you gave me."

"I'll leave you another before I leave." They were on Maphis's boat, in his untidy cabin, drinking rum, the only liquor he had available.

The cabin door opened, and a woman edged her way in. She was fairly young, but a slattern—brown hair untidy, face smudged with dirt, dress torn and filthy. There was an ugly bruise on her face. In a whining voice she said, "Simon dear, do you want . . . ?"

"Don't 'dear' me!" Maphis roared. "What are you doing in here, when I'm talking business with a mate? You come when I call for you, and not before."

"But I thought . . ."

"Don't think! I don't keep you around to think. I keep you around to warm my bed, and don't you be forgetting that little fact!" He raised a fist as though to strike, and the woman cringed, and started to sidle out the door, her fearful blue eyes never leaving Maphis.

There was something vaguely familiar about the woman. Brawley puzzled over it for a moment, and then, as her face disappeared behind the closing door, it came to him—she looked a bit like Catherine Carnahan.

He turned to Maphis. "That woman . . ."

Maphis gestured contemptuously. "Don't worry about her. She's just a slut I picked up to amuse myself with."

"No, that wasn't my meaning. I was struck by the fact that she looks a tiny bit like Catherine Carnahan."

Maphis scowled at him, and for a moment Brawley thought he would explode with anger. Then he motioned again, and made a spitting gesture. "That Cat! Someday I'd like to see her get what's coming to her."

"She's not in good favor with me, either. She snubbed me weeks back, and I don't take kindly to that. Also, there's a fellow working on her boat that I don't much care for, by the name of Morgan Kane."

Maphis shook his head. "Him I don't know."

"You wouldn't like him, even if you did. He thinks he's too good for the likes of us." He studied Maphis intently. "I was just thinking. . . . You have a score to settle with Miss Carnahan, and so do I, as well as with this Kane fellow. Why don't we settle it?"

Maphis stared at him, beginning to grin unpleasantly. "Just what did you have in mind, Tate?"

Brawley shrugged. "I should think you could dream up something. You know more about canals and canal boats than I do."

"Any number of things I could do, up to scuttling that damned boat of theirs, with them all on board. You want me to go that far?"

"I have no objections, so long as no blame is attached to either of us." He looked at Maphis intently. "No offense, Simon, but you tend to barge ahead, without thought of consequences. This has to be planned carefully."

Maphis was scowling. "You willing to help plan it?"

"So long as you go along with any scheme I concoct, agree to obey my orders."

"Why not? You're the educated gent, with all the brains. I'm just a poor, unlettered canawler. I'll be happy with any plan that will eliminate the Carnahans, father and brat." Maphis was grinning evilly now, and he rubbed his hands together briskly. "So let's get on with it."

Brawley held up his hand. "Easy now, Simon, easy. Let's don't rush into anything. Clever planning, that's the ticket. And I promise you I'll come up with a plan that will finish the Carnahans and their canal boat."

Chapter Seven

BUFFALO was a bustling town, and there was an air of the raw frontier about it. Cat, again in her mother's dress, unconsciously moved closer to Morgan, clutching at his arm, as they walked along streets crowded with humanity: canawlers; riverboat men; trappers wearing greasy buckskins rank with a full winter's wear; gamblers in dandy attire, with their fancy women on their arms; sailors off the Lake Erie boats; soldiers in neat uniforms; and even a few half-naked Indians. Many of the buildings were new, with raw, unpainted false fronts. Vehicular traffic clogged the street, sending up clouds of dust. Men shouted curses at horses, mules, and oxen, and snapped whips.

Scarf held up before her face as protection against the billowing dust, Cat glanced sidelong at Morgan. He was wearing the clothes he had been wearing the night she had rescued him; but they had been cleaned and repaired, and Morgan looked splendid in them. And handsome, she had to admit that; strikingly handsome.

Cat forced herself to look away from him. A gunshot sounded in the distance, and she flinched. "It's a little frightening, isn't it?"

"Frightening?" He flicked a glance at her. "You must have been to Buffalo numerous times before."

"Well . . . not really. Sure, to the loading docks, but I never strayed far from the *Cat* and the canal."

He patted the hand on his arm. "Don't worry. I know it looks a little rough and ready. As I mentioned before, not only is it a canal terminus, it's also the jumping-off place for settlers moving West, but nothing will happen to you; I'll protect you. With my life, if necessary," he finished with a smile.

Cat's temper flared, and she pulled her arm from his. "Don't sound so patronizing, so damned . . . male! I can fend for myself, thank you. I've managed so far."

He sighed, rolling his eyes skyward. "You're so prickly, Cat. So thorny. You're like a rose bush, beautiful when in bloom and at a distance, but when you get close, you'll get pricked."

After a moment she relented, and linked her arm with his again. In a small voice she said, "I'm sorry, Morgan. I suppose I do bristle too much. If somebody offers me harm, I'll accept your protection, and gratefully. All right?"

"All right. Let's hope it doesn't happen," he said in a neutral voice. "Here's where we'll be dining, anyway."

He indicated a two-story hotel with a nod of his head. The building was a little more elaborate than most Cat had seen along the street, with a brick front and an awning extending to the edge of the wooden sidewalk. Morgan was evidently familiar with the hotel; inside, he led her through the lobby and into a quiet dining room, lit by many candles and filled with a quiet hum of conversation.

Cat was unaccustomed to such fancy dining accommodations, and she was in awe of the place. Determined not to show it, she stood with her head high, while they waited in the entranceway as a man hurried toward them with menus under his arm.

As he stopped before them, his face suddenly blazed with recognition. "*Monsieur* Kane! How nice to see you again. It has been a long time."

"It has been, hasn't it?" Morgan said casually. "I don't remember. Just how long has it been?"

The man thought for a moment, then his face brightened. "Almost two months to the day, *monsieur*."

"That long, is it? Well, it's nice to be back." Morgan motioned to Cat. "This is Miss Catherine Carnahan."

"Welcome to my establishment, *mademoiselle*. I am Pierre." He bowed over her hand.

Morgan said, "Do you have a table for us, Pierre?"

"But of course, *monsieur*! Please to follow me."

They followed Pierre across the room to a secluded table half-hidden from the other diners by a potted fern.

With a flourish Pierre presented a menu to Morgan. "Perhaps a cocktail, *monsieur*, *mademoiselle*?"

"A bottle of wine, perhaps." Morgan glanced questioningly at Cat. "Pierre has a marvelous wine cellar, all shipped direct from France."

"That sounds fine, Pierre," Cat said regally, composedly; but inside she wanted to shriek with laughter. Cat Carnahan, the hoyden of the Erie, ordering wine in an elegant French restaurant, and addressing the owner familiarly!

She got herself under control, and sat with a perfectly straight face until Pierre was gone; and then she said, almost accusingly, "You've been here before, Morgan."

"It would seem so, wouldn't it?" he said ruefully.

"But you don't remember?"

"No. Not the place, nor Pierre."

"Yet you bring me here for dinner. You come here, and you are recognized. That strikes me as strange."

He shrugged. "Perhaps, but that's the truth of it. I suppose I remembered it subconsciously." He tilted the large menu up before his face, consulting it until Pierre returned with two wine goblets and a bottle in an ice bucket. He poured a little into Morgan's glass. Morgan savored it, and nodded. "Very good, Pierre."

When Pierre had gone away again, Cat said, "And that's another thing. . . . You told me a moment ago that Pierre had a marvelous wine cellar. That's not remembering?"

Morgan sighed and shook his head. "All right, Cat.

When you get ahold of something, you worry it, don't you? I must confess that my memory does seem to be coming back, in bits and snatches."

"Why haven't you mentioned it?"

"It didn't strike me as all that important. I don't remember enough yet to amount to anything. Besides, I'm just as happy not remembering, just as happy with my life as it is right now." His gaze was intent upon her.

She looked away in some confusion. "I don't know what you mean."

"Yes, you do, Cat," he said. "You know very well what I mean. I'm more attracted to you than to any woman I've ever known."

She stammered, "How . . . how do you know that for sure? You may even have a wife somewhere." She looked at him again.

Morgan shook his head. "No, I'm sure I'm not married."

"That's one of the bits and pieces that you've remembered?" She gave her voice a cutting edge. "A very convenient memory, wouldn't you say?"

His gaze did not waver. "I just know, deep in my heart, that I have no wife; moreover, that I have never really loved a woman before."

Truly flustered now, her feelings running wild, Cat gazed down at her hands, twisted tightly together in her lap. Suddenly she was furious with herself. Was this Cat Carnahan—self-sufficient, needing no one?

She forced her emotions under control, and looked across the table. She said coolly, "Could we change the subject, please? You are being somewhat . . . forward, you know. What gives you the right to say such things to me?"

He spread his hands. "The same right any man has to express his admiration and attraction to any woman."

"And what if that woman does not welcome such attentions?"

He smiled slightly. "Doesn't welcome? Or is afraid to hear them voiced?"

"Afraid! Why should I be afraid?"

"I don't know, Cat," he said simply. "But that's certainly the impression I get."

"Impression?" she flared, her temper rising again. "You have a nasty way of taking everything I say and twisting it around to suit yourself. Besides"—she looked down at her hands again—"we've known each other less than a month."

"A month, a week, a day, it doesn't matter. I know how I feel, and I think that you know how you feel, if you'd only let yourself."

She raised her eyebrows, making her eyes cold, although she could feel her cheeks go hot. "You know how I feel? Such arrogance!"

"I don't consider it arrogance at all . . ." He broke off, much to Cat's relief, as Pierre came up to their table again.

Morgan and Pierre went over the menu and discussed various items, without once consulting Cat. This was a custom that irritated her, as if a woman did not have sense enough to decide what food she wanted to eat; but for once she was grateful for being ignored. What on earth was happening to her? She felt as though she were being irrevocably drawn into something against her will. And yet *was* it wholly against her will? Intellectually, the attraction between them, and Morgan's boldness in bringing it out into the open, frightened her; but at the same time there was a physical pull that excited some part of her that she had kept dormant, a pull toward a secret pleasure and delight that had only had free rein in her dreams in the dark hours of the night, dreams that she usually denied to herself in the practical light of day.

Morgan was speaking: "Is that all right with you, Cat?"

"Is what all right with me?" she asked blankly.

"Duckling, I've ordered duckling for us."

"Why, yes, Mr. Kane," she said sweetly, "that would be fine. I always did have trouble making up my poor mind about such weighty matters. I am indeed fortunate to have a man along to do it for me."

Morgan squinted at her suspiciously, but he waved Pierre off, with instructions to bring duckling for both of them.

And then Morgan began talking of what he thought they should do on their return trip to Albany. "If we can't get a proper cargo for the *Cat*, I'm sure I can find another load of something to trade along the canal. On consignment again, if nothing else."

"Then you are planning to continue on with the *Cat*?"

His face became still. "I'd like to, unless you don't want me along."

"It isn't that. It's just that I wasn't sure you liked canal life. As I said, I'm sure you're not a canawler by trade."

"I imagine you're right about that. But then, since I can't remember what I did before, I can't very well return to that life, now can I? And I do like the Erie. I'm coming to understand why you love it so. It has a sense of freedom not found in most professions nowadays. There's romance to it, you're always on the move, with something new and strange every day. One thing I am curious about, Cat. What do you do in winter, when the canal is frozen solid?"

Taken aback by the sudden and mundane shift in the conversation, Cat blinked at him. "Well, the canal is drained, and the boats set on the bottom, usually, waiting for the spring thaw. It's damned boring, and sometimes we have trouble stretching money and food to last. I've heard there is something new—canal boats fitted out with ironclad prows to act as ice breakers. I understand they have high hopes for them. If they work, we can use the Erie the year round."

A waiter came with their food, ending the conversation for the moment, as they both ate hungrily. The food and wine were quite good, and Cat relaxed into a mellow mood; yet, a small part of her remained wary, waiting for Morgan to put matters on a personal level again. However, the talk remained general, and they left the restaurant arm in arm, replete and content, although Cat was vividly aware of the contact of his body whenever it touched hers.

It was a balmy night, but instead of walking, Morgan hailed a carriage for hire.

"It's not all that far," Cat said in surprise. "We walked here with no difficulty."

As they settled into the closed carriage, he said, "It can get rough here at night, especially down near the canal. There's no use taking chances. Oh, I'd defend you, my dear," he said with a laugh, "but I've dined so well, I don't know how effective I'd really be."

The carriage started up, throwing Morgan lightly against her. He remained where he was, without moving, his thigh touching hers. It was dark and private in the carriage, warm and close, and Cat felt her heart beating erratically. She found it difficult to breathe, and all her senses were acutely aware of his nearness. The odor of bay rum was pungent and pleasant in her nostrils; she could hear his shallow, rapid breathing; and although her hands lay quietly in her lap, her fingertips tingled, as if she were actually touching him.

Then he turned a little, shifting in the seat, his right arm going around her shoulders. Just as his arm settled lightly on her, the carriage rumbled over a pothole in the road, and his arm closed around her firmly. Involuntarily, Cat turned her face up to his, and without her ever knowing how it happened, he was kissing her.

She did not struggle or try to protest; this seemed the inevitable conclusion to the evening. She had never felt a man's lips on hers before, and it was more than pleasant. The tingle she had felt in her fingertips now spread throughout her entire body, and somewhere, in the core of her being, a vortex of confusing feelings began.

She realized that this was not proper conduct for a lady—letting a man, nearly a stranger, kiss her in the darkness of a closed carriage. Yet Cat was not hypocritical; she was enjoying what was happening to her, and had no thought of pretending otherwise, or of trying to fend

Morgan off. Not just yet, at any rate. She was curious to see what would happen next. Besides, she thought with an inward smile, she laid no claim to being a lady.

It ended all too soon. The forward motion of the carriage stopped, barely registering in Cat's chaotic thoughts, and Morgan leaned away from her mouth. He whispered, "We're here, Cat."

"Oh." She moved slightly away from him. Although he had scarcely touched her except on the lips, she felt mussed and disheveled, as though his hands had roamed all over her body; and she knew her face was flushed. She patted her hair, and pulled and tugged at her clothing, while he got out of the carriage. Dimly, she heard him discussing the fare with the driver, and then Morgan was back, leaning into the open door.

He extended a hand. "Come along, my dear."

She took his hand and let him help her to the ground. She sent a furtive look around, certain that anyone observing her would know of her wanton behavior in the carriage. But the area was dark and deserted, and Cat knew that the boat was deserted as well; Mick was off to the nearest tavern, and Timmie was supposed to be spending the night with a relative—he appeared to have relatives in every town and hamlet along the Erie.

With this realization a daring thought came to her. Taking Morgan's arm, she tried to push that thought out of her mind, but it kept nudging her as they made their way onto the canal boat. Why not? She was twenty-three years old, a woman grown, and never one to accommodate herself to the norm. The longing she felt to experience again the warmth and pleasure she had felt in Morgan's arms was almost uncontrollable. Why not, indeed?

At the door to her cabin Morgan stepped away from her and said formally, "I enjoyed your company this evening, Cat. Very much indeed. I will say good night now. . . ."

"Morgan . . ." She took his hand, suddenly bold. "Let's don't say good night just yet."

"I don't understand. . . ." He stared at her with arched

eyebrows, and then his slow smile came. "A gentleman never argues with a lady."

She led him into the dark, close confines of her small cabin. The window slits were open, letting in a faint breeze, but it was still quite warm; and the fever in Cat's blood made her even warmer; she felt a sheen of perspiration on her body. She reflected upon a phrase she had once read in *Godey's Lady Book:* "Horses sweat, men perspire, and women glow." Well, she was certainly doing more than "glowing," so she obviously was no lady.

She turned to close and bolt the door; and as she faced around again, Morgan caught her in his arms, bringing her hard against him. His kiss was like sweet fire, and this time his hands did roam over her body, touching lightly here and there, and Cat moaned softly, pressing herself closer to him.

She felt a growing hardness pressing against her belly, something she had only heard about in hushed whispers from the few women of her acquaintance. She supposed she should have been shocked, even revolted, yet she was not. She felt faint, the blood roaring through her head like a rushing cataract.

Then he was undressing her, with tenderness, with infinite care, but soon his hands became urgent.

She sighed softly, and stood back. "Let me, Morgan. You'll tear something." She gave a shaky laugh. "I don't have that many dresses to spare."

He stepped away from her; and as she finished removing her clothes, Cat heard rustling sounds as he took off his own clothing. She had to marvel at herself—undressing in her cabin for a man! It was something she would not have dreamed of earlier. She was not totally ignorant, even though she was a virgin; canal people were frank talking, and she had a vague idea of what took place when a man and a woman made love. She was trembling harder now, and it was partly from fright; but she had to admit to herself that it was mostly in anticipation. She could still feel the imprint of his mouth on hers, and the touch of his hands on her breasts and thighs.

She climbed into the bunk, instinctively pulling the sheet up over her nakedness. The bunk was quite narrow, and she wondered if they could manage; yet her bunk was no smaller than those on other canal boats she had visited, ones inhabited by both man and wife.

She heard Morgan moving. In the dark he banged against the edge of the bunk, and uttered a smothered curse. "We could use some light. Isn't there a lamp? Or even a candle?"

"No, please, Morgan," she said in a small voice. "Leave the cabin dark, please. This is . . ." She cleared her throat. "This is the first time for me, and I am embarrassed enough."

He fumbled along the length of her body. "Well, at least we don't need this." He stripped the sheet from the bunk, and then stretched out beside her. It was a close fit, and they both lay on their sides. Morgan's hands found her face and brought it to his, and she experienced his kiss again; and then his hands were on her body, stroking tenderly. Her nerve ends came alive, and she felt herself vibrate to his touch. The kiss continued, and she strained to get closer to him. His hand drifted down across her stomach and touched her in that most intimate place. At this strange male touch she gave an involuntary cry and flinched away, holding herself back from him.

"It's all right, Cat," he murmured in her ear. "I won't hurt you, I promise. I do love you, you know. I wasn't lying to you about that, just to . . ." he laughed softly, "just to have my way with you."

However, she was reluctant, lying rigid and still. Morgan found her lips again and began to caress her body with knowing hands—her back, her taut breasts, the flat plane of her belly.

Slowly, she relaxed under his ministrations, and gave herself up to the fiery sensations his touch aroused. Soon she was ablaze with want; she felt that she was on the trembling verge of some great discovery, some revelation that would change her entire life from this moment on. Morgan lowered his head, and his tongue found her nipples, gently caressing them, going from one to the other.

Cat moaned aloud, clutching the back of his head, forcing his mouth closer. Of course she had always known that her nipples were sensitive, but until now she had not realized just how much. After what seemed an endless time, time that was gradually becoming a torment for her, his hand once again moved lower. He touched the insides of her thighs, just the tips of his fingers stroking; and she trembled at his touch, but not from fear this time, and her thighs fell apart, opening to him.

Taking that as a signal, Morgan moved between her spread thighs. Cat tensed at the first tentative probing of his maleness.

"Just relax, Cat," he said soothingly. "It will be all right."

"I believe you," she said huskily. She reached up to run her hands down his braced arms. "Go ahead, I want you to."

She felt a brief burn of pain as he entered her, and then she forgot about it as she felt him thrust inside her, fully. We are so close, she marveled; his body is inside of me; that is as close as two people can get!

He was still for a little, and Cat gloried in the moment. She was a woman now; she had taken a man inside her!

Morgan began to move, slowly at first, and Cat savored the various sensations his thrustings aroused in her. She felt the beginning waves of pleasure, moving and spreading outward through her entire body. Why was this union of man and woman spoken of only in whispers, or as a subject of vulgar humor among men? It was nice, it was a warmth and a sharing, it was . . .

Suddenly, as Morgan began to move more rapidly and his breath quickened to a pant, it was no longer just *nice*. It was glorious, a rapturous delight! An involuntary cry escaped her, and she reached up and clutched him to her, seeking his mouth.

Her pleasure mounted and mounted, myriad sensations assailing her until it became almost torture. She felt that something was about to happen, should happen. Why did it not?

His tempo increased, his breathing raspy now, and the sound fueled her own passion. For the first time she began to move in counterpoint with him, her body taking over, all thoughts leaving her. All that existed was that marvelous feeling in her lower body, and she gave way to it, experiencing it to the fullest.

The feeling built and built to a point where she felt she could not bear it any longer. "Morgan, I . . ."

"Yes, my sweet, sweet Cat, I know," he whispered.

And then she felt him throb mightily in her, and she rose to meet him in a great convulsion, a sunburst of ecstasy that forced a strangled cry from her. It seemed to go on and on, a time without time, and yet she knew with the small part of her mind that remained sane that it lasted only moments. Morgan fell heavily on her, his face buried in the curve of her shoulder, his breath hot on her skin.

Her loins shuddered again, and then she was finally still. She felt weak, exhausted, her heart thundering in her breast; and she could not speak. There were many things she wanted to say—the wonder of it; the unspeakable pleasure he had given her; and the emotion that must be love for him. But *was* it love? If she spoke of it now, she might be speaking under the influence of her intense pleasure.

In the end, she said nothing. Moving away to lie beside her again, Morgan was the first to speak. "Did I hurt you, darling Cat?"

On the contrary, she thought; but she simply shook her head.

"I do love you, Cat." He caressed her face with his

fingers, fingertips lingering on her lips. "Do you love me in return?"

She did not answer.

"You must feel something for me to lie with me like this. Most women do not lie with a man unless they love him."

Feeling pressured by his insistence, Cat spoke for the first time, her tone a trifle tart. "I am not most women, Morgan. You should know that by now."

"Oh, I know *that* well enough," he said wryly. "And I suppose that's part of your charm, but you can be most exasperating at times."

"Because I wear men's clothes and like to do a man's work? Because I don't act like you think a woman should?"

"All of that, and more."

Restlessly, she turned her face away from him. "I am what I am, Morgan."

"I just want to know if you love me."

"I can't answer that right now, Morgan. Give me time to sort things out in my mind. This is all so . . . so *sudden*. This is all new to me."

"It's happened to men and women since the beginning of time. It's the way of things, Cat."

"But it's never happened to me, and I don't want to be pushed into something I may regret later."

"Regret?" He sat up on the edge of the bunk.

She sighed, some of the pleasure of the last moments fading. "Morgan, just don't push me! Give me time!"

He remained sitting on the edge of the bunk, and she felt that somehow he had moved away from her.

"Very well, Cat. If that's what you want. I'd better go now, before Mick comes back."

Silently, he rose and began to dress, and Cat, sorry now for offending him, remained silent also, wishing there was some way to make him understand. She *did* care for him. She had received profound pleasure from what they had just done; but was that love? She almost called out to him. She wanted to say something to ease the breach her words had caused; but before she could get the words out, he was gone, and she was alone in the cabin.

She felt tears sting her eyes, and she blinked angrily. It had been so beautiful; why had he not let things alone? And why had she recoiled from his question? She fell asleep with tears upon her face, and the signs of their lovemaking upon her body.

Timmie Watkins was returning to the *Cat* after having supper with his aunt. He was hurrying to get back to the boat. Although he had a dozen or more relatives living along the Erie, Timmie had been an orphan since the age of three. Up until a year ago he had lived with first one relative, then another; although they all treated him well enough, he had never been really happy until he went to work for the Carnahans. It had seemed to him that he had finally found a home at last, and he had been very happy—until recently.

He had fallen hopelessly in love with Cat, and he had had hopes that someday she might return his love. Those hopes had been dashed when he had seen her all dressed up the night she had gone to dinner with the stranger several weeks ago. Timmie had always thought Cat was beautiful, but he had never realized just how beautiful until he had seen her dressed in proper women's clothing. How could she ever love a mere hoggee?

And then, of course, there was the stranger, Morgan Kane. Timmie had seen the way Kane looked at Cat, and Timmie knew that any chance he might have with her was hopeless as long as Kane was around.

As the *Cat* appeared in the dim moonlight, Timmie started to step on board, then froze as he saw the door of Cat's cabin open and a figure emerge. He saw that it was too large to be Miss Catherine and realized that it had to be a man. He tensed, suddenly worried that some man had done harm to Cat.

Then the man turned about, and Timmie recognized Morgan Kane. Timmie shrank back into the shadows as

Kane jumped onto the bank and headed in the direction of town. Timmie stood staring after him, fists clenched, in the grip of a trembling fury.

He knew what had just taken place, and it made him sick to his soul. How could Miss Catherine do such a thing? In that moment his love began to sour, and started to turn toward hate.

Chapter Eight

THE next morning was glorious, clear and sunny, heralding the approach of full summer. It was a day to match Cat's feelings. She woke late, and was for a moment puzzled as to why she felt so good. Then the memory of last night flooded back to her, and she stretched like a contented kitten.

She dressed quickly and went up on deck. Everything seemed sharper this morning—the air smelled like wine; the songs of the birds along the canal bank sounded sweeter than she remembered; and everything she touched had a different feel to it. It was as though her passage into womanhood had sharpened all her senses, and it was wonderful to be alive.

Mick, looking disheveled and hung over, was sitting by the tiller, sipping at a mug of hot tea. Timmie was exercising the mules along the towpath, but Morgan was nowhere to be seen.

"Good morning, Mick. Where's Morgan?"

"How should I know? I'm not the lad's keeper," he said grumpily.

"But haven't you seen him?"

"Nope. He didn't even sleep in the cabin last night. Leastways, he wasn't in his bunk when I came back, about midnight. Never did show up." He gave her a look edged with malice. "Maybe the boyo decided he'd had enough of canal life, and snuck away in the night."

Hiding her alarm as best she could, Cat said, "Did he take his things?"

"What things? All the bucko has is the clothes he was wearing." He gestured and turned away, without looking at her again. "I'm thinking it's good riddance if he is gone."

She opened her mouth to retort hotly, mentioning the business Morgan had gotten them, but she refrained, afraid that she might give herself away if she said too much.

She turned away and mounted the towpath, staring up toward the town. Her good spirits had vanished. Cat knew that if Morgan *had* left, she would miss him sorely. But would he just sneak away in the night? That was not like him. . . .

And then she saw him striding along the towpath toward her. Her heart gave a great leap of joy, but she had herself composed by the time he reached her.

"Good morning, my dear," he said gravely, his eyes searching hers. "How are you this grand morning?"

"I'm fine," she said in a neutral voice. "I was just wondering where you were."

"I had things to do. I've been searching for a cargo for the *Cat*."

She wanted to ask him where he had been all night—surely he could not have looked for a cargo at night—but again she held her tongue.

"Did you find anything?"

He nodded, smiling. "Oh, yes, a load of grain. I took it at a price lower than the going rate. I hope you don't mind. I figured that was better than going back empty."

"I don't mind at all; I think it's wonderful. You're a born canawler, Morgan!" She experienced a sudden desire to reach out and touch him, and then he spoiled it.

"The wagons will be here in about"—he took out his watch—"an hour."

"You were pretty sure of yourself, weren't you?" she

said testily. "I gave you no authority to make such decisions!"

"But you just agreed that it was a good deal," he pointed out.

"All right, all right. But next time you might consult me first."

"I had to act quickly, Cat. Two other canal-boat owners came in while I was there. If I'd left to consult with you, without an agreement being reached, the grain merchant might have given the cargo to one of the others."

Knowing that he was right did not wholly appease her, but she said nothing more; instead, she turned toward the boat, calling out, "Timmie, get the mules fed. We have a cargo coming, and will be departing before too long."

As she stepped onto the boat, Mick said, "What cargo, daughter? I didn't know you had arranged anything."

"I didn't, Morgan did," she said curtly. "That's where he's been this morning."

"By my sainted mother!" Mick began to grin for the first time that morning, and slapped his knee. "The boyo is showing his worth. Maybe I was wrong about him all along."

"Don't get carried away," she said sourly.

He peered at her shrewdly. "What's wrong, daughter? Beginning to like the lad, are you?"

She looked away. "I like him well enough."

"A few days ago, I might have objected, but I'm beginning to take to young Kane. He's turning into an upstanding young fellow, in my judgment. It's past time for you to find a young man, I'm after thinking."

"And only a short time ago, you told me I was making a mistake taking him onto the *Cat*." She glared at him in exasperation.

"A man can always change his mind, can't he?" Mick said airily. "I'm thinking maybe we should consider giving him something more than just his bed and board. A man always works harder when he thinks he's appreciated."

"Now he's appreciated, is he?" she said angrily. "Well, we'll see."

To her relief, wagons began pulling in alongside the boat, ending the conversation, which was growing uncomfortable for Cat. They all pitched in, and five wagonloads of grain were soon stored below. Cat was introduced to the grain merchant, a plump, harried-looking individual named Fredricks.

"This man of yours, Miss Carnahan," Fredricks said, "is a pretty convincing fellow. If he hadn't been, I might have given my grain to another hauler. One man there offered to haul it much cheaper, but I'd already agreed to let you have it. I hope I don't have cause to regret my decision."

Cat felt her face flush at the phrase *this man of yours*, but she returned the merchant's gaze steadily and said, "You won't have cause to regret it, Mr. Fredricks, I promise you."

As they got under way, Morgan came to Cat at the tiller and said, "You know who one of those other two canawlers was? I'm sure he was the one who offered the lower rate. It was Simon Maphis."

"Maphis? And you beat him at his own game? Oh, I could kiss you for that, Morgan!"

"Why not?" he said jauntily, glancing around. "No one's looking."

Cat turned to tilt her face up to his, and he kissed her full on the mouth.

Simon Maphis was burning, infuriated that *Carnahan's Cat* had gotten the load of grain instead of the *King*. He had argued with the stupid grain merchant in vain, offering a much lower rate; but Fredricks had doggedly insisted that he had already given his word to Morgan Kane.

Now, at the end of a long day's futile efforts to find another cargo, Maphis trudged back to his boat. He was going to have to return to Albany with an empty hold; and he had Cat Carnahan, and her fancy fellow, to thank for that. Damn her to hell and gone!

Well, she was going to pay for that, and pay dearly. It was almost dark when he boarded his boat. He found his hoggee asleep on deck. He gave him a brutal kick in the ribs, booting him awake, and snarled, "Get the mules hitched, damn you, we're moving out!"

The hoggee got to his feet, whining. "But, Mr. Maphis, it's soon dark."

"I don't care about that. I want to catch up to *Carnahan's Cat*."

"But she left early this morning. I saw her."

"That's why I'm traveling all night. She's loaded, damn that woman to hell, and I'm not. We'll catch her. We'd better, or I'll pound your head to a bloody pulp!"

Soon they were under way, two burning lanterns bobbing in the bow like huge fireflies. Maphis had one other crew member, a drunken lout who was off in some tavern, no doubt; but Maphis left him behind without a thought. When he had to hire another hand, Maphis could pick up some derelict in the Side-Cut who would serve his purpose just as well.

For what he intended to do now, he needed little help; and he wanted no more witnesses than necessary. He had no fears that the hoggee would tell on him; he was only a cowed lad, and a half-wit at that. Maphis had no definite plan—the only thing he had in mind was the destruction, or at least the disabling, of *Carnahan's Cat*. He recalled Tate Brawley's words of caution, that any action against the Carnahans' boat should be planned out carefully beforehand. Well, to hell with that! It was not in Maphis's nature to be cautious, especially when his temper was running high, as it was now. At the moment he felt angry enough to tear the *Cat* apart with his bare hands, timber by timber, and strangle anyone who got in his way.

He stood at the tiller, tall and forbidding, letting the *King* move along at will, heedless of any other canal boats out at night. If any happened to be in his way, he would ram them. Early on, he had plated the hull of the bow with iron. He had considered ramming the *Cat*, but he wanted to destroy her totally, not just to cripple her; at the slow speeds a canal boat could obtain, it was unlikely that ramming could do enough damage to sink her. No, he would have to think of another way.

He kept the *King* running all night. Once, the hoggee dropped back to complain, "The mules are worn out, Mr. Maphis. We keep going without resting them, they'll drop in their traces."

Maphis snarled, "They drop, let them drop. I'll get more. You just keep them moving."

They were stolen mules anyway, and he could always steal another pair. Above all else he wanted to catch up with *Carnahan's Cat*.

Shortly after sunrise he mounted to the top of the cabin and squinted up ahead, shading his eyes against the sun's glare. There she was, two canal boats ahead!

He called the hoggee back and said, "All right, I've spotted her. We can slow down a little. Let the animals rest now and then. I just want to keep the *Cat* in sight until she ties up for the night."

"I'm hongry, Mr. Maphis," the hoggee said timidly.

"All right, I can eat, too. We'll stop for a bit whilst you fix us something to eat."

Maphis was tired from the long night without sleep, but he had the stamina of an elephant; and his anger was such that he knew he could last throughout the day and into the night, with maybe a short nap. He did not plan on doing anything until well after dark, when the *Cat* was moored and all aboard were asleep.

Thinking of the night reminded Maphis of the lanterns on the bow. Lashing the tiller into place, he made his way forward to blow them out. As he blew out the last one, he froze, struck by a sudden idea. Fire! That was the solution! He should have thought of it before. All canal-boat owners were terrified of fire; a good blaze could consume a canal boat within a short time. Yes, that was it, that would put the Carnahans out of business for good.

Chuckling to himself, Maphis went back to the tiller and settled down to sit out the daylight hours, waiting impatiently for darkness.

Cat selected a small side-cut, and they tied up there shortly after sundown. She watched Morgan help Timmie stable the mules, while Mick went below to prepare supper. She studied Morgan covertly, watching his well-muscled body in graceful movement, observing the sure quickness of his hands; and she shivered slightly as she remembered those hands on her body last night.

For the first time in a long while, she felt relaxed, without concern about where their next cargo was coming from. She felt confident that Morgan would always manage to find them something to earn money. Although she had little faith in luck—in her opinion, a person made his own luck—she had the feeling that the presence of Morgan Kane on board the boat was a talisman of a brighter future.

The spot where they had moored was lovely; off to the right was an area parklike in its beauty—a small glade, with trees in full leafage, and wild flowers and flowering shrubs.

Her thoughts were interrupted as she saw Morgan coming along the towpath toward where she sat by the tiller. He made the jump onto the boat easily; and watching him, Cat suddenly wanted him, a want that was a sweet ache. She wanted to be in his arms again; she wanted again what she had experienced last night. He stopped before her, and as she looked up, his face went still, his eyes staring down into hers; and she realized that her want must be naked on her face. At that moment she did not care; she wanted him to know!

"Cat . . ." He reached out to touch her, and then the moment was shattered by the sound of a bell clanging on the canal. With a start Morgan glanced around at a small boat hurrying east, pulled by a team of four horses. A bell hung on the bow, and a man was standing beside it. Even as Morgan watched, he clanged it again.

"What the hell is *that*?"

Cat laughed. "That is a hurry-up boat."

"And what is a hurry-up boat?"

"Troubleshooting boats. There's either a breach upstream in the berm or the towpath. Or they could be going to the rescue of a 'mudlark.' And before you ask, a mudlark is any boat that has run aground."

Morgan's attention returned to her again, but before he could speak, Mick's head poked up from below. "Food's ready, folks! Shall we eat on deck, as usual?"

Struggling for composure, Cat nodded. "Of course, Mick." She started to rise. "I'll help you bring it up."

"No, you sit there." Morgan's hand closed on her shoulder, squeezing intimately, his burning gaze still locked with hers. "I'll help your father."

"There's a bottle of wine hidden in the galley, Morgan," she called after him. "Hidden in a flour bin on the top right-hand shelf."

Mick stared at her in disbelief. "A bottle on board? I thought you were opposed to that, daughter."

"I am, usually, but I bought one in Buffalo." She shrugged defensively.

The wine and the simple but hearty food that Mick had prepared further relaxed Cat. She sat quietly, listening with amusement as her father told Morgan tall tales about the Erie, a sure indication that Mick not only accepted Morgan as one of them but that he liked the man.

"There was this mad sea captain," Mick said, "who spent good money for a dead whale that had been washed up on a Cape Cod beach. Now this bucko figured that he was going to get rich off'n that dead creature, by showing it to people along the Erie, charging a goodly fee, o'course. Trouble was, after the thing had been out in the sun for a week or so, it began to stink something terrible. Nobody would go within a hundred yards of this feller's boat, much less pay to go and see the bloody carcass. The captain tried to get rid of the stinking carcass by dumping it into the canal at night. But a canal walker spotted him, reported him, and the captain was fined two dollars for interfering with canal traffic. You know what finally happened?" Mick laughed uproariously. "He found a farmer about as mad as he was, and convinced him that the whale would make good fertilizer for his crops. He sold the whale to him for eight cents! Jaysus, no telling how much that captain was out of pocket, towing that great carcass all that way!"

Morgan laughed appreciatively, and Cat joined in, although she had heard the story many times. Morgan's glance met hers, and again Cat felt the stirring of desire. She moved restlessly, hoping that Morgan would make some move to get her alone, but Mick was rambling on.

"You've probably heard how the Irish built the old Erie. The bogtrotters, more than three thousand of them, put their blood, sweat, and tears into the building of it. Many a one of them died of it, working in that devil's own swamp, the mosquito- and malaria-infested Montezuma Marsh west of Syracuse, wearing only trousers, boots, and a slouch cap to protect them from the broiling sun. And for all this, bucko, they were paid the king's ransom, four shillings a day, seven days a week. Rainless days, that is. For if it rained, they couldn't work, you see. At night they slept with a dozen other bogtrotters on the floor, in shanties, which cost next to nothing to build. They ate the coarsest and the cheapest food the contractor could find. Oh, yes, I'm after forgetting. . . . They also had the jigger boss, which was a half-gill of whiskey or rum doled out to them sixteen times a day. That was to be sure they kept going. The poor lads, many of them didn't; they died in their tracks, knee deep in muck. Aye, it was no child's play, the building of the Erie."

When Mick had finally run out of steam, and had taken the dishes down to the galley, Morgan said, "Would you like to walk for a little, Cat? It's a nice night, and we might sleep better for a bit of a stroll."

Cat rose to her feet eagerly. "I'd like that very much, Morgan."

As she let Morgan help her off the boat, Cat happened to glance back. She saw Timmie staring at her with a strange, intense look, and she wondered if he suspected what was going on. She dismissed any concern for Timmie Watkins with a mental shrug; despite the fact that he had been mooning over her, he had no hold on her, and she had certainly never once had any romantic thoughts about the hoggee. Cat was not a snob—the fact that he was a hoggee had no bearing—but he was several years younger than she, and seemed little more than a callow youth to her.

She took Morgan's arm, and they strolled along the towpath. There was a slice of a moon, which gave a little light filtering through the trees shadowing the path. Insects hummed in the warm darkness, and somewhere a frog croaked hoarsely.

Morgan said, "I do believe that Mick is coming around to approving of me, finally."

Cat smiled up at him. "You can be sure of it. When he banters with someone like he did with you tonight, he likes that someone."

"Well, the feeling is mutual, Cat. I like your father."

"I like him, too, most of the time. Like I told you, he's an easy man to like." She sighed plaintively. "If only he'd ease off on the drink."

Morgan shrugged. "Well, we all have our faults, some to a greater degree than others."

"And you, you seem to have taken to canal life well enough. Have you given any more thought to how long you'll stay with us?" She held her breath for his answer.

"I think I'll stick around for a while." He squeezed her arm.

"But what if your memory comes back and you find you're . . . Well, if you find you're an important man somewhere, with a good job and responsibilities?"

"Somehow I'm sure I don't have any responsibilities,

nothing to take me away from the Erie, and you, if I chose to stay."

"I'm glad you feel that way, Morgan." Her breath was coming fast, and her heartbeat was erratic.

Morgan turned them back toward the boat, and he did not speak again until they neared the side-cut. "Shall we walk over in that direction, toward that glade?"

She nodded mutely, already anticipating what was about to happen. Her body turned soft and hot with need. She wanted this man with an intensity that she would not have thought possible.

"There's one bad thing about canal boats," he said in a low voice. "They're so cramped, there's almost no privacy."

"I know," she said, detesting the tremble in her voice.

He led her into the secluded area and under a spreading tree. Cupping her face between his hands, he kissed her, lightly at first. She came against him hard, returning his kiss with ardor, hands pressing his back.

"Dear, sweet Cat," Morgan murmured. "You have been in my thoughts all day, and I would become passionate just thinking about last night."

"I know. Me, too," she said shakily.

He stepped back from her, and removed his coat, spreading it on the thick grass. Cat sank to her knees on it, and Morgan dropped down beside her, taking her into his arms again. They embraced like that, swaying back and forth in their mounting passion. His hand moved under her shirt, seeking her breasts.

Cat said, "Wait, let me."

"Those damned trousers and shirt are like a suit of armor," he grumbled.

She did not answer, but quickly divested herself of the trousers, shirt, and undergarments, then lay with pounding heart while he undressed. His tall, muscular body had the look of a statue, dappled by the moonlight filtering through the leaves. Somehow, being out in the open like this, with the night like a warm pulse beating around them, made it seem more natural to Cat, completely without any coloring of shame.

Then he was beside her, his hands on her breasts, his mouth on hers. Cat, emboldened, reached down between them, and for the first time touched a man's organ. Morgan gasped at her touch, and Cat gloried in her ability to arouse such a reaction. The hardness of him was smooth and silken warm to her stroking fingers.

With a groan he moved to enter her. Cat was ready for him, and this time there was no stab of pain; their loving this time had a practiced ease, as though their bodies had thus engaged countless times before.

She locked her arms around his shoulders, and held him imprisoned there, his wildness restricted by the contraction of her thighs around him. As her pleasure increased, Cat became abandoned, her wildness matching his own, until her convulsions of rapture began. Morgan groaned loudly, his arms tightening around her as he began to shudder out his ecstasy.

"Ah, my sweet Cat, my sweet wanton, how I love you!"

When he finally lay beside her, she said musingly, "You called me wanton, Morgan. Am I?"

"I think so, but I meant it in the nicest sense, and there's nothing wrong with that. It's as it should be, and I love you the more for it."

She stirred uneasily. "But, a wanton . . . A woman who is that is not considered a good woman. Landsmen think of most canal women as wantons, or tarts."

He traced the line of her jaw with his finger. "Ah, but *wanton* can mean many other things. It can mean playful, capricious, unrestrained, and you are all those things. Besides, names mean very little. It's a label people put on other people they don't like, or understand. It's what a person feels about themselves that truly matters. Do you feel like a *bad* woman?"

She thought for a moment. "No, I feel good about myself, I feel good about what's happened to me." Blushing furiously, she hid her face in the crook of her shoulder.

"Then it's all right, isn't it? Besides, love, you told me, many times, that you care little about what other people think of you."

"But this is something different. I just didn't want you to think that I'm . . ."

"Hush." He covered her mouth with his hand. "I think you're the best woman I've ever known, and I love you."

There was an expectant pause, and Cat knew that he wanted her to answer in kind; but she could not, not just yet. She stirred and sat up. "It grows late, and Mick and Timmie will soon begin to wonder. We'd best get back."

"As you wish, Cat." There was an edge of disappointment in his voice.

He got up, picked up his clothes, and began to dress. In a few minutes they were ready to go back, and Cat took his arm as they strolled back toward the boat, both silent, busy with their own thoughts.

Climbing up the towpath, they soon could see the *Cat*. The boat was dark, and Cat assumed that both Mick and Timmie were bedded down for the night, for which she was glad; she was positive that there was a glow about her, and Mick could surmise from one look at her what had just occurred.

Then she stopped, blinking, and pulled at Morgan's arm. "What's that glow?"

Morgan followed the direction of her pointing finger. "Fire, it must be fire!"

He began to run, with Cat right on his heels. As they drew near, Cat saw a dark figure squatting in the shallow water by the bow. Even as she watched, she saw the figure toss a pail of liquid against the boat, and the fire flared. The *Cat* was on fire; someone was putting the torch to her!

Morgan bellowed, "Hey there! What the hell are you doing?"

Without waiting for a response, Morgan launched himself off the towpath. Cat saw the squatting man turn up his face, and in the light of the flames she recognized

Simon Maphis. Then Morgan collided with him, knocking him flat. They rolled over and over, tumbling together into the deeper water.

Cat did not pause to watch. She leaped on board the boat, screaming, "Fire! Mick, Timmie! Fire! Get buckets, quick!"

They always kept a few buckets on deck, some filled with water, others with sand. Fire was a constant threat to canal boats. Fortunately, the water of the canal kept the wooden hulls wet; but once a fire got a good start, it was difficult to put out.

She grabbed a pail of water, ran to the rail, and dumped it onto the burning planks. Out of the corner of her eye she saw Morgan and Maphis struggling in the water, but she had no time to spare for them. As she turned back, Mick charged up on deck, wild of eye, hair tousled, and Timmie came running up behind him.

Mick demanded, "What is it, daughter?"

"Simon Maphis put a torch to the bow. At least one plank is on fire."

"Timmie, grab a bucket, and let's get down to the bow. There we can dip water out of the canal. It'll be easier and faster." Mick picked up a bucket, vaulted to the bank, and scrambled down out of sight. Timmie followed him with another bucket.

The threat of disaster had turned her father into the old Mick—commanding, quick to make a decision, and sure of himself. Cat felt a flush of pride in him.

By the time she reached the bow with another bucket of water, the two men stood hip deep in water, busily filling their buckets with canal water and splashing it against the burning planks. Even as Cat watched, the flames went out. Smoke roiled up from the charred wood, and the odor caused her to hold her breath.

Mick dumped another two buckets against the bow, then stepped back for a breath. Cat called down, "What's the extent of the damage?"

"Not too bad, girl. Just a couple of planks scorched. It's fortunate we are to discover it in time. We probably won't even have to replace them."

Cat drew a sigh of heartfelt relief, and then with a start she remembered Morgan and Simon Maphis. She looked around and saw them struggling in the shallow water near the bank of the cut. Morgan seemed frail and slender compared to Maphis's bearlike bulk. They were locked together like two wrestlers, swaying back and forth.

As she watched, they broke apart. Maphis aimed a blow at Morgan's head, bringing his arm around and down like a club. If the blow had landed, it would have knocked Morgan senseless; but he eluded the clumsy blow easily, ducking down and away. Then, still in a half-crouch, he came up under Maphis's flailing arms, and drove his fist deep into the other man's belly. Although the two men were too far away for Cat to hear, she knew that the blow must have driven the breath from Maphis, for he doubled up, clutching at his belly.

Morgan stood erect, locked his hands together, raised them high, and brought them down across the back of Maphis's neck. Maphis seemed to give a great sigh and fell face down into the water, disappearing from sight. Morgan stood waiting, poised over the spot where Maphis had sunk. Cat held her breath, wondering if Maphis was drowning. She started to call out to Morgan to pull him out; as much as she despised Simon Maphis, she did not wish to see him dead, not like this.

Then Maphis emerged from the muddy water, spluttering and gasping for breath. In the dim light Cat could see his white face turned up to Morgan. As Morgan started to hit him again, Maphis scrambled away, on his hands and knees, splashing water, and began clawing his way up the bank of the cut. Morgan stood without moving, watching Maphis as he reached the top of the bank and ran toward the towpath of the main canal. There, he turned left and soon disappeared into the night. Morgan made a dusting motion with his hands and turned toward the *Cat*.

"Are you all right, Morgan?" Cat called.

"I'm fine, just a little beat up and out of breath." He began to wade toward the bank.

"Ahoy, the boat!" a voice called from Cat's left.

Startled, she swung that way and saw a smaller canal boat across the narrow cut. A man stood at the tiller, his hands cupped around his mouth. "Are you in trouble?"

"Everything is fine now," she said.

"I saw the flames just as I started past the cut. Thinking your boat was on fire, I turned in here to assist if I could."

"No, it's all right, thank you anyway. We managed to put out the fire in time."

"That's good. I also saw the fight in the water. Did you catch someone putting the torch to your boat?"

"Yes, we did."

"Your man—does he need medical attention?"

"No, he's fine, as well." In the faint light Cat could see that the man was young, well dressed, and she could see lettering on his boat, but could not make out what it said.

"The reason I asked, I'm a doctor. Dr. Anthony Mason, at your service, ma'am, anytime you require medical attention. Pardon me if I seem to be drumming up trade." He laughed with a flash of white teeth. "The fact of it is, I suppose I am. I need all the patients I can get."

"You must really be new on the Erie. Most of us don't travel at night."

"Oh, I am aware of that, but the canal walker along here told me that a woman is badly in need of medical attention on a boat moored about a mile along the canal. So, if you have no need of my services, I shall be on my way. Perhaps we shall meet again. What is your name, ma'am?"

"I am Catherine Carnahan. My father, Mick Carnahan, and I own this boat."

"I am pleased to have met you, Miss Carnahan."

"And I you, Doctor. I'll keep you in mind, in case we ever need doctoring."

Cat faced around as Morgan, dripping wet, ranged alongside her. "Who is that?"

"A Dr. Anthony Mason."

Morgan said dryly, "If I remain on board the *Cat* much longer, he might be a nice fellow to know. I may need his services."

Cat took his hand. "I'm glad you're all right, Morgan. Simon Maphis is such a monster, I was afraid for you."

"Mick tells me that the damage is slight. I guess we're lucky. And I gather from what you've told me before that it would do little good to report the incident to the authorities."

"None whatsoever. If someone had been killed, or even seriously hurt, they might have taken some action, but damage to a canal boat is not considered worthy of their time and effort. Morgan, you'd better get out of those wet clothes before you catch your death of the influenza."

Simon Maphis was still seething with frustration and rage when Tate Brawley rode up to the *King* two days later. As he watched Brawley dismount and prepare to board the boat, Maphis debated with himself whether he should tell the man about the fiasco with the *Cat*. Maphis well knew that he had let his anger push him into premature action; his impatience to torch the Carnahan boat had led him to move too quickly. When conceiving his plan, Maphis had determined to wait until after midnight; but when he had scouted the moored boat shortly after nine that evening, there had been no lights showing, so he had surmised that all aboard were asleep. He had then hurried back to his own boat, filled a pail with coal oil, stuffed his pockets with sulfur matches, and hastened back to do the deed.

How could he have known that Morgan Kane and the girl were not on board? It was rotten luck that they had not been, and had caught him in the act. If Kane had not taken him so by surprise, he would not have been able to whip him in the fight that followed. That galled Maphis more than anything else—Kane beating him! No one on the Erie had ever been able to do that before!

But if he did not tell Brawley what had happened, the lottery broker would eventually hear about it anyway; and that would likely end their friendship. Maphis did not want that to happen; he had been making good side money peddling lottery tickets. However, he knew that Brawley would be displeased with him.

Brawley was more than displeased with him. "You're a fool, Maphis, a complete fool," were the first words he uttered when Maphis had told him the tale. "When we first discussed this, we agreed that we would have to move carefully, devise a clever plan. Nothing about your plan was carefully considered!"

"We agreed to that before they took my cargo away," Maphis said sullenly. "I wasn't able to get another load in Buffalo and had to leave with an empty hold. I had reason to torch their damned boat—they attacked my livelihood!"

"It seems to me they're just sharper at getting business than you are," Brawley said coldly. He began to pace the narrow confines of the deck, absently fingering his side whiskers. Suddenly he wheeled on Maphis. "Do you still want to do them harm?"

"You're damned right I do! Now more than ever."

"I also have reason to see the Carnahans, and Morgan Kane, suffer, but I also don't wish to fail. So, if we're still to be associates, you have to follow my lead."

Maphis said eagerly, "Do you have a plan?"

"Not at the moment, but I will think of one, you can be sure. But first, I want your word that you'll do exactly what I tell you from now on."

"You have it. But I don't want to wait too long."

"You won't have to. But remember that old adage, Maphis: Patience is a virtue. Too hasty to act has seen many a man ruined, if not dead. You losing the tussle with Kane should tell you that."

"He caught me by surprise. It won't happen the next time. The next time he'll be the loser. Nobody whips Simon Maphis without living to regret it!" Maphis drew himself up arrogantly. "I am the King of the Erie, and it'll pay Kane not to forget it."

Chapter Nine

MORGAN decided it was past time that he began doing the job he had come to the Erie to perform. He had been so engrossed with learning canal-boat life, and with courting Cat, that he had neglected his investigation. He also felt guilty over the fact that he had not told her of his purpose here, and because he had let her believe that he still had not regained his memory. However, he realized that it was too late now to tell her the truth. He had let too much time elapse; she would be absolutely furious with him, believing that he was making a fool of her, and she would be right.

After giving much thought to it, Morgan realized that the best way to continue his investigation would be to form some sort of alliance with Tate Brawley. It was obvious that Brawley was the busiest ticket broker along the Erie, and he also represented the Union Canal Company, the company his uncle was after. Morgan was sorry now that he had antagonized the man, although he did detest him. He made up his mind to make contact with Brawley at the very first opportunity.

His chance came in a tavern in Albany, after the *Cat* had delivered the cargo of grain. Morgan was scouting the merchants in Albany for some kind of cargo to haul west. After a long, hard day with no success, he headed back for the *Cat.* Passing a tavern, he decided to stop in for an ale. The tavern was nearly empty, redolent of spilled beer and liquor. When Morgan received his mug of ale and had paid for it, he faced about to scan the room; and that was when he spotted Tate Brawley alone in a booth in the rear. Brawley had a bottle of whiskey at his elbow and a glass, and his head was bent over a small ledger book as he scribbled in it with a pen.

Morgan debated for a moment, then went down the room carrying his ale. He stopped at the booth and waited for Brawley to glance up. Brawley did, and scowled when he saw who it was. "What do you want, Kane?"

Morgan gestured, and said diffidently, "Mind if I join you?"

"I do mind," Brawley said curtly. "We have nothing to talk about. You've made that plain the times we've met."

Morgan strove for the right apologetic note, unhappy at having to debase himself before this scoundrel. "I'm sorry about that. I sometimes act on impulse." He grinned abashedly. "It often gets me into trouble. But I thought if you would accept my apology, we could start over on a more friendly basis."

Brawley leaned back, clearly beginning to enjoy himself. "Now why on earth should we want to do that? Can you give me one good reason?"

"Speaking for myself, yes. I need to earn some extra money. Working a canal boat doesn't pay much. I thought perhaps I could sell lottery tickets for you as a sideline. I understand that some of your salesmen are doing well."

"They are all doing well. Men working for me, Kane, always do well," Brawley said complacently.

"Then I would think that you could always use more."

"Possibly, but I don't just take on any gent who walks into a tavern. Why don't you sit down, and we'll discuss it." Brawley waved a hand.

Morgan slid into the booth across from the ticket broker and took a sip of his ale.

Brawley said, "From a couple of snide remarks at our previous meetings, I gather you don't approve of lotteries."

"That's not exactly true. I was just trying to impress Miss Carnahan," Morgan lied, sending up a silent prayer: Forgive me, Cat.

Brawley peered at him narrowly. "I know nothing of you, Kane. For instance, what did you do before you went to work on a canal boat? It strikes me that you're a man of some education. Why stoop to working on a canal boat?"

Morgan hesitated for a moment, staring down into his ale. Should he tell the same lie he had told Cat? After a moment he looked up, doing his best to put on a face of candor. "That may be true, but I don't know, you see."

"I'm afraid I don't understand that remark."

"Well, you see, I was attacked by thugs in the Side-Cut, and as a result, I don't know who or what I am. Miss Carnahan was kind enough to come to my assistance. That is the reason I am working for her."

"That's a pretty wild story, if true. But I do understand that you were shrewd enough to steal a cargo right out from under the nose of Simon Maphis. That shows some cleverness on your part."

"I learn fast," Morgan said slyly.

"Evidently you do." Brawley was silent for a bit, toying with his whiskey glass, studying Morgan intently. Then he nodded decisively. "All right, Kane, I'll give you your chance. Twenty percent commission on every ticket you sell."

Morgan knew that the commission figure was outrageously low, and he displayed dismay. "That's not a very good commission, Mr. Brawley."

"It's what I pay rank beginners. You get some experience, prove your worth, I'll up the ante." Brawley gestured curtly. "Take it or leave it."

"Oh, I'll take it," Morgan said hastily. He stood up and extended his hand. "It's a deal, Mr. Brawley."

Brawley hesitated for a moment, then gingerly shook Morgan's hand.

As Morgan strode out of the tavern, his mind busy with plans for his investigation, he failed to notice Timmie Watkins, the hoggee, huddled in a booth in a dark corner. Timmie had come to the tavern to fetch a bottle of liquor for Mr. Carnahan. He had spotted Mr. Kane and a strange man deep in conversation in the booth in the rear, so he had hidden back in the corner. And he had observed them strike some kind of a bargain and shake hands on it. As he waited for Mr. Kane to get a good lead on him, Timmie mulled this information over in his mind, wondering how he could use it to discredit Morgan Kane in Miss Catherine's eyes.

The next day Morgan managed to find a load of produce to haul fifty miles toward Buffalo. Canawlers did not like to haul fresh produce, since it tended to spoil easily in the heat of the stuffy holds; but Morgan bargained for a good haulage rate, with the promise that they would travel day and night until the load was delivered.

When Morgan returned to the *Cat*, he was leading a team of mules. Cat frowned at them. "What are those extra mules for?"

"I got a load of fresh produce for us, Cat, a fifty-mile haul."

Cat shook her head disapprovingly. "You know that's not a good idea. It can easily spoil, Morgan, and then we're responsible for it."

"That's why I hired a team of mules. We'll travel day and night, trading off the mules. I'll spell Timmie on the towpath."

"Hiring mules had to cost a great deal. Where's our profit in that?"

"I managed to get a good rate. We're getting enough to more than pay for the hire of the mules."

Mick, standing nearby, slapped his leg. "By the saints, bucko, you are becoming a blooming good canawler!"

Morgan said, "You know, it seems to me that a second team would be a good investment, Cat. I was talking to one canawler who has two teams, and he claims he averages fifteen to twenty miles a day extra with a trade-off team."

"Mules cost money," Cat said shortly.

"But they would soon pay for themselves," Morgan argued.

"Money we haven't got," she retorted, and turned away, dismissing the subject.

Morgan's behavior over the next two weeks mystified Cat. They still made love whenever the chance presented itself—which was not too often, given the constant presence of Mick and Timmie—and that was as pleasurable to Cat as ever; but there was a distracted air about Morgan that she did not understand. The first two times he had made love to her, there was no doubt that every part of his being was concentrated on her and nothing else; but now she had the feeling that his mind was on something else at odd moments, and he struck her as evasive when she questioned him.

Of course, whenever they were not moving he was quite busy, occupied with getting cargo for the boat. Somehow, he always managed to find something; sometimes the cargo was unusual for a canal boat, yet Cat was getting accustomed to that. They were beginning to show a profit now, and that was the important thing. They had reached an agreement: as soon as their profit margin was steady, Morgan was to receive a commission on every cargo he got for them.

However, in some cities, Morgan was gone from the boat from dawn until long after dark, and he appeared preoccupied on his return. On their arrival in Buffalo the mystery was cleared up—cleared up by Timmie, much to Cat's surprise.

These days Timmie spoke to her only when necessary for the operation of the boat, and he moped about with a sullen, resentful air. Cat knew the cause of it, and she was sorry for the lad, yet it was a fact that he would have to get used to. She owed nothing to Timmie, and her life was her own to do with as she saw fit.

She had noticed over the past few days that Timmie often disappeared about the time Morgan did, usually coming back before the older man did; but Cat thought little of it, since Timmie had relatives in almost every town along the Erie; and he had few duties to occupy him when they were docked, unless there was a cargo to load or unload.

On this day, their second in Buffalo, Cat was lounging on deck by the tiller when she saw Timmie hurrying up. Since the days were now quite hot, a canvas awning had been rigged over the stern, shading Cat from the sun while she sat at the tiller; and she usually took advantage of the shade whenever she could.

Somewhat to her surprise, Timmie came down the boat toward her. His expression was a mixture of trepidation and gloating. "Miss Catherine," he began hesitantly, "there's somethun' you should see."

"What's that, Timmie?" she said with little interest.

"It be better for you to see yourself first. Likely you wouldn't believe me, should I just tell you."

"Is it that important?" she asked irritably. "It's awfully hot in the sun today."

"It's almighty important," he said eagerly. "You'll know, once you see."

"All right, let me get a parasol."

She made her way forward to her cabin for a parasol. As she left the *Cat*, following the hoggee, it never occurred to Cat that it might appear incongruous, a person scarcely recognizable as a woman, in men's clothing, carrying a parasol.

Timmie led her along the waterfront and shortly stopped before a tavern. He indicated the tavern with a nod of his head, and started to push open the door for her.

"Wait." Cat placed a hand on his arm, staying him. "I can't go into a place like that. Ladies aren't allowed."

"To see what you have to see, Miss Catherine, you must go inside. It's all right, I'll be with you."

He took her arm with a firmness that surprised her, pushed open the door, and escorted her inside.

And then something caught her attention that drove everything else from her mind. Standing at the long bar was Morgan Kane, his back to the door; and gathered around him were several men, all listening intently as he talked glibly. "Gents, buy a ticket from me, and your fortune is made! The Union Canal Lottery Company has paid out some thirty million dollars over the past twenty years in prize money. Now, for the price of a ticket, just five dollars, you can win some of that prize money." Morgan waved a fistful of tickets over his head. "If you don't have the whole five dollars, talk to others interested, and split it up between you. You can share in a prize-winning ticket for as little as sixty-three cents!"

Cat could only stare, stunned. This was a Morgan she did not recognize—slick, sleazy, fast talking. She felt anger rising like a tide in her.

Now Morgan was chanting, "If Lady Luck is good to you / You will feel no pain. / Buy a diamond for your girl Sue, / If you deal with Morgan Kane!"

Now some of the men gathered around Morgan had taken notice of Cat, and were scowling at this intrusion of a woman into their territory. Morgan, evidently sensing that he was losing their attention, faced around slowly. His mouth fell open, and he paled slightly.

Recovering, he came quickly down the room toward her. "Cat, what on earth are you doing in here?"

"I might ask the same of you, Mr. Kane," she said icily. "What is this you're doing without my knowledge?"

"Cat, it's not the way it looks. I can explain."

"I need no explanation. I can see for myself what you are doing. It's bad enough, selling lottery tickets. You well know how opposed to that I am. But you're doing it as an employee of the *Cat*. Everyone along the Erie will naturally think I am sanctioning it. That is despicable,

Morgan!" Cat forced back a hot rush of tears. "I would never have believed you capable of such a thing!"

"Cat . . ." He tried to take her hand, but she snatched it away. "Let's go someplace where we can talk privately."

"I wouldn't dream of taking you away from your . . . business!" She almost spat the word. "I want you packed and off the *Cat* within the hour, and I never want to see you again."

He said desperately, "Cat, please give me a chance to explain."

"No!" she said violently. "I will never listen to your lies again, never! Come along, Timmie, take me out of this horrible place!"

Timmie, grinning openly, took her arm and escorted her out. Outside, he put on a grave face. "I'm sorry, Miss Catherine, but I thought you should be knowing what he was about."

"Yes, Timmie," she said dully. "You did the right thing. Thank you . . ."

"Cat, dammit, wait a minute!"

She ignored Morgan's voice and hurried on. Then he had her by the elbow, whirling her around to face him.

Timmie tried to intervene. "Don't you dare harm Miss Catherine!"

"Timmie, this is none of your business," Morgan said through gritted teeth. "Now be off with you!"

Timmie looked uncertainly at Cat, who gestured to him. "Go on, Timmie, I'll be all right."

The hoggee finally trudged off, looking back over his shoulder from time to time.

Cat looked at Morgan with unrelenting eyes. "Nothing you can say, Mr. Kane, will make any difference. Besides what you were doing in there, something else just occurred to me. The manner in which you were hawking those tickets makes it clear to me that you are no stranger to the trade. What about your loss of memory, sir? How did you know what to do?"

"There was never any loss of memory, Cat," he said. "I

should have told you, but I let it go on too long. I am sorry for that."

"So you are a liar as well," she said in a flinty voiçe. "You have made a fool of me all along." She was close to tears again, and she was angry with herself.

"Cat, please give me a chance to explain. Maybe you won't be able to forgive me, but hopefully you'll understand my reasons."

"I shall never forgive you, Morgan, never," she said with her head thrown back.

"What happened between us means nothing at all, then?"

"It means that you used me, and now you have betrayed me."

"Cat, I love you. You must believe that, no matter what."

"Love me?" she said angrily. "How can you expect me to believe that, when you've lied about everything else? Goodbye, Mr. Kane. I shall expect you to have your belongings off the *Cat* within the hour."

"You are behaving foolishly, Cat, but I have said all that I intend to say," he said in a harsh voice, his own anger blazing now.

Cat turned and walked toward the waiting Timmie, never once looking back.

Morgan stood staring after her, his anger slowly dissipating, replaced by a great sense of loss and sorrow. He had never really loved a woman before Cat, and now he had lost her. For a moment he damned Uncle Sherman, and all canal lotteries in particular; if not for his business on the Erie, this would not have happened. On the other hand, but for his purpose here, the likelihood of his ever having met Catherine Carnahan was small.

Well, at least he would be around the Erie for some time to come; perhaps Cat would change her mind and forgive him when her temper had cooled. He well knew how volatile her temper was, how changeable her moods. However, he sensed deep in his heart that it had all come to an end right here.

He sighed, and turned back into the tavern, shoulders slumping; but once inside, he straightened up and put a bright smile on his face.

"Excuse the interruption, gents," he said jovially. "Let's take up where we left off, shall we?"

One man, a little the worse for drink, leered at him. "That Cat, she's something, ain't she now? Seems to me you'd be wise to stay on her good side, if you know what I mean."

Morgan tightened up inside, framing a scathing retort; then he recalled that Cat was no longer his concern, and he curbed his tongue. He said, "Miss Carnahan was right to be upset. She is not sponsoring my sale of lottery tickets. In fact, I wish to make it known here to one and all that I am no longer associated with the Carnahans or their canal boat. Now . . ." He flourished a bundle of lottery tickets. "How many of you gents are interested in buying a ticket?"

On the way back to the boat Timmie began strutting a little, crowing about how Morgan Kane had finally been shown up for what he was. Annoyed, Cat said sharply, "You did the right thing, Timmie, in telling me. But I want to crush any illusions you may have. . . . Performing this favor for me does not earn you undue privileges, is that clearly understood?"

Timmie looked puzzled. "I don't know as I do understand, Miss Catherine."

"I mean you are still the hoggee," she said harshly, "and I run the *Cat*. That is the extent of our relationship, now or at any time in the future."

He looked crushed and lagged behind as she strode on toward the canal boat. She found Mick lolling under the awning by the tiller.

"It's worrying I was, girl," he said. "You hied yourself

off without telling me. And where's Morgan? I haven't seen the lad all day, not since early morning."

She folded up the parasol and jabbed it viciously against the bulkhead. "You won't be seeing Mr. Morgan Kane again, Mick. Not ever, if I have anything to say about it."

He peered up into her angry face. "Now what does that mean, pray?"

"It means that I caught him selling lottery tickets."

"You did? By my sainted mother! But then I guess I'm not too surprised, come to think about it. We've come to know that he's an enterprising bucko." A smile tugged at his lips.

"Selling lottery tickets is not enterprising, in my opinion," she snapped. "It's a criminal offense, as you well know."

"Oh, well." He shrugged negligently. "Nobody does anything about it. Everybody sells them, and everybody buys them, it seems."

"Not everybody. And him selling tickets while working for us will cause people to think we're in cahoots with him. And that's not all. I learned that he's been lying to us all along. He never did lose his memory."

"Well now, that does surprise me a wee bit." Mick scrubbed his chin, frowning. "Why would he do that now?"

"How should I know? I just know he did, he admitted it."

"But he must have had a reason, Catherine. Did he explain it to you?"

"He tried to explain, but I refused to listen," she said. "I was not interested in any explanation he could offer."

"Ah, Catherine, it's a stubborn woman you are. And hard. I am sad to see that in you."

"What explanation could he possibly have?" she cried out in despair. "He lied before about losing his memory. Any explanation he could offer would only be another lie."

Mick stood up, his face softening. "He touched your heart, the lad did. I suspicioned that between you. I warned the bucko to be careful, not to break your heart." He reached out for her hand.

She tore her hand from his grasp. "You told him that? How dare you say a thing like that about me to a stranger?"

"I'm thinking he wasn't such a stranger after all. And I was only concerned for your welfare."

"I can take care of myself, thank you," she said wildly. "I always have before, and I will now."

"Catherine, Catherine." He shook his head sorrowfully, his eyes filling with compassion. "You have so much to learn of life."

"If you mean learning that a man can lie to me, or betray my faith in him, I've learned my lesson, thank you. You can be sure that it won't happen again." She turned her face away from him.

After a moment she heard him walk away, and she sank down into the seat he had vacated. Once again she felt the onslaught of tears, and she determinedly fought them back. She sat on, staring along the canal with unseeing eyes. She had never felt so wretched in her life; and although she would never admit it to her father, she knew that Mick was right—Morgan Kane had touched her heart, and now it was breaking.

Well, she would just have to be more careful the next time she became romantically involved with a man, if there was a next time. She knew, deep in her heart, that another man would come along eventually; she was a woman now—at least she had to credit Morgan for that—and she could no longer simply ignore her sexuality. . . .

A voice halted her from the wharf: "Hallo, the *Cat*!"

She turned, glancing around, and saw a man standing there. He was a stranger, and yet there was something dimly familiar about him. He was slender and dark, dressed in a dark suit; he was bareheaded under the hot sun, his well-shaped head crowned with a shock of black curly hair. He was certainly no canawler, Cat thought. He smiled, showing a gleam of very white teeth. "You probably don't recognize me, Miss Carnahan, since it was night when we met. I'm Dr. Anthony Mason."

Cat got to her feet. "Oh, yes, Dr. Mason, I remember you. Won't you come aboard?"

"Thank you, I will."

He came down the gangplank, and up close she saw that his eyes were a golden brown, his smile was charming, and humor lines radiated out from his eyes. He was a little past thirty, Cat thought.

Cat indicated the bench by the tiller. "Won't you sit down? Would you like a cooling drink? I have some lemons, and could make some lemonade in a few minutes."

"That would be nice, if it's no trouble."

"It's no trouble. I'm glad for the company, and would like to hear about your experience as a doctor on the Erie. You're the first, I believe, to travel the canal by boat."

When she returned she found Dr. Mason smoking a pipe. He motioned with it. "Do you mind, Miss Carnahan?"

"Not at all, Doctor." She was carrying a tray with glasses, a pitcher of lemonade, and a plate of cookies that Mick had made last night. They had bought a block of ice in town, which was fast melting, but there had been enough left for the lemonade.

She served the doctor, then sat down beside him on the narrow bench. "Now, tell me about being a doctor on the Erie."

He made a rueful face. "There isn't much to tell, I'm afraid. Not very many patients yet. I've only been at it a couple of months, and people seem to shy away from me."

Cat nodded in understanding. "Canawlers are clannish, you'll find. But they'll come around in time, if you're a good doctor." She smiled. "*Are* you a good doctor?"

"I believe so. Of course, if a doctor doesn't believe he's good, it's likely he won't be. Confidence in yourself is a required trait in the medical profession."

"I'm curious as to why you chose to set up practice on a boat on the Erie. It's unusual, I think you'll admit."

"I needed a change." For the first time a shadow of

sadness passed over his face. "I've lived along a canal the past five years, the Schuylkill Canal, on the outskirts of Philadelphia. That's where I first opened my practice. I got married the moment I was out of medical school. We were happy for four years, Laura and I, and my practice was flourishing. Then she took the swamp fever and died. There was nothing I could do to save her, nothing." His faced twisted in anguish. "Can you imagine what it's like? It's hard enough on a conscientious doctor to lose any patient, but to lose your own wife is pure hell."

"Oh, I am so sorry. That must have been terrible for you." Impulsively, she moved closer to him, and placed a hand on his arm.

A faint motion of the boat told her that someone had stepped on board. She glanced up to see Morgan on top of the cabin, staring at them. She glared at him defiantly, moving even closer to the doctor, and she did not remove her hand from his arm. Morgan's face turned cold and hard, and he turned away and went below.

Dr. Mason continued, "I knew that I could no longer stand living in the same place where Laura had died. So I closed up my practice and came here. It somehow appealed to me, moving about freely on a canal boat, and since I know nothing else but doctoring, I began my practice again. I'm sure that I will gain the confidence of the canal people in time. . . ."

Cat continued to listen as he talked on, his voice a pleasant murmur in her ear, but she kept an eye out for Morgan. In a short while she saw him emerge from the cabin, a carpetbag in his hand. Mick was with him, talking rapidly, with many hand gestures. Now Morgan glanced her way, and Cat turned her face deliberately to the man by her side, and smiled into his face. In a moment she felt the *Cat* rock a little as Morgan and Mick stepped onto the gangplank and then onto the wharf. She did not take her gaze from Dr. Mason's face to look after them.

Chapter Ten

MICK was hurrying to keep up with Morgan's long, angry strides along the wharf. "Morgan, me lad," he said in a pleading voice. "There must be some reason you can offer that will calm Catherine down a wee bit. I'm thinking it wouldn't take much to change her mind."

"I'm sorry, Mick. I've said all I'm going to say."

Morgan wanted to confess everything to the older man; he liked Mick, and hated to leave him like this, having Mick think him the worst kind of rogue. However, Morgan well knew how Mick's tongue wagged when he was full of liquor; and Morgan had no doubt that if he told the man his real purpose on the Erie, soon everyone along the canal would know.

"Morgan, wait." Mick laid a hand on his arm, staying him. "I've come to look upon you almost as me own son. You can't be leaving us like this. We've come to depend on you, my daughter and me."

"You'll manage, Mick. You always did before."

"Not really," Mick admitted ruefully. "We were just getting by, scratching for a dollar where and when we could. We've done better since you came along than ever before, and here it is hard times."

"Again, Mick, I'm sorry," Morgan said in a softer voice. "But it's time I was moving on. There is a reason, a good reason, believe me, but there's also a very good reason why I can't tell you about it at this time. Hopefully, there will come a time when I can."

Mick stared at him worriedly. "I believe you, lad, but there's Catherine to consider. I'm thinking that you've found a place in her heart."

Morgan said tightly, "It would appear not. If that were true, she would have more faith in me. And from the way she was cozying up to that fellow back there, any place I might have in her affections would appear to be easily filled." Remembering the way Cat had looked at him so coldly, then turned her bright smile on the other man, fueled Morgan's anger again.

"Ah, that." Mick gestured negligently. "The ways of women are strange. The girl was just trying to hit back at you, I'm thinking."

"And I think you're wrong, Mick. In any case . . ." Morgan hefted the bag in his hand. "It doesn't matter. It's better for everybody concerned that I go my own way now. Goodbye, Mick. I hope you'll always be my friend." He extended his hand.

Mick took it with a sigh, and said dolefully, "It's missing you I'll be, bucko. May the saints watch over you."

Morgan nodded, and turned away toward the heart of town. After a few yards he glanced back and saw Mick heading toward the waterfront, instead of back to the *Cat*. Probably to the nearest tavern, Morgan surmised; and he would come stumbling back to the boat tonight. And Cat will blame me for that, he thought bleakly—another black mark added to the list.

Cat, too, was worried about her father. She watched him walk off with Morgan, after they were far enough away that Morgan could not see her watching. She saw the two of them stop and talk briefly, then saw Morgan stride on alone, as Mick walked off toward the row of taverns instead of returning to the boat. She sighed inwardly, resigning herself to spending the rest of the day here, waiting for Mick to return sodden with drink.

"Miss Carnahan?"

"Oh, I am sorry!" She turned to face Dr. Mason. "I was just wondering where my father was going."

"Shall I fetch him for you?"

She shook her head. "Oh, no, he'll be back when . . . well, when he gets back." She took a sip of lemonade, and tried to free her mind of all thoughts of Morgan and her father. "How did you become a doctor?" She smiled slightly. "May I call you Anthony?"

"You certainly may, if I, in turn, may call you Catherine."

"I prefer Cat, and you certainly may."

"Cat?" He considered for a moment, his head to one side. "Yes, I think I like that. You asked how I became a doctor, Cat. Like most others, I suppose. First, I apprenticed to another doctor. I have swept floors, curried horses, mixed medicines, and helped hold down patients for amputations and such. In the beginning you are little more than a servant!"

"Hold down patients for amputations?" Cat shivered. "That sounds dreadful."

He nodded. "It isn't pleasant. Laudanum helps, but many doctors don't have an adequate supply, and so resort to brandy or rum, getting the patients drunk before they amputate, but often the pain is so severe they wake up. . . ." At her pained expression he said, "I'm sorry, Cat. I realize this isn't a pleasant subject for a lady's ears."

"I'm not all that delicate," Cat said with a shrug. "Go ahead, Anthony, this is interesting."

"Well, as I was saying, in exchange for this menial work, the young apprentice gets to peruse the doctor's medical books, if he has any." Anthony's smile was wry. "And is benefited by what medical advice the doctor is capable of dispensing.

"After three years of apprenticeship, supplemented by attendance at a medical college, such as Harvard Medical School, which I attended, the apprentice becomes a full-fledged medical doctor. Not a very efficient system, I must admit. If a young man can afford it, it is better to go to Europe and attend a medical college on the Continent. They are more advanced there. There are a great many doctors practicing in this country without a bona fide diploma from *any* medical school, particularly the older men who did their training under the older system wherein they simply served as an apprentice to an established physician until the older doctor considered them accomplished enough to start practice on their own. At least the training now is *somewhat* better."

"I've never had the need of a doctor's service," Cat said. "But I suppose if I ever do, I should first make sure that he has a diploma before I let him treat me."

"Unfortunately, Cat, even that won't assure you of good medical care. There are many diploma mills, so called, all over the country now, since our population has grown and the need for doctors is more acute. These diplomas aren't worth much, so you need to be sure that any diploma has been issued by an accredited medical college. And even then"—he sighed—"you can't be sure that you have a good doctor. The requirements for graduation from even some of the best medical schools aren't very strict."

He ticked them off on his fingers with the stem of his pipe. "One, you must be twenty-one years of age. Two, you must have attended only two full courses of medical lectures given by the particular institution. Three, you must have attended one full course of anatomy in a dissecting room. Four, the candidate must have been apprenticed to an accredited doctor for three years. And five, he must write a medical thesis and submit it to the faculty two weeks prior to graduation.

"As you can see, that at least grounds the student in medical practice, yet it's a far cry from what is really necessary for a respectable medical practitioner."

"I guess the best thing then is just not to get sick," Cat said with a smile.

"That is always the best thing, of course," Anthony

agreed. "But there are some good doctors practicing, and the medical profession is setting stricter standards for itself all the time. You know what some doctors do when they set up practice in a new town? The first thing they do is visit the local cemetery and check the gravestones to see what the deceased died of. That way they'll have a rough idea of what diseases they may be confronted with. Of course, they always have to take into consideration that the attending doctor may have made a wrong diagnosis. That's one thing I can't do here, since the Erie doesn't have a common burial ground, like a town." He was smiling, humor lines radiating from his eyes.

Cat found herself drawn to Anthony Mason. Although the subject of his conversation was sickness and death, he seemed to find some humor in it. What she had told him was true—she had never needed the services of a doctor—but Mick had on occasion; and all the doctors she had seen were dour, humorless men, for the most part, as if they despaired of ever defeating death in their patients.

She felt someone step on board the boat, and looked up to see Mick coming toward them along the top of the cabin. She was quite surprised to see him back this soon. As he drew near, she saw that he was sober, which surprised her even more.

Beaming, he said, "I got us a cargo for Albany, Catherine."

"You did!" Cat jumped up to embrace him. "Mick, I'm proud of you! What did you get for us?"

"Well . . ." He knuckled his chin, looking somewhat sheepish. "Following Morgan's example, I went around town looking for merchants with a lot of dress cloth on hand, and I got a full load to sell on the way back to Albany. On consignment, just like Morgan did."

"You didn't!" Cat began to laugh helplessly.

"Well, it worked for him," Mick said defensively. "I'm thinking it's better than traveling the Erie with empty cargo holds."

Cat struggled to contain her laughter. "What happened

to all the indignation? What happened to your scorn of peddlers?"

Mick said gruffly, "A man can change his mind, can't he?"

"But who is going to do the selling?"

"I'm thinking I'll be the one to do it. A girl like you can't be running around doing it."

Cat shook her head, still amused. "Mick Carnahan, peddling cloth goods. It's a miracle, that's what it is."

"It's no bloody miracle. I've decided it's time I was doing my bit. Besides, if that boyo can do it, so can I."

"I'm sure you can, Mick, and I *am* proud of you. You don't know how happy this makes me, even if you don't sell a single bolt of cloth."

"Now I'm not going to be doing it forever, girl. Just until business picks up."

"Oh . . . I forgot. Mick, I don't think you've met our guest." She turned to Anthony, who stood up. "Mick, this is Dr. Anthony Mason. Anthony, my father, Mick Carnahan."

Anthony extended his hand, and Mick warily took it, eyeing the doctor askance. "Doctor, is it? Where do you practice?"

"On the canal," Anthony said with a smile. "I have my own canal boat."

"A doctoring boat on the Erie, is it?" Mick shook his head. "Circus boats I've seen on the canal, even dentists, but a doctor is something new. But I'm thinking we could use one. A good one." He peered at Anthony suspiciously.

Anthony smiled. "I'll do my best to measure up, Mr. Carnahan."

"It's close to suppertime, Mick," Cat said brightly. "Could you stay for supper, Dr. Mason?"

"I think I would like that, Cat."

Mick scowled at his daughter, then shrugged, made his way across the boat, and went below.

"I'm not much of a cook, you see. My father does most of the cooking."

"For a woman of your beauty, that is enough," Anthony said gallantly, and bowed over her hand.

Cat, blushing deeply, started to pull away her hand, then allowed him to keep it.

A month later, Morgan had acquired a fine horse, new clothes, and a pistol, which he carried in his saddlebags. He was fairly well known along the Erie now, and he was prospering. Even Tate Brawley was pleased at the rate at which Morgan was selling lottery tickets. One thing that helped a great deal was the end of the business slump; business was beginning to boom along the Erie once more.

Morgan often wondered how Cat and her father were doing these days. He had seen the *Cat* a number of times along the canal, with Cat at the tiller and Timmie with the mules. From the way the boat rode low in the water and the manner in which the mules were laboring, he gathered that they were getting plenty of cargo.

He had heard that Mick was emulating him, taking whatever goods he could find and selling them along the canal; and he had also heard that the Irishman was not drinking as heavily as before. So at least one good thing had come out of the whole affair.

The only time he had seen Cat was when she was at the tiller of the moving boat, and one other time, when the boat was moored at the wharf in Albany. Morgan, riding past, had seen her in animated conversation with the man he had learned was Dr. Anthony Mason. Even at a distance it had struck Morgan that there was a certain intimacy between them.

On this particular afternoon, Morgan was on his way west out of Schenectady; he had spent several days there, selling a large number of lottery tickets. He was slowly gathering new data on the lottery operations, especially those of the Union Canal Lottery Company; and he calculated that by the end of autumn he would have gathered enough information to take to his uncle. In the beginning

Morgan had been a little apprehensive that his name might be sent in by Brawley to the company, and that they would recognize at headquarters that a Morgan Kane had once worked for them as a ticket broker. This would not cause any problems there, but it might arouse Brawley's suspicions. However, the weeks had passed and Brawley had said nothing; so Morgan had concluded that any dealings he had with the broker were strictly between them, and that the company had no knowledge of his, Morgan's, connections with Brawley.

It was late August now, and sweltering along the Erie. Morgan rode slowly, letting the horse pick its own gait; he rode with his hat pulled down over his eyes, half-dozing in the saddle.

Suddenly he heard something in a grove of trees off to his left. He reined in the horse and listened intently. There—there it was again. It sounded like the cry of a child. It was never a good policy to nose into someone's troubles along the canal; yet, if someone, especially a child, was in distress, he could not just dismiss it and ride on.

The sound came again, a scream this time, quickly cut off, but clearly a scream; it was not a child, but it was definitely female. Deciding, Morgan rode down the slope of the towpath bank. At the edge of the grove, he slid off his horse, tied the animal off, and dug the pistol out of his saddlebag. Since he often ventured into places like the Side-Cut nowadays, he had decided that a weapon was a necessary precaution.

The cry came again, muffled but distinct. Moving as quietly as possible, Morgan made his way through the thick underbrush. Now he glimpsed, off to his right, a horse and buggy. The buggy was empty, the horse cropping grass.

After a few yards, the underbrush thinned out and he could see a distance ahead. He had a glimpse of movement among the trees, and soon saw two figures struggling in a small clearing, a large, burly man and a small woman.

As Morgan stealthily approached the clearing, he saw the man's heavy hand paw at the woman's breast, as she struck at him with small fists.

The man was guffawing at her feeble defense as Morgan, stuffing his pistol into his belt, moved silently up behind him, and fastened both hands in the man's thick, greasy hair, yanking brutally. The man yelped in pain as Morgan threw him aside.

He rolled over and came up in a crouch, his face scarlet with rage. "Who the hell are you?"

Morgan said dryly, "I don't think that really matters. What *does* matter is that the lady is objecting rather strenuously."

"That is between us, and you have no right nosing in."

The man rose and came at Morgan in a rush. Morgan sidestepped nimbly. By the time the other man had pivoted, Morgan had the pistol out and leveled. "Now hold it right there. Another step and I put a bullet in your leg."

The man froze, eyes showing fear.

"That your horse and buggy over there?"

The burly man nodded mutely.

"Then I suggest you hop into it and depart immediately. Your presence is no longer required here."

The man backed away slowly, his gaze riveted on the pistol. Then he turned and hurried off. Morgan did not lower the gun until he saw the man whip up his horse, sending the buggy careening away. Only then did he return the pistol to his belt and turn to look at the woman.

To his astonishment he saw that she was Lotte Pryor. She was panting slightly, and her face was flushed. The buttons at the waist of her dress were partially undone, and Morgan caught a glimpse of white lace and pale flesh. He wondered that she made no immediate effort to repair the damage. He said, "Are you all right, Miss Pryor?"

"Yes, I'm fine, Mr. Kane, thanks to you. You arrived just in time." She gave him a wan smile.

It struck Morgan that she was not quite as upset as she might have been, as many women would have been in her circumstances. Apparently she was made of sterner stuff. He said, "What happened, anyway? How did you get all the way out here alone with that fellow?"

"It was foolish of me, I know. Papa left me alone in an inn in Schenectady. He went off somewhere with Mr. Brawley. Over a week Papa's been gone, and I was getting bored and lonely, with nothing to do. Mr. Rawlins . . ." She gestured. "He's the man in the buggy. He's a traveling peddler, and he's been staying at the same inn the past few days. Well, he seemed nice enough, and very friendly. He offered to take me for a ride along the canal in his buggy." With a provocative slowness she began doing up her buttons.

Morgan said reprovingly, "It wasn't very wise of you, Miss Pryor, buggy riding with a man practically a stranger."

"I realize that now, but everything was fine until he pulled the buggy into the trees here. He said the horse needed a breathing spell, and maybe we could walk for a little. Well, then he just seemed to go crazy, and I suppose you know the rest of it."

"I can guess," Morgan said grimly. "I should have shot him. Such a man deserves nothing less."

"Oh, no, what you did was enough. I'll be forever grateful to you, Mr. Kane." She smiled suddenly, a dimple appearing and disappearing in her cheek, and she got a saucy look. "To kill Mr. Rawlins would not have been a Christian act, as Papa would say."

Morgan had to laugh. "Speaking of your father, we'd better see about getting you back to town. If he should return suddenly and find you gone, he would be worried. I have no buggy, Miss Pryor, so I'm afraid you'll have to share my horse."

"That would be fine, Mr. . . ." A faint blush colored her cheeks as she gave him a demure look. "May I call you Morgan? Or would that be bold of me?"

"Not bold at all. I would like that, if I may call you Lotte in return."

"You may." She tucked her hand under his arm. "That will make us friends, won't it, Morgan?"

He said gravely, "It will indeed, Lotte."

He escorted her to his horse, mounted up, then reached down to help her up behind the saddle. She said, "Should I put my arms around you, Morgan, so I won't fall off?"

"That seems like a good idea."

Her arms went around his waist, and she snuggled close to him as he started the horse in motion. Morgan soon discovered that this closeness was disturbing. He could feel the fullness of her breasts against his back; they were taut and full, and apparently had very little covering. He was sure he could feel the stiffness of her nipples tracing erotic patterns on his back as she bobbed up and down with the motion of the horse. To take his mind off the images that conveyed, he said, "How's your father's church lottery proceeding?"

"Very well. That's where Papa and Mr. Brawley went, looking for a canal boat to buy, to convert into a tabernacle. Mr. Brawley raised sufficient money with the lottery."

"Did Brawley take a commission on the ticket sales?"

He felt her shrug. "I really don't know. I try not to concern myself with church affairs."

Morgan felt like asking her what she did concern herself with, but decided it would be an improper question. Instead he said, "You were with your father in Africa, I understand?"

"Oh, yes. I was born there."

"How did you like it?"

"I hated it, every minute of it. The heat, every disease imaginable, the poverty and the ignorance of the natives . . ." She shivered. "I was never so happy in my life as when Papa said we were returning to America."

"It must have seemed strange to you, an American born in Africa, and never before seeing this country."

"It was strange, yes, but wonderful."

"How do you think you will take to life on the canal?"

He felt her shrug again. "I don't really know, but one thing about being a missionary's daughter, you learn to adapt to almost anything. If you can't adapt, you'll go mad. I saw that happen in Africa, to missionary wives and daughters."

"That must have been hard on you," he said sympathetically. "You won't have those problems here, but you may find the winters a little rough, after being all your life in Africa. The Erie usually freezes solid in winter, from two to four months. That's how bad the winters are."

"We were in Ohio last winter. I didn't mind the cold. It was a refreshing change." As though the thought of winter made her cold, Lotte snuggled even closer; and for a moment Morgan feared that she would try to squeeze into the saddle with him. He gave a soft sigh of relief when she did not.

They were entering the outskirts of Schenectady now. Lotte directed him to the inn where she was staying, and in a very short time they rode up before it.

Lotte said, "I don't see Mr. Rawlins or his buggy anywhere. I was afraid he might be waiting for me."

"He probably just kept right on going. No, Lotte, I don't think you need fear he'll bother you again."

But someone else was waiting for them—the Reverend Luther Pryor and Tate Brawley. They were waiting just inside the entryway of the inn.

When the reverend saw his daughter, he stepped toward her with a black scowl. He took her arm and shook her roughly. "Where have you been, girl? Mr. Brawley and I came back an hour ago, and found you'd gone kiting off with some fellow in a buggy." He glared at Morgan. "Is this the scoundrel?"

"No, no, Papa, this is Morgan . . . uh, Mr. Kane. You must remember meeting him."

Pryor was still scowling. "That doesn't mean that he isn't the blackguard."

Behind the reverend, Tate Brawley was smiling gleefully at Morgan's discomfort.

Lotte rushed on, "I went for a buggy ride with a man staying here at the inn, a Mr. Rawlins, a traveling peddler." She pouted prettily. "I was lonely here, and bored, all by myself. He seemed like a nice man, and it was a pretty day for a ride out into the country, so I accepted his kind offer."

Pryor seemed somewhat mollified. Despite his stern manner, he apparently melted when his daughter turned on the charm. Then the reverend frowned again. "But where is this peddler? Why did you come back with Mr. Kane?"

"Mr. Rawlins became . . . uh, rather hard to handle." A pink flush stained her cheeks. "It was a fortunate thing that Morgan came along in time to intercede." She beamed a smile at Morgan, then looked back at her father with a shiver. "He was an awful man, this Mr. Rawlins, Papa. And I know that it was foolish of me. I won't be so foolhardy again, I promise." She rushed at him, hiding her face against his shoulder. A sob was wrenched from her.

Pryor patted her shoulder awkwardly. "There, there, it's all right, daughter, so long as no harm came to you. But you must be very careful. I have warned you about men, strange men. The wicked flourish along this sinful canal."

She looked up into his face, eyes dewy with tears, and Morgan suddenly realized that she had missed her calling—she should have been an actress; she had a great deal of talent in that direction.

Now she stepped back, turning slightly toward Morgan. "Papa, I believe you should thank Mr. Kane properly. Morgan came to my rescue just in time."

Reverend Pryor inclined his head slightly, and said stiffly, "You have my gratitude, Mr. Kane, as well as our Lord's. And that reminds me, daughter." His face lit up with a fervor. "Today we are the proud owners of a good-sized boat, which Mr. Brawley assures me may be easily converted to our purposes. Come along, and I shall tell you about it."

Pryor took his daughter's arm and hustled her away. Lotte went, looking back over her shoulder at Morgan. In a moment Morgan saw them across the way; the reverend was talking animatedly, but Lotte's gaze was still on Morgan.

Brawley remained where he was. "It appears that you have gained the lady's admiration."

Morgan shrugged negligently. "It was no more than any decent man would have done."

"I'm not sure that I approve of an employee of mine contriving to gain Lotte's affections," Brawley said tightly. "I have my own eye on the little lady."

Morgan stared at him in puzzlement. "Contrived? For God's sake, Brawley, she was in distress, and I just happened to come along. You think I set the whole thing up?"

"It strikes me as a rather strong coincidence. I have learned what a clever fellow you are."

"Saying that I did go to such lengths, what could my motive possibly be?"

"The girl is a ripe little wench. What other reason would you need?" Brawley's expression was a lascivious leer. "It strikes me that our dear Lotte is a virgin, and I reserve the privilege of deflowering her."

Morgan was suddenly sick of this man, of his conniving ways, his lechery, his blatant dishonesty. "I work for you as a ticket salesman, Brawley, but that does not give you the right to select my friends."

"Who's talking about friends?" Brawley said with a smirk. "I'm talking about a woman. If you want, you can have her after I'm finished with her."

Morgan knotted his fists, swept by a strong desire to smash them into Brawley's face. In a low, angry voice he said, "And you, Brawley, can go straight to hell. You disgust me!"

Brawley reared back, his face reddening. "You don't talk that way to me. You work for me, goddamn you!"

"Not anymore, I don't. I quit right now. I can get a job with another lottery company. I've proven how good I am."

"I made a mistake taking you on," Brawley said in a choked voice. "You're too clever by half. Simon told me I was a fool. For once, he's right."

Morgan said in surprise, "Simon Maphis? What do you have to do with that blackguard? You'd better stay away from him. He tried to torch *Carnahan's Cat*."

"As you so aptly said, Kane, I'll pick and choose my own friends, thank you. As for you, I'm going to make life hell for you along the Erie. I have much influence. Take my advice and pick another canal to work."

"It so happens I like the Erie, so I think I'll stick around." Morgan grinned, beginning to enjoy himself. "Maybe I'll offer you a little competition. I sure as hell intend to make it as rough for you as I can."

"You have no idea how rough it can get," Brawley said in a hard voice. "I don't do battle according to any rules. For me, there are no holds barred."

Still grinning, Morgan retorted, "You trying to frighten me, Mr. Brawley? I don't frighten so easily. Neither does Cat Carnahan, as your friend Maphis found out."

"Why bring up the Carnahan woman?" Brawley said in a goading voice. "She has a new gentleman friend, or hadn't you heard? She's being squired around by a young doctor. Fellow has his own boat and everything. The way I hear it, they make an attractive couple."

Morgan refused to be goaded. "That's her affair, isn't it? I have no hold on her."

"That's not the way I understood it . . ."

Brawley broke off as Pryor and his daughter came up. The reverend said, "Mr. Brawley, shall we take Lotte down to inspect my boat? I am eager to get started. The Lord's work doesn't wait for idle hands."

"Certainly, Reverend," Brawley said heartily. "I am willing to aid you in every way I can."

Pryor inclined his head toward Morgan. "Good day to you, sir."

Lotte dimpled at him. "And I do thank you for rescuing me, Morgan."

"It was my pleasure, Lotte." Morgan had a sudden impulse. Sending a mischievous glance at Brawley, he said, "Reverend Pryor, may I have the privilege of calling upon your lovely daughter someday soon?"

Morgan saw Brawley stiffen and begin to scowl; then he glanced at Pryor, and saw the reverend wearing a look of displeasure.

"Please, Papa!" Lotte clutched at her father's arm. "Pretty please? Mr. Kane is a respectable man, and I'd like that very much."

Still wearing a stern look, Pryor nodded grudgingly. "I shall consider it, daughter. But for the present, Mr. Kane, we are both going to be quite busy getting our tabernacle in condition to accommodate our new flock of worshippers."

Chapter Eleven

FEELING awkward and out of her element, Cat entered Alband's Lady's Shop hesitantly, staring rather truculently at the plethora of women's clothing around her. She had been enticed inside by a dress she had seen on a clothes dummy in the window, a blue dress that would just match her eyes, cut in a graceful style that showed off a tiny waist, and with lace at the throat, neck, and shoulders.

Now, looking at the feminine apparel on display all around her, Cat felt overwhelmed. Everywhere she looked in the small shop, she faced bonnets and ribbons, and ruffled waists, skirts, dresses, capes, and coats. There was simply too much to choose from, and her inexperience made her feel very ill at ease.

The shop owner, a plump, pretty woman in a lovely, wine-colored silk dress, bustled up. "May I help you, miss?"

Cat, feeling deeply uneasy, could only nod. Surely this sophisticated woman must see right through her and must somehow know that she, Cat, was a canal hoyden, with no real knowledge of feminine things.

The woman said, "Is there something special you are looking for, something in particular you wish to try on?"

Cat nodded once again. "The dress in the window, the blue one. I think it is about my size."

This time it was the woman's turn to nod. "An excellent choice, my dear. I just received it today. I will remove it from the window. The changing room is just there, behind those pink curtains."

Cat, glad that she had washed her underthings and petticoats, looked at herself in the mirror to see if there were any tears or worn spots that could embarrass her. There were none, and it was with a bit more confidence that she accepted the blue dress and the shopkeeper's assistance in putting it on.

When the last button was fixed, Cat turned slowly in front of the mirror, her cheeks flushing with pleasure. She loved the dress; but the price was outrageous, far in excess of any price she had ever paid for something to wear.

The proprietress, hands clasped over her midsection, beamed at her maternally. "It looks grand on you, dear, simply grand! It brings out the blue of your eyes, and it's a lovely fit, hardly needs any altering at all."

"I like it, I must admit," Cat said. "But the price . . . it's terribly expensive."

"But it will last, you see. The material is the very best. And it's the latest fashion, right from Paris, France."

Cat very much doubted the last. She well knew that by the time any new fashion in ladies' wear reached the Erie, it was at least a year out-of-date. But what did that really matter?

She said suddenly, "All right, I'll take it!" Business had been good the last few weeks, and she had available cash now. "And I'll need a new pair of shoes, and other accessories to go with the dress."

"We can provide everything you need, my dear," the woman said happily. "And may I say it's a pleasure to serve such a lovely lady as yourself."

By the time Cat was completely outfitted, she had spent well over fifty dollars. In days past she would have been horrified at even the thought of spending that much money on clothing. At the same time, she felt such a glow of pleasure and anticipation at the idea of wearing the new garments that any concern over expenses was unimportant.

As she paid the bill, she smiled to herself, wondering what her father would say when he learned of her expenditure. If she knew Mick as well as she thought she did, he would be pleased. Whatever else he was, her father was no tightwad, and he had been after her for years to buy ladies' clothing for herself. Cat was happy at the change in Mick since Morgan had left. Oh, he had far from reformed overnight; but he was not drinking as heavily as before, and he had taken over the business where Morgan had left off, doing most of the outside work now, finding cargoes for the *Cat;* and he was doing very well at it.

Arms laden with packages, Cat started toward the door. A hatbox atop the other packages obscured her view, and without warning she collided with someone, sending the packages tumbling to the floor.

Flushed with annoyance, she glared at the young woman blocking her way, and saw that it was Lotte Pryor. Behind Lotte stood Morgan Kane.

"We're sorry, ma'am . . ." Morgan began, and then broke off as he recognized Cat. His smile came slowly. "Good afternoon, Cat. How are you?"

Ignoring him, Cat bent to scoop up her bundles.

Morgan stepped forward. "Here, let me help you."

"I can do it for myself, thank you very much!" she snapped.

She gathered up her bundles haphazardly; and as she started to straighten up, she lost her grip, and they fell again. "Damn blast and hell!"

"Still refusing help from a man, I see," he said sardonically. "But I don't suppose I should have expected you to change all that much." He bent down and retrieved her packages. "Here, hold out your arms."

Gritting her teeth, Cat held out her arms, and he stacked the packages neatly. Grudgingly, she said, "Thank you, Mr. Kane."

"You're welcome, Miss Carnahan," he said with a dip of his head.

Off to one side, Lotte was glaring daggers at Cat.

And then, just as she started out the door, Morgan said, "Are the new clothes so you can dress up for your doctor, Cat? You never did that for me."

She opened her mouth to retort angrily, then changed her mind and stormed on out of the store.

Part of her anger was occasioned by the fact that Morgan was right. She *had* bought the new outfit because of Anthony. He too was in Albany, with his medical boat, and he had invited her to supper. This would be the second time she had gone to dinner with him, and she could not continue to wear the same old dress every time they went out together. She did not mind him seeing her in her usual garb aboard the boat, but for social occasions he had a right to expect her to dress like a lady.

Still, it was none of Morgan's business, and so like him to give his opinion when it was not wanted or asked for. She had been right to sever relations with him. He was an impossible man!

Morgan watched Cat go, amused. Angry as she was, Cat was still beautiful, and she still stirred his blood; he knew she always would. Not only that, he reflected with melancholy, he was still in love with her. That had not changed, and probably would not for a long time, if ever.

"Morgan?" Lotte said plaintively. "Have you forgotten about me?"

He turned. "Of course not, Lotte. Now whyever should I do that?"

"Were you and that canal girl sweethearts?" she asked with a pout.

"Now you really don't wish to know that, do you, Lotte? Besides, if there was anything between us, it was over before I met you." And it would seem to be over for good, he added to himself.

Lotte gave him a smile of satisfaction. "I wouldn't care to play second fiddle, is all."

"Speaking of sweethearts, how about you and Tate Brawley?"

"Oh, he's just Papa's friend," she said with a shrug.

"I'm sure Brawley has more in mind than that."

She looked at him with interest. "Do you think so?"

Morgan had already learned that Lotte was a vain creature, loved flattery and male attention, and had very few interests outside of herself and her own pleasure. He was certain that she only pretended to have an interest in the church just to appease her father. At the same time, she was a pretty thing, good company—as long as no serious matters were under discussion—and he suspected that she was a passionate woman, although their relationship had not yet reached that point. Withal, she was attractive enough on his arm to draw envious male glances when Morgan took her out, and there was enough male vanity in his nature to enjoy that.

He said, "Hadn't you better shop for your new hat? You know your father is expecting you at the grand opening of his canal tabernacle tonight. And I want to hear you sing your solo. I haven't had that privilege yet."

"Oh, yes, you're right." Lotte turned and walked over to the woman who owned the shop, and began talking animatedly, with many gestures.

Morgan leaned against the door frame and watched Lotte with amusement. He watched for a half-hour as she tried on one hat after another, turning back and forth before the mirror. He wondered if Cat spent as much time agonizing over her choice of clothes. He had the strong feeling that she did not, since she was totally inexperienced at purchasing clothes, at least to the best of his knowledge.

But why was he thinking of Cat? That was finished; if he had not realized it before today, he did now. Cat had made her feelings quite plain, and evidently she had found another gentleman friend. Morgan determined in that moment that he would never again allow himself to become so involved with a woman. From this time forward it would be nothing more than a pleasant interlude; he certainly intended no strong commitment to Lotte Pryor.

After all, Cat claimed she needed no one, he thought glumly. If she could hold herself aloof from emotional alliances, so could he!

Cat was also thinking of Morgan, as she got dressed for her dinner engagement with Anthony. She had often wondered if she had been too hasty, too quick to anger, in sending him away without letting him explain. But what had there been to explain? Whatever he had to say would only have been another lie. And from all appearances today, he was suffering neither from pangs of remorse nor from lack of female companionship.

She stood back from the warped mirror, eyeing herself critically. The dress, slippers, and hat were very becoming, she thought. Strange, before Morgan came into her life, she would not have dreamed that she would take pleasure in looking at herself in new finery; but now she had to admit that it was a good feeling, dressing up, as Mick would have said, "as a proper lady should."

As she had surmised, her father had been happy that she had purchased new clothing. Not only had he made no comment about the price, but he had not even asked what she had paid, which had moved her to comment, "These garments came dear, Mick. I spent more money for clothes today than I've spent on clothes in my entire life."

"Thank the saints for that, Catherine. I'm thinking it's about time. As for the money, you've earned it. All these years you've worked like a man, and hardly a penny did you spend on yourself."

It was time for Anthony to arrive. With a minor adjustment to her hat, Cat went up on deck. The moment she opened the cabin door, she smelled Anthony's pipe tobacco.

She found him in the stern with Mick, listening as her father spun one of his yarns of the Erie. Cat paused a moment to listen.

". . . Mostly Irish built it, you see, fresh off the ships from the ould sod. They worked for four shillings a day, and the jigger boss, which was a half-gill of whiskey for each man sixteen times a day. They earned it, cutting through the Montezuma Marsh, a hell of snakes, mosquitoes, punkies, black flies, stinking mud, and the miasmic fever. Thousands died.

"A few years ago, when the old Erie was first in full flower, boats were so thick a fellow could just walk across, from towpath to the opposite bank. There were a lot of hoodledashers—"

"Hoodledashers? What's a hoodledasher?"

"That's a long string of empties towed in tandem. By the saints, did *that* cause problems, especially at the locks. . . ." Mick broke off as he saw Cat, and nodded at her with a proud smile. "There she is, Dr. Mason. Me own daughter, and a pretty creature she is, you must agree."

Anthony turned, taking the pipe from between his teeth. "Yes indeed, Mr. Carnahan. Your daughter is a lovely lady. My compliments, Cat," he said with a bow. "I'll be proud to be seen with you tonight."

"It's proud you should be," Mick said. "Catherine is the prettiest girl on the whole length of the Erie!"

"Now stop it, Mick!" Cat scolded. "You're both embarrassing me."

"You see, Anthony me lad, Catherine is unaccustomed to compliments," Mick said with a broad wink. "For years I've been trying to get her out of those castoffs of mine, and what bucko in his right mind would be complimenting her in such attire?"

Cat ignored him, her cheeks flaming, and took Anthony's arm. "Shall we go, Dr. Mason? I'm sure you don't wish to spend more time listening to Mick 'stretching the blanket.' "

They left the boat, with Mick's loud bellow of laughter

trailing them. Anthony said, "What does 'stretching the blanket' mean?"

"It's canal talk for telling tall tales. Actually, it means stretching the truth a bit, sometimes all out of shape."

He laughed. "I figured it was something like that."

The *Paradise* was moored down the towpath a way, and that was where they were having dinner. Cat would have preferred almost any other place, yet she could not complain to Anthony that she wished to avoid the *Paradise* because that was where she had first dined with Morgan. Besides, it was the only decent eating place in the area.

It was just growing dark as they strolled along the towpath. It had been a very hot day, and the faint breeze off the canal was a welcome relief. Once or twice they met canawlers of Cat's acquaintance, and she took note of their stares at her finery with a feeling of smugness.

She could not help but compare Anthony to Morgan, stealing furtive side glances at him. He was not as handsome as Morgan, yet his dark good looks were attractive enough. He lacked Morgan's bold manner and insouciant charm; however, his face showed intelligence and kindness, and good humor, whereas Morgan's sense of humor was often perverse, sardonic, and mocking.

Cat dreaded what Samuel O'Hara would say when he saw her with another man. As usual, he was standing on the gangplank, greeting his customers as they arrived. At the sight of Cat on Anthony's arm, his eyes widened, but the only thing he said was, "Catherine, lass, you are lovely tonight. Aye, a rare sight for these tired old eyes."

"Thank you, Samuel," Cat said gravely. "This is Dr. Anthony Mason. He is new on the Erie, offering medical services on his canal boat."

Samuel held out a large hand, and they shook. He boomed, "And I am Samuel O'Hara, in food services, as you can see. We serve the finest of food, Doctor, as I'm sure Catherine will agree." His eyes twinkled. "Is it that you might trade your services for mine? I'm getting on, you know. Ah, the ailments, the aches and pains afflicting this old body of mine." He sighed lugubriously, rolling his eyes.

Anthony laughed. "It's possible, Mr. O'Hara. I've only been on your canal a short time, but I have already learned that the barter system is popular here, since cash is sometimes in short supply."

"Aye, that it is, that it is. But go on in, you are most welcome to my establishment." As Cat started past, Samuel caught her arm and whispered in her ear, "You're a popular lass these days. Aye, that you are."

Feeling flustered but complimented nonetheless, Cat went on into the floating restaurant with Anthony. Samuel had already motioned a waiter forward, and they were escorted to the same table she had occupied before with Morgan and her father. By coincidence or design? Samuel O'Hara had a leprechaun's fey sense of humor.

Cat determined not to let it bother her, pushing all thoughts of Morgan out of her mind, and concentrated all her attention on Anthony across the table from her.

He lacked Morgan's flair for ordering wine and the like, but he did consult her about the menu when it arrived, which pleased her. They settled on trout, which the waiter assured them was fresh, caught only the day before.

"Caught where, I wonder?" Anthony asked when the waiter left with their order. "Surely not the canal?"

"I certainly hope not, with all the garbage that's dumped into it daily." She gave a mock shudder. "There are few fish in the canal, only those that come in when fresh water is let in from the feeder canals to keep the water level constant in the Erie, and those don't last long. No, these trout came from one of the lakes nearby, I'm sure."

Wherever the fish came from, it was very good, as Cat had known it would be; true to his boast, Samuel O'Hara served only the best. Anthony was not a great conversationalist; he tended to talk mostly about his profession and the practice of it along the canal. His new life was still so fresh to him that he found it fascinating; as Cat listened, her attention wandered from time to time. She caught herself looking around the dining room. Looking for Morgan?

When the music started up, she clapped her hands and said gaily, "Let's dance, Anthony. This is about the only chance I get." She did not add that she had only really danced once before, with Morgan.

Anthony looked dubious. "I've not had much practice dancing, Cat. Becoming a doctor leaves very little time for such frivolities."

"I'm not very good myself, to be truthful." She jumped to her feet. "So we'll start out even. Come on, Anthony." She moved around the table to take his hand.

Reluctantly, he stood up. "All right, Cat, but I think you'll be sorry."

The music was a stately waltz, and Anthony took her into his arms awkwardly. He had told the truth—he was not a very good dancer. Now that she thought about it, he was far from graceful in movement, although his hands were slender and supple, and very gentle in their touch. Again her thoughts jumped back to that night she had danced in Morgan's arms. How graceful he was; what a delight to glide across the floor in his arms!

Damn blast and hell! Was Morgan Kane going to sneak into her thoughts all evening? Angry with herself, determined that this would be the last time tonight that she would think of Morgan, Cat missed a step, and almost stumbled, gripping Anthony's shoulder for support.

"I'm sorry, Cat," he said ruefully. "I told you I was a terrible dancer. In fact, I lack most of the social graces."

"It's not your fault, Anthony. It's been a long, exhausting day, and I've discovered that I really don't want to dance after all."

"Then shall we go?"

"If you don't mind too much."

"Not at all."

Anthony paid their bill, and they made their way to the gangplank. Samuel O'Hara was still there, greeting latecomers. He called after them, "Come back anytime, Cat. And you too, Dr. Mason."

Cat took Anthony's arm, and they started along the towpath. He said solicitously, "I'm sorry you're tired, Cat."

"Not really that tired. I just found I wasn't in the mood for dancing." On impulse, she squeezed his arm and said, "Where is your boat tied up, Anthony?"

He looked down at her in question. "Only a short distance from the *Cat*."

"Could I see it? It's early yet, and I've never seen a doctor's canal boat."

His face registered surprise, then began to brighten. "I would be most happy to show you my boat, Cat. I've done an awful lot of work on it, and I'm proud as punch."

Even from the outside of his boat, Cat could see that he had cause to be proud. It was more on the order of a passenger packet than a cargo boat, with a high cabin in the center, with more windows than would normally be the case, providing air and light; the entire boat had recently been painted a cheery yellow. A sign burned in wood was fastened to the cabin at the top of the gangplank: DR. ANTHONY MASON: ALL DISEASES TREATED: SURGERY.

And across the side of the boat was the name in bold letters: THE PARACELSUS.

"What does that name mean?" Cat asked.

"Paracelsus was a Swiss physician practicing in the sixteenth century. He was a controversial figure in his time, but he is now considered the Father of Medicine by a great many."

Cat had to smile. "I doubt that many of the canawlers will understand what the name means."

"Probably not, but then they're distrustful of doctors in any case." He shrugged, spreading his hands. "In the past, people went to witches and midwives when they needed doctoring, and that superstitious way of life is difficult to overcome."

"Especially along the Erie, where all canal people are distrustful of land people to begin with."

"I am aware of that, Cat. That is something I will have to overcome, but I sincerely believe that in time they will come to trust and have faith in me. I've already converted a few here and there. Not many, I'll admit, but hopefully the word will spread."

She put her hand on his arm and said softly, "I should think you are a man anybody can trust, Anthony. If I'm ever sick, I wouldn't hesitate to come to you for help."

His color heightened, and he placed his hand over hers. He said simply, "Thank you, Cat. Now . . ." He became brisk. "Come on aboard and I'll show you around."

As they topped the gangplank, he gestured to the main cabin. "This is where I have my examining rooms, my surgery, and my office. The smaller cabin up front—the bow, I think you canallers call it—is my personal quarters."

The rooms in the larger cabin were neat as a pin, the waiting-room area painted in bright, cheerful colors, with reasonably comfortable chairs. The few doctors' offices she'd been to with Mick had been dark, forbidding, and very uncomfortable. She said, "You have every reason to be proud of everything, Anthony."

"This is the last room, the one I use for what little surgery I perform. Mostly amputations and the like, and some emergency surgery. People are terrified of being operated on, and even within the medical profession there is still much controversy about the advantages and disadvantages of surgery to remove diseased organs. Personally, I think it is the future of medicine. Unfortunately, the philosophy of most doctors is purge, blister, and bleed."

The other rooms had various odors that Cat could not identify, but those odors were faint, and not really unpleasant, but in the surgery the odors were strong and immediate, and rather nauseating.

Anthony noted her reaction and apologized. "I'm sorry, Cat. I know the smells are strong. I keep most of my drugs and medicines in here." He gestured to shelves along the walls, filled with bottles and vials. "And some odors, like carbolic acid, for instance, are almost impossible to eliminate completely."

There was one large chair in the room, resembling a barber's chair, and a narrow, high table with a thick pad on it. There was one other item in the surgery—a tall cabinet with several shelves with glass doors. Cat could see various instruments on the shelves.

Anthony said, "That is my meager supply of instruments. Since surgery is frowned upon, there are no supply houses, except for bone saws and other instruments for amputation. The others I have I either devised myself and had made, or are copies of what other surgeons have devised. I have a set of wooden forceps for extracting teeth, bullets, and other foreign matter in wounds. I am quite proud of it." He took an involuntary step toward the cabinet, then stopped. "No, I doubt you'd really be interested in seeing it. Let's go back into the other room before you become faint."

Cat stiffened. "I don't faint all that easily," she said sharply.

Anthony stared in surprise at her tone, and Cat silently scolded herself, remembering how her prickly independence had irritated Morgan. In a softer voice she said, "I'm sorry, I didn't mean to sound offended. I suppose that the odors are a little stronger than I'm accustomed to."

"It's all right, Cat, I understand. You've seen everything there is to see, anyway." He led the way into the larger room and started toward the main cabin door. "In fact, you've seen all there is to see." He looked back over his shoulder. "Except for my own quarters, but then I don't suppose you'd care to see those." There was a look of wistful hope on his face.

"I don't see why not."

"It's usually not considered proper for a lady to visit a gentleman's rooms alone."

"In some quarters I'm not considered all that proper."

Then, realizing how the remark must sound, she hastily added, "What I meant was, I'm not offended by your suggestion."

His face brightened. "Then you will? I think I have a glass of port to offer."

"That sounds fine. Just so long as you don't think I'm not a 'proper' lady."

He shook his head vigorously. "Oh, I would never think that, Cat. It's just that I've never known how to conduct myself around women. The only one I ever knew . . . uh, intimately was my wife, and Laura has been dead now for over a year."

"Tell me about your wife, Anthony. What was she like?"

His shoulders went rigid, and for a moment she feared that she had somehow offended him. Then he relaxed. "Forgive me, Cat. Since her death, I've never talked about her. Frankly, it hurts even to think about." As he opened the cabin door, he turned to her with a musing smile. "I've never *wanted* to talk about her, but now, all of a sudden, I find that I do wish to tell you about Laura. Perhaps that tells you something."

Cat felt herself flush, and was glad when he faced around to usher her inside. She was being forward, she knew that, and she also knew the reason for it. Then they were inside, and she put the thought out of her mind as she glanced around.

Like the rest of his boat, his living quarters were clean, well lighted and ventilated, freshly painted, and surprisingly large. Evidently, two or three small cabins had been ripped out to make one good-sized room, which had several pieces of comfortable furniture; a woodburning stove and cooking quarters were shielded by a curtain.

Anthony motioned to a chair. "Please sit and make yourself comfortable, Cat, and I'll fetch the wine."

Crossing to the galley section, he drew aside the curtain. Cat sat down, her glance going to the bed against the far wall. It was not the usual canal-boat bunk, but a regular-size bed. With flaming cheeks she tore her gaze away just as Anthony returned with a wine decanter and two glasses.

Anthony poured the wine and sat down opposite her. He held up his glass in a toast. "Here's to a wonderful evening, Cat. I thoroughly enjoyed myself."

"As did I."

They sipped at their wine, then Anthony put down his glass, lit his pipe, and assumed a serious expression. "You asked about Laura. She was a lovely girl, warm, outgoing, and we had known each other since childhood." He smiled fleetingly. "I suppose you could say we had been in love all our lives. Laura had a special interest in medicine. In fact, ever since she was a little girl, she wanted to be a doctor. I can remember her as a child . . . we would play doctor. Oh, I don't mean in the usual sense." His cheeks turned pink. "We would play with dolls, pretending they were hurt, and we would tend to them. Laura was good at it. When she could read, she found an old medical book and studied it until the pages fell out. There came a time, when we were old enough, that she could dismember her old dolls, pretending to amputate a diseased limb, then sew it back onto the doll. She had the touch—she was born with it. In my belief she would have made a wonderful surgeon."

"Then why didn't she?"

He gave her an incredulous look. "A woman become a doctor? It's almost impossible, and to become a surgeon is unthinkable. I think there are maybe a half-dozen women practicing medicine out West, on the frontier, but I doubt that any have a medical degree. Probably most of them worked as nurses, and then later put their scant medical knowledge into practice. To my knowledge, no accredited medical school in the United States will accept women as students. As a woman, Cat, you should know how difficult it is for a woman to enter most professions."

She nodded glumly. "Yes, I do know, very well."

"Laura did help me in my practice, as a nurse, and by the time she died she knew almost as much about medicine as I did. That's one thing I'm even more sorry about. We both wanted a family, but we were young, and she wanted to work with me for a while before she bore children." He looked so sad that Cat wanted to reach out and comfort him. "Raising a child on my own would have been rough, I know, but at least I would have had a part of Laura with me today."

"Do you use a nurse now?"

"No; nurses, good nurses, are difficult to find. Most doctors get by using their male apprentices. Besides"—he smiled slightly—"can you imagine how canallers would take to coming to see me and finding a woman working with me? They'd turn and run."

"You're probably right in that. But it must be hard to do everything alone."

"I don't have all that many patients as yet." His smile was wry. "When I build up a practice and people get accustomed to me, I will then think of employing a nurse." He looked at her, his stare intent. "I have a strange feeling that you'd make a wonderful nurse, Cat."

She said lightly, "You're not by any chance proposing, are you, Anthony?" For a moment she thought she had gone too far, and she chided herself. Her anger at Morgan had pushed her into being rash.

His expression was empty and still for a long moment, then he said in a shocked tone, "Oh, no, Cat! I would never presume to do such a thing on such a short acquaintance."

"A friend once told me that time has little to do with it, that a man and woman know almost immediately if they are attracted to each other."

"Oh, I am attracted to you, Cat, very much so. I think I was that first time, even with only the moonlight to show your features, and you wearing men's clothing."

She retreated now. "I do hope you don't think I'm being too forward, speaking of such matters."

"Not at all." He began to smile. "I rather admire such forthrightness in a woman. Many of today's women are beginning to speak frankly on matters that would have shocked their peers not long ago."

"And still do, I imagine."

"Yes, that is quite true. But a doctor sees too much of the world, of mankind at its worst and best moments, to be shocked. I much prefer frankness to the coy simpering that seems to afflict all too many women."

His face suddenly got a set and determined look; and he got up and crossed to her, and reached down to lift her to her feet. He kissed her firmly. Somewhat taken by surprise, Cat was momentarily at a loss for words. But then this was what she had not only expected but asked for, was it not?

His mouth was passionate and demanding, the strength of his arms around her beyond what she had expected. She detected a strong sexual hunger in him, and she realized that he was being truthful when he had said he had known only his wife intimately.

There was not the immediate arousal, the strong, almost overpowering desire that Morgan's mere touch had sent sweeping through her; and this disappointed her a little.

But she returned his kiss with a growing ardor, and she was breathless when he finally broke the kiss. His face was flushed in the lamplight, and he was breathing heavily. "Forgive me, Cat. I really hadn't intended doing that, but it has been a long time since I've held a woman in my arms, and you are a beautiful, desirable woman."

"There's no need to apologize, Anthony," she murmured. She reached out to touch his face gently.

He seized her hand and pressed it to his lips. "Will you stay, for a while? I very much want you to, dear Cat. I need you; I want you."

"Yes," she said in a whisper. "Yes, Anthony, I'll stay."

Without another word he led her to the bed, and then began to undress her. Despite the desire that she knew was raging through him, he took his time. Whatever urgency he felt, he curbed; unlike Morgan, he did not pluck at her clothing with haste; his surgeon's hands were skillful, and found each button and hook without fumbling.

And when they were naked together on the bed, those same hands caressed her artfully, always gentle; sometimes his fingers touched her body as softly as the fluttering of a butterfly's wings. Cat showed none of the boldness she had displayed with Morgan; since she, in large part, had initiated this, she was fearful that any further boldness from her would displease Anthony.

He seemed to sense that she was uncertain, and he took his time, building her passion slowly but skillfully. He was a good lover, certainly not as forceful as Morgan, but infinitely more gentle and patient; and soon she forgot that she had begun this out of anger at Morgan, to pay him back in some small measure, and her body began to respond to Anthony's ministrations.

Again, without a word from her, he seemed to know when it was time, when she had attained a full arousal, and he moved to enter her. His mouth locked to hers as he started to move inside her, thrusting slowly, but with an ever-increasing rhythm; and sensations sparked along her nervous system like tiny shocks.

Her pleasure mounted and mounted until nothing was in her mind but the achievement of that final moment of rapture that she felt approaching with astounding speed. Then she was there, a bursting of ecstasy inside her that forced a muted cry from her lips; and she rose to meet him a final time. They cleaved together, shuddering. Anthony, with the art of a consummate lover, had timed it perfectly.

As the last shiver of pleasure passed, Cat stroked the back of his head with her hands. He stretched out beside her, and once again she reflected how nice it was in this bed, instead of on her bunk on the *Cat*.

He said huskily, "I suppose you could tell that that *was* the first time I've been with a woman since Laura died. You know, it's really a strange thing." He took her hand and held it tightly. "After her death I felt no need of a woman. I thought I'd never experience desire again. I decided that I would be content buried in my work, seeing to other people's needs instead of my own." He laughed quietly. "That was before I met you, Cat. Shows how wrong a man can be."

"I'm glad I was the one, Anthony."

"There is one thing, though. . . ." His voice changed. "I am in no position to marry at the present. Every cent I had to spare is sunk into this boat. I'm barely earning enough yet to be able to feed myself, much less two."

There it was again, she thought resentfully; was that the first thing a man thought about?

She started a hot retort, then choked it back. "Don't worry about it, Anthony. Don't think that I practically invited myself into your cabin to trap you into marriage."

"Oh, I would never think that, Cat," he said in a shocked voice.

"I'm not ready for marriage either. I'm perfectly content with my life on the *Cat*."

"That's good." There was a faint note of relief in his voice. Then he said in alarm, "But we will see each other again?"

Now it was her turn to squeeze his hand. "I'm sure we shall, Anthony. In fact, I'm looking forward to it."

Chapter Twelve

MORGAN stood at the tiller of the Reverend Luther Pryor's floating tabernacle, which the reverend had named the *Waters of Christ*. Morgan had rigged a strip of canvas over the stern to ward off the sun; and Lotte sat beside him, holding a parasol over her head even in the shade, twirling it as she talked.

Morgan scarcely listened to her idle chatter, concentrating on the canal ahead, and thinking back with amusement on how it had come about that he was operating the canal boat for the Pryors.

When the reverend had finally finished converting the packet he had bought into a tabernacle, and was ready to launch his long-cherished dream, he found himself confronted with a problem—he knew nothing whatsoever about running a canal boat.

Morgan, who had been squiring Lotte during the past few weeks, brought her home one evening to a fully completed water church. After Lotte had gone below to her cabin, the reverend approached Morgan diffidently.

"Mr. Kane, I find myself in somewhat of a quandary," he said a touch pompously.

"And what is that, sir?"

"When I made plans for my water tabernacle, I failed to

consider one thing. I know nothing at all about operating such a craft."

"You can find hundreds of men to run your boat for you, Reverend," Morgan said with a shrug. "The Erie abounds with them."

"They're all roughnecks, sinners of the worst sort," the reverend said with lofty disdain. "I could never trust them."

In Morgan's estimation, there was little of value to steal on the *Waters of Christ*, but he reserved comment, sensing what was coming.

"Besides . . ."—the Reverend Luther Pryor looked off in embarrassment—"I don't have the funds to pay them, not at the present time."

"Just what did you have in mind, Reverend?"

"I thought perhaps you, out of Christian charity, might give me a hand with the Lord's work."

"You mean, you'd want me to work for nothing?"

"Oh, I would provide food and lodgings," Pryor said hastily. "It is my understanding that you worked for the Carnahans under such an arrangement."

"That was in the beginning. When I started getting cargoes for them, I was to receive a commission. I never received any, true," he added wryly. "But that was because I left rather suddenly, shall we say." He stared at the reverend intently. "Then, of course, there are my lottery tickets. You know that I make my living as a lottery-ticket broker."

"Well, that was something of what was in my thoughts," the reverend said, embarrassed again. "I thought, as we traveled up and down the canal, you could still sell your lottery tickets. My tabernacle would even be providing free transportation for you."

"That won't bother you, my peddling lottery tickets from your boat?"

"I imagine that the Lord will understand and be tolerant, so long as we are both doing His work. After all . . ."—the reverend permitted himself a slight smile—"but for a lottery I would not have my tabernacle."

Morgan was not a particularly religious man, but he did try to adhere to what he *did* believe. The hypocrisy of some people always amazed him. Here was the Reverend Luther Pryor, a fanatical man of God, willing to bend the laws of his God for his own convenience. He said, "How *about* Tate Brawley? Mightn't he object? We're not on the best of terms, you know."

"I discovered that you were right about Mr. Brawley. Although I am grateful for what he did for me, I have since learned that he took a percentage from the sale of every ticket. An exorbitant amount, in my opinion."

"That's Tate Brawley for you, Reverend. He never does anything out of the goodness of his heart."

"Also, it is my belief that he is lusting after Lotte," the reverend said indignantly.

If you only knew, Reverend, Morgan thought sardonically. Aloud he said, "All right, Reverend, we have a bargain. I will try it for a time, but I cannot promise to stay too long. I warn you that I may have to leave at any time, on a moment's notice."

Now, staring at the canal ahead, a tiny smile played across Morgan's mouth. Brawley was lusting after Lotte, was he? Morgan had managed, without any great difficulty, to become intimate with Lotte Pryor soon after the day he had rescued her from the clutches of the traveling peddler. He also had some news for Brawley—Lotte Pryor was far from being the virgin Brawley thought she was. She was not only a passionate woman, but she had the skills of an accomplished courtesan. Where she had gained her experience, Morgan had no idea, and he had not inquired; but he certainly knew now that her touching him that day in the buggy had not been inadvertent. He had been on board the church boat for almost a week now, and he had taken her to bed on two occasions when the reverend was absent. Morgan knew from the signs that she was itching to be bedded again.

The *Waters of Christ* had originally been a packet, and it was fair sized—sixty-five feet long and nine feet wide. What had once been the passenger cabin had been converted into the meeting house and would seat a good-sized crowd. The forward section was much the same as that of the *Cat*—with two cabins for sleeping and a tiny galley. Morgan slept on deck at night.

He was fairly confident that the reverend would leave the boat tonight, when they stopped at Lockport before going through the Lockport Five, that awesome staircase of lock combines necessary to lower a canal boat over the Niagara escarpment. It was Pryor's intention to hold services there for at least two evenings; and as had happened in the other towns where they had stopped, he would leave the boat for an hour or so to spread the news of his arrival. Morgan had tried to explain that this was really not necessary, since the "towpath news" would have spread the word of his imminent arrival. Word of any coming event could spread from Albany to Buffalo far faster than a boat could travel the distance, carried by mouth from one canal walker to another. However, the reverend always yearned to get out among "the brethren."

Now, as they entered the outskirts of Lockport, Pryor came up on deck. Morgan sent a sidelong glance at Lotte and was amused at what he observed. Where before she had been sitting loosely, knees apart, her ankles showing, a touch of the wanton about her, now she sat up primly, dress touching the deck, hands folded in her lap, looking prim and proper.

The Reverend Luther Pryor said ponderously, "We have arrived, I see."

"Just about, Reverend. We'll be tying up shortly."

The reverend rubbed his hands together gleefully. "I can't wait to get out among the sinners and announce to them that the word of God will be spoken here tonight." He was already dressed in black, his black hat set squarely on his head, the tight, reversed collar so restrictive that the folds of loose flesh about his neck were pinched painfully.

He said, "I have never traveled the Erie this far west."

Morgan nodded. "It's wilder here, closer to the frontier. Not only will you find frontiersmen here and in Buffalo, but also boatmen off Lake Erie. They're all a rough lot."

"All the better for my work, Mr. Kane, all the better." The reverend rubbed his hands together again.

Morgan turned to Lotte. "Going through the locks here, Miss Pryor, is a little frightening for the first time. It's something like going down a very steep staircase, as the boat drops from lock to lock as we go over the escarpment. I would suggest that you might care to walk down the first time. Also, you can get a better perspective that way."

"I'm not so easily frightened, Mr. Kane," Lotte said pertly.

"You will do as Mr. Kane says, daughter," the reverend said severely. "While I may be the captain of the souls in my church, he is the captain of our vessel. A captain's orders are always obeyed to the letter."

"Yes, Papa," Lotte said submissively, her eyes cast down.

Ahead Morgan could see the end of the line of boats waiting to pass through the locks; they were backed up for a half-mile or more. It would soon be dark, and the locks were always closed before that time; so the canallers wanted to pass through today, if possible, so that they would not have to wait in line all night. For this reason, the canallers and lockkeepers were always at odds.

Morgan called across to the hoggee, pointing out a spot up ahead where they could moor out of the way of the other boats. As they nudged into the wooden wharf, and Morgan tossed a mooring rope to the hoggee, he could hear a voice singing from one of the waiting boats: "Oh, the E-ri-eee is a-risin' / And the gin is a-gettin' low, / I scarcely think / I'll get another drink / Till I get to Buffalo!"

Pryor waited impatiently until the gangplank was run out. "Don't wait supper for me, daughter. I shall fast tonight, in preparation for the morrow. I am never hungry when I am doing the work of the Lord."

As he walked briskly out of hearing, Lotte said with a pout, "He treats me like I'm a child, Papa does."

"But we know better, don't we, Lotte?" Morgan said with a knowing smile.

"I don't know what you mean, sir," she said archly.

Without answering he reached down for her hand. She dropped her parasol with a clatter and came into his arms urgently, mouth turned up expectantly.

"I think we'd better wait a minute. It's a little public out here."

"Oh." She drew away from him. "I never thought."

She walked sedately ahead of him, the epitome of a minister's daughter; but the instant her cabin door was closed behind them, she came into his arms eagerly. Her lips were hot and seeking, and her fingers worked frantically on the muscles of his arms.

"You are so strong, Morgan," she whispered. "So strong!"

Then she turned away toward the bunk, undressing as she went. As he began to remove his own clothes, Morgan said, "I hope the good reverend never comes back unexpectedly. There'd be hell to pay, in more ways than one."

She shrugged. "Once Papa leaves to go about collecting his flock, he never returns early."

"There's always a first time."

She did not answer, and Morgan wondered, as he had before, whether Lotte really cared. It had struck him that, perhaps unknowingly, she *wanted* her father to catch her. It could be that she was wearying of playing the pious daughter of a minister and would be relieved to stop the charade and perhaps go her own way.

By the time Morgan was undressed, Lotte was ready and waiting, lying on the bed with one knee drawn up, watching him with bright, hot eyes. Underneath the prim clothes she wore, her figure was surprisingly lush. But, each time, Morgan could not stop himself from comparing her with Cat. Lotte's breasts were larger, her hips broader, and her body was soft, whereas Cat was lean and supple, with not an ounce of excess flesh on her; hard work on the canal boat kept her body honed down.

"You've looked long enough." Lotte beckoned insistently. "Come here. You're ready for me, that's plain to see." She laughed richly as he came toward her.

She reached out for his erect organ and drew him down to her. There was seldom any need for preliminaries with Lotte; she was always ready and open for him. She locked her arms around his neck, pulled his mouth down to hers, and raised her hips as he entered her. A guttural moan came from her.

She attained a climax almost at once, ripping her lips away from his to utter a stuttering cry; but she was lax for only a moment before she rose to meet him again, her body adjusting to his movements.

Morgan held a rein on his passion, knowing from their other times that she would reach a second peak again in a short time. As he felt her body began to quicken again, he let himself go, groaning as a mighty spasm seized him. She rose and clung to him, crying out once more, her body shuddering in ecstasy.

Her bunk was somewhat wider than the one in Cat's cabin, so there was room for Morgan to stretch out beside her comfortably, his arm under her head. She turned her face against his chest, warm breath stirring his chest hairs.

"Morgan," she said breathily, "you probably think I'm terrible."

"Now why should I think that, my dear?"

"Because I don't behave like a minister's daughter. You probably think I bed down with any man available."

"Well, I certainly hope not." He chuckled, he hoped convincingly. "I'm more particular than that."

"There haven't been that many. Only two before you. I hope you believe that."

"If you say it's true, I believe you."

"It is true," she said vehemently. She stirred restlessly.

"It's not an easy life, being a missionary's daughter. And with Papa . . . well, you know Papa."

He said dryly, "Oh, yes, I know Papa."

"Life in Africa was horrible. There was nothing to amuse. It was church, church every day. I had to do something, or go mad. There was this other missionary. . . ." She gently stroked his chest with her fingertips. "He was young, single, and quite attractive. He helped Papa. He was lonely, and he also hated the life there. Well, it . . . it just happened. It lasted about six months, and I had found something that relieved the tedium a little. But Paul, he was all torn up with guilt. Tortured, really. He wanted to marry me, but I just couldn't!" She shuddered. "Being married to a missionary would have been worse than being the daughter of one! And then . . ." Her voice became more subdued. "Paul went off into the jungle, and he never returned. He died out there somewhere in that hell. I think he went off to die, full of guilt. I always blamed myself for his death.

"But at least Papa never suspected a thing. When we came back to the United States, I met another man where Papa got his parish. I thought I might even marry him. But when I hinted at it, he laughed at me and said a terrible thing. 'Why marry the cow when the milk is free?' "

She clung to Morgan. "I was absolutely mortified. Since then I've behaved myself, until you came along."

Morgan patted her shoulder in compassion. He sensed how easily her sensual nature, vanity, and lack of worldly experience could lead her into disastrous affairs with men.

She went on, "At least you were honest with me in the beginning. You told me at the start that you weren't interested in marriage. I appreciate that."

She turned her face up to kiss him.

He said, "How about Tate Brawley? I had the feeling that he had his eye on you, and you seemed to like him."

"Not really. I only pretended to, to please Papa. Mr.

Brawley is a cold man. There is something sinister about him."

She has more common sense than I gave her credit for, Morgan thought in surprise.

"I like a man with warmth. Like you, Morgan." She kissed him again, and her hands began to roam over his body. "Of course, other things count, too, like strength, and . . ." Her small hand closed around him, and she laughed softly.

"You're an insatiable wench, you know that, Lotte?"

She laughed wickedly. "With you I am, Morgan, but never before, believe me."

He rose up to take her, and she welcomed him with a groaning sigh.

A few hours later, Morgan stood in the back of the reverend's tabernacle and grinned to himself as Lotte stood beside the small piano on the platform at the far end of the room. She was dressed demurely, hands crossed before her, her eyes cast heavenward, as her father sat down at the piano and began to play a hymn.

The Reverend Luther Pryor was a poor piano player, but his daughter had a marvelous voice. A clear, sweet soprano, she sang like an angel, and looked like an angel. Her voice soared, filling the room with bell-like notes, sending a shiver down Morgan's spine. Remembering her in bed only a short while ago, he could scarcely believe this was the same woman.

The room was about half-filled, and the crowd was made up mainly of women. Even if they are not inspired by the reverend's sermon, Morgan thought, their evening will not be wasted, just listening to Lotte sing.

Two days later, they started through the locks, on their way to the next town. Against Morgan's advice, Lotte chose to remain on board; the Reverend Mr. Pryor, exuberant over his success the past two nights, was in too good a mood to set his foot down. Lotte stood beside Morgan at the tiller. The reverend was below in his cabin, preparing his next sermon. "I am too busy doing the Lord's work to play the part of the gaper," he had told Morgan. "I shall take your word, Mr. Kane, that the locks are a wonder. But none of man's work can approach the wondrous deeds of our Lord."

The Lockport Five was five pairs of double locks cut through solid rock, through which ascending and descending boats passed so close together that a conversation could easily be held between two passing canallers.

As they entered the first lock and the gates closed behind them, Lotte gasped and clutched at Morgan's arm, as she realized just how steep their descent would be.

Morgan said, "I warned you, Lotte."

"Oh, I'm not frightened, Morgan. I think it's thrilling!"

The boat descended slowly from one lock to the next, and eventually they were through the bottom lock, the canal flowing level before them. Their hoggee and the mules were waiting for them at the bottom. Morgan threw him the tow rope, and the hoggee fastened it to the harness. He shouted, and the mules strained in their traces. The *Waters of Christ* began to move slowly, safely on its way to their next destination.

Morgan grinned faintly; he could hear Luther Pryor's voice all the way from his cabin in the bow, as he bellowed out his practice sermon: "To be saved, you must give your soul to Jesus. He said, believe in me and ye shall be saved!"

Chapter Thirteen

HARD times were definitely over, and business was booming along the Erie. The Carnahans were now able to get all the cargo they could handle. New canal boats were seen on the Erie; and old ones, abandoned for some time, Cat was sure, were patched up and put back into service. Once more traffic along the canal was so thick that at times a person could walk across the Erie at any given point without once touching water. The only bug in the ointment, as Mick would have said, was that there was increased friction between the canallers and the lockkeepers, because the boat operators were agitating for the locks to remain open at night. However, they were having little success with that demand.

Cat was gratified that she was kept busy from dawn to dusk. Sometimes they even traveled at night, from lock to lock. The reason she was happy to be so occupied was that it kept her from thinking of Morgan. She had sworn to herself that she would forget him; but of course that was not possible. She still longed for him, with her body and her heart; she knew now that she did love him. Many times, in the still of the night, in her bunk, she thought of getting word to him, with the idea of listening to his explanation; and if it was at all plausible, forgiving him, and taking him back onto the *Cat*, and into her bed and her heart.

But with the arrival of daylight she always changed her mind. She knew about Morgan living on the Reverend Luther Pryor's boat and running it for him. She had seen him at the tiller a number of times that summer; and once they had even passed so close that Morgan had tipped his hat and given her a wink.

"Good morning to you, Miss Carnahan," he had said breezily. "A fine day, isn't it?"

Face flaming, she had looked away, refusing to respond to him.

It was quite clear to her that he was not suffering any grief at their parting. Unbidden, a thought had slipped into her mind: Was he bedding the prim Miss Pryor? Was he pleasuring her? Were his hands and mouth on Lotte Pryor at night? The images this thought created caused her to writhe inside with jealousy and anger.

No, she would never seek to reconcile with Morgan Kane! Damn and blast him!

And yet she found herself missing him at odd moments, and to blot the image of him from her mind she would throw herself into her work again. She worked with such a frenzy that Mick even commented on it. "You're going at it too hard, Catherine. I think you've even lost a few pounds, and I wouldn't be thinking that possible."

"We have to earn money while we can, now that times are good again, to make up for the past year. Don't fret about me, Mick, I'm fine."

"I'm thinking you're not so fine," he said in a grumbling voice. "But well I know 'tis a waste of time to argue with you." He peered at her shrewdly. "It's missing young Morgan you are, ain't it?"

"No, I'm not missing young Morgan," she snapped.

"This doctor fellow now, he strikes me as a fine, upstanding lad," he said musingly.

"Mick, will you stop worrying about my personal life? You

keep trying to marry me off. You want to be rid of me that badly?"

"A lass your age should be married; but getting rid of you, no. I'm thinking no such thing."

"What do you think, then—that Dr. Mason will marry me, and come live happily forever after on the *Cat*?"

Mick straightened up, offended. "If it's me that's worrying you, don't. I can manage very well by meself."

"Now you sound just like me." She laughed affectionately and gave him a rare kiss. "I do love you, Mick. Just stop concerning yourself about me."

In truth, she was proud of her father. Although he still drank, he had not come home drunk since Morgan had left. He did his share of the work, and got most of the cargoes they hauled nowadays. It seemed to Cat that Mick somehow felt responsible for Morgan's leaving, and was doing everything he could to make up for it.

As for Anthony Mason, Cat had seen him only twice since that night on his medical boat; she had simply been too busy. After their last meeting, Anthony had said with a wry grimace, "We're like two ships that pass in the night, Cat."

At neither of those two meetings had they made love. Both times they could only talk for a few minutes; both times the *Cat* was loaded, Cat was in a hurry to get to her destination, and Anthony was on his way to treat a patient. She had gathered from the few words they had exchanged that his practice was still far from flourishing.

Cat longed to see him again, for an evening. She was lonely; Anthony was a spirited companion and a good lover. Also, the summer was ending; it was into September now. Another two months and winter would be upon them. Cat dreaded the coming winter more than she ever had in the past. She feared that when the Erie was drained and they had to lay idle, she would go out of her mind. It had been bad enough before, three months or more with nothing to occupy her time; but after all that had happened this summer, she well knew that her mind would be full of it. She loved to read, and always hoarded what books she could get her hands on for the winter layoff; but the supply of books along the Erie was scarce. At least this winter they would not have to suffer from want; the summer had been good to them financially. However, that very well-being could cause another problem; the other winters, money had been in short supply, and Mick could not drink so much. She feared that, with ample money in his pocket, he would revert to his old ways.

Then, in Rochester, where they had just unloaded a cargo of farm equipment brought in from Albany, Cat was happy to see Anthony's boat tied up at the wharf, as the *Cat* pulled in to unload. She saw no sign of Anthony; but just as they finished unloading and were putting the boat in order, she saw him swinging along the wharf with long strides.

She greeted him with a glad cry. "Anthony! Dear Anthony, I'm so pleased to see you again!"

He took her hands. "And I you, Cat. It seems forever. I've missed you."

She peered at him. "You seem in an unusually fine mood today."

His smile widened. "I am, Cat, I am! I think I've finally broken through. I saved a woman's life last week. She had terrible abdominal pains. Other doctors had given up. They diagnosed her pain as 'knotted bowels,' and gave her only days to live. But I knew it was a burst appendix. I persuaded her to let me operate. I took an awful chance, I know. There have only been a few such operations, and none successful, that I know of. Usually, by the time the surgeon gets in there, it's too late."

He laughed exuberantly. "Her husband and a friend didn't want me to operate, but *they* weren't suffering her awful pain, and she insisted. The two men stood outside my surgery all the time with pistols, and they swore they'd kill me if she died. But she lived, she lived! I was successful!" He sobered a little. "Of course, I was fortunate in one respect. There was another doctor, a land doctor, who did agree with my diagnosis, and he assisted in the operation. I could never have done it alone."

"She was a canal woman, I gather?"

"Of course, the wife of a passenger-packet captain."

Cat started to smile. " 'Land doctor.' You're beginning to sound like a true canawler at last, Anthony. You're thinking of people on land as separate from us."

He looked startled, momentarily, then nodded slowly. "You're right, I am. But the thing is, you see . . ." His exuberance broke through again. "With this happening, I've finally gained the trust and respect of the canallers. I've already noticed it. More and more people are coming to me for medical attention."

"I'm glad for you, Anthony." She squeezed his hand.

He swung her arms back and forth between them. "I'm happy you're in Rochester, Cat. I have something to really celebrate. Will you have dinner with me tonight?"

"I will be more than happy to."

"I don't know what eating accommodations Rochester has to offer, but we'll find out." His eyes crinkled. "To be honest, to be with you tonight, they could serve sawdust, for all I care. I'll pick you up at eight, all right?"

"Fine, Anthony."

With a wave he was gone, his stride vigorous as he walked away along the wharf. Smiling fondly, she stood watching him until he was out of sight. She *was* fond of him, but she doubted that it would ever go beyond that. And yet, she thought, it would not be a bad life, married to Anthony Mason.

She shook off the thought and went about finishing her chores.

She was not quite finished dressing when she heard Mick greet Anthony on deck; and when she finally did come up, she found her father telling another one of his Erie yarns. With a smile at Anthony, Cat stood back, waiting until the story was finished.

"It was something, Anthony lad," Mick was saying,

"that opening day of the Erie, October 25, 1825, for them that observed it. O' course, sections of the canal had been open before that day, but that was the day she opened her full length. There was close to a five-hundred-mile celebration. It started in the Erie Basin, the packet *Seneca Chief* leading the parade of boats, carrying symbolic kegs of water from round the world. Many bigwigs were on board the *Chief*, but the biggest of all was DeWitt Clinton, the governor of New York State, the bucko mainly responsible for the building of the Erie.

"Clinton stood in the prow as the *Chief* slipped past the signal cannon, pulled by a prize team of horses, their hoggee the champion driver on the Erie. The cannon went off, and then the second cannon to the east, placed within hearing distance, was fired, and so on all down the line. 'Tis said that New York town had the word within eighty minutes that Governor Clinton and the *Chief* were on their way.

"You know, lad, that the legal speed on the Erie is five miles the hour. Even so, it was an eye-filling spectacle, a long line of boats following the *Chief*. I know, I was there in Buffalo, where it all began, and then we put the *Cat* into the tail end of the line. Catherine there"—he grinned at Cat—"was only fifteen at the time, but I'm sure she recollects it well."

Smiling, Cat said, "Oh, yes, I remember it very well. It was a great sight."

"Aye, a grand sight it was," Mick resumed. "O' course, we didn't average near four miles an hour, you understand. There was a celebration in every town along the canal, and we had to stop in each and every one, else they be offended. All but Schenectady." Mick laughed heartily. " 'Old Dorp' it was called by many folks. Old Dorp didn't join in the celebration."

Anthony took his pipe from his mouth. "Why was that, Mr. Carnahan?"

"Well, it was like this, you see. The Durham boats were built there. The whole town of Old Dorp, back then, depended on that single industry. The folks figured that their industry was doomed because canawlers would be using the long boats that carried more cargo. Schenectady held a mock funeral when the *Seneca Chief* passed by. They were wrong, o' course. Nowadays Old Dorp depends on the Erie for its livelihood as much as any other town.

"I'm thinking that more whiskey flowed that day than Erie water." Mick laughed again. "Aye, a grand ball was had by all, all the way to New York town. Most folks hardly had the energy to even be aware when we finally all reached the Hudson and New York. There, the grand finale of it all was called the Wedding of the Waters, when the water kegs were emptied into the harbor to mingle with the waters of the Atlantic Ocean. Ah." Mick sighed, shaking his head dolefully. "We'll never see the likes of that ever again, I'm thinking."

Cat said tartly, "And I'm thinking that Anthony has heard enough of your blarney for one day."

"You hear that, Anthony me lad? How ungrateful a daughter I have, her that can talk to her own da in that fashion."

"Come along, Anthony, don't pay any attention to his blather."

Anthony stood, offering Cat his arm. As they left the boat, Cat glanced back, and Mick gave her a wink. She stuck out her tongue at him.

Two hours later, after an unsatisfactory meal, they were on the *Paracelsus*, in Anthony's cabin.

As Anthony closed the door, he said, "I am sorry, Cat. It was a wretched meal. I must have picked the worst restaurant in town."

"I doubt there are any good ones. Don't worry about it, darling." She laughed softly and stepped to him. "Besides, we both know that the food wasn't that important. This, now, is what is important."

"I have missed you, Cat."

With a groan he took her into his arms. She accepted his kiss hungrily, glorying in the warmth and softness of his lips and the hardness of his body.

He proceeded to undress her with delicate care. She could imagine those sensitive, supple fingers exploring an ailing body, searching out the site of illness; and those same hands were now bringing her to the fullness of life. She shivered, clinging to him as he lowered her onto his bed. His touch might not send her to that almost instant peak of searing desire as did Morgan's touch, yet Anthony knew well how to build her passion slowly, until she was trembling with need of him; and soon she beseeched him with blind hands to enter her.

"Yes, Cat," he murmured. "Oh, yes!"

She sighed softly at his entry. He was inside her with one long thrust, and she rose and fell with him as their rhythm quickened, and quickened yet again. She gave a muted cry and rose to cling to him fiercely as the first shudders of ecstasy shook her.

"Ah-h, Anthony," she said in a guttural voice. "That's it! Yes, yes!"

Hearts pounding in the same furious tempo, they melded together and became one body, one person, for several moments of joyous rapture.

She kissed the nook of his shoulder, and she felt his panting breath stir her hair.

"You're a passionate woman, Cat. Even Laura . . ." He cut off the rest of the sentence abruptly.

Cat did not press him to finish what he had started to say; she realized that he had been about to speak of something private, perhaps even sacred, between him and his dead wife, and she felt no inclination to pry.

He lay beside her, his breathing even now, and a lassitude stole over Cat. She must have slipped into sleep, for she sat up with a start at the pounding of a fist on the cabin door. Her first thought was that it might be her father. Yet she knew that Mick, even if he suspected that

Anthony was her lover, would never be so crass as to force himself upon them at such an inopportune time.

Then a strange voice said, "Doc? Dr. Mason, are you in there?"

Anthony sat up, a little groggy from sleep. "Yes? What is it?"

The voice said urgently, "I have my friend out here who needs attention real bad, Doc. He has a bad cut on his thigh."

Anthony was already up and dressing quickly. "I shall be right there." To Cat he said, "You'd better get dressed. You can slip out while I'm tending this fellow in my surgery."

Anthony hurried out, leaving the door slightly ajar, taking a lantern with him. Light flared outside as he lit the lantern.

As she dressed, Cat heard their voices, as Anthony said, "This looks bad. How did it come about?"

Cat heard loud groans of pain now, as the other man spoke. "We was scouring the countryside for some wood for our stove on the boat, Doc. Jed here had the ax. It grew dark on us, and he was chopping on a dead tree. He slipped and fell just as the ax came down, slicing open his thigh, as you can see. . . . My God, look at all the blood!" Cat heard sounds of retching.

Anthony said sharply, "How long ago did this happen?"

"Just a few minutes ago, Doc," the man replied, gagging again. "We'uns are just down the canal a ways."

"It's a nasty cut. I'm afraid he nicked an artery. Here, help me tie a tourniquet around his thigh until I can get him into my surgery and repair it."

"I can't, Doc," the other man wailed. "I can't stand the sight of blood. As you just saw, it makes me puke."

"But I need another pair of hands here. I'm using pressure from both of mine to stop the bleeding. Otherwise, your friend may die."

"I can't, Doc!" the man wailed. "Hate to say this, me

not being a woman, but I've been knowed to faint at the sight of blood."

Dressed, Cat stepped out of the cabin. "I'll help you, Dr. Mason."

Anthony was kneeling beside the man prone on the deck. The wounded man's trouser leg had been torn away, and Anthony was pressing his thumbs against the artery on the inside of the thigh. There seemed to be blood everywhere. The second man, pale and shaken, gaped at Cat. At least his was not a familiar face; so he could not identify her.

Anthony looked up at her doubtfully. "I don't wish to impose on you. It's not your place to . . ."

"You said he might die if you didn't have help."

He nodded. "That's true enough. He might die anyway. I don't know how much loss of blood he's suffered. But if I don't block off the artery flow until I can repair the damage and stitch up the wound, he most certainly will die."

"Then I must help. Tell me what to do."

"You sure you can manage?"

"I'll manage," she said steadily. She knelt beside him. "Just show me what to do."

"Here, right where I have my thumbs. That's the nicked artery. If you can do it, place all the pressure you can on the artery, just until I can fetch a tourniquet to tie around his thigh."

Gingerly, Cat reached down to the spot indicated. The sweetish smell of blood made her stomach turn, and the hot, slippery feel of it almost made her change her mind. Steeling herself, she found the pressure point Anthony showed her, and pressed down.

"Press down with all your strength," he said, getting up. "I'll be right back with a tourniquet."

Cat felt the artery pulsing mightily, as if the blood was trying to find a way past her fingers. She closed her eyes tightly, and pressed down until her arms began to ache.

Mercifully, Anthony was back within minutes. "Hold on

just a moment longer." Kneeling beside her, he quickly placed a length of rubber tubing around the man's thigh, just above the wound, and tied it off tightly.

"Now let go, but slowly, until I see if it is working."

Cat slowly eased her pressure. Anthony held the lantern close to the cut. In a moment he nodded in satisfaction. "Good! The flow has stopped." He got to his feet, giving Cat a hand up. She swayed, feeling faint. He asked anxiously, "Are you all right?"

Gulping a lungful of the night air, she nodded and straightened up. "I'll be all right. It's just . . ." She gestured vaguely.

"I know." He whirled on the other man. In a commanding voice he said, "Now you have to help me get your friend into my surgery room. I can't work on him out here."

"I can't, Doc," the man said weakly.

"You can and will, or by God I'll get my pistol out and shoot you dead on the spot. Do you understand me?"

The man nodded sullenly.

"Just inside the door is a stretcher. Fetch it. Move, damn you! I have to work on him at once."

The man scurried into the main cabin, and Anthony turned to Cat. "Can I impose on you a bit more? I need someone to hold a light for me. If I depend on that fellow, he might faint on me and leave me in total darkness."

"Of course, Anthony. I'm all right now." She was far from all right; her stomach still roiled, and she felt faint, yet she was determined to brave it through.

The man came back with the stretcher, and together the two men lifted the wounded man onto it. He groaned and raised his head, mumbling something Cat could not understand. With Anthony at one end and the wounded man's friend at the other, they picked up the stretcher and started inside, with Cat holding the lantern high so they could see. They carried the patient the length of the main cabin and into Anthony's surgery. There, he was placed on the high table.

Anthony took a squat bottle from his medicine cabinet and thrust it at the man. "A bottle of rum," he said contemptuously. "Leave us and stay in the other room. That should keep you occupied."

Anthony closed the door, and said to Cat in a low voice, "I don't even own a pistol, but the threat worked."

He picked up a wooden stethoscope and held it over the man's heart, listening for a few moments. "Heart seems sound enough. For the moment at least. Surprisingly strong, in fact, considering the amount of blood he must have lost."

Next, he took a small vial from the cabinet, raised the patient's head, and forced him to swallow. "Laudanum," he explained to Cat. "There'll be quite a bit of pain while I'm working on him. Let's just hope this keeps him unconscious."

He lit two oil lamps and gave them to Cat. "Stand at the foot of the table and hold them low enough so that I'll receive the maximum amount of light."

He went to a washbasin in the corner, poured some alcohol into it, and proceeded to wash his hands thoroughly. "Paracelsus had a theory, all those long years ago, that many surgeons themselves infected their patients by carrying germs into the wound from dirty hands. He was scoffed at then, and still is today. In fact, many doctors still call his theory rubbish, but I believe he had a valid point, so when I treat someone, especially when I perform surgery, I make sure my hands are as sterile as possible. I remember watching an operation once, where the surgeon operated while smoking a cigar, dropping ashes all over everything." He made a sound of disgust and dried his hands on a clean towel.

From the cabinet he removed a pair of scissors, a needle, suture, and a scalpel, all of which he proceeded to rinse in a fresh basin of alcohol. After drying the instruments, he placed them on a clean towel beside the man, who was now unconscious and snoring strenuously.

Cat held the lamps so Anthony could get the best

advantage of them as he bent over the patient. With the scalpel he cleared away enough flesh that the nick in the artery was fully exposed. Very gently, with fingers as sensitive as if they had eyes of their own, he probed into the wound, cleansing it of blood. With the artery blocked off now, there was only a small seepage.

Threading the needle with very fine suture, he sewed up the nick in the blood vessel, using infinite care. Then he straightened, picked up the scalpel, and dipped a soft cloth in alcohol. Quickly then, he cleaned the wound again and swabbed it out with alcohol, as the man on the table twitched and groaned several times.

"Even through the opium," Anthony commented, "he's feeling pain now. I have to hurry up."

Using another needle and a coarser suture thread, he quickly but methodically stitched up the cut, drawing together the edges of the wound and sewing at the same time. Cat marveled that he was able to do everything at once without three hands. Finally, he straightened up with a sigh. With the wooden stethoscope he again listened to the wounded man's heart.

"It's still beating strongly," Anthony said with satisfaction. "Apparently he was fortunate in that he didn't lose too much blood. I think he will be all right, so long as infection doesn't set in. That's the worst enemy of the surgeon, infection. Someday we'll find some solution to that, something to completely sterilize the wound and operating conditions. This man's survival will depend on his constitution and his ability to fight off infection. Some people, the fortunate ones, have it more than others."

He closed his eyes, placed his hands in the small of his back, and arched back his neck while rotating his torso. Opening his eyes, he saw Cat still standing there holding the lamps. "Cat," he said gently, "it's over now; you don't need to hold the lamps any longer."

"Oh," she said with a start. "I guess I didn't realize." As she started to put down the lamps, she glanced down at herself, and saw with horror that the whole front of her dress was smeared with blood. "Damn blast and hell! What will Mick think when he sees that? He'll be sure that I've been attacked and nearly killed."

"Oh, I am sorry, Cat. Here . . ." He crossed to the washbasin for a pitcher of water and a cloth. "Most of it will probably wash off. You may be going home with a wet dress, but it'll come out easier now than later."

She stood still while he sponged off the front of her dress. His own hands were still bloody from the operation. In ordinary circumstances she would have been repulsed, but while watching him perform his magic on the wounded man, her admiration for Anthony had mounted; and she somehow felt complimented that he was using those very same hands to perform such a mundane task as sponging her dress. And that was what it had been, she thought—sheer magic. True, she had never before observed a surgeon at work, yet she knew instinctively that what she had just witnessed was a master surgeon at work.

In washing her dress his hand moved over her breasts, and she shivered, suddenly faint with a powerful surge of desire. For just a moment she toyed with the thought of luring him back into his cabin; but then he said, "I'll escort you back to your boat, Cat, then I have to return here and watch over the patient for the rest of the night. If he wakes up, I'll have to dose him with laudanum again. I may even have to strap him down to the table, to keep him as immobile as possible until it's safe for him to move about without tearing out the stitches."

"There's no need for that, Anthony. I can make my way home alone. It isn't that far."

"I won't hear of it. No lone woman is safe along the wharf at night. There, that's about all I can do for now." He returned to the basin and quickly washed his hands clean of accumulated blood.

He gave her his arm, and smiled. "If your father questions you about the soiled dress, I'll tell him you just helped to save a man's life."

In a chair in the main cabin, the wounded man's friend

was nodding, the rum bottle held tenderly in his hands. Anthony woke him with a prod of his toe. "Your friend will likely be all right. He's sleeping now, but he might wake up at any time. I have to see the lady home. I want you to stay right here, and if your friend does wake up, I want you to go in to him, and keep him there. If you're not both still here when I come back, you'll regret it, understand?"

The man bobbed his head, smiling loosely. "I'll wait right here, Doc, promise on it," he said in a slurred voice. He held up the rum bottle. "And thanks for the medicine. I needed it."

Anthony snorted, and went on out with Cat. As they walked along the wharf, he said, "I want you to know how much I appreciate your help, Cat. Not very many women would have done what you did. They would have swooned at the first sight of blood. Not only are you beautiful, but you are a strong woman."

"Coming from you, Anthony, that is a great compliment. Watching you at work was a revelation. You are a great doctor."

He laughed. "That sounds like some of your father's blarney."

"No, it's not." She squeezed his arm. "It's the absolute truth."

"You know something, Cat?" he said musingly. "You *would* make a fine doctor's wife. That fact was really borne home to me tonight."

Chapter Fourteen

SIMON Maphis, with a belly full of rum, was roaring his way through the Cut. His pockets were full of money, and he was having a high old time for himself. It had been a good year for him, everything considered; and although it was December now, the weather had been relatively mild, until today.

It was cold enough tonight to freeze, and Maphis was sure that the Erie would be drained before the week was out, stopping all canal traffic; but with the hot rum flowing through his blood, he was not feeling the cold. Unlike most canallers, Maphis did not mind the advent of winter, for he could still make money selling lottery tickets. In fact, since the annual prize drawings were held right after the first of every year, this was the best time for selling tickets, especially since most of the canallers, after a good summer, were flush with money.

The Cut held no fears for Maphis. He knew that no thief or cutthroat would dare attack the King of the Erie. He felt as safe here among his own kind as he would in any canal town; and here he could do just about any damned thing he cared to, without anybody getting into an uproar about it.

He swaggered along the rutted street from tavern to tavern, shoving people aside if they did not get out of his way, knocking them to the ground if they did not move fast enough to suit him. It was his night to howl; and if anybody got in his way, they would suffer for it. He was about ready for a woman, but so far he had failed to find one who suited him.

He went from place to place, getting into two fights, neither of which lasted very long. The first was with a man he knocked out in Sadie's Place with one sledgehammer blow; the second was with two men in a tavern aptly named the Bucket of Blood. This time he grabbed a head in each hand, like a melon, and slammed them together. That ended the fight; one man staggered out the door, leaving his chum cold on the sawdust-covered floor.

Maphis, roaring with laughter, stepped over the prone body, strode to the bar, and hammered his fist on it. "A bottle of your best rum, barkeep. And it had better be your best, or you'll end up on the floor alongside that fool over there."

The bartender placed a bottle before him, and Maphis picked it up by the neck, drinking straight from the bottle.

A woman's voice said beside him, "You're some battler, you are, love."

Maphis looked around and down, expecting a woman coming about to the middle of his chest. Instead, the woman who stood beside him was large and voluptuous, and he hardly had to look down at all to stare directly into her bold blue eyes. She was a little above the average in looks for a woman in the Cut, and Maphis knew this was the one he wanted.

"I'm by God the best man along the Erie," he boomed out. "I'm King of the Erie, Simon Maphis by name."

"And I'm Bertha. Big Bertha, if you like. The King, eh? I've always wanted to meet a king face to face."

"Now you've met one, woman. How about a drink?" He waved the rum bottle.

"I'd love one."

"What'll you have?"

"Whatever you're having will be fine."

"I'm drinking rum. Powerful stuff."

"If you can drink it, I can."

Maphis roared with laughter. "A glass for the lady, barkeep."

"I have a glass at my place," Big Bertha said with an insinuating smile. "It's more comfortable there."

He squinted at her, sobering slightly. "How much?"

"For the King of the Erie, nothing, love." She tossed her head, heavy black hair swinging. "I'd consider it an honor. A man like you doesn't come along every day."

A strumpet giving away her favors? Maphis could scarcely believe his good fortune; and he was not about to spurn her offer, even if she had been pocked and ugly, which she definitely was not.

"Ah, you're the one for sweet talk, ain't you, Bertha? But I like that now." He slung an arm around her shoulders, and they went out of the tavern, one of his arms still around her shoulders, the other carrying the rum bottle. He took a swig, then offered it to Bertha.

She took it without a word, tipped back her head, and drank. "Wow! You were right, King, that's powerful stuff!"

Laughing, he squeezed her shoulder. "I like you, Bertha." He also liked being called King. Not only did it make him feel all-powerful, it made him randier than ever. He was going to give this wench a tumble she would never forget!

Bertha had quarters in a building up the street. From the outside, it did not look like much—an unpainted, dilapidated structure, with a crudely lettered sign, ROOMING HOUSE, creaking in the wind.

Bertha led Maphis down a dim hall to a room in the back. When she lit a lamp, he was a little surprised to see that the room was clean and comfortably furnished. The rooms of the other Side-Cut whores that Maphis had seen were as sad as their inhabitants.

The big woman did not give him much time to inspect his surroundings. She took the bottle from him and placed it on a side table. "We'll drink that, after," she said huskily. "Watching you in action, King, got me fired up.

It ain't often that I see a husky brute like you in the Cut, love."

"Brute, eh?" he growled. "You like that, eh?"

"I like that, love. I like it as rough as you can give it to me."

Maphis was certainly no accomplished lover. He liked his loving simple and uncomplicated; and most women who would take him into their embraces were either plain whores or sluts, and they lay still as logs while he rutted atop them.

He soon found that Big Bertha was unlike any whore he had known. She also liked it uncomplicated, but she did not lie like a log. She fell athwart the bed, hoisting her skirts up above her waist. She wore no undergarments, and the sight of her ample, milk-white flesh aroused him fully. He hastily removed his breeches and fell upon her. She received him with a grunt, and then went crazy under him. She clenched and unclenched powerful thighs around him, and rose to meet his every thrust, crying out, "That's it, King! Rough, that's the way I like it!"

When they had both experienced their pleasure, Maphis realized that he had met his match in bed. As he collapsed, panting, beside her, he considered taking her with him on the *King*. In Maphis's experience with women, this was the first time he had known one to receive any kind of pleasure with him, and he had come to believe it was not possible. True, a few had tried to convince him otherwise, but he was no fool—they were all faking; but this woman was not; she had enjoyed it every bit as much as he had. Strangely, for that very reason, he was a little intimidated by her; he had the feeling that this would somehow give her a measure of control over him. No, he decided, it was best he leave her in the Cut. Besides, he knew where she was, if and when he wanted her again. Once reduced to living in the Cut, women of her stripe seldom made it to the outside world again.

Bertha sat up on the edge of the bed, shoving down her skirts. "I'm going down the hall for a few minutes, love.

Then we'll finish the rum. Don't go away now, the night is far from over. I want some more of what you just gave me."

As the door closed behind her, Maphis sat up, looking curiously around the room. Unaccustomed to cleanliness himself, either of his person or of his surroundings, he was amazed at how clean the room was, and he wondered, uneasily, if he should have bathed first.

What the hell! He smacked his fist against the bed. What was wrong with him? Wondering if he should have taken a bath before tumbling a whore! With a grunt he got out of bed in order to reach the table and the rum bottle. A little unsteady on his feet, he stumbled slightly, lurching against the small table. He snatched up the rum bottle before it could fall to the floor, and then paused. Behind the table, now askew, was a black leather valise, expensive from the look of it. Curious as to why a woman like Bertha had such a valise in her possession, he bent and picked it up. The lock on the valise had been broken; without the least compunction, Maphis opened it.

Inside was a sheaf of papers. Maphis had never learned to read; he could read figures and decipher names that he was familiar with, but that was the extent of it. He leafed through the papers idly. They were covered with handwriting. His brief scanning picked up a few figures, but they meant nothing to him. Then his gaze stopped, caught by a name written at the bottom of one page—Morgan Kane!

Just then he heard Bertha reenter the room. Without trying to hide what he had done, he turned, with the papers in his hand.

"Where did you get this valise, Bertha?" he demanded.

She shrugged carelessly. "Some man came in with it a couple of weeks ago. He didn't have enough money to pay me, so he bargained, swapping me that thing. It looked like it might cost a penny or two, so, like a fool, I took it, thinking I might sell it somewhere." She shook her head in disgust. "I should have known better. Who in the Cut has the money, or even the need, for something as fancy as that?"

"Was the man's name Morgan Kane?"

"How do I know, love? I don't ask after their names. I don't even *want* to know. I probably wouldn't have asked yours. You told me, remember? I didn't ask."

"Was he a dandified gent, wearing fancy clothes?"

"Gawd, love!" She snorted softly. "The day's long past when I attract a gent like that, especially here in the Cut. No, he was a ratty-looking fellow. Come to think of it, he smelled like one, too."

"I'll buy the valise from you, Bertha. Here." He dug into his pocket for a handful of coins. "That enough?"

"Sure; it's more than I'll get somewhere else." Carelessly she tossed the coins onto the table. "Take the thing and welcome to it. Now come on, let's sample the rum and then have some more sport."

Maphis was torn. He wanted to snatch up the valise and go looking for Tate Brawley; he knew in his bones that the ticket broker would be interested in the papers. On the other hand, he had no idea where Brawley was at the moment, and he wanted this lusty wench again. Brawley could wait.

He put the papers back into the valise, dropped it onto the floor, and picked up the rum bottle. He advanced on Bertha with a leer. "A tot of rum, and then the sport, eh?"

It was several days before Maphis saw Tate Brawley, who came by the *King* later in the week to collect for the ticket sales Maphis had made.

"Come into my cabin, Tate, I have something to show you."

He took Brawley into the cabin and dug out the valise, showing it to him.

Brawley looked from the valise to Maphis. "What's this, Simon? I have no need of such."

"It's what's inside that's important." Maphis turned the valise upside down and dumped the papers into the bunk.

Brawley gave him another dubious glance, then picked up several sheets of paper and began to peruse them. Maphis chuckled gleefully as the ticket broker's expression changed.

Brawley began to curse in a low, angry voice. "That two-faced, conniving son of a bitch! To think that I trusted him! I should have killed him long ago."

"What is it, Tate?" Maphis asked eagerly. "What's on them papers?"

Brawley looked up. "Don't you know? Didn't you . . .? Oh, I forgot, you can't read." He waved a paper under Maphis's nose. "Our Mr. Kane is on the Erie investigating lottery operations. As best I can make out, he's working for some state legislator over in Pennsylvania."

Maphis frowned in puzzlement. "But I don't understand. This ain't Pennsylvania, this is the state of New York."

"But the Union Canal Lottery Company is headquartered in Pennsylvania, you idiot," Brawley said in a snarling voice. "And from these papers, that's the company Kane seems to be mostly interested in."

Brawley continued to sift through the papers, stroking his side whiskers as he did so. Finally, the papers in his lap, he simply sat, staring straight ahead, his expression cold and forbidding.

After a bit Maphis said impatiently, "Well, what are we going to do about this fellow, Tate?"

Brawley's head came around, his eyes flat and deadly as a reptile's. "Why, I'm going to kill him, of course."

"Good, good!" Maphis said with great glee, rubbing his hands together briskly. "Then maybe we can take care of Lady Bitch Carnahan, eh, Tate?"

"We'll see," Brawley said curtly. "But first things first." He rose to his feet abruptly. "I saw Pryor's tabernacle at Albany on my way here."

Maphis said quickly, "Can I go with you? You may need a hand."

"I can handle Mr. Kane myself." Brawley was stuffing the papers back into the valise. "You can come along if you wish. But what'll you do about your boat? I'm going by horse; a canal boat's too slow."

Maphis shrugged. "What the hell, I'll leave it here. There was ice on the canal last night. They'll probably be draining it afore long, and I'll be beached for the winter anyways."

"All right then," Brawley said in a hard voice. "Come along. I want to get my hands on Kane before he goes back to Pennsylvania with what information he has collected."

"But, Morgan, you can't just go off and leave me this way!" Lotte said plaintively. "What'll I ever do without you?"

Morgan said dryly, "Oh, I'm sure you'll get along just fine, my dear Lotte. I haven't the least doubt about that."

"But I love you, Morgan, you know that." They were standing in the stern of the moored boat, and Lotte moved close to him, touching his hand.

He shook his head, amused. "No, you don't, Lotte. Think about it, and you'll know that isn't true. You'll find another man who can serve your purpose."

She recoiled, tears in her eyes. "That's cruel! I never thought you'd say something like that to me."

"I know you're a good actress, Lotte, so don't try acting with me. It won't work. One thing I've always liked about you, you're honest with yourself, and so have you been with me. . . ."

He stopped as he saw the Reverend Luther Pryor coming from the bow. In a low voice Morgan said, "Quiet now, here comes your father."

She whirled around. "Papa, Morgan is leaving us! Don't let him!"

The reverend stepped down beside them, looking in dismay at Morgan. "Is this true, Mr. Kane?"

"I'm afraid it is, sir. I told you in the beginning that I might be moving on at any time. Well, now is the time. I must go to Pennsylvania. I have urgent business there, and also I'd like to spend Christmas with my uncle. He's my only living relative, and I've waited so late now that I'll just have time to make it."

"But you promised me some notice," Pryor said in distress. "I have to find somebody to take your place."

"No, you don't, Reverend. Don't you remember what I told you? Winter is here. As a matter of fact, it's come late this year. They'll be draining the canal, and you'll be going nowhere. You'll be on the bottom until spring, when they flood the canal again. Your best bet is to spend the winter right here. People now know about your church, and they'll come from all around for your services."

"Of course, I don't wish to keep a man from his duties," Pryor said slowly. "I do want to thank you, sir, for all you have done for me. I do not think I would have managed without you." He smiled fleetingly and extended his hand. "Our Lord can work miracles, but occasionally a helping hand from man is necessary."

Morgan, also smiling, shook the reverend's hand. "You're most welcome, Reverend Pryor. It has been my great pleasure to know you and your daughter."

"But you are coming back, aren't you, Morgan?" Lotte said anxiously. "After your business is finished, I mean?"

Morgan hesitated before saying slowly, "I'm not sure, Lotte. I certainly can't promise anything. Now, if you will excuse me, I'll go pack my things."

As he packed his few belongings, Morgan pondered Lotte's question. He really had not given much thought to coming back to the Erie once his business was done with Uncle Sherman. He wondered if there would not be too many painful memories for him here, memories of Cat and their brief love affair. Since that was finished for good, he might be better off going somewhere else. The western frontier was slowly opening up, and he had heard there were many opportunities for a man with initiative. He had been playing with the idea of going there when Uncle Sherman and his scheme had sidetracked him. He could even return to the Mississippi and the riverboats, although perhaps he had seen too much of what gambling could do to its victims.

He hefted the valise stuffed with his notes. The lotteries had left damaged people strewn the length of the Erie. Many people had gone without food and clothing to buy tickets, hoping for the big bonanza when the tickets were drawn in January; but if his uncle was accurate in his assessment of the Union Canal Lottery Company, very few, if any, would win grand prizes. In the valise Morgan had case history after case history of people who would be destitute if they failed to win any big prize money. That should certainly be enough to convince the state legislature of Pennsylvania that it was time to move against the Union Canal Lottery Company.

At least, Morgan figured, he had done all he possibly could; now it was up to Sherman Morrison and the other legislators.

It was late afternoon when Brawley and Simon Maphis rode up to the *Waters of Christ*. The decks were deserted, which was not surprising since the day was gray, overcast, and quite chilly.

Dismounting, the two men walked up the gangplank, and Brawley knocked on the cabin door. There was no immediate answer, and Brawley began to curse in a low voice. "Where can they be?"

The door to the tabernacle opened, and the Reverend Luther Pryor said, "In what way may I help you gentlemen?"

When Brawley faced around and Pryor recognized him, the reverend's welcoming smile became a frown. "What are you doing on my boat, sir? I made it quite clear that I wanted no more dealings with you."

Brawley motioned impatiently. "I'm not here to see you, Reverend. Where is Morgan Kane?"

"Mr. Kane left about two hours ago."

"When will he be back?"

"I haven't the least idea, sir. From what he said, he may not be back at all."

Brawley tensed. "What do you mean?"

"From what I gather, he has business elsewhere, and also he has it in mind to spend our Lord's Day with his relations."

"Business where, dammit?"

"Do not curse me, sir!" Pryor said with outraged dignity. "But to answer your question, I do believe Mr. Kane left for the state of Pennsylvania. Exactly where, he did not see fit to inform me."

"Goddammit to hell!" Brawley pounded his fist against the bulkhead.

The reverend drew himself up. "Do not blaspheme on my boat, Mr. Brawley! This is sacred ground."

"Sacred ground, my aunt fanny. But for me, you wouldn't have this damned boat, so don't give me orders." He advanced on Pryor threateningly, his face working in frustration.

Pryor stood his ground. "I will not deny your help, and the Lord and I are grateful, but now I must ask you to leave my church."

"You defy me, preacher? I could squash you and your damned boat like a bug. Ah, the hell with it! I don't have time to dally with you. Come on, Simon." He turned toward the gangplank, then whirled back to glare at the reverend. "But you'd better not be lying to me about Kane. If I learn he isn't gone, I'll destroy you and your damned boat. You keep that in mind, preacher man."

He walked away with long strides, so rapidly that even Maphis had to trot to keep up. "What are you going to do now, Tate?"

"I'm going to Pennsylvania and smash that damned Kane. I have to be there for the prizes drawing, anyway. I know what he's up to—he's trying to get the company into hot water. Well, others have tried and failed. But I still intend to see that he pays for what he's done to me, and for what he intends to do to Union Lottery." Brawley plunged on with long strides, heading toward the lights of a tavern up ahead. "Right now I'm going to have a drink, several drinks, while I think a bit."

Maphis was silent until they were in the tavern, a large glass of whiskey before Brawley, a glass of rum before Maphis.

They both drank deeply before Maphis spoke. "But what about the Carnahans? You promised to do something about them, and here it is winter. If the canal is drained and they're beached until spring, it'll be harder to do anything."

Brawley glared at him with hot eyes. "I have my own problems to worry about."

"But you promised to help me figure out a plan," Maphis whined. His voice took on a note of cunning. "Besides, you said you owed them, especially the girl. And don't forget, if the girl hadn't saved Kane's life, and taken him onto her boat, he wouldn't have been around to plague you."

Brawley looked thoughtful, stroking his side whiskers. "You're right about that, I do owe the Carnahan woman. And I suppose another day or two won't matter all that much. Kane already has a good start on me. I should have no trouble finding him, since I know where he's headed. I'm sure he'll be at the ticket drawing, causing all the trouble he can."

"Then we'll do something about the Carnahans and their boat?"

"I told you I would help, and I will." Brawley took a drink of whiskey, banged on the table for a refill, and then sat staring off into space while he waited to be served. Maphis also waited, squirming impatiently.

When his drink was served, Brawley finally focused on Maphis again. "You've had a good year, right? At least you did well for me."

Maphis said cautiously, "I've got a few dollars in my pocket, yes. But what does that have to do with any plan?"

"It has this to do with it. What I have in mind will

require hiring a few toughs from the Cut. But they come cheap, and I'll pay my half. Putting the Carnahans out of business will benefit you financially, Simon. All it will do for me is get back at that snotty Cat, but I'm still willing to pay my share." He eyed Maphis thoughtfully. "Are you in?"

Maphis nodded reluctantly. "I wasn't thinking of paying out good money, but I reckon it's worth it."

Brawley nodded, and leaned forward to speak in a low, confidential voice. "Now listen close. Here's what I have in mind. The clever thing about it is, neither of us will be directly involved. They'll do all the dirty work. . . ."

Carnahan's Cat was moored about a half-mile from the *Waters of Christ*, and Cat and Mick were trying to decide where best to spend the winter. Cat had just received word that the Erie was going to be drained within three days.

Mick wanted to try to make it to Buffalo. "I'm thinking it's a livelier place, more things going on. . . ."

"More taverns, you mean."

"Now, daughter, that's not fair." He gave her a reproachful glance. "No such thought was in my mind. I was thinking there'd be some jobs there, maybe, where I could earn a few extra dollars for us this winter."

"I'm sorry, Mick, that was a nasty thing for me to say, and not true, I know. But I still much prefer Albany. It's more civilized. As for a job, your chances are as good here as anywhere. You know that there are a half-dozen men for any job that comes available along the whole stretch of the Erie. Winter throws hundreds of men out of work."

He looked at her shrewdly. "You're sure it's not just because this doctor bucko is wintering in Albany that makes you want to stay here?"

She felt her color rise, but she stared back at him defiantly. "That may have something to do with it, yes. At least Anthony provides some civilized company. He can talk about things besides the canal and related activities, which is all the canawlers can talk about. You know they'll spend the winter either telling tall tales about last summer or boasting about what they're going to do come spring."

He was nodding. " 'Tis true. Canal talk gets bloody stale around the woodstove in winter. All right." He spread his hands in agreement. "It's here we'll be staying then."

"If nothing dire happens, we should be able to make it through the winter all right," she said. "We have enough put away for food and our other needs."

It was a chill evening, and they were in Cat's cabin, with the galley door open, the heat from the woodstove keeping the two small cabins cozy. Cat was mending some of her older clothes, and Mick was enjoying one of his rare pints of ale. Finishing the pint, he leaned back and dozed. Cat watched him fondly. The *Cat* was a much happier boat now that he was behaving himself—most of the time.

A footfall on deck brought Cat's head up. Timmie was supposed to be spending the night with relatives. "Mick," she whispered. "I think someone just came on board." Even as she spoke, another pair of footsteps sounded.

Mick came out of his chair as a splintering sound came from above. They were tied up in a side-cut out of Albany, at a location where they figured it would be ideal to spend the winter, not too far from other boats for neighborly visits, yet far enough from town to be away from wharf ruffians.

Mick was on his feet, reaching for the ax handle he always kept handy in case of trouble. Cat had her Colt hidden away beneath her bunk. Just as she started for the bunk, the cabin door crashed open, and a grinning tough stood in the doorway. In one hand he carried a huge club.

Mick roared, "What are you doing here? By the saints, I'll bash your head in!" Raising the ax handle as high as he could, given the small size of the cabin and the low ceiling, he started to swing it.

The shorter man moved in low, using the end of his

club like a battering ram, connecting solidly with Mick's belly. Mick grunted in pain, his breath whooshing out.

Cat was at the bunk now, scrabbling under it for her pistol; but as she swung around with it, another man barged into the cabin. With a cruel laugh, he casually knocked the pistol from her grip, wrapped powerful arms around her, and carried her out of the cabin. She fought with all her strength, but it was to no avail. All the while she had been dimly aware of crashing sounds on deck, but she was appalled at what she saw.

Four other men were running about, carrying axes, chopping at everything in sight. Already the end of the cargo cabin was in splinters, and now one man clambered monkeylike atop the cabin and began to chop away at it.

The man holding Cat yelled, "Jack! You and Red take your axes down into the hold. Chop the bottom out of her and let the water in."

Cat screamed as loudly as she could, hoping to attract someone's attention. The man holding her clamped his hand across her mouth; she fastened her teeth around the fleshy part of his hand and bit down hard. The taste of blood filled her mouth, and her captor yowled in agony. He turned with her, slamming her brutally against the bulkhead. Pain burst in her head like a bomb, and she lost consciousness for a moment. Only a few minutes must have passed before she regained her senses, for the first thing she saw when she opened her eyes was Mick staggering up onto the deck.

He gazed around dazedly for a moment; then his vision cleared, and he gave vent to a thunderous roar when he saw what was happening to the *Cat*. "You bloody sculpins, what are you doing to my boat? I'll strangle every one of you!"

"You ain't strangling anyone, old man," said the man who had knocked Cat down. He raised his voice. "Caleb, take care of the old geezer. Shut his mouth!"

"Old geezer, is it?" Mick looked toward the source of

the voice, and saw Cat on the deck. "Catherine, what did he do to you?"

He lurched toward Cat. Cat saw the man called Caleb advancing on her father, and she screamed, "Mick, look out!"

Her warning came too late. Caleb swung his club, hitting Mick on the right arm, and Cat heard the sickening crack as a bone snapped. Caleb swung again, this time slamming the side of Mick's head, and Mick fell headlong to the deck. Cat screamed again and started to scramble across the deck toward him. The man beside her reached down, grabbed her by the hair, lifted her up, and hit her a stunning blow in the face. She spun down into darkness once more.

The first thing she was conscious of was the stench of something burning, and she awoke choking on smoke. The deck was shrouded with smoke, like a thick fog; and then she saw flames licking out of the gray billows. She was lying flat, and she could tell from the tilt of the deck that the *Cat* was listing. They had holed the bottom and set her on fire!

She had to get off the boat before it sank or the flames reached her. She managed to get up on her hands and knees, and started to crawl toward where she hoped the gangplank was. In the confusion and smoke she was badly disoriented.

Then she froze as she remembered. Mick! He was back there somewhere, either unconscious or dead. She called, "Mick, can you hear me?"

She held her breath; there was no answer. She waited, trying to get her bearings. The space between the hold cabin and their living quarters was not large; but Cat did not know how much time she had before the boat sank or went up in flames.

Still on her hands and knees, she reversed direction and began to crawl again, feeling both ways in front of her. Nothing. Despair filled her, and she began to weep, both from frustration and the smoke; tears streamed from her eyes.

She kept going, her hands out before her, feeling for her father. She shouted again, "Mick!"

This time she thought she heard something—a groan. Yes, there it was again.

She moved in that direction, faster now. Then her hand encountered a body. It was Mick, still as death. "Mick, please wake up! We have to get off the boat, but you must help me!"

Her father did not move. She positioned herself, both hands under his armpits, and began to drag him. It took all her strength to move him, inch by inch. She had never realized just how heavy he was, and of course she was very weak. She coughed rackingly, choking on the smoke. She felt a blast of heat, and glanced around to see tongues of fire eating their way across the deck toward them.

In desperation she stood and, half-bent over, began pulling him along a little faster. All at once the backs of her legs struck something. The steps up to the gangplank! There were only three steps, but how on earth was she going to hoist him up that high? Her strength was fast ebbing, and she feared that she would faint at any minute.

She shouted as loudly as she could, "Help! Somebody please help me!"

Miraculously, a voice answered, "Is some'un on board there?"

"Yes! At the gangplank. My father is unconscious. Please help me!"

Footsteps pounded on the gangplank, and two men emerged out of the smoke.

One man helped Cat to her feet. "Here, miss, I'll help you off. Bob, you take the big fellow there, you're bigger than me."

The man with Cat led her to the gangplank and off. As she went she looked back over her shoulder, and felt weak with relief as she saw a big man half-carrying, half-dragging Mick along the gangplank.

Then they were on the wharf, several yards distant from the burning boat. Cat knelt by her unconscious father, and looked back at the *Cat* just as it began to sink; every part of the deck and cabins was blazing now. She knew with a sick feeling that the boat was done for: what the fire did not do, the water would finish. Everything they owned was being destroyed before her very eyes. And she remembered something else—all their money, the money they had worked so hard for, the money that was to see them through the winter, was in her cabin. It was gone, too.

She turned back to Mick. He looked so white and still, and blood seeped from a lump on his head. She could not tell if he was breathing.

She turned her face up to the men gathered around and said in a pleading voice, "Please, somebody fetch Dr. Anthony Mason. His boat is just a hundred yards along the canal."

Simon Maphis had hidden in the shadows of a warehouse some distance from the *Cat*, and watched as the thugs he and Brawley had hired crept aboard the boat to commit their destruction.

After they had hired the six thugs, Tate Brawley had departed immediately for Pennsylvania. He had warned Maphis, "Now you'd better stay clear, Simon. These toughs will do the job without supervision. If you show yourself, you'll be in trouble. They'll make the connection between you and the toughs. So be wise for once, and stay clear."

But Maphis could not resist. He had to watch the destruction of Cat Carnahan and her precious boat.

He clapped his hands with glee as he heard the axes begin to chop. His delight increased as he saw the flames start to consume the boat, and then as the boat started to list to the port side. He lingered to watch the thugs run off the boat, one by one. He watched, squinting his eyes against the smoke, his gaze on the gangplank; but no one appeared. Cat and her father were taken care of!

Suddenly he saw men running toward the burning boat from both directions along the canal, and decided that it was time to take his leave. With a last, gloating look at the *Cat*, Maphis slipped farther back into the shadows and walked quickly away, unseen.

Chapter Fifteen

It was a cold, snowy Christmas Day in Pittsburgh, and Morgan was content to sit in his uncle's parlor before a blazing fire. They had just eaten a sumptuous holiday dinner—a fat goose with all the trimmings—and Morgan was stuffed to the point of drowsiness.

Each man had a glass of brandy, and Sherman Morrison was smoking a cigar. "Damned doctors tell me I should cut out the cigars," he had grumbled to Morgan earlier, "but if a man can't enjoy a good cigar after dinner, what's to live for, especially after a fine Christmas feast. I have few enough pleasures left in life, anyway."

At the moment he was deep into Morgan's notes; his only comment concerning them so far was a disgusted grunt from time to time. Morgan gazed sleepily into the flames. He was tired; it had been a long train ride to Pittsburgh, and he had arrived very late last night.

Listening to the wind moan around the outside of the house, he wondered how it was along the Erie tonight. It had been quite cold when he had left, and he was sure that the canal had been drained by now, before it had a chance to freeze solid. The last he had heard, the *Cat* was in Albany, and he supposed the Carnahans would winter there. It would be nice right now if Cat were by his side, his arm around her shoulders as they stared into the fire. He missed her terribly, dammit, and he was swept by a feeling of desolation every time he thought of her. He still had not decided where he would go after his business with his uncle was finished.

Sherman Morrison said angrily, "It's a blasted shame, the way these lottery companies are bleeding people who can't afford it. I've never been one for trying to legislate people's morals, and I've certainly never been opposed to people gambling—not for those who can afford it. Hell, I enjoy a good poker game myself, and I figure if a man with money is fool enough to gamble it away, it's on his own head. But this . . ." He hefted the papers in his hands. "You've done a good job, nephew. You've accumulated some dandy material here."

"But will it accomplish anything?"

"It'll help, that's for certain." His uncle dipped the moist end of his cigar into the brandy, then puffed away.

"What do you plan to do with the material now that I've collected it?"

"I'm going to my committee with it first, then to the full legislature. I'm going to read it into the record, every word of it," Morrison said grimly. "If nothing else, it'll be a matter of public record, and I think I can interest some of the newspapers in publishing most of it. Several of those newspaper fellows owe me a favor or two."

"Do you think the legislature, or your committee, will act on it?"

"Who can predict something like that? The lottery companies have powerful lobbies in the capital, and I'm sure they're bribing some of my fellow members. But I think there's a good chance, a strong chance, that some legislation will come out of it."

"You have more faith in politicians than I do, Uncle Sherman."

"Not faith in politicians per se, nephew, but in myself. With what you've brought me, I'm confident I have enough power in the legislature to swing it." Morrison took a swig of brandy. "Which reminds me, what are your plans now?"

Morgan shrugged. "I have none, really. I've been thinking of heading out West—the *far* West."

"You could probably make it out there. It's rugged country, I'm told, but you have the courage and the intelligence." He drew on his cigar. "But I would like to offer you an alternative. I could use you on my staff, nephew. The pay is good, and the work isn't too hard, most of the time."

Morgan shook his head. "No, that sounds too tame for me."

"Ah, you young hotbloods." Morrison sighed. "But I would like for you to remain with this project for a while longer. For instance, the drawing for prizes by the Union Canal Lottery Company is held in January, as you know." Morrison gave a bark of laughter. "It's held on the landing of the main stairway leading up to the second floor of the State House at Harrisburg. That shows the gall of the company. They hope that by doing this it gives the whole thing an air of legitimacy, that we in the state government condone the whole charade. I've been trying to put a stop to it for years, without success. Anyway, Morgan, I'd like you to be there. I'll be there, too, of course."

Morgan stirred in annoyance. "Uncle Sherman, what purpose could I possibly serve there? I've done all I can do with this business."

"Two reasons why I want you there. First off, I want your direct testimony before my committee. And secondly, I want you to observe the ticket drawing. Maybe you can spot some irregularities. Remember, I told you that it's been rumored that about half the ticket stubs in that drum are purchased by the company itself—the ticket holders are its own employees. If we could catch them at that . . . Well, that's definitely criminal fraud."

Morgan shrugged. "All right, I'll go. But I don't know of any way to catch them out at such shenanigans . . . not and prove it."

"Some of the fraudulent ticket holders may well be men

you know, maybe even some of their own ticket brokers you met along the Erie."

"They'd have to be pretty damned stupid, Uncle, to have the gall to do that."

"Nephew, I'm an old man, and I've learned a few things dealing with greedy crooks over the years. They tend to get cocky to the point of foolhardiness after they've been getting away with something for years. They begin to think they're invincible."

"That's true enough, I've noticed that myself." Morgan was thinking of Tate Brawley. Would he be there, with a fistful of fraudulent tickets? Under the law, any ticket broker or salesman was forbidden to participate in a lottery drawing for which he had peddled tickets; but Brawley was pretty arrogant; he just *might* be there. The thought of catching Brawley at something illegal enough to send him to jail was more than reason enough to journey to Harrisburg!

By the time Morgan and his uncle had journeyed to Harrisburg, the weather had moderated. It was still very cold, but it was clear and sunny, and the streets had been swept clear of snow.

They arrived three days early for the drawing, since Morrison had called for his special committee to sit, not only to consider the material Morgan had collected but to hear his verbal testimony if they so wished. Morrison had a suite reserved the year round in a hotel within walking distance of the State House.

The first day, Morgan was free while his uncle held a closed session with his committee. He wandered through the streets, and he noticed that there was already a carnival atmosphere in the city. People were arriving in droves for the drawing. Everywhere he overheard people talking excitedly about what they expected to win.

He reflected on the greed and stupidity of mankind. The total prize money was supposed to be eighty thousand dollars, and would be divided in two hundred ways, starting with ten grand prizes, the exact amounts not known until the drawing took place, then scaling down to over a hundred small prizes of five and ten dollars. Since the tickets cost five dollars apiece, the two hundred winners could do little more than get their money back, except for the grand-prize winners; and the chances against winning a grand prize were astronomical. If his uncle was correct, the drawing would be rigged so that those ten grand prizes would be won by lottery-company men, who would then return them to the company coffers.

So, the vast majority of the thousands of people gathered for the drawing would go away empty-handed, with shattered hopes. Unfortunately, Uncle Sherman was correct about something else—wealthy people seldom purchased lottery tickets; it was usually those who could not afford it.

When Sherman Morrison returned from his committee session, he was glum. "They went through your material, and despite the facts you had collected, I couldn't muster enough votes to get the committee to recommend a bill banning lotteries to the legislature as a whole. Damn the close-minded bastards!"

"Then it was all a waste of my time, and yours," Morgan said bitterly.

"I still want you to testify tomorrow. They agreed to listen to you, at least."

Morgan threw up his hands. "Uncle Sherman, what more can I tell them? It's all there, in my notes."

But in the end Morgan agreed to testify. He discovered that the committee was split roughly 40–60, the majority opposed to Morrison's stand. Morgan already knew that his uncle had to have a majority to vote the proposed bill out of committee.

The questioning he underwent was both hostile and friendly, as was to be expected. He did note that his uncle wore a somewhat smug expression this morning. Morrison sat throughout the questioning in silence, asking no questions of his own, his face hidden most of the time behind a screen of cigar smoke.

One of the hostile and most persistent of the questioners was a plump, pompous individual, a state senator named Corrigan. He had challenged most of Morgan's notes on the hardships suffered by lottery players, saying that Morgan's claims were exaggerated. Now he said, "You know, Mr. Kane, I'm Irish, like most of the folks you mention in your report. My own parents came over from Ireland a generation ago. Myself, I worked hard, pulled myself up by my bootstraps to where I am today. Most of those bogtrotter Irish are a shifty lot. Their chief occupations in life are whoring, drinking, and gambling. You deprive them of one way to gamble, they'll only find another. Would you agree with that assessment?"

Morgan shrugged. "I wouldn't know, Senator. I don't judge people by their race or origins." He was getting fed up with this man's arrogance. "I was given a job to do, and I did it. You may draw whatever conclusions you wish. After all"—he smiled slightly—"as you said yourself, they're your people. You should know them better than I do."

Corrigan bristled. "Now you look here, young fellow! Don't you go getting insolent with me. That wasn't what I said at all. . . ."

The man on Corrigan's right, one of the friendlies, laughed. "Seems to me that's exactly what you did say, Corrigan. The Bible says, 'Judge not, lest you be judged.' "

Corrigan aimed a glare at his colleague. "Don't go quoting Scripture at me, Bartlett. I'm more of a Christian than you are, any day."

Bartlett ignored him and looked at Morgan. "In essence, Mr. Kane, you are telling us that you observed many cases of hardship brought about by lottery-ticket purchases?"

Morgan nodded. "Yes, a great many . . ."

Corrigan snorted. "Five dollars is a hardship?"

"To many people along the Erie," Morgan said stolidly, "five dollars is hard to come by. And with the high-pressure sales practice by the more-unscrupulous salesmen, most of them buy more than one ticket before the year is over. Just yesterday I walked the streets of Harrisburg. Do you gentlemen realize just how many hundreds, perhaps thousands, of people have spent money to come here just for the drawing, with great expectations of winning a grand prize?"

"That's their problem," Corrigan grumbled. "Most of them came here from New York State. Why should we concern ourselves with people from out of the state? I, for one, am certainly not concerned!"

There was a brief silence, which was finally broken by Sherman Morrison. It struck Morgan that his uncle had been waiting for just such an opportunity.

"As to that, Senator," Morrison said softly, "I heard something just this morning that may be of interest to you, sir. To all of you."

Corrigan looked at him warily. "What might that be?"

"The Union Canal is a Pennsylvania project, would you not agree? And its welfare should certainly be of concern to us here, should it not?"

"And so? That's the purpose of the lottery run by the Union Canal Lottery Company—to raise funds for the Union Canal. In my opinion, it has served that function very well. We all know that, so what are you getting at, Morrison?"

"The report I heard is that the lottery company took in around a million dollars this past year, yet the Union Canal is only getting around sixty thousand, which by any calculation leaves nine hundred and forty thousand unaccounted for. Less the prize money, of course, which certainly doesn't amount to all that much. Now where do you suppose the rest of all that money went?"

Corrigan's face reddened as the men around the table stirred, muttering incredulously. "Where did you get your information, Morrison?"

"A secret source," Sherman Morrison said promptly. "I'm not at liberty to reveal it as yet."

"A secret source! How many times have I heard *that*? It's nothing but another rumor," Corrigan scoffed. "Another scurrilous lie, an attempt to discredit the Union Canal Lottery Company. Well, it won't work, Morrison. It's been tried again and again and didn't succeed. It won't succeed this time."

Morrison shook his head. "I've heard all those rumors, we all have, and I've always suspected there was a great deal of truth in them, but this time the story is true. I can't prove it at the moment, but I soon will, be assured of that."

Corrigan thumped the table angrily and rose to his feet. "Well, until you can show me solid proof, I'm not voting for your goddamned bill!" He stalked out of the committee room, slamming the door.

Senator Bartlett said, "Is it really true, Sherman? Or did you just say that to shake Corrigan up a little?"

"My information is solid. It came from a source inside the Union Canal Company. Preliminary word has been received from the lottery company that sixty thousand, after the lottery tomorrow, is about all they can expect to receive. We will certainly know the true facts within a few days, after the drawing, and when it comes time for the lottery concern to settle accounts."

Bartlett began to smile. "If that is true, then there has been some high chicanery going on, and the public outcry will be enough to force those reluctant committee members in our midst to finally act." Grinning, he glanced around the table. "Agreed, gentlemen?"

Morgan's glance went from face to face. By now he could identify those siding with his uncle's cause and those opposed. From the glum faces of the opposition, he knew that Bartlett was right—the days of the Union Canal Lottery Company seemed to be numbered.

Morrison rapped his knuckles on the table. "I think that does it for today, gentlemen. Unless someone has something to add, I move that we adjourn."

The committee members got up and departed in a body, leaving Morgan and Sherman Morrison alone.

Morgan's uncle glanced at him with a self-satisfied smile. "It would appear that our side is about to win, nephew. So I suppose you may leave whenever you like, without staying for the drawing tomorrow. Unless," he added hopefully, "you'll reconsider and go to work for me?"

"I think I'll hang around for the drawing anyway, Uncle Sherman. There's one particular fellow I want to watch for. I'm positive that he'll attend the drawing."

In anticipation that he might encounter Tate Brawley, Morgan went to the drawing armed; but when he saw the mob of people gathered, he despaired of ever spotting Brawley. The mass of people spilled out of the State House and onto the street outside. Morgan slowly worked his way through, and was the recipient of much grumbling and complaining by those people he had to push past.

The drawing was just starting as he managed to squeeze his way inside the building. Two representatives of the Union Canal Lottery Company stood beside a drum. One spun the drum; when it stopped, the second man reached down into it for a ticket stub. He would read off the number and shout it out in a loud, carrying voice, and yet a third man, standing by the doors, passed the numbers along to those outside the building. Each time a number was called, a cheer went up from the lucky winner, and groans and curses came from the losers.

Morgan continued to press forward, his eyes scanning the crowd for Brawley. He knew that the ten big prizes would be the last stubs drawn, both to keep the suspense high and to prevent a possible riot; he was confident that the instant the last grand-prize stub was drawn, the men on the landing would slip away with the drum, to escape any possible repercussions from the crowd. Morgan suspected that the man dipping into the drum would palm the winning stubs for the grand prizes, stubs with numbers matching those on the tickets held by their confederates in the crowd, much in the same manner as a crooked gambler slips an ace out of his sleeve.

By the time Morgan had worked his way to the foot of the broad staircase, they were ready to draw the last stub. It was then that he saw Tate Brawley. Brawley was standing on the third step from the bottom; and, sure enough, he had a lottery ticket in his hand. Morgan would have wagered his last dollar that the numbers on his ticket matched up with the last stub numbers called. Morgan worked his way up to the step below the ticket broker but did not announce his presence yet; and Brawley, intent on the men at the drum, did not notice him. Morgan drew his pistol, hiding it from view by holding his coat over it.

The stub was drawn and the number was read off. Brawley waved his ticket, opening his mouth to call out.

"I wouldn't, Brawley," Morgan said into his ear. "We both know it's rigged for you to win."

Brawley froze, his mouth open. "Kane!" He started to turn.

Morgan moved up to the step beside Brawley and rammed the pistol into his side. "Don't turn around, and don't call out your number."

"You bastard!" Brawley said in a choked whisper. "I know all about you. I came across the valise you lost, with all your notes. You've been working against me and the company all along."

"That's right, I have," Morgan said softly. "I know all about the chicanery, the crooked operations. And if you call out the number of that ticket in your hand, I'll announce to the people present that you're a broker for the Union Canal Lottery Company, and that the drawing for the grand prizes is rigged. What do you think they'll do to you? I'll tell you . . . . They'll tear you limb from limb."

"When I came across that valise, I swore I'd kill you, Kane."

Morgan laughed. "Well, you're hardly in a position to do that right now, are you? What we're going to do is work our way out of here, Brawley. Then you'll have a choice. . . ."

He was interrupted by the man on the landing, who again read off the number, a note of desperation in his voice. "Isn't the person present with this winning number?" There was a brief hush as the crowd seemed to hold its collective breath. Then the lottery-company representative laughed nervously. "Well, it seems the winner isn't present. Under the rules, we have to hold the final prize-winning ticket until it is claimed. . . ."

Voices were raised in anger. "No! If he ain't here, draw another number!" Other voices echoed the same sentiment.

The man on the landing held up his hands for quiet.

As the crowd slowly quieted, Morgan spoke again into Brawley's ear: "As I was saying, you have a choice. I can take you to the law and charge you with fraud. Or you can come with me to see State Senator Morrison, and agree to testify as to the fraudulent practices of your company. I'm sure he'll grant you immunity from prosecution, if you'll tell the truth."

"No! Damn you, Kane, I'm not going to do it."

Before Morgan could respond, the man on the landing spoke again. "I'm sorry, good people, but under our drawing rules, the winner, if not present, has to be notified of his winning ticket. It's the only fair thing to do. . . ."

"No, it ain't fair!" several voices shouted in unison. "Draw another stub! Give us all a chance!"

A woman standing only a few feet away from Morgan screamed. "I've lost everything, everything!" She screamed again and began tearing at her hair, her head swinging back and forth so that Morgan could glimpse the madness in her eyes.

Now people began to surge about and shout curses. Fights broke out as people tried to storm the staircase and the drum.

A shot suddenly rang out. Morgan looked to his right and down. He saw a man waving a gun. People backed away from him, leaving a cleared space, and Morgan saw another man on the floor, blood pouring from a wound in his chest. The man with the pistol glanced about wildly; and then, without warning, he put the pistol to his temple and pulled the trigger, and fell to the floor, joining the other man in death.

Morgan's brief inattention gave Brawley the chance he had been seeking. He bolted, shoving Morgan aside, and bulled his way through the crowd. The shove sent Morgan off balance; by the time he had righted himself, Brawley was almost at the front doors.

The whole lower floor around the staircase was a madhouse now, with people screaming and shouting, fighting and clawing at one another.

Knowing that it probably was hopeless, Morgan set off in pursuit of Tate Brawley. He had literally to fight his way to the doors, so furious with his own stupidity that he struck out blindly, until he finally gained the doors.

The melee was as bad outside the building as inside. People were shouting, scuffling, running back and forth. Morgan stood on the steps, looking both ways. He could not see Brawley anywhere. He noticed people looking at him strangely and shying away, and he realized that he was still holding the pistol. He stuck it in his belt, and wandered through the crowd aimlessly, knowing that now it was indeed hopeless—Tate Brawley had gone to earth. After what had happened here today, Morgan was sure that the Union Canal Lottery Company was doomed; and Brawley would certainly realize that, and would not hang around Harrisburg. More than likely he would head back to the Erie. He would have no difficulty finding employment as a broker with another lottery company.

When Morgan returned to the hotel, he found his uncle already there, waiting for him in the lobby. They retired to the bar for a drink, while Morgan filled him in on the scene at the State House.

Morrison had already heard about it, and he agreed with Morgan's judgment. "Yes, this will finish off the Union Canal Lottery. I'm confident that with what happened today, coupled with the fact that most of the money they collected this past year has vanished down a rat hole, I will have no trouble in getting the bill banning lotteries in Pennsylvania out of my committee and onto the floor of the legislature. I wouldn't be at all surprised to see the bill made into law within the month. Thank you, nephew. I salute you for a job well done."

Morgan shrugged. "It seems to me that it would have happened anyway, without me."

"Not necessarily." His uncle took out a cigar, dipped one end into his glass of brandy, then lit up. "The material you gathered could well be what I need to tip the scales in my favor." Blowing smoke, he stared at Morgan intently. "So what are your plans now? Have you decided yet?"

"Just about," Morgan said, nodding. "I appreciate your offer of a job, Uncle Sherman, but that's not for me. And there's nothing for me along the Erie now." He thought briefly of Cat, then made an effort to cast her from his thoughts. "I think I'll head west, somewhere beyond the Mississippi, maybe even farther west than that. As the mountain men say, I'll see the elephant, if nothing else."

"It's winter, Morgan. A little cold to go that far west at this time of the year, wouldn't you say?"

"I'll probably winter in New Orleans. I've never been there. Then, come spring, I'll move north and west."

Chapter Sixteen

IT proved to be a long, dreary winter for Cat. The boat was destroyed, along with their money; and Mick had been badly injured. He had a broken arm, which was healing slowly, and the blow on the head had given him a concussion. He had lain in a coma for days, and Cat was convinced that but for Anthony's medical skill, her father would be dead.

They were now living in a poor hotel in Albany, not too far from the *Paracelsus*, so that she could take Mick once or twice a week to see Dr. Mason. Anthony had wanted them to live on board his boat with him, but Cat's pride would not allow her to accept his charity; and although Mick did remain on the medical boat until he was well enough to move around, he was equally adamant about not accepting Anthony's largess.

Cat had gotten a job as a barmaid in a tavern near the hotel. It was a degrading job, since the waterfront rowdies harried her—in their estimation, all barmaids were fair game. However, after she had been there a couple of weeks, Cat had displayed enough spirit, and the ability to fend them off, so that she not only gained their respect, they left her mostly alone, even coming to her defense when a stranger wandered in and made advances to her.

Still, it was hard, menial work, and the type of people

who frequented the tavern were far from the best. Even when the men left her strictly alone, Cat could feel their eyes always on her; and she knew they were wondering what she would be like in bed, and probably mentally undressing her as they watched her move about with her wooden serving tray.

The other barmaid, Amy, was coarse and vulgar, flirting with every man who came in; and Cat knew that she often made assignations with men after the tavern closed. Amy viewed Cat with contempt, sneering at her for being "too good for the likes of us," and eventually their mutual dislike grew to the point where they never spoke to each other except in the course of business.

Since Mick was still more or less incapacitated by midwinter, he was not really aware of the surroundings where she worked. But Anthony knew. He came into the tavern whenever he could, sipping at a single glass of ale for hours, watching over her, fearful of what might happen to her. When he could, he would accompany her home, or back to the medical boat, for a brief time of love. This did not happen too often; Cat was usually exhausted by the end of the evening; and Anthony too was tired, since his day started early, and often she did not get finished until midnight or later.

One evening, after they had made love, he burst out, "I can't bear to see you work there any longer, Cat!"

She said wearily, "I have little choice, Anthony. I tried for other jobs, but naught were available. You know how few jobs are open to women. I'm actually fortunate to have found this one, so I must make the best of it. At least I earn enough to pay for our room, and to feed us. I'm only sorry that I haven't the money to pay your medical fees."

He motioned impatiently. "I've told you, forget about that. If you never pay me, I won't be worried."

"Well, it worries me!"

He groped for her hand. "Cat, I thought we meant more to each other than that."

She drew away her hand. "You mean, my being in bed with you like this is pay enough?"

"Cat . . ." He sighed. "You *are* a trial sometimes. Of course I meant nothing of the sort, and you know that very well. Knowing you, I'm sure you'll insist on paying me every penny. But there's no hurry. I'm doing fine right now, and when you get back on your feet . . ."

"Which may be never," she said gloomily. "I can't see any way Mick and I can get together enough money to replace the *Cat*. Even if he was well and could work, together we couldn't earn enough money for our purpose."

"Somehow or other, I think we got off the subject here, and I suspect that you did it purposely," he said dryly. "We were talking about you working in that tavern. It's just not fitting."

"And I'll tell you again, I have no choice."

"Cat . . ." He eyed her speculatively. "Where is the indomitable Catherine Carnahan I first met? Nothing daunted you then. Now you seem taken with a lack of spirit. In short, you seem to have given up. That's not like you."

"I know . . ." She drew a hand across her eyes. "I'm not always this disheartened. Some days I'm sure we'll manage to replace the *Cat*. Other days, I'm like this. Maybe it's this damned winter. It's a terrible winter—no life anywhere, nothing green or growing, no water in the Erie. Maybe when spring comes around again I'll have a brighter outlook on life."

"There's something I wish you would consider very carefully. I would have mentioned it before, but I was afraid of how you'd react, knowing that pride of yours. Now, this is a legitimate offer, no charity intended."

She looked at him in open suspicion. "Offer of what?"

"A job. I want you to go to work as my nurse."

"Your nurse?" She stared. "I've had no training of that sort, you know that."

"I'm at the point now where I need someone, and as for training, I've talked of that before. There's no such thing as a trained nurse, certainly not around here. Whatever you need to know, I can teach you. Watching you that night while I repaired that fellow's thigh told me that you'd make a fine nurse."

"Why haven't you mentioned this before?"

"Two reasons. One I just told you: I was afraid you'd think I was doing it out of charity. The other reason is simple. I haven't been able to pay a nurse. But my practice is such now that I can. And as always happens, there is more illness in the winter, the grippe, pneumonia, and other ills. God, I'd hate to think what would happen if an influenza epidemic struck here. There aren't enough capable doctors to handle it. Will you do it, Cat?"

She was still wary of his motives, suspecting that he *was* making the offer out of the goodness of his heart, but there was another, more compelling reason why she felt she could not accept. "I don't think it would do your reputation any good, Anthony, my working with you like that. It's hard to keep a secret along the Erie, and I'll wager a number of people already know that we are lovers. If word spreads of that, it may lose you patients."

He laughed, batting a hand at her. "Usually it's the woman who is concerned about her reputation, Cat, not the man."

"Your being a doctor makes a difference. As for myself, I care very little. I've always gone my own way, done whatever I please."

"Then if you're not worried about yourself, I'm certainly not concerned about what people think of me."

"But you should be, that's the whole point. No, I won't be responsible for hurting the practice you've worked so hard to build up."

"But, Cat . . ."

"Hush, Anthony." She put herhand across his mouth. "We'll talk about it no more. Now, make love to me."

She took away her hand and kissed him demandingly.

*   *   *

Two nights later, in the tavern, Cat saw a new customer come in and take a rear booth. She had seen only his back, and did not know who it was until she rounded the booth with her tray and looked down into the newcomer's face. "You!" She recoiled with a gasp.

"I heard you were working here, missy," Simon Maphis said, grinning hugely. "I had to come see for myself. Cat Carnahan, a serving wench in a waterfront tavern. You are finally brought down to the level of the rest of us, eh?"

"You were responsible for the destruction of our boat, I'm as sure of that as anything! And my father was almost killed."

"You didn't see me about, now did you, missy?" he said smugly. "You can't prove a thing."

"Maybe not, but I still know you were behind it, Maphis. Who else could it be? You're the most contemptible person I've ever known in my life."

His face went ugly. "Don't be bad-mouthing me, Missy Carnahan! I won't stand for it."

Without another word she started to turn away.

"Wait a minute now!" He reached out and grabbed her arm. "I came in here to be served a bottle of rum. Now fetch it!"

She tried in vain to jerk her arm free. "Fetch it yourself. I'm not waiting on the likes of you."

"You're the serving wench, ain't you?" Grinning again, he began to twist her arm, forcing her almost to her knees. "Eh? You fetch me a bottle, or you'll be on your knees before me. I think I'd like that, Lady Carnahan on her knees before Simon Maphis."

The pressure steadily increased, and Cat knew that she would indeed be on her knees in the sawdust at his feet in a minute. In a blaze of anger she exerted all her strength and pulled her arm out of his grasp; but rather than running away, she gripped the wooden tray in both hands, and brought the edge of it down across his arm on the table. He yelped in pain; and then she began to rain blows on the top of his bowed head, banging the edge of the tray across his skull again and again. Trapped in the booth, Maphis could only defend himself by holding his hands and arms around his face and head.

The uproar had already attracted attention, and through Cat's anger she heard laughter and hoots of derision at Maphis's plight.

"What gives, King of the Erie? You letting a slip of a girl beat on you?"

"Look at the roughest, toughest man on the Erie!"

"Haw, Simon! You be needing some help?"

Then Amy was at Cat's side, seizing the tray and trying to wrestle it away. She hissed, "What do you think you're doing, Miss Goodheart? You can't be thumping on a paying customer like that!"

"Damn blast and hell!" Cat said angrily. "Leave me alone! You don't know what terrible things this man has done to me."

Then a man had her in a strong grip. Looking around, Cat saw that it was Prudhomme, the owner of the tavern, a huge bear of a man. Usually of good temper, his face was red and angry now. "Amy's right. It don't matter none what he's done to you, girl! Simon Maphis is a customer in my place. None of my girls abuse a customer in my place."

Cat sagged in his strong grip, the anger draining out of her.

Maphis reared up out of the booth. "Let me get my hands on the bitch! She's shamed me before my mates. I'll teach her a lesson she'll never forget!"

Prudhomme stepped between them. "No, Simon, there'll be no harm coming to the girl here. I do ask pardon for her behavior, but I'll not see you lay a hand on her. She's discharged, as of this very minute. You'll have to be content with that."

Maphis was not appeased. "I can't lay a hand on her, but she can whack on me as she damn pleases, eh? That hardly seems a fair way to handle it." He took another threatening step forward.

"It's fair in my estimation, Maphis," Prudhomme growled. "I don't allow women to be abused in my place. Now sit down, and you'll get your bottle of rum, on the house. Amy, fetch it for him."

"Yes, dearie, just sit down, and Amy will tend to your needs. Anything you need, just come to Amy," she said insinuatingly. She took Maphis's big hand and coaxed him back into the booth.

Prudhomme was already leading Cat away. She could feel Maphis's murderous glare on her back as she walked off; but she was more concerned now about her job.

"You're not really going to discharge me, are you, Mr. Prudhomme?"

"You leave me no choice, Miss Carnahan," he said gruffly. "I can't allow my serving girls to abuse the customers. It'd give my place a bad name along the Erie. Can't afford that."

She laughed scratchily. "Abuse *him*? Abuse that monster of a man? He outweighs me three times. And you can't know the things that man has done to me. I'm sure he was behind the destruction of our boat and injuring my father."

"I know Simon Maphis is a blackguard, you don't have to tell me. And you're probably right about what he has done. But none of that has any place in here. Any troubles between you two should be handled out of my tavern. I'm truly sorry, Catherine. It has to be this way."

Cat started to ask him what she was supposed to do; she knew it was unlikely that she could find another job. But she refused to beg.

She shook her arm free of his grip, and said with as much dignity as she could muster, "I still think you're being terribly unfair, sir, but if that is the way you want it . . ."

He said regretfully, "I'm sorry, Catherine, I really am."

When she returned to their hotel room, Mick was surprised. "Why are you back so early, Catherine?"

She started to brave it through, but, to her chagrin, she burst into tears. "I was discharged, Mick."

"Ah, it's sorry I am."

They were sharing a small room, with a cot for Cat. Mick was well enough to get around now, and his arm was almost healed. He opened his arms to her, and Cat went into them, crying on his shoulder. It was the first time since the death of her mother that Mick had held her in his arms.

After she was finished weeping and sat back, he asked, "What happened, daughter? I can't understand why anyone would discharge you. I've never known a harder worker."

"It had nothing to do with my work." All at once she was telling him everything, letting it all pour out. Now that she was no longer working in the tavern, it could hardly matter that he knew.

"That double-damned Maphis!" He pounded the bedpost with his uninjured arm. "Is that black-hearted scoundrel to hound us for the rest of our lives?" Then the rest of what she had told him seemed to register, and he glared at her. "You were working as a serving girl in a waterfront tavern? My own daughter, without telling me? Have we sunk so low?"

"We had to eat and shelter ourselves, and this was the only job I could get to earn what we needed."

"A shame it is, a great shame!"

"I didn't feel any shame," she lied. "At least it was honest work."

"No, Catherine, no." He shook his head. "The shame I'm feeling is mine. I should be the one earning our bread, not my daughter. Instead I'm an old sot banged up and worthless."

She looked at him suspiciously, thinking that he was putting on an act; it was the first time that he had ever made such a confession. Then she saw that he was perfectly serious, and she felt contrite. Touching his unhappy face gently, she said, "It wasn't your fault, Mick, that that bunch of villains destroyed our boat and burned all our money."

"If I had been the man I should be, I would have stopped them."

"One against six? Don't be ridiculous, Mick." She smiled. "Don't you think you're stretching the blanket a bit?"

Suddenly they were both laughing helplessly. Mick hugged her. "I am boasting a bit, ain't I, Catherine? Me, taking on six thugs?" Sobering, he patted her shoulder. "But don't fret, it's healing I am. I'll find something."

Cat knew that no one would hire him, in his condition, even if there were jobs available, yet she said nothing. Her father was indeed a changed man, and she had no wish to discourage him. . . .

A sharp knock on the door startled both of them. Cat spun around quickly, her thoughts immediately jumping to Simon Maphis. Had he found out where they were lodging and come to gain his retribution?

Then a voice said, "Cat? Are you in there? Mick, is Cat home?"

Cat went weak with relief; it was Anthony's voice. She said, "Yes, Anthony, I'm here. Come in."

He rushed in, looking worried. "I went to the tavern to escort you home. You weren't there, and all I could find out was that some sort of altercation had taken place. Are you harmed?"

"Nothing but my pride," she said with a shaky laugh, rising to her feet. "I was discharged tonight, Anthony."

"Tell me what happened."

In as few words as possible, keeping a tight rein on her emotions, she told him what had occurred.

"This man Maphis is despicable," Anthony said angrily. "He should be made to account for his villainy."

"What do you intend to do, Anthony?" she said dryly. "Take that nonexistent pistol of yours and go hunting him?"

"No, of course not," he said quietly. "I have never been

a man of violence. But I was thinking of going to the authorities."

She had crossed to him and now took his hand. "It will be a waste of effort, Anthony. The authorities do not care. You are one of us now, and you know what little regard they have for canawlers. Besides, we can prove nothing," she added bitterly.

"I know the situation, but it's still not right." He shook his head in disgust. "I think we should make an effort to do *something* about this Maphis."

"We have learned the hard way, Anthony. We take care of our own problems. Someday, some way, I will even matters with Simon Maphis," she said in a hard voice. Then her thoughts turned to the more immediate problem. "Our worry right now is to find a way to earn money to feed us."

"My offer still stands," Anthony said. "It's the solution to all your problems."

Mick cocked his head. "What offer is that, lad?"

"Didn't Cat tell you?" Anthony shook his head at her. "No, I can see that she didn't. I need a nurse on the *Paracelsus*. Cat would do admirably. Now wait, Cat." He held up a hand as she started to object. "Both your father and you can live aboard my boat. There is room. With Mick there with us, how can that cause any scandal?"

Mick began to scowl. "What scandal?"

Anthony said quickly, "She's afraid there'll be talk if she goes to work for me."

Mick said vigorously, "By the saints, if anyone dares to blacken my daughter's good name, I'll rip out their tongues!"

"That would do little to quiet the gossips," Cat said, "but your idea may be a solution, Anthony. With Mick and I living on the boat, people may not see anything wrong with the situation."

Anthony said a little sharply, "I fail to see that it would be much different than when Morgan Kane was living on the *Cat*."

Cat felt herself flush, and she had no answer for him.

Mick guffawed. "He has you there, Catherine! As for myself, I'm thinking it would be grand to be back on a boat again, instead of in this hovel of an inn. And I'm also thinking we should be grateful to the boyo here. It would not be charity, since you'd be working for the lad, and soon I'll be able to lend a hand here and there, I'm sure."

Cat sighed, knowing that she had no more arguments to offer. There had never been any logical reason for her stubborn refusal to accept his kind offer, anyway; except that in some strange and maddening way, it had seemed a betrayal of Morgan. Angry at herself, she said, "All right, I accept, Anthony. And you do have our gratitude."

Morgan was happy that he had selected New Orleans as the place to spend the winter. He was only sorry that he had not visited the city before. It was a town built for and dedicated to pleasure, especially the French Quarter. Women of great beauty, with flashing eyes and seductive ways, were plentiful; and he never lacked for female companionship.

He made his living, a very good living, by reverting to his former profession—gambling. His conscience did not bother him, however; almost every night a high-stakes poker game could be found in one or another of the hotels in the Quarter, and the players were all men of wealth and could easily afford their losses. Some of them seemed actually to *enjoy* losing. Also, there were many professional gamblers in the Quarter, and Morgan was able to test his skill against a professional or two at every game.

He won steadily enough to live comfortably, and even put aside some money. Sherman Morrison had paid him well for his task, enough for a very good stake. Morgan had received a letter from his uncle, telling him that his efforts to ban lotteries in Pennsylvania were successful. The state legislature had acted promptly, passing a strong law against lotteries in the state; and the Union Canal Lottery Company had gone out of business.

Morgan even thought occasionally of remaining in New

Orleans indefinitely. He had a suite in one of the better hotels in the Quarter, he ate and drank well, and he had entered into a pleasurable relationship with a Creole woman named Marie Renaud. She was slender and quite attractive, wore clothes beautifully, and was a consummate artist in bed. Marie did not pretend to be anything but a woman of pleasure, a courtesan of the old school; she had been reared to cater to the needs of men. She had expensive tastes, but Morgan knew he could afford her.

However, he grew restless before the winter had run its course. Although he was harming no one by gambling for high stakes with men who could afford it, he knew deep in his soul that he would never settle for gambling as a way of life. It was a soft, easy life, there was no physical challenge to it, and he had known enough professional gamblers to know that it ate away at the moral fiber of a man. No matter how much a man might rationalize, gambling was not quite respectable, and it gave him no sense of real accomplishment. Many gamblers Morgan had known proclaimed their honesty to one and all—they would *never* stoop to cheating; but sooner or later every gambler lost his bankroll, and in desperation would resort to palming an ace or any other crooked maneuver that would recoup that bankroll. So far, Morgan had been fortunate; he had never found it necessary to play crooked poker, but he knew it was only a matter of time. Also, he kept remembering the scene in the State House in Harrisburg—the woman going mad, and the fellow who had killed another man and then shot himself.

The Mardi Gras celebration relieved the tedium somewhat. It was a time of madness and fun; the Quarter thronged with out-of-town visitors for the week-long celebration. The parties went on round the clock, most inhibitions were shed, and a marvelous time was had by all. Morgan joined in the fun, and he enjoyed himself hugely.

On the last night, he attended one of the many grand balls with Marie. She had dreamed up costumes for them that had cost Morgan a pretty penny, but he did not mind too much—two nights before he had won five thousand dollars in a poker game, his biggest win yet.

Marie attended the ball as Marie Antoinette. "Who else, *chérie*?" she had said with a wicked grin. "I was named after her, did you know that?"

She persuaded Morgan to go to the ball as Napoleon, complete with wig and tricornered hat. He had commented dryly, "It strikes me that I'm a little tall for Napoleon. But what the hell, anything to please you, dear Marie."

They made quite a dashing couple, they drank champagne and danced until dawn, and they were still in good spirits when they returned to the hotel as the sun rose. The Quarter still thronged with revelers, and the narrow streets were packed. Doorways were littered with revelers passed out, still clutching bottles in their hands.

In the lobby of the hotel was a huge bowl of chipped ice holding bottles of champagne for the guests. Marie detoured around to pluck a bottle out of the melting ice. She hastened back to Morgan's side, with the bottle cuddled like a baby in the crook of her arm.

"Don't you think you've had enough of that?" Morgan asked. "We've been drinking champagne all night."

"I never get enough of *anything*! Have you not learned that yet, Mr. Kane?" she said archly. "I am greedy, yes, but we do not live forever, and I wish to have all the good things of life while I can."

She hooked her arm in his as they went up the stairs. Marie was about ten years older than Morgan, at least that was his estimation of her age; and she had the universal terror of all women of pleasure—she was afraid that age would destroy her physical appeal. Somehow, this thought made Morgan think of Lotte; there were several points of similarity between Lotte and Marie, which was amusing, since Lotte was a minister's daughter. It was the first time he had thought of Lotte since leaving the Erie.

His suite was on the second floor, facing east, and it was

flooded by pale winter sunlight as they entered. Marie went to fetch glasses while Morgan bolted the door.

When he faced around she had already taken off her dress and slippers, and stood in her stocking feet and a thin undergarment, pouring the champagne. The garment was sheer enough to reveal the swell of her breasts and the soft contours of her figure. His blood began to quicken.

Marie gave him a glass and held hers up. They clinked glasses, and Marie said provocatively, "A toast to the rest of the night. May it be as good as the beginning."

"The beginning?" He grinned. "The night's long past, Marie."

She said huskily, "It is not over until you have made love to me."

"That we'll take care of at once." He drank half of the glass of champagne, then began to undress. He removed his wig with a grimace. "I must have already been drunk to have agreed to wear this damned thing. No telling who's had it on before me."

"I thought you were most attractive tonight, Morgan."

"If you're fishing for a compliment, which I suspect you are, I consider myself honored to have been with the most beautiful woman at the ball tonight."

"I know you are lying, Morgan," she said, suddenly misty of eye. "But I do most appreciate it." She made a small curtsy, finished her champagne, and began removing the rest of her clothing.

She started to take off her white stockings, then stopped, looking up at him wickedly. "Shall I leave them on? I seem to remember that I did one night, and it pleased you."

"It does add a certain piquancy, I must admit."

With a nod she tumbled back onto the bed. When Morgan joined her, she locked her arms around him, her mouth seeking his feverishly. She pulled him as close to her as was humanly possible, and Morgan could feel the softness of her breasts flattened against his chest, and the wiry prickle of her mound pressing against his stomach.

In a little while she urged him over onto his back. "Now just lie still," she commanded.

Amused as always when she did this, Morgan watched with some detachment as she made love to him with her lips, her hands, and, incredibly, her breasts. She knew all the secret places on a man's body that inflamed desire to a high pitch. Her long hair trailed over his body, tickling and exciting him.

Soon his detachment vanished, and then the amusement, as his entire body, from head to toe, was afire with need; but as he made to rise, she muttered deep in her throat and pushed him back down. "Not yet, not just yet!"

She continued what she was doing, until all thought left him; and he was all sensation, blind and deaf to anything but the intense pleasure she was giving him.

She said gutturally, "Now!"

She rose, flinging herself onto her back on the big four-poster, and Morgan moved to enter her. She was the only woman he had ever known who could so arouse a man that the act of penetration was almost an anticlimax. Moaning, she surged against him, and they were both in the throes of ecstasy almost at once. Crying out, she convulsed, shuddering, and Morgan uttered a loud groan as the first mighty spasm of pleasure seized him.

They remained together until the final tremors of passion had passed. Then she reached up to kiss him lingeringly, and laughed complacently. "Now, darling, *now* the night is over!"

She immediately turned over, and Morgan knew that she would be asleep within seconds. He lay quietly beside her, but he was not yet ready for sleep. After a little he got up, put on his breeches, and went out onto the tiny iron-railed balcony outside the window.

The sun was well up now. The streets of the Quarter were almost deserted, except for a few drunks still lying in doorways, like fallen logs. Last night had been the climax of Mardi Gras, and Morgan knew that the city would not revive for several days; and most of the visitors would be gone shortly.

Looking out over the empty streets, Morgan thought it had a dead look, like a battlefield after a fierce battle; and he realized that he felt as dead inside. The gambling, the fine food and liquor, the lovemaking—nothing had really reached the heart of him. He had not felt really *alive* since the days with Cat on the Carnahan boat.

He stirred, mentally shaking himself, uttering a low curse.

It was time to leave New Orleans. Winter was almost over. By the time he could get out of town and on his way north, or west, or wherever, spring would be upon him. Since he had been traveling lightly, he had nothing much to pack, except his winnings, which amounted to a considerable sum by now. All he had to do was buy a good horse, traveling clothes, and perhaps a new pistol, and he could be on his way.

From inside the room came Marie's sleepy voice: "Darling, aren't you ever coming back to bed?"

She would be ready for him again, Morgan knew. Well, why not? One last bout of love, and that would be the end of it. "I'll be right in, Marie," he said.

Chapter Seventeen

CAT was of two minds about living on board the *Paracelsus*. She enjoyed working as Anthony's nurse and discovered that she had a surprising aptitude for it. Under Anthony's tutelage she soon became quite proficient, and she was proud of the fact that she was a great help to him. And Mick had now recovered sufficiently to do what chores were needed to keep the boat in top condition for the spring, when the Erie would be operable again.

On the other hand, living on the same boat with Anthony and her father made it more difficult for them to find private moments in which to make love. There was a furtiveness about it; and where before she had not experienced guilt, Cat now felt a vague shame each time it happened.

She confided this to Anthony one night in the privacy of his cabin. Mick had gone into town for a few hours, providing them with some time alone. Cat had the feeling that her father had manufactured an excuse to leave them alone; although he had never breathed a word to her, Mick was far from stupid.

After she had told Anthony, he gave a slight shrug. "There's always a solution. Marry me, Cat. God knows I've asked you enough times."

"And I'll give you the same answer, Anthony. No, I won't marry you."

"And I fail to understand why," he said in exasperation. "I love you, and you must feel something for me. You've proven that a number of times."

"I do care for you, Anthony." But not enough, she said silently; not enough to marry you. She touched his cheek with the back of her hand. "I am very fond of you, my dear. But I am just not ready for marriage yet. Perhaps sometime, but not now. First I have to see if Mick and I can get a canal boat for when the canal opens."

"I suppose you think that I'm offering to marry you out of charity," he said grumpily.

"No, I don't think that at all."

"Or maybe it's because the first time I made love to you, I said I couldn't afford to have a wife." He looked at her closely. "Is that the reason?"

"Anthony, does there have to be a reason, beyond the fact that I just don't care to get married at this time? Look, if the time ever comes, I'll let you know. Until then, I'd rather you didn't ask me again."

Before he could speak again, she sealed his mouth with her lips. Deep in her heart, Cat knew that she was moving closer to giving in all the time, giving in and just accepting his proposal. It would not be a bad life, married to Dr. Mason, as she had thought before; but something held her back from making the final commitment. Maybe it was fear of losing her independence, or maybe it was because she did not love him enough; but she was fearful that if he kept at her, she would finally weaken and agree to be his wife.

Then all thought ceased, as her passion spiraled under his ministrations, and she sought forgetfulness in his embrace. She welcomed him inside her with a soft sigh, and gave herself over totally to intense pleasure. For a little while nothing else existed but this man in her arms.

When their passion broke, she sank into sweet sleep. Their day had been a long, grueling one; it seemed to Cat that the patients grew more numerous with every passing day.

When she woke some time later, she smelled Anthony's pungent tobacco smoke. He was on the other side of the small cabin, in the rocking chair, his face occasionally lit by the dim glow of his pipe. Cat lay quietly for a while, without letting him know that she was awake. He sighed now and then, and she knew that he was troubled by something.

She finally said softly, "Anthony?"

"Yes, Cat? Did I wake you? If so, I am sorry."

"No, I woke on my own. Something is on your mind, I can tell. What is it? I hope it's not my spurning your proposal again?"

"No, not that. I'm worried about something else. I'm not sure, but I think I had a case of cholera yesterday."

"Cholera?" She sat up in alarm. "I've heard terrible things about cholera. Wasn't there an epidemic somewhere not too long ago?"

"Yes, in New York, in Virginia, and other places, last summer. Almost four thousand people died from it in New York, and six thousand in New Orleans. There is nothing, you know, that carries an epidemic quicker than a water vessel, traveling from place to place. Cholera is a disease of the digestive system and can be carried by food or drink. And if it has by chance been carried on a canal boat to the Erie, it can spread like wildfire."

"But I'm a little puzzled, Anthony. How can you say this disease is spread by boats, when not a single boat has passed along the Erie since before Christmas?"

"That doesn't mean much. It could have been infected food or drinking water that was brought here earlier. Cholera has existed in parts of Asia for thousands of years. India has had many cholera epidemics. It is believed that that is how cholera was brought to the United States last summer, by ship from India to New York Harbor."

"This patient you mentioned . . . how do you know he, or she, has it?"

"It was a man, and I'm not all that sure, as I said. But he had many of the symptoms—severe diarrhea, muscle cramps, and a high fever. He hadn't reached the vomiting stage yet. That's usually when death occurs, from excessive and constant vomiting, and overwhelming dehydration. The incubation period is short, usually from two to three days after the contaminated material is taken into the body. I tried to question him about what he'd eaten the past few days, but he got skittish and left before I was done with him."

"Then how are you ever going to know?"

"Two ways. First, cholera runs a quick course. If he really has it, he'll be dead shortly, if untreated. And the second way we'll know is if he has infected anyone else. The disease is highly contagious. The likelihood of its being an isolated case is very small."

"And that would mean the epidemic you're fearing?"

"Precisely. God grant that it doesn't happen." His pipe glowed as he drew on it. "Statistically, there's about a fifty percent fatality rate in untreated cases, and I've read that during some epidemics, as high as ninety percent have died."

"There is no treatment, no cure?"

"Not really. As I said, death comes about through extreme dehydration brought about by diarrhea and vomiting. Replacement of the body fluids is absolutely essential. I've heard that the most effective method so far developed is an injection of a salt-and-water solution directly into the veins. I've also read in medical journals about a theory that dead cholera germs injected into a person can prevent the disease, but not cure it, although that theory is dismissed by most physicians as poppycock."

"Then I suppose we can only wait and pray. Do you know the name of the man who came to you?"

"Yes, one Henry Jenks."

Two days later, Anthony received word that Henry Jenks had died the day after his visit to the medical boat.

Immediately, Anthony left the boat to try to contact any friends or relatives of the dead man who had been in intimate contact with him, or who might recall sharing food with him that could have been contaminated. "I also want to learn if anyone has the early symptoms."

He returned to the *Paracelsus* after dark, weary and disgusted. Mick was cooking supper and Cat was mending clothes when Anthony stormed into the cabin, carrying a bottle of whiskey.

"What a miserable day I've had! I'm going to have a rare drink." He waved the bottle. "Mick, would you like one?"

Mick hesitated; and then, as Cat looked at him, he said, "I'm thinking I'd better not, boyo. I'm finding that I'm better off without the liquor."

Cat said, "What happened, Anthony?"

With a weary sigh Anthony sat down with a glass of whiskey. He took a hearty swallow before replying. "I found out that Henry Jenks had only recently arrived from the Side-Cut. He'd been working there as a bartender in one of the taverns. I'm sure now that he died of cholera, and I'm equally sure that's where he caught the disease."

"Why do you think that?"

Anthony was filling his pipe. "Well, I told you of the epidemic last summer. What I didn't mention was that most of the victims were the poor. They all lived in slum neighborhoods. For instance, of the hundred deaths in a single day in July, ninety-five of them were buried in potter's field."

Puzzled, Cat said, "I fail to understand what that has to do with it. Not that I'm not sorry for the poor souls, but how did where they lived have anything to do with it?"

"There is a theory, which I subscribe to, that cholera strikes hardest in those areas that are terribly overcrowded, with people living in shacks, many sharing the same unsanitary privies, drinking tainted water and swill milk, and garbage stinking in the streets. These sections are the most susceptible to any contagious disease. In addition, these slums are the habitat of prostitutes, criminals, and other social outcasts."

"Oh, now I begin to see. You think that since the Side-Cut is also filled with just that sort of people, one of them may have carried the cholera from New York?"

Anthony nodded grimly, his pipe glowing now. "Precisely, Cat. God knows why it has taken so long, since the incubation period is short. I can only surmise that someone brought it in with food, perhaps some kind of liquid, or maybe even on his, or her, clothes. But the bad part of it is that if Jenks died of cholera, others in the Cut will also, as well as people here in Albany. There is only one saving feature. Cholera is generally a hot-weather disease. I can only hope that it won't spread too quickly, or become too widespread, in winter."

"But that doesn't tell us why you had such a bad day, Anthony."

"Nobody will listen to me." He struck the arm of his chair with the palm of his hand. "Oh, some agreed that Jenks may have died of cholera, but you know what they say? That it is God's will."

"God's will? I'm afraid I don't understand."

"In the epidemic last summer, people believed that it was the moral dereliction of the slums, rather than the conditions. Poor people and moral outcasts lived there. Ergo, it was their moral decay that brought the disease down upon them." He laughed curtly. "Ministers preached from the pulpits that it was God's will. God's wrath had fallen upon the wicked to teach them a lesson. And they preached that it was not only useless to fight God's will, but impious as well. The thing that is so frustrating is that the poor people believe that hogwash themselves. That's what I faced today."

Mick said, "That surprises me a little, lad. We canawlers are a clannish lot, but pretty independent of thought. And we're a proud people—too proud to admit that a sickness is a punishment from the Almighty for our sins." He laughed. "Most of us are proud of our sinning."

Anthony finished his drink. "Most of the people I talked to today, Mick, aren't canallers, but townspeople, warehousemen and the like. Hard working, but poor and, unfortunately, ignorant."

"Well, I'm thinking it will be all right. Maybe this epidemic you speak of will not be so bad. Anyway, supper's ready. Nothing picks up a man's spirits better than a good hot meal."

"I certainly hope you're right, Mick," Anthony said gloomily. "But I have a bad feeling about it."

Anthony's gloom was justified. The very next day three people came to see him. After examining them, he took Cat into his tiny office and told her, "They have cholera. They have all the symptoms, no doubt of that."

"It's strange, Anthony. They wouldn't listen to you, yet now they come to you."

"Sickness changes a person's viewpoint. God's will or not, they come hoping for a miracle, and I have none to offer."

"What are you going to do?"

"I'm going to keep them here, bed them down on the floor in the main cabin, and do what little we can for them. I can't let them go about spreading the sickness any more than they have already done." He looked at her with a frown. "I'm concerned about you, though. I think you and your father should leave the boat until the epidemic is over."

She said in dismay, "Leave? But I thought the arrangements were working fine."

"It's not that, Cat, but cholera is highly contagious. I've told you that. I'd never forgive myself if you contracted the disease, you or Mick."

"But how about you?"

"I'm a doctor," he said simply. "Any doctor who would run and hide from an epidemic is not worth his salt."

"You need me here now more than ever."

"I can manage somehow."

"You're a doctor. Well, I'm a nurse. You've made me one. I could never live with myself if I left you to face it alone. No, I am staying by your side."

"But, Cat . . ." Then he reached out to pull her into his arms. "Ah, Cat, darling Cat! I love you!"

Without speaking she hugged him tightly. In truth, his words had frightened her. What if she *did* get the disease? But she could not, would not, leave him.

By the end of the week there were ten people lying on pallets on the floor of the main cabin. Anthony and Cat worked tirelessly, often far into the night, with Mick doing what he could. Four patients had died, and three others had recovered.

Anthony said, "There's not a great deal we can do. Sponge them down often with cold water, to fight the fever, and get them to drink as much liquid as possible. As for you, Cat, I want you to drink a lot of water every day, with a small amount of salt in it."

In addition, Anthony devised a sort of mask for both of them to wear—several layers of soft, porous cloth saturated with a mild solution of alcohol; it was placed over the mouth and nostrils and tied behind the head. "I haven't the least idea whether this will prevent us from breathing the contagion, but it should help some."

Cat soon came to view the main cabin as a scene out of hell. It stank badly of evacuated bowels, of sweat and vomit, and the cabin was never quiet. The discomfort of the patients was so severe that they could sleep little, but tossed and moaned at all hours. The only ones who were quiet were either unconscious or dead.

By the middle of the second week, five more people had died. Cat was discouraged and exhausted. She moved from patient to patient, kneeling beside them, bathing them with cold water, and constantly cleaning up after them. To get them to swallow water, or any fluid, she and Anthony usually had to work together, with Anthony holding the patient still and forcing the jaws open, while Cat got as much liquid down them as possible.

To Cat's surprise, Anthony was cautiously optimistic. "I would have expected many more people to be struck down, many more than we could accommodate on the *Paracelsus*. Naturally, I'm sad about those we have lost, yet the majority are surviving; and perhaps you hadn't noticed, Cat, but fewer patients came in this week than last."

"No, I hadn't noticed," she said dully, wiping her brow. "There hasn't been time to count."

"Poor Cat, you have been working hard, and you have been marvelous," said Anthony. "I don't know what I would have done without you."

They were having a few minutes' respite in his office. He kissed her gently on the forehead. Cat was suddenly swept by a wave of longing; they had not made love since the first cholera victim had been taken on board. Pressing herself against him, she lifted her face; but he took hold of her shoulders and gently pushed her away.

His voice husky, he said, "Dear Cat, as much as I want you, I don't think it wise. If either of us has picked up the contagion, we could pass it on to the other."

Despite his words of caution, Cat wanted him in that moment. She needed desperately to forget all the sickness and death around her; a time of sweet oblivion in his arms would restore her.

He was speaking again. "The situation could still turn worse. Until the last victim is well again, we must not relax our vigilance for a moment."

At the pulpit on his gospel boat, the Reverend Luther Pryor waxed eloquent. "The Lord has brought down a plague upon our heads," he thundered. "It is His retribution for those among you who have sinned. It is God's awful warning that you must mend your ways, or suffer this terrible sickness that is upon you. If you are taken by it, you will be sent down into the very pit of hell, and there suffer eternal damnation!"

He looked out over his congregation. Attendance was

meager this evening. Many people were fearful of leaving their homes lest they contract cholera. Ever faithful to his vow to succor them, to bring them the word of God, Pryor had gone among them, taking Lotte with him so that she could sing a hymn to lighten their spirits. He glanced back at Lotte sitting behind him. He was worried about her; she had been feeling poorly the past two days.

He turned back to his small audience. "I notice that many of the brethren did not attend this evening. Oh, ye of little faith! Our Lord would not visit His wrath upon any who came here to worship Him. Pass the word, brothers and sisters. All who come here are safe from harm. God will spread His wings over them." He threw his arms wide and raised his voice. "Tell those among you who are fearful to come here and confess their sins! They must come and ask forgiveness of our Lord. Only in that way will they find salvation, and then they will be protected from this epidemic that rages amongst us! Now, let us pray." He clasped his hands over his bosom and raised his eyes to heaven. "O Lord, please come to the aid of the poor sinners among us. They know not what they do. We beg of You to soften Thy wrath. Do not inflict them with this dread plague. We beseech Thee to look kindly upon us mere mortals. For that boon, I pledge myself to redouble my efforts among my flock, and bring more to salvation. Amen."

Pryor raised his hands in benediction over his congregation. "Now Lotte will sing a hymn for us, praising our Lord."

He crossed quickly to the piano. Sitting, fingers poised over the keyboard, he glanced at Lotte. She was still sitting, head down, as if she had not heard him. He said sharply, "Daughter, it is time."

Lotte gave a start and looked up. She stood, but as he struck the first chords, she began to sway. Then she gave a moan of agony, and doubled over, retching. Before Pryor could react, she had fallen to the floor. She lay curled up into a ball; and by the time the reverend had reached her, she was unconscious.

"Lotte! What ails you, daughter?" He felt her forehead and found that she was burning with fever.

He looked up dazedly at the members of his congregation gathered around him.

A man said, "I have my buggy here, Reverend Pryor. We could take her to Dr. Mason's medical boat. It is only a short distance away."

Not knowing what else to do, Pryor nodded. A short time later he was in the buggy with his parishioner, holding Lotte's head in his lap. Lights burned on the *Paracelsus*, with two torches blazing at the head of the gangplank.

The two men carried the unconscious Lotte on board. Dr. Mason met them at the head of the gangplank. "Reverend Pryor! What is wrong? Did your daughter have an accident?"

Even as he spoke, Anthony was leading them into the main cabin. The reverend explained as best he could what had happened. Inside the cabin he stopped, appalled at his first look about. People were lying in orderly rows along the floor, and now a woman rose from her knees beside one, and came toward them, removing a queer-looking mask from her face. Pryor recognized her as the woman who had formerly run the canal boat. For a moment he was strongly tempted to take Lotte out immediately; in some ways she was a weak vessel, and might be corrupted by the proximity of such a woman as Catherine Carnahan. But Dr. Mason had already begun his examination of Lotte.

Pryor hovered anxiously. When Dr. Mason shook his head and rose to his feet, the reverend said, "What is it, Doctor? Some female complaint, I imagine?"

"I'm afraid not, Reverend," Anthony said with a grave face. "Your daughter has cholera."

Pryor was stunned. "No! I can't believe that's possible!"

"There is not the slightest doubt, Reverend. You must

leave her here. We'll do what we can for her." He turned to Cat. "Prepare another pallet, Miss Carnahan."

Pryor dropped to his knees beside the unconscious Lotte. In a condemning whisper he said, "How could this happen, girl? You must have sinned in the eyes of our Lord, and this is His judgment upon you." He clasped his hands over his heart and gazed heavenward in supplication. "Forgive my wayward daughter, dear Lord. She is but a weak vessel, and knows not the depth of her transgressions. I humbly pray to You not to punish her too severely."

In her daze of exhaustion, Cat did not at first realize who Lotte was. When it did dawn on her, Cat was at the point of rebellion. This was the woman who had replaced her in Morgan's affections; this was the woman who she was certain had taken Morgan into her embrace. It is too much to ask of me, she cried silently, to nurse the woman who stole my love! To have to nurse her, bathe her, spoon-feed her, keep her clean! It was simply too much to demand of her!

So accustomed was she by this time to automatically obeying Anthony's commands, that she was already moving toward Lotte and her kneeling father as the rebellious thoughts went through her head. She reached them in time to hear the reverend's words, and her heart went out to the sick girl. It was bad enough to be inflicted by cholera, but for Lotte to have her own father blaming her illness on her sins was even worse!

Now the reverend got to his feet and strode out with a flashing, scornful glance at Cat. Slipping her mask into place, Cat knelt beside the girl. She pulled a pallet over and gently moved Lotte onto it, straightening out her limbs, then went about removing her clothing. Lotte was afire with fever; and although she was still unconscious, she groaned constantly. Cat knew that she must be suffering greatly.

She fetched soft cloths and a pail of water and began to

bathe Lotte. She covered her with a clean sheet, then continued to wash her burning face. From another pail of water she wet a cloth, and squeezed drops of water into the girl's open mouth. Lotte swallowed convulsively.

Lotte's eyes suddenly opened, and she looked at Cat with glazed, unseeing eyes. Cat said, "It's all right, my dear. We'll make you well again."

"Morgan, oh, Morgan," Lotte muttered. "Please come back to me. I'm ill, I need you."

Cat stood up quickly and began to back away, resisting a strong urge to slap the girl.

The next morning Lotte was conscious and fully aware when Cat came into the main cabin. As Cat brought water to her, Lotte looked at her with clear eyes. She frowned slightly. "I know you, you're Catherine Carnahan."

Cat nodded, forcing a smile. "That's right, Lotte, I am."

Lotte glanced around. "Where am I?"

"You don't remember?" Lotte shook her head. "You're on Dr. Mason's medical boat. Your father brought you in last night. You were quite ill. It seems that you fainted during his service. But you do seem to be better this morning. Do you feel like eating?"

Lotte shook her head vehemently. "My heavens, no! The thought of food makes me want to . . ."

Cat nodded, feeling sympathy for the girl despite herself. "I know. But you should drink water, as much as possible." She held out a cup of water. Lotte tried to raise her head, then let it fall back. Cat placed her hand under the girl's head, raised it, and held the cup to her mouth.

Lotte drank slowly but thirstily. When she was done, Cat said, "I have to bathe you now."

She reached out to draw down the sheet, but Lotte clutched at it.

"You must let me, Lotte. This is no time for modesty. Frequent bathing with cold water is essential. Besides, it's the doctor's orders."

Still clutching the sheet, Lotte said, "Did you undress me last night?"

"Yes, of course," Cat said impatiently. Her thoughts were angry: You undressed readily enough for Morgan. But she made her voice gentle as she said, "Lotte, this is hardly the time for false modesty. Besides, I'm a nurse. I've undressed and bathed all the people in here, both men *and* women."

"You're right, I am being foolish," Lotte said with a soft sigh.

She relinquished her hold, and Cat drew down the sheet. Lotte did have a lovely body, all soft and rounded, all pink and white; and Cat could easily see why Morgan, or any man, would find her attractive.

Willing her mind a blank, Cat briskly set about giving the girl a bath; but she was uneasily aware of Lotte's gaze on her all the time.

She had just finished and let Lotte draw the sheet back up when Anthony strode into the cabin, the wooden stethoscope dangling from his neck.

"Well, we're awake, I see," he said cheerfully. "We've never officially met, Miss Pryor. I'm Dr. Anthony Mason."

"How do you do, Doctor," Lotte said demurely.

"How are you feeling this morning?"

"Better, I think. I really felt terrible all of yesterday. I wanted to tell Papa, but I was afraid he would scold me. He doesn't believe in people getting sick."

"Well, you were a very sick girl last night, and I told your father so. Now, suppose I examine you, Miss Pryor?"

Cat moved off, tending to other patients, while Anthony completed his examination of Lotte. When she saw that he had finished, she came back. Anthony nodded at her with a pleased smile. "I do think Miss Pryor is one of the fortunate ones, Miss Carnahan. She seems to be over the worst of it. Her fever is down, and the bowel convulsions are not so severe. See that she gets plenty of water."

Cat turned to give Lotte more water to drink, but she

saw that the girl was sleeping quietly; and she decided not to disturb her—sleep would be the best thing for her right now. She followed Anthony as he went from patient to patient.

After his rounds, Anthony ushered her into his office and closed the door. "I think the epidemic has run its course; everyone here now seems out of danger. Actually, I suppose *epidemic* is a misnomer. We seem to have suffered lightly. I don't know about the other doctors, but we have lost relatively few patients. Not that that is much consolation to the poor devils who have succumbed to it. But it is certainly nothing on the scale of last summer's epidemic in New York and other places. The contributing factor must be that it is winter. We should thank God that it did not hit us in the summer!"

The improvement in their patients was even more marked the next morning, especially in Lotte.

She was bright of eye, long hair combed and lustrous, when Cat came in. She was sitting propped up against some pillows, and she smiled brightly at Cat. "Good morning, Miss Carnahan."

"Good morning, Lotte. How are you feeling?"

"I'm a little weak, but I feel much better. The doctor was just by to examine me, and he said I should be able to go home in a couple of days."

"I'm glad for you, Lotte," Cat said sincerely. She was over her pique at the girl. If she should be angry at anyone, it should be Morgan Kane. "You're probably hungry. I'll fix you something."

"Catherine . . ." Lotte smiled prettily. "May I call you Catherine?"

"Certainly. Or Cat, if you like."

"Could we talk for a bit?"

Cat hesitated, not sure that they had anything to talk about, but she could not be rude to a patient. "Certainly we may." She drew a chair up close to the pallet and sat down.

Lotte glanced around, lowering her voice. "You knew Morgan Kane, I believe?"

Cat said in a dry voice, "Oh, yes, I knew Mr. Kane."

"Were you . . . ? I know this is unforgivable of me, but I must know," Lotte said in a rush. "Were you . . . ?" Again she choked up, unable to continue.

"Were we lovers?" Cat said bluntly. "It's really none of your business, but I'll tell you anyway. Yes, Morgan and I were lovers."

Lotte blushed furiously. "I've been dying to know. I asked Morgan, but he evaded the question."

"I must say that surprises me a little. I would have thought he would have boasted to one and all."

"Oh, no, Morgan would never do that! He's too much of a gentleman," Lotte said, shocked. Then she looked subdued. "You don't think he really would go around telling people, do you?"

Cat smiled slightly. "You mean, about you and him?"

"How did you know about that? Oh!" Lotte clapped her hand over her mouth.

"I didn't . . . not for sure until this minute. It wasn't hard to guess, though. You spoke his name the night you were brought in here."

"I did? Oh, I am sorry, that must have been terrible for you."

"Not really. Morgan Kane means nothing to me anymore." To her astonishment, Cat found herself liking this woman. She was vain, she was not the brightest girl in the world, and, Cat suspected, her moral character was not of the best, in spite of her being a minister's daughter—or perhaps because of it?—yet there was an endearing, little-girl quality about her. And speaking of moral character, Catherine Carnahan, you have little right to sit in judgment, she reminded herself.

Lotte was saying, "Have you heard from Morgan since he left the Erie?"

"Not a word, nor do I expect to."

"I haven't, either," Lotte said petulantly. "I thought he'd come back after his business in Pennsylvania was finished, or at least write. But, nothing!"

"What business did he have in Pennsylvania?" Cat asked, trying to make it appear an idle question.

Lotte shrugged. "I don't know. He didn't say, only that he wanted to spend Christmas with his uncle, or somebody."

"Well, I expect we've seen the last of Morgan Kane," Cat said, suddenly feeling depressed.

Lotte moved restlessly, fluffing out her hair. "I haven't seen Papa once, have you?"

"Not since the night he brought you here."

"Papa doesn't like illness. He believes it to be a weakness." Lotte sighed. "He's been preaching about the cholera, you know. He thinks it's God's anger descending upon people for their sins. I guess he thinks that of me. Now he'll likely be suspecting that something happened while Morgan was living on our boat, and make life difficult for me." She stopped suddenly, peering at Cat closely. "But that can't be true, can it? *You* didn't catch the cholera."

"What?" Cat started to get angry as she caught Lotte's meaning, and then she began to smile. "You're right, I didn't. So your father's theory must be wrong, wouldn't you say?"

She began to laugh, and Lotte joined in. When Anthony came in a few moments later, he found them embracing, laughing helplessly.

Two days later, all the cholera patients were gone, including Lotte Pryor; and Cat was sitting on the deck, enjoying the luxury of nothing to do, no patients to tend, for the first time in what seemed an eternity.

Sitting there, Cat suddenly realized something—she was outdoors without a coat of any kind, and she was not chilly. It was the middle of March now, and the faint breeze she felt was almost warm.

The winter was over, and soon the gates would be opened, letting water into the Erie again; but instead of cheering her, this thought plunged her into despair. They were no nearer to having a new boat to replace the *Cat* than they had been the day after it was destroyed.

Chapter Eighteen

IT was the spring thaw by the time Morgan reached the Erie. The canal walkers were out in full force, each covering ten miles a day along the towpath, looking for danger spots in the berm, places where the winter might have damaged it, creating a leak.

The "fog gangs" were out. They were the first boats on the canal after the spring breakup of ice and water was let into the main body of the Erie. It was their duty to clean the canal of debris, which might snag the bottoms of the boats. Morgan noticed that the "scalpers" were already at work—the cargo agents who obtained cargoes for a fee. Morgan recalled Mick telling him once that they never used the services of a cargo agent: "They charge outrageous fees, bucko. They ain't called scalpers for nothing. Most wise canawlers hustle up their own cargo."

Morgan was looking for the Irishman, hoping to find him somewhere away from Cat, so that they could have a private talk. At Buffalo he had heard that the *Cat* had spent the winter in Albany; at another place he had heard that the *Cat* had been destroyed by fire shortly after he had left the Erie for Pennsylvania. He had this confirmed by a canal walker as he rode along the towpath a few miles west of Albany.

"Yup, the Carnahans lost their boat shortly afore

Christmas," the man said. "It burned and sank into the mud. Word was that somebody came on board and chopped her up. I reckon that part's true enough, since old man Carnahan has been laid up most of the winter."

Morgan tensed. "Was Cat . . . Was Miss Carnahan harmed?"

"Not that I heard about."

"Where are they now?"

"Last I heard, they were living on board that medical boat of Doc Mason's."

Morgan sat on his horse for a few moments, undecided. His first inclination was to turn the horse west and just keep going. He had ridden out of New Orleans nearly a month ago, intending to follow the Mississippi north to the Missouri, and then follow that river west until he found what he was looking for.

But when he reached Saint Louis, he changed his mind. He still loved Cat Carnahan, dammit! Maybe if he made one more try, she might have calmed down enough to listen to him, and to forgive him; although damned if he thought there was really anything to forgive. What had he done that was so terrible, except lie to her about losing his memory?

But now he learned that she was living on the same boat as Anthony Mason!

The canal walker had started on. Morgan called after him, "Are Cat and this doctor married?"

"If they are, I haven't heard about it. The way I understand it, she's working for him, as his nurse."

A nurse! Morgan was so astounded that he could not speak for a moment, and the canal walker continued on. But then, Morgan thought, why should he be surprised? Cat was a very capable woman, and he could see that she might make an excellent nurse.

Well, he had come this far, Morgan decided; he might as well go the rest of the way.

Flicking the reins, he rode on. The trees were beginning to leaf out, and already there was much activity on the canal, aside from the work boats. He began looking for the medical boat as he entered the outskirts of Albany. Then it came to him that he did not even know the name of the doctor's boat. He stopped and asked the first person he saw, and was told that the boat was called the *Paracelsus* and that it was located only a short distance along the canal.

He got off his horse and led him the rest of the way. When the boat came into view, he was torn by indecision. Should he just board the boat and announce himself to Cat? If only he could have a few words in private with Mick first . . .

Then the problem was solved for him. He saw Mick Carnahan leaving the boat alone, walking across the gang-plank to the wharf. Only a few yards away, Morgan called softly, "Mick?"

At the sound of his name, Mick stopped, his head swinging in Morgan's direction.

"It's Morgan, Mick, Morgan Kane."

Mick's face lit up. "Morgan! By the saints, it's glad I am to see you!" His voice boomed out.

Morgan motioned. "Not so loud. I'd like to have a few words with you before your daughter knows I'm here."

"Oh, I'm sure Catherine will be as happy to see you again as I am."

"Are you now?" Morgan said dryly. "I'm not so sure, after the last few things she said to me."

"You know Catherine's temper. . . ."

"Oh, yes, I know Catherine's temper."

"But it doesn't last. I'm sure she's over it by now."

"Has she told you so, in so many words?"

Mick looked uncertain. "Well, no."

"Then I don't want to risk it until we've had a talk. Where's the nearest tavern?"

"I don't drink much these days, lad. I'm reformed, I am." He added hastily, "Not that I was ever that much of a toper, mind."

"One mug of ale can't hurt, Mick." He took Mick's arm. "We have some catching-up to do."

Settled down over two mugs of ale in an almost empty tavern, the two men looked at each other.

"By the saints, boyo, I've missed you!" Mick slapped the table.

"And I've missed you, too, Mick."

"Then why did you go off and leave us like that?" the Irishman said explosively. "I tried to get you to explain, but you did the clam on me!"

"Mick, at the time, I thought it best that I didn't explain. It wouldn't have helped matters any with Cat. But now . . ." He shrugged. "Now I can explain. And you are right, I do owe you an explanation."

Succinctly, he told Mick the reason for his presence on the Erie and the ultimate results of his investigation.

"But why wouldn't you tell us, bucko? I'm thinking 'tis a grand job of work you did."

"Mick, I had to work as secretly as possible, and I was afraid . . ." He broke off in sudden embarrassment.

Mick peered at him. "You were after thinking I'd blab it around when I was in my cups? No, you were right to think that." He held up his hand. "When I take on too much of the drink, I talk too bloody much. But you could have told Catherine."

Morgan shook his head. "I wanted to, I even tried to, but she wouldn't listen. She probably wouldn't have believed me anyway, because I'd lied to her about losing my memory."

"Why *did* you let us go on thinking that?"

"Well, I kept postponing it, until it had gone on too long. I'll be honest—I suppose I kept living the lie to gain Cat's sympathy. Also, I thought if I told her, I'd have to leave the *Cat*, and . . . Well, it's all past," he said lightly. "What happened to the *Cat*, Mick?"

"One night a half-dozen toughs forced their way on board. They started busting up the boat with axes. When I tried to stop them, they broke my arm, knocked me out with an ax handle, and then set the torch to the *Cat*. I was fortunate that some fellows came by in time to help Catherine get me off."

"What's happened since? I understand you're both living on Dr. Mason's medical boat."

"Well, with me laid up, Catherine had to support us," Mick said somewhat defensively. "First she got a job as a serving girl in a low tavern, without telling me. She was discharged from that because of Simon Maphis, that scoundrel. Then Dr. Mason was kind enough to offer her a job as his nurse." Mick leaned forward animatedly. "She's a good one, is my Catherine. Did you hear about our epidemic?"

Morgan shook his head. "No, I've been . . . well, all the way down to New Orleans."

"It was the cholera. Several poor sods died, but Anthony and Catherine worked day and night, and saved a goodly many. It's proud I am of her, lad."

"I'm sure you are," Morgan said slowly. "About this doctor fellow . . . is there anything between the pair of them?"

"Nothing to be taken seriously, I'm thinking. He's asked her to marry him, that I know, and Catherine keeps refusing."

Morgan felt a leap of hope, but tried to keep his face inscrutable under Mick's sharp gaze.

Mick said, "The girl still has a soft heart for you, I'm thinking."

Morgan did not respond to the remark. Instead, he said, "You have no idea who was behind the pillage of the *Cat*?"

"An idea, yes. Simon Maphis, damn his black heart!"

"You're probably right. And I'm sure Tate Brawley also had a hand in it somewhere. The pair of them have been pretty thick. Is Brawley back on the Erie?"

"I heard that he was, brokering lottery tickets. But I haven't laid eyes on the fellow myself." Mick eyed Morgan keenly. "Why would Brawley be involved?"

"He's a vengeful man, and Cat scorned him once, you'll recall, on the supper boat last summer. And he might have thought he was striking back at me, harming Cat."

"You say you've been all the way down to New Orleans, lad. Why did you come back to the old Erie?"

"I didn't intend to, to be honest. But I changed my mind at the last minute. I had to see Cat one more time, Mick. You must know how I feel about your daughter."

"I had my suspicions." Mick leaned forward. "Then come with me now. She's there, on the doctor's boat."

"No." Morgan shook his head. "I don't think the time is right. I'd rather talk to her away from Dr. Mason's boat."

"That chance may never come, bucko. She sticks pretty close to that boat."

Morgan frowned. "Surely you're not intending to live there forever?"

"At the moment we have little choice." Mick spread his hands. "We had hopes of buying another boat to replace the *Cat*, but I'm thinking that won't be happening for a long time. Right now, we couldn't buy a rowboat."

Everything fell into place in Morgan's mind, and he knew what he was going to do. "What if I give . . . No, wait, that'll get your hackles up, I know. What if I *loan* you the money to buy another boat?"

Mick stared incredulously. "*You?* Where would you get that kind of money?"

Morgan gestured impatiently. "That's not important, I have it."

"Then *why* would you do it?"

"You know the answer to that, Mick."

Mick nodded slowly. "Because of Catherine, of course. But I'm not sure how she'll take to it, boyo. Probably get her back up."

"I don't want her to know."

Mick looked puzzled. "You don't want her to know?"

"Not now, at any rate. I don't want her to know that I had anything to do with it. She would indeed get her back up, and refuse to accept it. So for now, let's just say we're silent partners, all right?"

"But she'll be wanting to know where I got the money. What will I tell her? You can't get a good freight boat for less than fifteen hundred dollars."

"Tell her you found someone who had enough faith in the two of you to let you buy the boat and pay it off in installments. There's nothing unusual in that. Boat builders do it all the time. So long as she doesn't know I had anything to do with it, I'm sure she'll be happy to have her own boat again."

Mick nodded thoughtfully. "Aye, that she will." He broke into a broad grin. "As will I, Morgan lad, as will I!"

Morgan took out his purse. "I have bank drafts with me, on a Saint Louis bank. I'm going to write you out a draft for three . . . no, four thousand dollars."

Mick reared back. "I don't need that much. I can get a good freight boat, brand new, for half that."

Busily writing out the draft, Morgan said, "I have in mind a passenger packet."

"But that takes a crew of four or five, Morgan," Mick said in dismay. "And neither of us knows anything about operating a passenger boat."

"You can learn, can't you? It's a cleaner business all the way."

"But not always profitable. A man can't go out and hustle up passengers like he can freight. If you don't have a full load of passengers, you have to go with what you have. It's not very dependable, lad."

"I have an idea about that." Morgan handed the bank draft across the table to the Irishman, then leaned forward and began to tell him what he had in mind.

Mick was dubious. "If you can do it, that would be fine. But can you?"

"Anything's possible. It certainly won't hurt to try. I'll go to my uncle's right away. I'll be back in ten days, two weeks at the outside. Meanwhile, you buy us the boat, Mick. And not a word to Cat. Let's make it a surprise."

* * *

Sherman Morrison looked at Morgan in astonishment. "I didn't expect to see you again so soon, nephew. What happened to your plans for heading west?"

"I changed my mind, Uncle Sherman. Remember I told you that I worked for a time on a canal boat on the Erie in the course of my investigation?"

Morrison nodded, taking a cigar from the humidor on his desk.

"What I didn't tell you was, it was run by a woman, Cat Carnahan. I fell in love with her, until we had a falling-out, to put the best face possible on it. I swore to myself that I would never see her again."

Morrison grinned, blowing smoke as he lit the cigar. "But you did." He took on a reminiscent look. "I remember that very same thing happened with your aunt. We quarreled bitterly over something. God only knows what it was, I certainly don't recall after all these years. Anyway, I stormed off, swearing to myself that I'd never see such a stubborn, opinionated woman again. Well, needless to say, I changed my mind; and you know something, your aunt remained just as opinionated until the day she died. But we were happy, most of the time, and we loved each other. Are congratulations in order, nephew?"

"Hardly," Morgan said wryly. "Cat is certainly stubborn and opinionated, but I don't know if congratulations are in order, Uncle Sherman. I did go back to the Erie, but I haven't seen her yet."

Morrison's face registered his bewilderment. "You haven't? I'm afraid I don't understand."

"I discovered that the Carnahans lost their boat while I was away. Tate Brawley, I think, had a hand in it. Also, while I was away this winter I stayed in New Orleans, and went back to gambling. . . ."

Morrison peered at him. "Back to your old ways, eh?"

"Only temporarily, Uncle Sherman. But I had a good winter—I won quite a large sum of money. In Albany last week I talked with Cat's father and learned about their boat. I let him have the money to buy a new one."

Morrison grunted. "You're a generous fellow, I must say."

Grinning, Morgan said, "That's the creed of the gambler: easy come, easy go."

"So why have you come to me?" Morrison wore a faint scowl. "If you were so foolish as to give all your money away, don't expect me to . . ."

"No, no." Morgan held up his hand. "That's not it at all. I still have money. I don't want money, just a favor."

Morrison still looked wary. "What favor is that?"

"You once mentioned that you have some influence in Washington City."

"A little," Morrison admitted. "A few people owe me favors from the past."

"The U.S. mail is in sad shape, wouldn't you agree?"

Morrison grunted contemptuously. "It is absolutely dreadful. Like everything else the federal government undertakes, it ends up an awful mess. It sometimes takes a month for a letter to get from here to Washington City."

"How about the possibility of canal packets carrying the mail, Uncle?"

"Carry mail by canal boat?" Morrison said incredulously, and started to laugh. "You must be daft, nephew! What do they average, about four, five miles an hour?"

"I'm not necessarily talking about speed. I'm talking about reliability. At the moment, the mail is carried haphazardly, by horse, by train, by stagecoach, sometimes even on foot. Nothing is organized. Connections from one mode of transportation to another are seldom made. Often mail has to lay over for a week or more in one place before being transported on. Besides, there are ways of increasing the speed of a canal boat, especially a packet that isn't laden with freight."

"I still can't see it, but I can see that you've given this a great deal of thought," Morrison said.

"Yes, I have. There are enough connecting canals now

to transport mail throughout much of this part of the country. You know how bad the roads are once you get this far west. There are no decent connecting roads the whole length of the Erie, for instance. But if mail was placed on a canal packet at the Hudson River, it could travel all the way to Buffalo, even to Chicago, without once changing to another means of transportation."

"You're thinking of this boat you bought for your friends?"

"I am."

"But I still fail to grasp what you wish of me."

"You have friends in Washington City. I thought you could call in some of those favors owed you, and get the Carnahans a mail-carrying contract with the federal government. You see, Uncle, their boat will be a passenger packet, but passenger traffic is notoriously unreliable: a full load one trip, maybe half-full the next. A contract such as this would give them stability, something they could depend on for a guaranteed income."

"I don't know," Morrison said. "Trying to talk some bureaucrat into hauling mail by canal boat . . ."

"I should think the government would be delighted to have something like this. It wouldn't cost an arm and a leg, since it wouldn't be the Carnahans' sole source of income. After all, that's the way it works with stagecoaches, which carry passengers, also. I'm sure that if a stagecoach line could operate from the Hudson to Buffalo, the government would be glad to use it to carry the mail. This way is the logical solution, until roads are built."

"Logical? Since when has any government been logical, especially the federal government?" Morrison snorted softly. "But I'll give it a shot. Whether or not I get anywhere is a different matter."

Cat had been sorely puzzled for days by Mick's behavior. He disappeared for hours on end, sometimes all day; and when he was around, he was always smiling, as if hugging a delicious secret to his bosom. Now that spring was here, fewer patients came to see Anthony, which meant that

Cat had much less to do; and she was bored and discontented.

She stood on deck for long periods, watching with an unhappiness close to anger as boat traffic quickened on the canal with the arrival of spring. How she yearned to have her own boat again!

This only served to make her father's frequent absences and secretive smiles more maddening.

In exasperation she said to him one afternoon, "Mick, what *is* going on? You're gone all hours of the day, and you go around looking like a cat after a bowl of cream. At first I thought you were drinking again, but . . ."

"Catherine, how could you think that of me?" He got a hurt expression, but it lasted only a moment before the smug look returned. "For once, girl, you'll have to be having patience. I can't be telling you yet."

"You know I don't like secrets, Mick."

"Well now, if I told you, it would no longer be a secret, would it?"

"Damn blast and hell, keep your secret then!" she said with an angry toss of her head. "I don't care."

"Oh, you'll care, right enough, when I tell you."

It was an afternoon in March when he finally told her. Standing on the deck of the *Paracelsus,* she saw him swinging jauntily along the wharf. He saw her and stopped at the wharf end of the gangplank. Grinning, he waved to her. "It's time now, Catherine. Come with me."

"Time for what? And go where with you?"

"Time for me to be telling you what I've been up to. As for where, you'll see. Now come on."

She felt just stubborn enough to refuse him, yet her curiosity was whetted to a fine point. She said, "All right. But it had better be worth it."

"Oh, I'm thinking it will be," he said, his grin broadening.

She crossed the gangplank, and he took her arm. Nothing more was said until they had walked down near the end of the wharf. There he drew her to a halt before a spanking new passenger packet; the colors were blue and gold, glistening brightly, and the windows were so clean they sparkled in the afternoon sun.

Mick said proudly, "Well, girl, what do you think of her?"

Puzzled, Cat said slowly, "It's a beautiful packet, but why did you bring me all the way down here to . . ." She broke off with a gasp as she saw the letters painted on the side of the cabin: CAT II. She glared at her father. "Is this some kind of a joke?"

"No joke, Catherine. It's ours, *Cat II*. I'm thinking maybe I should have consulted you before naming her, but I was sure you'd want the name."

Totally bewildered, Cat said, "I don't understand any of this, Mick. Who does this boat belong to?"

"Why, to us, of course. You're not normally so dense, girl."

She tore her arm out of his grasp. "Dense, is it? How did you get the money to buy this? We had none."

"Didn't need money. You know how many boat builders are willing to sell on installments to people with good reputations. And it's well known along the Erie that the Carnahans are solid, dependable canawlers."

"But we know absolutely nothing about running a passenger packet, Mick!"

"What we don't know, we can learn."

Cat shook her head. "I still don't understand. Something doesn't *feel* right about this. Here we've been racking our brains trying to figure out a way to buy a freight boat, and here's this packet, at least twice the price, all ours! It's like a fairy tale, a dream come true, and I know from bitter experience that dreams seldom come true."

"Now you're sounding like a bogtrotter Irishman, girl, superstitious to the core. You know that the fates are sometimes on the side of the angels, Catherine."

"Fates! Angels!" she said scornfully. "Don't talk rubbish, Mick."

But her attention was distracted. She was staring longingly at the *Cat II*. It was such a lovely boat. She wanted to pinch herself to be sure she was not dreaming. Could it be true? Were she and Mick really the proud owners of this boat? How could it be possible?

She was still suspicious—something was not *right*—but for once in her life, she abruptly decided, she was not going to look with skepticism upon something good.

Mick said, "If you don't believe me, I have the ownership papers in my pocket. . . ."

"Oh, who cares? I'll take your word for it, Mick. Come on!" She seized his arm. "Let's go on board and inspect our new boat!"

Morgan had ridden on passenger packets before, but only for short distances; he had never spent the night on one or had more than one meal. When he was ready to leave Washington City, he sold his horse and decided to journey back to Albany on the Erie via passenger packet. Since it appeared that he was going to be involved in the passenger business, he should learn what he could about it; it was certainly advisable to find out what the competition had to offer.

He was not sure but what the trip to Washington City had been a waste of time. Sherman Morrison had written several letters to people in power in the federal government, outlining Morgan's proposal to use canal boats for carrying the mail. Morgan had decided that, since the mail service was so unreliable, it would be wise to carry the letters to Washington City by hand.

Since he was there on the behalf of Morrison, he was welcomed cordially by the recipients of Morrison's letters; but at every office he received the same response when he explained his purpose—the plan sounded promising, but others would have to be consulted, and it would take time to reach a decision. Morgan's uncle had warned him that this would happen, yet he was still disappointed. He did elicit promises that he would be informed by mail in Albany of what the ultimate decision was.

He boarded the first packet early in the morning, in

time for breakfast; the passenger packet was named the *Ark*, which Morgan thought apt, since it did bear some resemblance to the biblical Noah's Ark.

The only real deck, of course, was the roof of the main cabin, as was the situation with freight boats such as the *Cat;* but this cabin was higher, about fifty feet long, with chairs for the passengers to sit on if the weather was nice. In the bow, carefully segregated from the rest of the boat, were the tiny quarters for the crew.

In the stern was the galley, fronted by a bar. A Negro cook ran the galley and also worked as bartender. The main cabin served as a dining room and saloon by day and was converted into a dormitory at night, with the women's sleeping section separated from the men's by a curtain.

The fare was five dollars for a twenty-four-hour run.

The breakfast menu was surprisingly varied, and hearty, consisting of tea and coffee, heavy bread, several kinds of fish, liver, steaks, ham, and chops, potatoes, pickles, and black pudding. Morgan was to find before the day was over that the midday dinner and supper consisted of the same food; but even so, he thought, it was remarkable that one man and in such a tiny galley could prepare and serve such varied fare for the close to fifty passengers on board.

There was a backgammon board in the cabin, along with a small library of twenty books, all torn and dog-eared; but since it was a warm day, most of the passengers sat on top of the cabin, watching the scenery passing slowly by.

The crew consisted of the cook, a captain, a hoggee in charge of the mules, and two steersmen, one for the day shift and one for the night shift.

It seemed pleasant enough to Morgan, until evening came. Shortly after supper was served, at eight o'clock, everyone was herded out of the cabin unceremoniously. Morgan was puzzled and a little indignant at first, but the other passengers seemed resigned to it. Then he realized what was happening when he saw the crew members carrying bedding and other items—the cabin was being converted into a communal bedroom.

When they were finally allowed back in, two hours later, Morgan was aghast at what he saw. He had heard people say they never traveled by canal boat at night if it could be avoided, and now he saw the reason. The beds were little more than hammocks—strips of canvas stretched over narrow wooden frames. Each bunk was held by two iron rods projecting out of the bulkhead, and the front side was supported by two ropes fastened to the edge of the frame and suspended from hooks in the ceiling. There were three beds to a tier, one above the other, fastened by the same ropes. The tiers were set very close together all around the walls, and a red canvas curtain had been suspended from the ceiling at one end, to provide a minimum of privacy for the half-dozen ladies on board.

Morgan thought he had never seen anything that looked more uncomfortable. He wondered how the passengers selected their bunks, and then he saw the men crowding around the captain at a table at the opposite end of the cabin. The ladies were already retiring behind the curtain. Realizing what was happening, Morgan moved down to the table, the last man to arrive. The male passengers were drawing lots for the bunks. Even as he approached, several hurried away from the table, clutching small pieces of cardboard in their hands, searching for the bunks with corresponding numbers. Morgan noticed that most of them, the moment they had located their bunks, immediately removed their clothing, some taking off more than others, and crawled into the narrow hammocks.

As Morgan reached the table to draw his number, he was reminded of the faces of the people at the lottery drawing in Harrisburg; these faces bore the same eager, hopeful expression. In his opinion, none of the bunks was worth fretting over.

When he finally got his number and went in search of it, he found it along the port-side bulkhead. An enormously fat man stood beside it, wearing a doleful expression.

He looked around. "What number do you have, sir?"

Morgan glanced at the number on the cardboard and found that the corresponding number was that of the bottom bunk. "I have the bottom one."

"And I have the top. How the devil am I supposed to climb up there, with my heft? And even if I could, I will probably roll off once I'm asleep. At least on the bottom I wouldn't have far to fall. I don't suppose . . ." He glanced at Morgan in supplication.

Morgan hesitated, gazing dubiously at the top hammock. But what difference did it make? He already knew that he was going to spend the night on deck. He could not imagine anything more uncomfortable than these hammocks. With a sigh he said, "You may have the bottom bunk, friend. In case anyone questions you, here's the number." He handed over the piece of cardboard.

"Thank you, sir. I am most appreciative," the fat man said. He got a sly twinkle in his eye. "You are not a businessman, sir. I would gladly have bargained for the lower bunk."

Morgan smiled pleasantly. "I am not reduced, sir, to profiting from the hardship of others."

As he made his way out of the cabin, Morgan noted that some of the passengers were already asleep, as evidenced by the loud snores. Aside from the discomfort of the narrow hammocks, a man would hear snores, coughs, or any other noises made by his neighbors, he thought.

There had to be a better way to accommodate sleeping passengers; it would certainly be profitable to devise a better means of handling the situation.

The deck chair was not the most comfortable of beds, either, but at least the night was not too chilly; and Morgan noted that a number of the others joined him before the night was over. He dozed off and on all night in the chair, and woke with the sun, stiff and cramped. In only a few minutes there were sounds from below, and soon the rest of the passengers began coming up on deck.

The fat man saw Morgan and approached him. "They

are most rude on this packet. They herd you like cattle at night from the cabin. Now they're herding us all out again, to arrange the cabin for breakfast. I noticed that you did not occupy your bunk, sir."

Morgan shrugged. "I figured that it would be better up here. I've never been a man for crowds, and it certainly is crowded down there."

"I must beg your forgiveness, if I was the cause of any discomfort to you."

Morgan shrugged again. "I caught a few winks, enough to survive."

But after several nights spent on board the *Ark* and a second packet it was necessary to transfer to in order to reach Albany, Morgan was weary and not a little disgruntled when he finally stepped off the second boat carrying his valise. If anything, the second boat was more uncomfortable than the *Ark*, since it had been crowded to capacity.

Not only were the boats uncomfortable at night, they provided no facilities for bathing; Morgan even had to shave with cold water. He resolved that if his partnership with the Carnahans progressed, he was going to see to it that they carried a wooden tub of hot water for those passengers who wished to avail themselves of it.

He felt grimy, he smelled rank, and his clothes were rumpled and filthy. He had intended to look Mick up at once and see if he had purchased the passenger packet, and how Cat had taken to it; but it was late afternoon when he left the passenger packet, and he decided to find a decent inn, and have a hot bath and a good night's sleep before looking for the Carnahans. He made one stop first—at the general store housing the post office. There was no communication from Washington City, not that he had really expected a decision yet, but he could hope.

He found a decent room, had a long, hot bath, sent his clothes down to be cleaned and ironed, and slept almost twelve hours. After a hearty breakfast, he went in search of Mick. He saw a new passenger packet a distance away and had a hunch that it was the one. When he neared it, there was no longer any doubt; CAT II was painted in bold letters on the side of the cabin.

He stood where he was for a few moments, looking the packet over, savoring the moment. It was a beautiful craft, and he felt a pride of ownership, although he supposed it would be some time before he dared let Cat in on the fact that he was her silent partner.

He did not see anyone on deck, but there were sounds of activity from the cabin, and he assumed that the Carnahans were on board. Taking a deep breath, he stepped onto the gangplank and went on board.

As he stepped onto the deck, Cat came out of the open door. She skidded to a stop at the sight of him. "Morgan!" For just a moment a flashing smile of delight lit her face, and then all expression left her features.

"Hello, Cat," he said quietly. "You're looking well."

She was in men's clothes, her hair was mussed, and her face was smudged with dirt. In spite of all that, she looked beautiful, and his heart sang at the sight of her. At his words she flushed, and her hands came up to fuss with her hair.

"I never expected to see you again," she said in a subdued voice.

He grinned lazily. "You should have known better. Did you think you could get rid of me so easily?"

Mick stepped out of the cabin behind her. "Lad!" he boomed. "It's happy I am to see you. What do you think?" He swept a hand around the boat.

Morgan said, "I think you did just fine, Mick." The instant the words were out of his mouth, he realized he had made a bad mistake. He glanced at Cat and caught her glaring at him.

She looked at her father, then back at Morgan. As comprehension dawned, her anger blazed. "You!" She almost spat the word. "I'm stupid. I should have known you were behind it." She switched her gaze to her father. "Some boat builders are willing to trust the Carnahans, because we have such a 'fine' reputation! Not only is

Morgan Kane a liar, now he has made a liar out of you as well."

Mick sent Morgan a helpless glance as Cat started toward the gangplank. Morgan stepped forward to seize her arm. "Now wait a minute, Cat. For once, will you just listen?"

"Another explanation, Mr. Kane?" She flung off his arm. "I will not listen to another one of your lies. You bought and paid for this packet, so I'll leave it to you." She took three steps toward the gangplank, then whirled back around. "But I want my name off the cabin, do you hear? Paint it over today. I refuse to have my name in any way associated with you, or anything belonging to you!"

Chapter Nineteen

CAT strode along the dock, so blinded by tears that she could scarcely see where she was going.

Damn and blast Morgan Kane to hell!

Did he think that he could just stroll back into her life and buy her forgiveness, her love?

What made it even worse was that she had fallen in love with the *Cat II*. She was a beautiful boat; and operating a passenger packet, even with several inherent difficulties, could be so much more pleasant than running a freight boat, where you were often forced to haul any cargo available.

Now it was all over, her dream-come-true shattered in one stunning moment of revelation.

And where could she go now? Beg Anthony to take her back as his nurse? He had been deeply hurt and angry two weeks ago when she had told him that she was leaving the *Paracelsus*, that she and Mick had acquired a replacement for the *Cat* and were returning to their former occupation.

"You're leaving me after all this time?" he had said in dismay. "What am I to do without you?"

She smiled slightly. "I'm not going to the other side of the world, Anthony. I'll still be on the Erie. We'll see each other from time to time."

"But it won't be the same as on the *Paracelsus*. It'll be like it was before. We'll only be able to snatch a stolen moment now and then."

"Perhaps it's better that way. We're too close here. I feel . . . well, confined."

"Aside from personal considerations, what will I do for a nurse?"

"You'll find somebody else. Anthony . . ." She sighed. "I'm not meant to be a nurse. I get too depressed around sick people. You're a doctor, it's far different with you. It's your life."

"I had hoped that it would be your life as well," he said gloomily.

"No, never. I belong on the canal, but running my own boat. I was never so happy as when Mick showed me the *Cat II*. I'm sorry, dear Anthony." She reached out to touch his face. "I am fond of you, very fond, but I doubt I'd ever make a good doctor's wife."

"That's not true!" He caught her hand and pressed it to his lips. "Together we would accomplish a great deal. You're a wonderful nurse, Cat."

"I was . . . adequate. To be good at something, you have to love it, and the more I worked with sick people, the more I hated it. I love having my own canal boat. I know most people think it isn't a life for a woman, but it's my choice."

His shoulders slumped in defeat. "I know how useless it is, Cat, to try and talk you out of something. So go with my blessing." He threw his hands wide. "But I'm still going to be left without a nurse."

Cat had a sudden inspiration. "I know somebody who might work out fine. Lotte Pryor."

"Lotte Pryor!" He stared at her in shock. "Cat, what are you thinking of? The girl is a hummingbird. She has little more brains than a flea."

"That's not wholly true. That's what I thought at first, but I had a couple of long talks with her while she was here sick. She has brains. It's just that she's never had a chance to use them. It's the way she was brought up. A minister's daughter isn't *supposed* to think."

Weakly, he said, "She has no nursing experience, Cat."

"Aha! Neither did I. But remember what you told me?" She leveled a finger at him. "You said you could teach me all I needed to know, and you did. Besides, she has had some experience. In Africa, she told me, she often nursed the sick natives."

"She likely wouldn't be interested, anyway."

"I think she might. Oh, I guess I haven't told you. Mick told me recently that he heard her father wouldn't let her back on his boat. She's going to have to fend for herself. I think this would be ideal for her. . . ."

Cat's thoughts were interrupted by the sound of pounding footsteps behind her, and Morgan's voice rang out, "Cat! Wait up!"

She thought of running, but she knew she could never outrun him; besides, it would be undignified. By this time it was too late—he had her by the arm, pulling her to a halt.

Breathing hard, he said, "By God, this time you're going to listen to me, Catherine Carnahan, even if I have to hogtie you!"

"Listen to what?" she said icily. "More of your lies?"

"Oh, for God's sake, Cat," he said wearily. "Nobody's lied to you—not really. A little deception, perhaps." He smiled slightly. "But both Mick and I realized that if you knew right off that the money to buy the boat came from me, you'd balk like a towpath mule, which is what you just did."

Cat tried to pull her arm out of his grip, but he held her firmly. "I have a suggestion for you, Mr. Kane. If you feel the need of female companionship on your new boat, why don't you ask your friend Lotte Pryor? I'm sure she would be more than happy to oblige."

Morgan blinked. "What *are* you talking about?"

"You think I don't know about your affair with Lotte?

She had the cholera, you know, and I nursed her through it. We had several long, interesting talks, and one subject we discussed thoroughly was you, Mr. Kane."

"And so? You would have nothing more to do with me, and she was available."

Cat gasped. "You make it sound like I was to blame."

"In a way, you were."

"And saying that she was available—that's an awful thing to say!"

He nodded soberly. "You're right, it was. I shouldn't have put it that way. Lotte is all right, but she is not you, Cat." He grinned insolently.

"Will you let go of my arm?" She gave an angry jerk, but his fingers tightened.

"Not until you promise to listen to me, Cat. I think you owe me that."

"Owe you? I don't owe you a thing."

"Cat . . . Please, will you just listen for a little?"

"Mr. Kane saying *please*? I can't believe it." Cat knew, deep in her heart, that she wanted to listen. The first spurt of anger at him had passed, and she was achingly aware of his touch on her arm. "Well, since you put it so nicely, for you at any rate, I'll listen."

He breathed a faint sigh and loosened his grip, but he still watched her warily, as if fearful that she would bolt and run. When she made no move, he said, "Let's go over and sit down. This may take a while."

He led her to the wharf pilings and they sat down. He began then, and told her, step by step, everything that had happened from the day Sherman Morrison had broached his proposal. When he reached the point of the attack on him in the Side-Cut, Morgan said, "I did lose my memory for a while, Cat. Honest to God. I could remember very little the next morning when I awoke in your father's cabin. It wasn't until later that I finally remembered everything, and by then you thought I had lost my memory, so I just let you go on thinking that."

"But why, Morgan?"

"I'm not sure I can explain. It made it easier to go about my investigation, for one thing. I didn't know how you'd take to that, if I told you. And loss of memory gave me a ready excuse to remain on the *Cat*." He looked at her with such love that she was forced to look away, feeling heat rush to her face. "I wanted to stay around you for as long as possible. And then when we . . . when we became lovers, I was afraid I'd lose you if I revealed that I was living a lie. Which is exactly what happened, when you did find out."

Still not looking at him, she said quietly, "Continue. Tell me the rest of it."

He told her the rest, skipping over his liaison with Lotte. When he had finally brought her up-to-date, she said in a dry voice, "It strikes me that you kind of skirted around Lotte Pryor."

"I did, I'll admit it, but I didn't think you would want all the details."

"You're right, I don't."

"I'm no saint, Cat," he said tensely. "Lotte is an attractive woman, and the close proximity . . ."

"Oh, I can see how the temptation would be too much for a man like you," she said with a cutting edge. "As you said, you're no saint."

"Would you want one?"

Avoiding a direct answer, she said, "The money to pay for *Cat II*—you won that gambling, then?"

"I don't deny it," he said simply. "It's the way I've made my living most of my life. But I'm an honest gambler, Cat, I want you to believe that."

"They all say that. And you wouldn't say otherwise, even if you weren't."

"Probably not. But I'm good, and I've never found it necessary to cheat."

Cat knew that he probably was telling the truth; he did have a knack for doing everything well, including making love. Hastily, she said, "If you're such a good gambler, why invest in a canal boat?"

"Call it a love offering. Or a peace offering, if you prefer." He reached out to take her hand. "I want us to be friends, Cat, if nothing else."

She let him keep her hand as she gazed at *Cat II*. It *was* a beautiful boat, damn and blast! She so longed to be at the tiller again.

As if reading her thoughts, Morgan said, "We'll be partners, but you'll be the captain, Cat. Mick and I will serve as the crew, with maybe Timmie on the towpath, if we can get him back."

"Oh, Timmie's around," she said, her gaze still on the packet. "In fact, I've already promised him the hoggee job."

"Well then?" Morgan said cheerfully. "I can foresee no problems."

It irritated her that he was assuming that she had already capitulated; however, she knew, in some small part of her mind, that she had. She said tartly, "I can foresee a number of problems. For one thing, a passenger packet can be unprofitable, if not handled right. I've seen all too many fail. The expenses are twice as heavy as a freight boat, and if the passengers aren't there, you can't sell tickets."

"I have some ideas about that. One I told Mick about. Didn't he tell you?"

"No, he didn't."

"Well, I've been to see my uncle, the state legislator I mentioned to you. He wrote some letters to influential people in Washington City, and I delivered them by hand, telling them personally of my plan."

"Just what plan is that?"

"A contract to carry mail on the *Cat II*, from the Hudson to Buffalo," he said on a note of triumph.

"Carry mail on a canal boat? I've never heard of such a thing."

"Neither had anybody else, until I thought of it. But it'll work, I know it will. If we get the contract, it will mean extra profit on every trip."

"*If* we get the contract."

"I think the chances are very good that we will," he said confidently. "I was promised a decision soon. I'm just waiting to hear. I have some other ideas as well. Let's go back to the *Cat II*, and I'll show you."

He took her arm, and she went along willingly. Whatever reservations she had had were gone, swept away by his enthusiasm. It had always been thus, she mused, remembering how confident he had been that he could get cargo for them in last summer's bad times; he had been as good as his word. She felt a rise of hope; perhaps he could produce this time, too.

Morgan said, "I took a passenger packet to Albany this week. I wanted to observe how one was operated. In fact, I was on two, and both could stand a great deal of improvement. For instance, the sleeping accommodations are dire. Passengers are required to sleep in narrow hammocks stacked one on top of the other, almost like firewood. It's my thought to build more comfortable bunks and keep the cabin less crowded."

"That would mean carrying fewer passengers."

"True, but you wouldn't need quite so many with the additional income from the mail contract. And I think we could charge more, adding a couple of dollars to the five dollars per twenty-four-hour fare. And there were no baths available, not even hot water for shaving. I believe that adding a private cubicle for bathing, and providing hot water, would help even more in convincing people that it's worth the additional fare. A passenger packet can't be made as luxurious as an ocean liner, or even a riverboat, but a few comforts could be added. It would be worthwhile, I'm convinced."

He took her arm as they started across the gangplank. Cat said, "I would advise not getting too ambitious, Morgan, until we see what happens with this mail contract."

"Wrong," he said blithely. "I think we should proceed full steam ahead. I have enough money for the changes needed."

* * *

Over the next week, Morgan brought carpenters in to install the bunks, following the ideas he had outlined to Cat. He had two let-down bunks installed, instead of three to a tier, and had them made a foot wider; and he allowed two feet of space between each tier, instead of jamming them together. As a result, the *Cat II* could handle only thirty-five passengers instead of the customary fifty. Morgan also added two curtained bathhouses, one for men and one for women, along with a wood-fueled boiler to provide hot water.

The improvements cost a goodly sum. Cat was still dubious, but she voiced no more objections. After all, it was Morgan's money; if he wanted to spend it so lavishly, she saw no reason to object.

Although *Cat II* was larger than its predecessor, Cat's cabin and the one shared by Morgan and Mick were still cramped; but she did not mind.

One thing that did chafe her considerably before the week was out was Morgan's inattention to her. He was busy from dawn until dusk, supervising the work on the boat, and paid her scant heed. Mick trotted around in his wake almost worshipfully, Cat thought disdainfully.

She had anticipated that Morgan would approach her some night, demanding his due. Why else had he financed the whole thing? She was of two minds about how she would react. She could rebuff him with lofty scorn, or succumb to his charms and fall into his arms. But when he had made no move by the end of the week, she felt, perversely, like a woman scorned, and was furious. Once or twice, she caught him looking at her with an amused smile, as if he knew what she was thinking, and that only enraged her more.

Morgan made a trip once a day to the post office for the letter from Washington City. On Monday of the new week, after all the changes had been completed on *Cat II*, he came back with the expected letter. He was not as exuberant as Cat had expected him to be, and she soon found out the cause.

"It's the letter from the post-office official," he said. "But it's not exactly what I was hoping for."

Cat said, "We didn't get the contract! I told you we might not."

"That's not exactly it. They didn't turn us down flat. They're playing it cozy. They want a trial run first."

"Trial run?" Mick said. "What does that mean?"

"Well, according to this letter, we take a sack of mail, actually a dummy sack," Morgan said with a wry smile. "It seems that they don't trust us with real mail. We make the trip to Buffalo. If we make it with no hitches, and make the run in good time, *then* they will grant us a contract. If we agree, we're to let them know by return post, and a man will be sent here from Washington City to monitor us all the way. I assume he'll be a nonpaying passenger."

Despite the fact that Cat had more or less anticipated something like this, she was bitterly disappointed. She turned away, staring along the canal. She said, "So what do we do now?"

Mick said slowly, "I'm thinking it's not all that bad, Catherine. What's wrong with giving it a try? If we can't do what's required of us, we're not deserving of the contract."

"That had occurred to me, Mick, but I'm glad you mentioned it first," Morgan said. "Cat?"

She turned around. "I suppose we have to try, now that we've gone this far. But it must have also occurred to you, Mr. Kane, that they're going to demand a top performance. We're going to have to travel faster than normal, and if anything goes wrong, this monitor fellow is going to send in a bad report."

"Then we'll have to see that nothing happens, won't we? As for speed, I have a couple of things in mind."

"You always have something in mind, don't you?" she said acidly.

"I'm always trying," he said with an insouciant grin.

"Give the lad credit, Catherine," Mick said in exasperation. "He always comes through, I'm thinking."

"And I'm thinking that whatever he has in mind will cost us. Am I right?"

Morgan nodded. "More than likely. But it'll be worth the added expense over the long haul. And I'll take care of any extra expenses." He looked from one to the other. "Is it agreed, then? Shall I write back and tell them we accept their terms?"

Mick said promptly, "By the saints, yes, boyo!" He rubbed his hands together. "It can be exciting, I'm after thinking. Sort of like a race. Against ourselves, in a manner of speaking!"

"I suppose we have no choice but to proceed." Suddenly, totally unexpectedly, Cat caught fire. Mick was right: it *was* exciting. "All right, let's do it! Damn blast and hell, we'll *make* it exciting, Mick, more exciting perhaps than the parade to New York Harbor celebrating the opening of the Erie!"

Tate Brawley stepped out of his breeches and joined Lucy Crawford in her big bed.

Lucy opened her arms in ardent welcome. "It's been a long time, Tate." She pouted. "You've been back to the Erie for months and haven't dropped by to see me once."

"I've been busy, woman," he said curtly. "Since the Union Canal Lottery Company went under, I've had to scramble to make a living, busy day and night." He could not help adding boastfully, "But that'll be the day when they can keep Tate Brawley down."

It was true, he had had a rough time of it for a while after the Union Canal Lottery went out of business; but now he had built up a network of ticket salesmen along the Erie, selling tickets for other lottery companies, and he was doing just fine, thank you.

Only one thing galled him—Morgan Kane. He blamed all his misfortune on Kane. If he could just get Kane in his gun sight and wipe him off the face of the earth, everything would be right as rain again. But apparently Kane had vanished; undoubtedly too cowardly to come back to the Erie, damn his soul to perdition!

"Tate?" Lucy said in a complaining voice.

"What?" he said irritably.

"You're off somewhere, not paying attention to me." She was frowning. "I must say it's not very flattering."

"It's attention you want, is it?" He ground his mouth roughly on hers; and closing his hand around one ample breast, he squeezed cruelly.

Instead of objecting, Lucy wrapped her arms tightly around him, pulling him close. Brawley forgot about Morgan Kane and concentrated on the job at hand. One thing at a time, that was the ticket!

In a moment she had guided him inside her, and they were making the bed bounce and squeal in their violent passion.

Lucy's head rolled from side to side, her mouth wide. "Yes, oh yes, Tate! That's it, that's what I missed!"

As they neared a pounding climax, Lucy drummed her fists on his back and kicked her heels into the air. With a prolonged grunt, Brawley attained his satisfaction, then slowly relaxed. "Was that attention enough for you?"

"Oh, yes, Tate, oh yes!" she said breathily into his ear.

Before Brawley could move off her, a loud knock sounded on the door. Brawley tensed and whispered fiercely, "Who's that, one of your roomers?"

Wide-eyed, Lucy said, "I don't know. I don't think so; they know better than to come rapping on my door."

"You sure one of them hasn't been rogering you?"

"No, no, I swear, no one, Tate, no one but you."

Brawley did not believe her; all women lied; it was as natural to them as eating. He measured the distance to his clothes, and the pistol underneath them. . . .

The knock came again, and a voice said, "Tate? You in there? It's me, Simon Maphis."

Brawley relaxed with a muttered curse. "What the hell

are you doing here, Simon, coming around when I'm on private business?"

"It's real important, else I wouldn't have, you know that."

"All right, go downstairs to the parlor. I'll be down in a minute."

Brawley got out of bed and began putting on his clothes.

Lucy sat up, pulling the blanket up over her nakedness. "Who is that?"

"Just a business associate."

Her face reddened. "I don't know as I appreciate being interrupted in the privacy of my bedroom, Tate."

"I don't give a damn what you don't appreciate, Lucy," he growled. "If you appreciate me, just shut up, or I won't be back."

Buttoning his shirt, he went out, slamming the door, and clattered down the stairs. He found Maphis pacing impatiently in the parlor. Brawley snapped, "This had better be damned important, Simon. How did you know I was with her, anyway?"

Maphis assumed an injured look. "Why, you told me about the widow Crawford once, Tate. Don't you recall? And 'tis important; it's about Morgan Kane and the Carnahan woman. . . ."

"Shush, not here." He batted a hand at Maphis, sending a look up the stairs. "Let's find a tavern. We don't want our business known to one and all. Lucy has a lip as loose as a goose."

He would not let the excited Maphis talk until they were settled in over drinks in the tavern. With a light-fingered stroke of his whiskers, he said, "Now, what's this about Kane and Cat Carnahan?"

"Kane's back on the Erie, with a purse as fat as a hog ready for butchering." Maphis leaned forward. "He's gone in partners with the Carnahans, and they've bought a new boat."

Brawley cursed. "Damn those toughs we hired! They didn't finish the job they were paid to do. If they had, both Carnahans would be dead now. I should have hunted those bastards down and got part of our money back."

"It really wasn't their fault, Tate. They torched the *Cat*, bunged the old man up some, and sent the boat to the bottom. The Carnahans both would have been burned to a crisp, except some fellows happened by in time to save them."

Brawley squinted at him suspiciously. "How do you know all this?"

"I . . . I just heard about it," Maphis mumbled, his glance sliding away.

"No, you didn't just hear about it! You were there, watching. Couldn't keep away, could you?"

"I just had to see it happen, Tate, and besides, I thought somebody should see that we got our money's worth," Maphis said defensively. "Besides, no one saw me. It was safe as church."

"It had better be. If I'm ever connected with that business in any way, you'll be sorry, Simon." But what's done is done, Brawley thought; a man has to make do with what he has to work with.

Maphis got a mulish look. "Half of it was my money, Tate. I had a right to see what happened."

"Never mind, I guess no harm was done." Brawley stroked his side whiskers thoughtfully. "So the Carnahans and Kane are partners, are they?"

Maphis nodded, clearly relieved that the subject had been changed. "Not only that, but they have a passenger packet, not a freight boat."

Brawley arched his eyebrows in surprise. "A passenger packet? Wonder where Kane got all the money. That's going to make it harder, trying to do them damage with a load of passengers. If we were by chance to harm a passenger or two, we'd be in trouble. The law cares little about a canaller, but a load of passengers is a different kettle of fish."

"That ain't all. You haven't heard the rest, Tate.

Somehow, Kane managed to finagle a deal with the federal government to carry mail."

"Mail on a canal boat? How did he manage that?"

"It ain't set yet," Maphis said smugly. "Before they're given the contract, they must have a trial run, from Albany to Buffalo. If their performance ain't up to snuff, they don't get the job. The way I hear it, there'll be some fellow from the government on board all the way, to see how they do."

"A government man? Hell, that makes it even more difficult. We harm a federal man, we're really in trouble, up to our asses."

"Maybe we should do something before they start, before the government man gets here?"

Brawley's gaze sharpened. "You mean they're just sitting there, waiting for him? Where, in Albany?"

"Yeah, that's where they operate out of, but they're not just sitting there. They're already in operation, taking passengers, but just on short hauls, never more than a day or two away, so they can get back to meet this post-office fellow when he comes."

Brawley sighed. "That pretty much rules out doing them damage in Albany, since there'll be passengers coming and going."

"We're not just going to sit on our hands and do nothing, are we, Tate?"

"Not at all. Morgan Kane has plagued me enough, and I'm going to see to it that he pays." Brawley drummed his fingers against the ale mug. "It might be better anyway to wait until the government man is here, observing. Then, when they fail to get the government contract, they'll be the joke of the Erie. There're any number of things we can do to spoil their trial run. After that, they won't even be able to get passengers. That's when we strike and strike hard!"

"Tate . . ." Maphis fidgeted. "One thing: before we finish them for good, I'd like my chance at the woman.

Just ten minutes alone with her, then we can bury her head first in Erie mud."

Brawley grinned. "Fancy her, do you?"

"I do, I won't deny it." Maphis looked at him squarely. "She made *me* a laughingstock once. I want her to rue that day."

Brawley looked at him keenly. "Is that the reason you hung around the night the toughs attacked, hoping to get a chance at her?"

Maphis reddened, his glance dropping away. "I might have grabbed her, if the chance had come up. But it didn't, not when all the crowd had gathered."

Brawley considered the King of the Erie. He probably had made a mistake in allying himself with Simon Maphis. Maphis was little more than a brute, with subnormal intelligence, and a slave to his appetites; yet, he was vicious, willing to go any lengths to avenge what he considered a slight, and he was handy to have around when it came time for rough stuff.

Brawley said, "Well, as I've already said, that's in the past now. But from now on you follow my orders to the letter. You've got a good thing going, working for me selling lottery tickets. If you disobey me again, I'll take it away from you and give it to somebody else. Understood?"

Maphis nodded and said sullenly, "Understood, Tate."

"That's the ticket. We have to start making our plans, it's not too soon for that. It seems to me that I have heard that that hoggee of the Carnahans, Timmie something-or-other, is gone on the Carnahan woman. With Kane back in the picture, I wonder how the hoggee feels. Maybe we can use him to our advantage. . . ."

Chapter Twenty

"BUT we're not even coming close to making expenses, Morgan," Cat said unhappily.

"I didn't really expect to in the beginning," Morgan responded. "We need time to get established." He grinned. "Just think of it as a learning experience, Cat. By the time we get going good, we'll know all there is to know about the passenger-boat business."

"It's an expensive experience," she said glumly.

"Don't fret about it. I still have money left, enough to keep us going for several months."

"I know, but I don't feel right about that. I like to hold up my own end."

"Give that prickly pride of yours a rest, Cat. I don't mind, and if it makes you feel any better, you can pay me back out of your share of the profits we'll eventually be making."

"That's a mighty big *if*," she said, staring straight ahead.

She was at the tiller of the *Cat II*, as they approached Albany. They were nearing the end of a round trip to Schenectady. On the way west they had carried ten passengers, and now had only six on the return trip. The fares they had received barely covered the cost of the food.

At least wages presented no problem at the moment; the only person they had to pay was Timmie.

Mick was serving as cook and bartender. Much to Cat's surprise, he had volunteered for the job. "But by the saints, I'm not after doing it forever, only until we're on our feet and can afford a cook's wages."

Since they were making only short trips, there was no problem working the tiller. Morgan spelled Cat occasionally, and she and Morgan converted the cabin into a dormitory at night.

Morgan had objected strenuously to that. "You're the boat's captain, Cat. You're not supposed to be making beds. Working the tiller is bad enough, but making beds is undignified for a captain!"

"I've done things much more undignified. Besides, it saves an extra man's wages. And don't tell me again that *you* have the money to afford another man. For now, Morgan, this is the way it's going to be."

Although she had not admitted it to him, Cat had to concede that Morgan's innovations were a tremendous improvement over other passenger packets. Every passenger who had traveled with them had nothing but praise for the more comfortable sleeping arrangements and the bathing facilities. All had promised to pass the word along; and as Morgan had said, "Just wait until we have passengers on a long haul, for several days. That's when they're really going to appreciate everything."

Cat thought that he probably was right, but it did them little good at the moment. There was one factor they had not taken into consideration beforehand, although Cat thought they should have. While the majority of freight boats on the Erie belonged to individuals, the opposite was true of passenger packets: most passenger service was provided by companies, all operating several packets. These companies had been in business for a long time, they had the experience and the personnel, and they had ticket offices in all the major towns along the canal. They spent a great deal of money advertising; and whenever people wanted to travel by packet, they naturally gravitated to the large lines, instead of patronizing individual packets, even if the individual owners offered better bargains.

"Shouldn't we think about advertising?" Cat had asked Morgan, when they realized what was happening.

"I think it would be money ill spent at the present time, Cat. We're not on a regular schedule as yet, and won't be until we have our mail test run. It was my thought that we should spot several advertising posters along the Erie about that particular trip. Since it will be a special run, we should give all the public notice that we can. After that is successful and behind us, we can settle down to a regular schedule, and *then* we will spend money advertising. But for the present time we should just pick up what passenger traffic we can."

Cat supposed he was right, but it always upset her to operate at a loss. When that had happened with the original *Cat*, she had done something about it; she was not always successful, but at least she felt she was *doing* something.

As they neared the docking area, Cat risked a glance at Morgan, standing beside her. He was in profile to her, staring at the wharf, and keeping a watchful eye on Timmie. Cat knew that part of her dissatisfaction stemmed from Morgan's strange attitude toward her. Since that day on the wharf when she had agreed to become partners with him on the *Cat II*, there had been nothing of a personal nature spoken between them. At that time he had stated that he had returned to the Erie because of the love he felt for her, but since then . . . nothing!

He was friendly enough, without the slightest touch of aloofness, and was willing to talk about anything, except personal matters. Cat had waited patiently, confident that sooner or later he would attempt to make love to her. But as time passed, and there was still no move on his part, she became more and more upset. Where in the beginning she had intended to hold him off, soon she began to long for him. Just to be near him, as she was right now, ignited a fire of wanting inside her. She ached to reach out and touch him, touch his hand, stroke his cheek, any physical contact. What was wrong with him? Was it her fault, something she had done, or not done? She had contemplated making the first overtures, yet she cringed from that; it would be too humiliating if he spurned her!

And then, in that disconcerting way he had, Morgan turned his face toward her, and his eyes took on a warm glow. He moved a step closer, until she could feel his breath on her cheek. He was going to kiss her! She parted her lips, and she could already feel his mouth on hers.

Then the prow of the boat bumped gently against the wharf, and the moment was gone.

Morgan turned away, moving lithely across the top of the cabin to the bow, where their six passengers were already gathered, waiting impatiently to disembark. Disoriented, almost dazed, Cat stared after him. Instead of feeling anger, she was swept by a feeling of desolation.

By the time the *Cat II* was moored, and Cat had moved up to the bow, all the passengers were gone. Morgan had shaken the hand of each, cordially thanking them for taking passage on the packet and inviting them back.

As Cat came up beside him, she wondered if he would seize the moment and become intimate again. Mick was somewhere in the main cabin, and Timmie was seeing to the animals.

But a man, who had been waiting for the last passenger to leave, now started up the gangplank. He was a short, middle-aged man, well dressed in a suit and a flowing tie; and he carried a small traveling bag in one hand and a canvas sack in the other.

He spoke as he stepped onto the deck. "Morgan Kane?"

"Yes, sir, I'm Morgan Kane. What can I do for you? We won't be taking on another load of passengers until tomorrow morning, sir."

"I'm not a passenger, per se." The stranger smiled fleetingly. "My name is Lars Anderson. I've come from Washington City."

"From the post office?" At the man's nod, Morgan let out a whoop and shook his hand vigorously. "We've been waiting for you!"

"I'm sure you have," Anderson said in a dry voice.

Morgan turned to Cat. "This is Catherine Carnahan, my partner. And this"—he nodded as Mick came out of the cabin, drying his hands on a towel—"is her father, Mick Carnahan. Mick, this is Mr. Anderson, from Washington City."

"Mr. Anderson, is it?" Mick said, beaming. "It's glad I am to see you, sir!"

Cat had said nothing, merely nodded in greeting. She was studying the newcomer closely and she did not like what she saw. His brown eyes were unfriendly, and he had a Nordic, phlegmatic countenance, devoid of expression.

Now Anderson confirmed her opinion. "In all honesty, I must tell you, Mr. Kane, and Mr. and Miss Carnahan, that I did not approve of this scheme. But I was overruled by my superior, and ordered to come here. When I told my superior that I thought carrying mail by canal boat was an idiotic concept, he just smiled, and said it would be better to send someone who didn't like the scheme. That way, if you convince me, it's sure to be feasible. If someone came predisposed to like it, my superior would never be sure. So I must warn you people, I am going to take some strong convincing."

Morgan, Cat noticed, had been smiling all through the speech, and he was still smiling. Now he said cheerfully, "Then I guess it's up to us to change your mind, Mr. Anderson. That seems fair enough. I've always liked a challenge."

"That's one thing in your favor, at least. I admire a man who likes a challenge."

Morgan said, "We must ask a favor of you, Mr. Anderson. We have some preparations to make. Since we had no idea when you would be arriving, we couldn't just sit here idle, so we've been making short passenger hauls. Would it be all right with you if we had, say, a week to get ready for the trial run?"

Anderson considered his answer for several moments, then nodded ponderously. "That seems fair. I was given no time limit. I only hope there's a decent inn in Albany. I certainly do not intend to spend any more time than necessary on this boat." He wrinkled his nose, as if he smelled something nasty. "I hate boats, of any size or shape, always have."

Mick said quickly, "There's a fine inn just up the way, sir. It'd be my pleasure to show you."

As Mick escorted Lars Anderson off the boat, Cat said in a low voice, "Oh, that's just great! He hates boats!"

Posters appeared on buildings and posts along the length of the Erie all the way to Buffalo:

INAUGURAL VOYAGE—PASSENGER PACKET CAT II—ALBANY TO BUFFALO—FIRST ERIE CANAL BOAT TO CARRY UNITED STATES MAIL—BE A PART OF THIS GREAT EXPERIENCE—TRAVEL IN LUXURY—FARE SEVEN DOLLARS PER TWENTY-FOUR HOURS—TRAVEL ALL THE WAY OR PART WAY—DO NOT MISS THIS GREAT OPPORTUNITY—OFFICES OF THE CARNAHAN-KANE PASSENGER COMPANY LOCATED ON ALBANY WHARF!

It had been a week of feverish activity for Morgan and the Carnahans. Cat was occupied with getting ready for the onrush of passengers, if they came; she had to see to clean linens for the beds, and to purchase food and other supplies. If they did not fill the packet to capacity, she thought unhappily, they would be out of pocket for the unused food.

They had rented a small shack on the Albany wharf, put up a sign—TICKET OFFICE: CARNAHAN-KANE PASSENGER COMPANY—and installed Mick in the shack to sell tickets. Cat had no idea where Morgan was much of the time, since he was gone most of every day; and when she questioned him, he said merely, "There are many things to be done, Cat. I haven't the time to explain now."

She suspected that he did not want to explain, for fear that she would protest whatever he was doing; and whatever he was doing, she was certain, was costing money.

During the first part of the week, Mick reported that the ticket sales, while heavier than before, were still far below what they had hoped for.

They saw nothing of Lars Anderson, which suited Cat just as well; but Mick had gone to the inn to check on him, and had come back to report that he was still residing there.

Two days before their departure date, Morgan told her what he had been up to. "I've traded the mules in for horses, four horses in fact. Now just hold on, Cat! Sure, it costs additional money, but we need horses for more speed. I intend to have Timmie trade teams, about two hours on, two off. That way we will be able to average better than the usual five miles an hour."

"But you know that's illegal, Morgan. The legal limit is five miles an hour."

He grinned. "I hardly think anybody's going to check, for this one trip. Besides, it's my understanding that the speed limit is rarely enforced anyway."

She nodded reluctantly. "That's true, but I still don't like it."

"You don't have to like it, Cat. It's my doing. Not only that, but I contacted the captain of another packet, and gave him instructions, and the money, to rent several other teams of horses at numerous points along the Erie. Just in case we need them." His smile was wry. "He took some convincing, grumbling about giving a helping hand to the competition. I managed to finally convince him that if we won the mail contract, it would benefit all of us in the long run."

"But how about Lars Anderson? What will he think?"

Morgan shrugged. "How will he know that it's anything out of the ordinary? He's ignorant of canal boats. He admitted that he hates all boats."

"I don't know, it seems a little underhanded to me," she said uncertainly.

"Underhanded? Not really, Cat. It's been done before, the idea's not original with me. Other passenger packets use tradeoff teams."

"I thought speed wasn't all that important, that you were selling your idea on reliability?"

"That's true, but speed plus reliability will help sell this fellow. Besides, hating boats so much, the sooner he gets off, the happier he'll be."

By the morning of their departure, Cat was feeling better about the whole thing. There had been a spurt of ticket sales the last day, and they were filled to two-thirds of their capacity.

Morgan said, "And we'll pick up others along the canal as we go. I'll wager that we will have a full house by the time we get to Buffalo."

"Full house?" she said quizzically. "Poker talk?"

"Life is like that, Cat, didn't you know? Life is a game any way you look at it."

And love, she desperately wanted to ask; is love a game to you, too?

She said nothing, of course, and soon was too busy to think about it. A large crowd had gathered on the wharf; and much to her surprise, they gave the *Cat II* a rousing send-off. Lars Anderson was seated on the cabin deck, and she saw him glance at the boisterous crowd with a disapproving scowl.

Cat's astonishment increased the farther they proceeded. Crowds were gathered on the wharf at every town to cheer them on. She saw people with picnic baskets, waving as they passed; there was an air of a festive occasion about it, and Cat was deeply touched.

It appeared that everyone on the Erie knew what was taking place. Other canal boats stopped to let them pass, and many boats they met going east also stopped, unhitching their towlines from their towpath animals so that the

Carnahans would not have to go through the complicated maneuver of pulling in their own towline. And the canallers, one and all, cheered them on:

"Go get 'em, Carnahans!"

"Show that government man what a real canawler can do!"

Many women called, "And show them what a woman can do, Cat!"

Cat felt herself flushing with pride and affection for her fellow canawlers, and she had to admit that everything was going smoothly so far. *Cat II* moved along at a merry clip. Every two hours Morgan would hop onto the towpath and help Timmie unhitch the working pair of horses and harness up the second team.

Lars Anderson did not seem overly impressed. As they came abreast of another packet, the deck crowded with passengers cheering them on, he remarked sourly to Morgan, "If popularity would gain you points, Mr. Kane, you'd win out."

"Canawlers are like that, Mr. Anderson," Morgan said with his lazy grin. "Always cheering the other fellow on. Most of them are like that, anyway."

"Well, popularity doesn't deliver the mail, sir. It might pay you to remember that."

"Oh, I will. But it does give a man a good feeling, wouldn't you say?"

They made such good time that they were going to hit the first lock shortly after dark. Cat said with a sigh, "It's too bad we have to lay up until morning. If we could have gotten through this lock, we could have traveled most of the night."

Morgan said, "Don't give up the ship, Cat. Maybe we'll get through anyway."

She frowned at him. "But we can't reach it in time. It's another hour, and you know the locks all close before dark."

"We'll see," he said cryptically.

As they approached the lock shortly after dark, Cat was astounded to see that it was lit by torches set along the towpath, instead of being dark as was the custom; and instead of giving the order to find a place to tie up for the night, Morgan shouted to Timmie, "Keep the horses moving, Timmie, we're going right on through."

Before Cat could speak, she saw the wooden lock doors swing open for them. People lining the bank cheered lustily as they entered the lock, and she saw the lockkeeper give Morgan a jaunty wave. In a very short time the *Cat II* was through the lock and moving on along the canal. They would not reach the next lock, Cat knew, until well after sunrise the next morning.

"Morgan, how on earth did you manage that?"

Mick, standing close, said, "The lad's a miracle worker, Catherine. Don't you know that by now?"

"No miracle, Mick. Just a little persuasion, and the promise of a few free suppers, and the lockkeeper relented. Just this once, he said, but don't expect him to do it again."

"I'm thinking that if you bribed the rest of the lockkeepers all the way, we're in clover."

Morgan laughed. "I prefer the word *persuasion*, Mick, to *bribe*." He sobered. "Unfortunately, my persuasive powers didn't work too well. Most of the lockkeepers refused to go along. I knew there was animosity between canawlers and the lockkeepers, but I didn't realize it ran so deep."

Mick nodded. "It goes deep, lad, way back to the beginning of the Erie. Canawlers have always wanted to pass through the locks at night, and they've been known to sneak through in the dark, opening the locks themselves. That didn't go over well with the lockkeepers, needless to say."

"I didn't have time to contact all the lockkeepers personally, of course, but I did send word via the canal walkers, all the way to Buffalo. God knows how many will see fit to cooperate."

"Well, all I have to say is," Cat said, "we'd better not let Anderson find out."

"There's no reason he should find out. As I'm sure you've noticed, my dear, he isn't very communicative, and it's well known that all canal people dislike government men. So who'll blab to him?"

"There're some people I can think of who don't like us, who would do anything to cause us trouble," Cat said darkly. "Like Simon Maphis."

Morgan nodded. "And Tate Brawley. I've been expecting some trouble from them, but I haven't seen or heard anything of either one."

"It's not too late yet," Cat said. "We've just started. It's a long way to Buffalo."

"Don't you two go borrowing trouble. Whatever that mangy pair might try, we'll win out," Mick said confidently.

Timmie Watkins was a very unhappy lad, while two weeks ago he had been just the opposite.

After the destruction of the *Cat,* Timmie had spent a miserable winter—no job, no money; and he had been forced to live off the charity of his relatives, which he hated even more now.

And then—happy day!—Miss Catherine got another boat, and a fancy one it was. When Timmie approached her for the hoggee job and she promised it to him, he could not have been happier.

Then Morgan Kane had come back into Miss Catherine's life, and Timmie learned that he was her partner in the boat.

Jealousy began to corrode Timmie's soul like bitter wormwood. Every time he thought he had Miss Catherine to himself, Morgan Kane popped up. Timmie considered many options; he thought of killing Kane, but he well knew that he could never do it. He considered leaving, but what could he do? He knew nothing but canal work, and it was too late in the spring to get another hoggee job.

In the end he decided to stick it out. Maybe if he kept a close watch on Kane, he could discredit him again in Miss Catherine's eyes. After all, he had done so before.

Grudgingly, he had to admire Kane's cleverness with this project—the extra horses, convincing the lockkeeper to allow the packet through after dark, and so forth. However, this only further inflamed his hatred of Kane. He did have a sneaking pride in being the hoggee on such a momentous trip; for although he had no real sense of history, Timmie had the feeling that this voyage of the *Cat II* would become a legend along the Erie. Still, that did not ease his hatred of Morgan Kane. Every time Timmie saw Kane in Miss Catherine's presence, he burned inside.

At least Kane had not been able to talk all of the lockkeepers into letting them through at night, and there were twenty-seven locks on the first part of their journey; the second night they had to stop at the lock at Cohoes Falls, just out of Schenectady, having arrived a half-hour after the lock had closed for the night.

After Timmie had taken care of the horses and snatched a bite to eat in the galley, he bedded down close to the animals. There was not room for four horses on board the packet; and since the weather was growing warm, Timmie slept in his blankets near the picketed horses, so he could be close to them during the night, and also because he refused to sleep on the same boat with Morgan Kane.

He lay awake for a long time, listening to the sounds of gaiety coming from the boat. The packet was filled to capacity now with passengers, and they all seemed to view the trip as a cause for much celebration, keeping Mick busy behind the bar. Timmie smoldered with resentment as he listened. He had glimpsed Miss Catherine earlier, in a fine dress, circulating among the passengers, on Kane's arm; and Timmie had to wonder if they would retire together to her cabin for the night.

After a time he dozed as the sounds from the boat abated, and then woke with a start at a touch on his arm. As he opened his mouth to cry out, a big hand clamped around his lips, and a knee was planted on his chest, effectively pinning him to the ground.

A harsh voice said, "This is Simon Maphis, mule boy. You know who I am?"

Timmie swallowed, cold with fear. He nodded violently.

"Simon Maphis, King of the Erie. I'm rough on them that does me wrong. Now, I'm going to take my hand away from your mouth, mule boy. If you call out or shout, I'll break your neck like a stick! Nod if you get my meaning."

Again Timmie nodded. It was too dark to see the man's face, but Timmie had no doubt that it was Simon Maphis.

"All right now, just lay quiet and listen." Maphis took away his hand but did not remove his knee from Timmie's chest. "You know what that mistress of yours is doing right now, eh?" Maphis said in a sneering voice. "She's cavorting with Morgan Kane, that's what. I peeked into a cabin window some time back, and saw her with my own eyes. All arm in arm, lovey-dovey with him. It's dark over there now, so you can be sure they're tumbling in her bunk. You believe me?"

"I believe you, Mr. Maphis," Timmie said in a whisper.

"You been soft on her for a long time, ain't you?"

Timmie nodded mutely.

"Well, seems to me you'd jump at a chance to get back at the pair of them. I've got a way, not only to get back at them, but a chance to earn fifty silver dollars in the bargain, more'n you'll make all summer as their hoggee. You willing to listen to my scheme?"

"I'll listen, sir."

Timmie listened carefully as Maphis quickly told him what he had in mind.

* * *

Cat was awakened the next morning by the sounds of a commotion on deck, and far-off voices shouting. Since she had become accustomed to noise on the boat in the past two days, she was not particularly alarmed. She had gone to bed disappointed, and the same disappointment plagued her now.

Last night Morgan had squired her gallantly around the main cabin, introducing her as the captain. He had asked her earlier to wear her prettiest dress, and had told her that she looked splendid, his eyes warm and glowing as his gaze swept over her. To each passenger last night he had said proudly, "I'll wager you've never seen a more beautiful captain on any passenger boat you've ever ridden on, am I right?"

It had felt good, strolling on Morgan's arm and listening to his admiring words. She had begun to hope that the night would end in his arms. But he had escorted her to her cabin door and said formally, "Good night, Cat. Sleep well. It has been a long, hard day, and we'll start with the sun in the morning, the minute we can get through the lock."

He had not even kissed her good night! Now she whispered fiercely, "Blast you, Morgan Kane!"

Then her head came up as Mick's voice blared outside her cabin door, "Catherine! You'd better come. We have trouble!"

Quickly, she put on her working clothes and hurried on deck. Mick and Lars Anderson were standing by the cabin door, looking along the towpath. Morgan was not anywhere in sight.

"What is it, Mick? What's wrong?"

He turned a bleak face to her. "The horses are gone, girl. Not only the horses but Timmie as well."

She caught her breath. "What happened, do you know?"

"I'm thinking foul play, but I don't know. Morgan has gone scouting to see what he can find out."

Lars Anderson wore a small, cold smile. "If this is an example of how well a canal boat operates, Miss Carnahan, I think that I might as well leave you here and return to Washington City. This whole affair has the look of a fiasco to me."

Chapter Twenty-One

CAT tried to ignore Anderson. She moved to the edge of the deck to peer both ways along the canal. "I can't understand what could have happened. Timmie is a good, dependable boy."

"I'm thinking it could have been horse thieves, Catherine. You know how valuable horses are."

"But that still doesn't explain what happened to Timmie," she said, afraid of what the answer might be.

Before Mick could respond, Anderson said, "Did you hear what I just said, Miss Carnahan? You've failed the test, so I might as well pack up and go. I'll be very happy to be off this boat."

Mick's temper slipped. "You're not giving us much of a chance, bucko! And just how will you be getting back to Washington City, without the use of a boat? Shank's mare?"

"There are always stagecoaches," Anderson said stiffly.

"Not along here, there ain't," Mick said with scarcely concealed glee.

"Then I shall buy myself a horse, Mr. Carnahan," Anderson said. "I much prefer a horse to a boat any day."

"Landsmen!" Mick snorted. "You land people are all alike, I'm thinking. You never know what's good for you."

"Hush your squabbling, you two," Cat said excitedly. "Here comes Morgan with the horses."

As the two men ranged on either side of her, Cat realized that something was wrong. It was true that Morgan was leading four horses toward the boat; but they were not their own animals, and Timmie was not with him.

Cat hurried across the gangplank to meet him, with Mick right behind her. Cat was relieved to see that Anderson remained where he was.

"Those aren't our horses, Morgan," she said.

He nodded, smiling tiredly. "I know; these are four of the animals I arranged for in advance. Thank God I thought of doing that."

"But where are *our* horses, and Timmie?"

"I have no idea, Cat. I left the boat at dawn and have searched everywhere. There's no sign of either Timmie or the horses. I can think of at least three possibilities. He could have stolen the horses. . . ."

"No!" she said strongly. "Timmie would never do that."

He stared at her thoughtfully. "You're a strange woman, Cat. Sometimes you'll believe anything bad about a person—me, for instance—while at other times your faith is boundless."

She flushed, but said stubbornly, "I refuse to believe that Timmie is a thief."

"Then the two other possibilities are, one, somebody paid him to walk away, or, two, he was attacked and the horses were taken."

"I can't believe he'd do that, either, take money to quit on us. And who could be behind it?"

"Two people I can think of right off. The unholy pair, Tate Brawley and Simon Maphis. Don't you think they want us to fail, and would do anything to see to it? We've been wondering why we haven't seen hide nor hair of them since we started on this trip. They have to know about the trial run. If they don't, they're the only people along the Erie who don't know."

"But if they're behind it, I prefer to think that they overpowered Timmie."

"Think what you like. It's the same any way you look at it. Our horses are gone and so is Timmie."

"But don't you think they're capable of harming Timmie and taking the horses?" she persisted.

"Of course they're capable of it!" he said impatiently. "They're capable of anything. Cat . . ." He passed a hand over his mouth. "I'm sorry to bark at you, but I'm tired and annoyed, and we have to get moving."

"But how about Timmie?" she said in dismay.

"The boy will have to fend for himself. We have a trip to finish. Besides, I haven't the faintest idea as to where to look for him. . . . Oh, hell, here comes Anderson. What did he say, anything?"

Mick said, "He was all for leaving, lad, and giving us thumbs-down on the test."

"That figures," Morgan muttered. "Let's just hope he doesn't know one horse from another."

Stopping before them, Anderson said, "I see that you found your animals, Mr. Kane."

"Yes, sir," Morgan lied. "The boy took sick during the night, and the horses wandered off." He added brusquely, "You'd better get back on board, Mr. Anderson, we'll be moving out in a few minutes."

Anderson looked at him quizzically. "Who's to handle the horses, if your boy is gone?"

"I will, until we find a replacement." Morgan smiled slightly. "On the Erie, sir, we learn to make do."

"I don't know," Anderson said doubtfully. "I fail to see how just the three of you can manage everything."

"We'll manage, you'll see."

With a stiff nod, Anderson turned away and went back to the packet.

Cat said, "I don't see how you're going to manage, either, Morgan. We're going to start on the Long Level shortly, sixty-nine miles without a lock, and we'll be traveling day and night, you said. Then there's the other long stretch, west of Rochester, and that one is sixty-two miles without a single lock. You can't drive the teams all that distance by yourself, Morgan. It's impossible for one man!"

"Nothing is impossible, Cat. Not when something has to be done. Maybe I can find a hoggee along the way somewhere."

"It's not likely, lad," Mick said. "Not this late in the year. All the good ones are already hired, I'm thinking."

"Good ones or not, we'll use anyone we can find." Morgan smiled tiredly. "I'd hire an ape, if he could hold the reins in his hands."

"Well, I can always spell you, boyo."

"No, Mick," Cat said. "If there's any spelling to do, I'll do it. You have enough to do serving the passengers."

"You?" Morgan stared in consternation. "Cat, I can't have you doing that. You're the captain, it's not . . ."

"Don't you dare say it's undignified, Morgan Kane," she said hotly. "We're in this together, all three of us."

He broke into a slow grin. "Right, Miss Carnahan. We're in it together, come hell or high water." He cupped her face in his hands and kissed her quickly, his mouth warm and tender. "Now back to the tiller, we're moving out."

He turned away, clucking to the horses. Cat stood without moving, his kiss leaving her in a rosy daze.

"Catherine," Mick said sharply, "you heard the lad. Let's get under way."

"The bastard had extra horses stashed?" Tate Brawley slammed his ale mug down onto the table, the brew sloshing out. "Damn the fellow anyway!" Then he smiled slightly. "I do have to admire his cleverness."

"Admire him all you like," Maphis said. "But that doesn't help matters a bit. Now what are we to do?"

Maphis sat hunched over his ale across the table, and Timmie Watkins was huddled in the inside corner of the booth, staring down morosely at his hands.

Brawley said, "How are they managing without him?" He nodded contemptuously at the hoggee.

Maphis said, "Kane is driving the animals, most of the time, with the woman relieving him." He grinned unpleasantly. "They're going to be one whipped pair by the time they reach the end of the Long Level."

"Maybe they won't reach the end of it," Brawley said thoughtfully. "The woman, anyway."

Maphis licked his lips. "We going to take her, Tate?"

"Watch your mouth, Simon." Brawley batted a hand at him, and glowered at Timmie, his anger rising. "Why didn't you tell us, boy, that they had fresh horses stashed all along the canal?"

"Because I didn't know, Mr. Brawley," Timmie said, shrinking away. "Nobody told me, honest they didn't."

"Ah, away with you, you nitwit. You're of no use to us. Beat it, that's the ticket."

"But what about my fifty dollars?"

"What fifty dollars?"

"Mr. Maphis here, he promised me fifty dollars," Timmie said stubbornly, "if'n I'd help him steal the horses."

Brawley laughed gratingly. "But stealing the horses did us no good, now did it? So you get nothing, not a cent. Simon, get rid of him."

Maphis stood up, reached down a huge paw, seized Timmie by the arm, and yanked him out of the booth. "On your way, mule boy."

"But my fifty dollars!" Timmie wailed. "You promised! Without it I'll starve."

"I promised nothing; you must have been hearing things. And what do I care if you starve? You heard Mr. Brawley. You're of no use to us."

Maphis swung his free hand, cuffing Timmie across the side of the head and sending him reeling across the room. He fell to his hands and knees, blood pouring from one ear. He shook his head dazedly, whimpering.

The tavern keeper charged across the room, a bludgeon in his hand. "Here now, no rough stuff in my place!"

Maphis scowled at him. "Innkeeper, you get back behind your bar, or I'll take that club and smash your head as flat as a cow patty."

The tavern keeper took a long look at Maphis's massive physique and murderous eyes, and scuttled back behind the relative safety of his bar.

Maphis switched his baleful gaze back to the hoggee, still on his hands and knees. Maphis took a threatening step toward him. "On your way, or you've got worse coming to you."

Timmie got to his feet and staggered out of the tavern. Maphis dusted his hands together and swaggered back to the booth.

Brawley smiled faintly. "That's the ticket, Simon." And then, as Maphis sat down, he leaned forward and said, "But you've got a loose lip."

Bewildered, Maphis said, "What'd I say, Tate, what'd I say? Eh?"

"Blabbing our plans to that boy. Who knows who he might tell?"

"What plans? I didn't know we had any plans."

"About taking the woman."

Maphis's face lit up. "Then we are going to take her, Tate?"

"First, I'm putting you on notice. You talk to nobody about what we're going to discuss."

Maphis looked offended. "Tate, you know I wouldn't go blabbing. I'm not that sort of a fellow. What happened a bit ago was just a slip. I didn't know you were really planning anything like that."

Yet again, Brawley questioned the wisdom of working with Maphis. But if anything was to be accomplished at this time, he had little choice. He took a drink of ale and said, "All right, here's what we'll do. Working short-handed like they are, Kane and the Carnahans will be worn thin by the time they near the end of the Long Level. They'll be too tired to be cautious, so we'll watch for our chance, and . . ."

* * *

By the time the *Cat II* had finished the Long Level and started on the second sixty-two-mile stretch without a lock, word had been flashed by the canal walkers both ways along the Erie, back to Albany and forward to Buffalo—the *Cat II* was on its way to setting a speed record.

It had not come easily. Cat, Morgan, and Mick had worked practically round the clock, catching an hour's rest whenever they could; anything to keep the boat moving. Morgan had not been able to find a replacement for Timmie, and of course Cat had been right—he could not be on the towpath twenty-four hours a day. He had managed most of the Long Level, with Cat spelling him for two hours during the day; but he was staggering with exhaustion when they began the second long level. He realized that he could not do it alone, and had ceased arguing, except for forbidding her to work the horses at night; but as they started on the second long level, she won out on that as well.

It came to a head one evening just after sundown. They had to stop the boat for a half-hour twice a day, to feed and water the animals, and Morgan and Cat were on the towpath, attending to that chore.

"You're not thinking straight, Morgan," Cat said. "You can't handle the horses most of the day and then work all night, too. You're dead on your feet as it is."

"Maybe we should just stop at night."

"And lose what we've gained? Even Lars Anderson is impressed by our progress. And do you know what I heard?" she said excitedly. "We're setting an all-time record!"

Morgan laughed and shook his head. "You've really entered into the spirit of this, haven't you? Well, I've always known that you had a competitive nature. But it's not safe, a woman out here alone on the towpath at night."

"I can fend for myself, thank you. And I knew there

would be some risk when I agreed to this crazy test run. Mick can't relieve you, you know that. At least he can handle the tiller, while I'm driving the teams and you're catching some rest."

"I suppose I can't argue with the logic of that. I must admit that I'm bone tired. At least on the last part of the journey, after we're past this stretch, there'll be some lockkeepers who won't let us through at night, so we'll be forced to stop for all night." His bark of laughter was raspy; he had grown hoarse from shouting at the horses.

Cat's heart went out to him. She had never seen a man work harder; and his face was drawn thin, since he had lost weight on the long trek, and from the long hours. "If I've been sharp with you, Morgan, I want to say that I'm sorry. What you've done has been far beyond the call of duty. You've been wonderful."

He looked at her soberly. "Does that mean that I'm forgiven?"

She made a startled sound. "Forgiven? Of course you're forgiven! There really isn't anything to forgive . . . except for Lotte. I doubt I'll ever really forgive you for that."

"She never meant anything to me, not in the way I love you."

"Love?" She began to tremble. "Do you realize that it's been weeks since you mentioned love to me? I thought that you . . ."

"Cat, you knew, you must have known. That's what all of this is about." He made a sweeping gesture with his hand. "You think I'd do all this for any other reason?"

"But you haven't said a word, not since that day on the wharf when I agreed to your plans," she said softly. "You haven't even . . ." She hesitated, then took the plunge. "You haven't even kissed me."

"I was afraid you'd be angry if I tried."

"You, Morgan? Afraid?"

"You can be rather intimidating, Cat. I don't think you realize." He began to grin. "But I can remedy my neglect in short order."

He opened his arms, and she came into them. He held her tightly; and as his mouth came down to meet hers, some of her longing eased. He did love her!

His kiss was tender and sweet, and she responded with the same tenderness, realizing that this was hardly the time or the place for anything more than that. If only there were a grove of trees where they could find seclusion and make love! But there was not; the surrounding terrain was rather flat and without vegetation, the canal running straight as an arrow into the distance.

Morgan took away his mouth with a groan. "I do love you, Cat, and you don't know how much I've missed touching you, kissing you. If only . . ."

"I know, darling." She touched his lips with her fingers. "There will be time enough when we reach Buffalo. . . ."

Mick's shout sounded from the packet: "Supper is ready, you two. Come and get it!"

Cat stepped out of Morgan's arms, laughing shakily. "Trust Mick to always pick the wrong moment." She reached out to touch Morgan's face again. "I'll go first. Then, when I'm finished, I'll take over the horses for three hours or so while you eat and rest for a bit."

An hour later, Cat was walking behind the horses, urging them on to greater effort. She was wearing a dress, which did not please her too much, but Morgan had been adamant about that. "It is simply not fitting, Cat, for the captain of a passenger packet, and a lady, to be seen wearing men's clothes."

The night was very dark and overcast, and patches of fog drifted off the water, like blowing smoke. The lanterns on the bow of the *Cat II* behind her were reassuring. There was also a lantern suspended from the harness between the two horses, but sometimes the drifts of fog were so thick that its light was momentarily obscured. The spare team of horses, tethered to the packet's railing, plodded along in the boat's wake.

Cat was very tired, and her feet were sore and painful, but she kept moving. She had a choice, of course: she could ride one of the horses, which would be easier than walking; yet she knew from past experience that this was not a good idea. On horseback, a tired person had a tendency to doze off, and when that happened, the horses slowed to a plodding walk or stopped altogether. After all, the animals were weary, too.

As long as she kept walking, she would be forced to stay awake, and keep the horses moving. . . .

She blinked wearily, squinting forward. The patch of fog had drifted away, yet she could not see the lantern. Either it had gone out, or it had been . . .

She gasped at a sound behind her, and started to whirl around, when a powerful arm wrapped around her, and a hand clamped over her mouth. A voice said roughly, "Not a peep out of you, woman, or I'll pop your neck like a chicken's!"

Morgan was in a deep sleep of exhaustion, yet his subconscious mind was attuned to the motion of the boat. When it stopped suddenly, he bolted awake. Still groggy with sleep, he sat for a moment, trying to figure out what had awakened him. Before it became clear in his mind, he heard Mick shout, "Morgan! You'd better get up here on the quick, lad!"

Morgan had gone to bed fully dressed except for his boots. He pulled them on quickly and hurried from the cabin. Mick was pushing out the gangplank, and Morgan was amazed to see Timmie Watkins helping him. A quick glance in the direction of the horses told him nothing, since a heavy fog bank hid them.

"What is it, Mick?" he said urgently. "Why have we stopped?"

Mick straightened up after shoving the gangplank onto the towpath and turned a worried face to Morgan. "It's Catherine, lad! Something's happened to her!" He was already hurrying across the gangplank.

Morgan ran after him, with Timmie right on his heels.

As he caught up to Mick, he demanded, "What's Timmie doing here?"

"He came to warn us about Catherine, but I'm thinking he was too late."

Morgan could see the horses now, standing still, heads drooping, and his heart almost stopped—Cat was nowhere to be seen.

He plowed to a stop, his gaze taking in the fact that the harness lantern was gone. Cupping his hands around his mouth, he shouted, "Cat! Where are you?"

Beside him, Timmie gasped and said, "It's Simon Maphis, Mr. Kane! He's took her, I know he has!"

Raging with fury, Morgan seized the boy by the shoulders and shook him hard. "What do you know? Tell me, and be quick about it!"

Timmie began to tremble in Morgan's grasp. "I done a bad thing, Mr. Kane. Simon Maphis came along and threatened me into stealing your horses. I won't lie to you, he also promised to pay me. . . ."

"I had already surmised that," Morgan said impatiently. "But that's not the important thing. What do you know about Cat?"

Stumbling over the words, Timmie related what had happened in the tavern and the words he had overheard about Cat. "That was back a ways, Mr. Kane. I hurried as fast as I could, but I had no horse and had to hoof it, getting a ride now and then. But they have horses, you see, and were ahead of me all the way. I guess I was able to almost catch up to them tonight 'cause they been lurking around, awaiting their chance."

"Timmie . . . this is important. I don't doubt that Brawley and Maphis are behind it, but did you overhear anything else, anything that might give us an idea of where they may go with her?"

Timmie was silent for a moment, thinking hard. Then he bobbed his head. "It could be they're taking her to Maphis's boat, the *King*. I did overhear them talking about having left Albany a week afore we did so they could always be ahead of us. They left the *King* somewhere along this stretch, then doubled back on horseback, keeping pace with us."

Morgan chewed his lip thoughtfully. "That sounds like the logical place to take her and hole up. Are they aware that you know this?"

"I don't think so, Mr. Kane. It was afore we were in the tavern that I overheard them talking. They didn't know I was listening."

Morgan nodded. "It sounds like my best shot. Let's just hope I'm right!" He became brisk, motioning for Mick and Timmie to follow him back to the *Cat II*. "I'm going after them as soon as I pick up my pistol."

"I'm going with you, lad," Mick said vehemently.

"No, Mick, you stay here. Somebody has to stay with the boat. If anything happens to it, you know how Cat would feel."

"My daughter's welfare is more important than any bloody boat!"

Morgan smiled thinly. "I can't argue with that, but I can travel faster alone, Mick. Speed is of the essence now. The longer it takes to catch up to them, the more danger Cat is in. They're going to be in a hurry, and I'm wagering she'll be all right until they reach Maphis's boat, where they'll think they're safe."

"But you can't handle those two alone!"

"I can and I will," Morgan said grimly. "I'll have the element of surprise in my favor. They'll expect us to come haring after them, but they won't realize that we know their destination. I just hope to God I'm right about that part!"

Timmie said eagerly, "Maybe I should go with you, Mr. Kane. It's me to blame, anyways."

"Not really, lad." Morgan patted his shoulder. "This would have happened, one way or another, without you. It's partly my fault. I should have been more on guard, knowing that pair like I do. No, you stay here with Mick. The pair of you see what you can do to keep the *Cat II* moving. You know, Mick, that Anderson only needs an excuse to turn thumbs-down on us."

They were at the gangplank, and Morgan started across at a brisk pace.

Mick said unhappily, "I'm thinking it's not right to let you go chasing that pair of villains by yourself, bucko."

On deck, Morgan faced him squarely. "Mick, you're forcing me to be brutally frank, but this is not the time to be polite. You'd only be in the way. You're an old man, Mick, and not yet fully recovered from the attack on you. I am going alone."

Mick recoiled with a hurt look, and his mouth opened and shut as he tried to speak and could not.

"I'm sorry, Mick. You know how close you are in my affections, but I'm telling the truth, and you know it, in your heart." He clasped the Irishman's shoulder, squeezing.

Mick nodded, blinking back sudden tears. "Yes, I know you're right. Good hunting, lad. May the saints watch over you."

Ten minutes later, Morgan, his pistol in his belt and spare cartridges in his pocket, rode one of the fresher horses up the towpath at a gallop, leading another. He was riding bareback, since there were no saddles available. He railed at himself for not having had the foresight to bring along a riding horse and saddle; these two horses were work animals, not built for speed. He judged that Maphis and Brawley had a good half-hour lead on him and were certain to be riding saddle horses. There were two things in his favor. On such a dark and foggy night, they dared not risk riding too fast, and probably Cat had been forced to double up on one of the horses, unless they had thought to bring a spare.

But if he had guessed wrong, if they were heading east instead of west . . .

He shook his head, forcing such thoughts from his mind. They *had* to be heading in this direction.

He pushed the animals to their limit, heedless of the dark night, changing horses every hour or so.

* * *

Cat, still slightly befuddled from the cuff Maphis had given her on the head when she had fought him, rode in front of him on his big horse. She was gagged, her hands tied behind her back, and Maphis had his arms around her as he held the reins. Every time she tried to struggle, he clamped his arms like a vise, squeezing the breath from her; and she finally realized that it was useless to struggle in her present position, and rode quietly, her head drooping, her mind filled with despair. The fate that was in store for her unless she managed to escape was too terrible to contemplate. Brawley and Maphis had quarreled about that as they rode.

After a few miles along the towpath, Maphis had said hoarsely, "When are we going to stop, Tate, so I can have at her?"

"Not now, you idiot," Brawley hissed. "Do you think they're going to just let us ride off and not follow? Kane is not a fellow to give up that easily."

"But how're they going to know which direction we went? In this fog they didn't see which way we took."

"Kane will know we'll follow the canal, so he'll have a fifty-fifty chance at guessing right. If he does guess right and comes this way, he's right back there on our heels."

"But when, Tate?" Maphis whined. "When do I get her?"

"Curb your appetites, Simon, that's the ticket. There'll be time enough when we get to your boat."

"Kane'll never find us once we get to the *King*," Maphis said confidently. "He won't have an idea in hell as to who took her."

"He's not stupid, he'll know we're the likely ones."

"That ain't good enough. Once we do get to my boat, he won't dare do anything, not knowing for absolute sure."

"Just be quiet and ride," Brawley said tersely.

They rode on into the night. Cat was sure that Morgan would come after her, but what if these two were right? Once they had made it to Maphis's boat, Morgan would never find her. She vowed that Maphis would never have her; she would fight him to the death.

Even as she thought this, one of his hands groped for her, finding her breast and squeezing hard. Cat squirmed, trying to cry out through the gag.

Brawley must have heard something, for he said, "What's up over there?"

Maphis chuckled hoarsely. "Just sampling the goodies, Tate."

"Dammit, can't you wait? Concentrate on moving."

Maphis removed his hand, but from time to time he managed to touch Cat, brushing her thigh or her breast as though inadvertently. Soon it grew light, and Cat sighed with relief. He would have to keep his hands to himself now, or Brawley would notice. From time to time, as surreptitiously as possible, she strained against the bonds around her wrists, as she had been doing since she had been captured. It seemed to her that the bonds were looser than they had been at the start, yet that could be wishful thinking on her part.

As the sun came up, Cat craned around to look back, trying to see if Morgan was behind them. There was no one in sight along the towpath as far as she could see, yet there was still some fog lingering along the ground.

Maphis slapped the side of her head. "Eyes forward, missy," he said jeeringly. "That man of yours ain't never going to find you."

"But others might see us, and wonder what we're doing carrying a woman tied and gagged," Brawley said worriedly. "How much farther? I thought your boat was closer than this."

"Just a little farther, Tate. Don't fret, nobody will be up and about this early. It's too early even for the canal walkers. We'll get there safe and sound. And then, missy, we'll have us a high old time." He gave Cat a hard shake. "The King will make you forget Morgan Kane!"

Cat's heart plummeted. How would Morgan ever find

them once they were hidden away on Maphis's boat? She was going to have to rely on her own resources, that was all. Well, she had thwarted Simon Maphis once before, and she was determined to do so again.

True to Maphis's word, they soon came to a side-cut leading off the canal. At a word from Maphis, they rode along the cut for about forty yards. He had maneuvered the *King* into some high rushes, and it was partially hidden.

Brawley looked around as he slid off his horse. Maphis also got down, then lifted Cat off the horse. After riding for so long, Cat's legs were weak, and she would have fallen if he had not held her by the arm.

"Hide the horses over there, Simon, in those trees." Brawley motioned to a grove of small trees to the right. "Hide them well. I'll take the woman on board."

"Why can't I do that, Tate? She's mine, you promised!"

"I won't touch a hair on her head, Simon. I like my women willing. You're the expert on canals, you can place the animals out of sight better than I can."

Grumbling, Maphis complied, leading the horses away; and Brawley shoved Cat ahead of him toward the *King*. Under his breath Brawley said, "An animal, that's all he is. I should never have . . ." He raised his voice slightly. "I would advise you to submit to him, Miss Carnahan. If you do not, I can't be responsible for the consequences."

Stepping from the gangplank onto the deck, she faced him, trying to articulate words through the gag.

"Oh, I am sorry." He removed the gag. Almost apologetically, he said, "We had to do that; we couldn't risk your screaming."

Taking several quick gulps of fresh air, Cat said, "I will never submit to him, never! He *is* an animal, as you seem to realize, so why are you in cahoots with him?"

"One has to make do in this world," Brawley said with a philosophical shrug. "Please go down below; I don't wish to force you."

"No? I didn't realize you were such a gentleman, Mr. Brawley."

"I was once, but circumstances changed me." His voice hardened. "Miss Carnahan, do not mistake me. I am not your savior. I will not interfere with Simon's plans for you. I may not wholly approve, but I will not interfere."

Hoping to sting him into being incautious, she said, "You're a fraud, you know that? You make a pretense at being a gentleman, yet you're as much a brute as Maphis is!"

His eyes flashed dangerously, and he raised a hand to slap her, then used it to stroke his side whiskers instead, smiling coldly. "You are trying to provoke me, but it will not work."

"I don't understand why you're doing this then, if not for what Maphis has in mind."

"Why, to get at Morgan Kane, of course. I want to hurt him any way I can. He's the cause of all of my misfortunes of late. But do not mistake me again. I care little what happens to you. I shall be honest—you will never leave this boat alive."

Cat went cold all over as she stared into his implacable eyes.

He said, "But I am not interested in sexual congress with you, Miss Carnahan. You had your opportunity, and spurned me. For that you will suffer, but at Simon's hands, not mine. He wants the Carnahans to suffer, and I want Kane to suffer. Our immediate aim is to disrupt your trial run for the mail contract, and I think this will accomplish that. Kane will come looking for you, and I doubt that your father can operate the packet alone."

He was interrupted by the heavy tread of Maphis's footsteps on the deck. "The horses are well hidden, Tate. What's this, you haven't taken her below yet?"

Brawley turned his cold smile on Maphis. "I was waiting to give you that pleasure, Simon."

"Gladly. Let's go below, eh, missy?"

Maphis stepped to her, picked her up in his arms, and started to manhandle her below. She managed to scream once, piercingly, before he clamped a hand over her mouth.

"You shouldn't've ungagged her, Tate. The bitch's scream can be heard a mile."

Morgan had almost reached the point of complete despair; he was beginning to think that he had ridden in the wrong direction. When the sun came up, he could see nothing ahead except patches of fog. And then a freshening breeze came up, dispersing the fog, and he could see all the way to the lock at the end of this level stretch. There were no horses on the towpath; and although he could see a half-dozen canal boats waiting to pass through the lock, he did not think that Brawley and Maphis would have the gall to take the *King* through the lock with a captive woman on board.

If he had to ride back the other way in search of Cat, it was hopeless. He had only one horse left; the other one had collapsed just before dawn, and the one he was riding was nearly finished.

As he came up to a narrow side-cut leading off the main canal, Morgan reined in, trying to calculate his next move. He supposed he should at least question the canal people to see if they had seen the *King* anywhere. He had started to drum his heels against the weary horse's flanks when he was arrested by a shrill scream somewhere down the cut. It was Cat, it had to be!

Imbued with exultation, tempered by the fear that the scream meant that he was too late, he urged the horse down the treacherous bank of the cut. The cut had apparently been abandoned for some time, since trees grew over the bank, with high rushes sprouting out of the rank water. Then, about thirty yards along the cut, he saw the outlines of a boat. He pulled the horse off into the trees and quickly dismounted. Pistol in hand, he advanced cautiously through the rushes, finally parting them a few feet from the boat, and his heart began to hammer as he saw the lettering on the side of the boat: KING.

The boat was eerily quiet, seemingly deserted. Had they come and gone, or had they not come here with Cat after all? Then he saw fresh hoofprints in the soft earth around the end of the gangplank on the bank. He thought for a moment, debating exactly how he should proceed. If she was still alive, it would not be wise to make his presence known until he could locate her on the boat; they might kill her the instant they knew he was close to them. Morgan knew that it was very difficult to step on board a canal boat without causing movement and thus being detected, but he had no choice.

He stepped onto the gangplank and began to inch forward a step at a time, treading as softly as possible, alert for the slightest sound.

The moment they were all inside Maphis's cabin, Brawley shot the bolt on the door. Cat was appalled at the condition of the cabin: it was filthy, with molding food on the table and a layer of dirt on the deck. The single bunk was unmade, and the blankets were a dingy gray—and that was where Maphis was carrying her! She struggled, kicking out with her feet, trying to butt his chin with her head.

Maphis laughed. "Feisty little wench, ain't you?" He tightened his arms around her.

Cat subsided, furtively straining against her bonds again. Had they given a little?

Maphis dumped her onto the filthy bunk and stood back, his sausagelike fingers working at the buttons on his breeches.

Brawley said in disgust, "Can't you even wait a bit?"

"I've waited long enough, Tate. No more waiting. If you don't want to watch, go outside. Or turn your head."

Past him, Cat could see Brawley watching, his eyes bright and hard, and she had to wonder, despite his protestations to the contrary, if she would not have to endure his attack upon her body as well. She was sickened by the thought of both of these animals taking turns at her.

Maphis dropped his breeches and she saw his member stiff and throbbing. It was huge . . . frighteningly huge. His face was red, and he was panting loudly.

He put one knee on the low bunk, and let it rest there for a moment while he shoved her dress up to her breasts. He pawed at her, seizing a handful of her undergarments and ripping them from her. The sight of her nakedness inflamed him, and he braced a hand on the slat railing at the side of the bunk, as he prepared to hoist himself on top of her.

Without further thought, Cat drew one leg up as far as she could, and kicked out viciously, her booted foot smashing into his groin.

Maphis howled like an animal feeling the cut of the lash, and rolled off the bunk. His flailing hand gripped the slat, loosening it, and then he was on the deck. Still howling with agony, he doubled over, holding himself.

Cat aimed a glance at Brawley and saw that he was laughing. Then his gaze drifted to her, and at the sight of her exposed body, his eyes glazed with lust. He took a single step toward her, then froze as the boat trembled slightly, and Cat heard the sound of running footsteps overhead. Brawley drew his pistol and stood poised as the steps stopped at the cabin door and Morgan shouted, "Cat! Are you in there?"

Brawley moved with the speed of a cougar, clamping his hand over her mouth before she could cry out.

"Brawley? I know you and Maphis are in there with Cat," Morgan yelled. He pounded on the door. "Timmie told me you were taking her and coming to Maphis's boat. If you so much as harm a hair on her head, you won't live long enough to regret it!"

Brawley's face flushed with anger, and he whipped around at the moaning Maphis, forgetting about Cat. "You loose-lipped idiot! I told you to keep your mouth shut around that hoggee! Now look at the fix you've got us in!" He aimed the pistol at the big man's head. "I kept telling myself to dump you."

He fired. The bullet tore into Maphis between his eyes, staring up at Brawley in sudden fear. He arched up off the floor, then fell back, as his blood mingled with the dirt on the deck.

Cat felt bile rise to her throat, and time seemed frozen, as Brawley stared down at the man he had killed. Even Morgan was quiet beyond the cabin door. Cat was the first to break the stasis. She strained against her bonds with all her strength, and they snapped. She was free! At the same time, Morgan threw himself against the heavy door. Brawley spun around, his weapon pointed at the door. Unnoticed, Cat sat up, looking wildly around for a weapon, for anything she could use.

Her elbow grazed the side slat Maphis had loosened in falling. Her hands had little feeling left in them from being bound so long, and she did not know how much strength she possessed. She gripped the slat and yanked; it came free easily. She got to her feet; and holding the slat high, she brought it whistling down across Brawley's extended arm. There was a snapping sound, and the pistol fell from his hand and clattered to the deck.

Brawley stared down at his arm, dangling at an odd angle. Then he looked at her in disbelief. "You broke it, you bitch, you broke my arm!"

Cat was already sidling around him toward the door. Without once taking her gaze from him, she bent and scooped up the pistol, but he was no longer interested in her as the pain hit him. With a whimper he dropped down onto the bunk she had just vacated, tenderly cradling the broken arm.

Cat backed up to the door, fumbled behind her for the bolt, and drew it back, just as Morgan charged the door once more. It burst open, and Cat managed to step out of the way just in time. Pistol in hand, Morgan stumbled past her and skidded to a stop. His glance took in the still Maphis on the deck, and Brawley on the bunk, holding his arm.

"Cat?" Morgan said on a rising note of alarm. "Where are you?"

"Over here, Morgan," she said with a shaky laugh. "And I'm fine. You came to my rescue just in time."

"But what happened in here? Maphis looks dead, and Brawley is not in too good a shape either." He turned to stare at her. "Did you do all that?"

Cat smiled wanly. "I can't take credit for all of it. . . ." Suddenly weak, she groped for a chair at the table and sat down.

Keeping a wary eye on Brawley, Morgan stepped to her. "Are you sure you're all right?"

"Not really, but it's just the reaction setting in. I'll be all right in a bit. To finish answering your question, Brawley killed Maphis, and when you distracted him, I broke his arm with the side slat from the bunk."

Morgan shook his head in wonder. "It would appear that I really didn't need to come to your rescue at all."

"Not true, Morgan." She took his hand and squeezed hard. "It wouldn't have turned out like this if you hadn't come battering on the door. Maphis was about to . . . attack me. I did save myself from that."

"That's when you screamed? But for hearing that, I likely would never have found you."

"No, I screamed when Maphis started to haul me into the cabin."

"And Brawley just shot Maphis in cold blood?"

"Pretty much," she said, nodding. "I gathered that Brawley has been displeased with him for some time, and when you shouted that Timmie had told you where to find us, that seemed to trigger something in him. He seemed to blame Maphis for that, for talking too much, I guess."

Morgan was smiling at Brawley in satisfaction. "I think we can safely turn him over to the law now, Cat. Not only did he abduct you, a crime in itself, but he killed his own partner in cold blood, not even in self-defense. He'll pay and pay heavily for that."

She said doubtfully, "I'm not all that sure, Morgan. You know the low esteem the law has for canawlers."

He was shaking his head. "That doesn't apply in this instance. The whole Erie is proud of the Carnahans and what you're doing. For someone to try and discredit us on the mail run, committing murder in the bargain, will not be tolerated. You'll see."

"That reminds me. Where is the packet? And is Mick all right?"

"So far as I know, he is. *Cat II* is somewhere back behind me, but moving this way, I hope."

"Did Timmie really come back and tell you about Maphis and Brawley?"

"Yes, but I'll tell you about that later. Right now, let's get Brawley to the nearest constable. They had saddle horses, I assume?"

"Oh, yes. Maphis hid them nearby."

"Then we'll take them. They stole our animals, so I figure it's an even swap."

The day was almost over by the time they had found a constable, told him what had happened, and directed him to Maphis's body. The constable had promised to prosecute Brawley for abduction and murder to the full extent of the law. Finally, the sun lowering behind their backs, they rode east along the towpath.

Morgan stood in the stirrups and squinted ahead. "I had hoped they would be here by now," he said worriedly. "I pray that nothing has happened to them. Of course, they only have one team of horses, and they're worn out." He glanced over at Cat. "We'd better move along at a fast clip. They may be in some difficulty. At least we have saddle horses, and they're relatively fresh."

They urged the horses into a gallop, and rode along without speaking for a time. Cat damned the day she had let Morgan persuade her to wear a dress on the towpath. She had to bunch the dress up around her thighs, and she had no undergarments; Maphis had shredded them beyond repair. Morgan had sent one glance her way, then had averted his gaze, and had not looked at her since.

Strangely, Cat could not keep her mind on the plight of the packet, although she hoped nothing had happened to her father; her thoughts kept straying to Morgan. She knew that he was acutely aware of her dishabille, and this caused her to smile to herself.

At dusk she began to lag behind, and shortly Morgan noticed it. Several yards ahead of her, he reined in, letting his horse drop back beside hers. "Anything the matter, Cat? I suppose you're worn out; you've had a rough time of it."

"That's not it, I was thinking of something else. Does that remind you of anything, Morgan?"

They were abreast of a cut, and she indicated a copse of trees at the point of the triangle formed by the intersection of the side-cut and the Erie.

He followed the direction of her pointing finger, then looked at her curiously. "The place where we made love that night?"

"It does look like it, doesn't it?" she said ingenuously.

His grin came slowly. "But what about the *Cat II*?"

"I'm sure Mick and Timmie can manage for a bit longer."

He threw back his head and roared with laughter. "You, Catherine Carnahan, are shameless!"

"But isn't it customary for a gallant knight to claim his reward for rescuing a damsel in distress?"

"I don't know what fairy tales you've been reading, my dear. I certainly never read one that mentioned *that* particular reward. And as I said before, I hardly rescued you; but on the other hand, I've never been known to spurn a fair lady." He drummed his heels against the horse's flanks. "Come on, fair damsel!"

He rode recklessly down the bank, and Cat sent her horse after him. By the time she reached the trees, he had already dismounted. He held up his arms, and she slid off into them. He sought her mouth, and they kissed passionately. Pressing against him, she could feel his tumescence through his breeches.

"Cat, darling Cat," he murmured. "When I couldn't find you, I was near despair. I knew that my life would be over if I couldn't find you in time."

Lifting her high, he strode to the nearest tree, and stretched her out on the ground. Spring flowers were still growing, and Cat smelled the scent of crushed blossoms. She breathed deeply of the perfumed air, and waited impatiently for him to remove his clothes and join her.

On his knees, he stared down at her, his face luminescent in a splash of moonlight. "Must I undress you?"

"It isn't necessary." She pulled up her skirts. "Simon Maphis took care of that."

Staring down, Morgan sucked in his breath. "Ah, Cat, I am sorry. The filthy carrion!"

"When I knew he was about to ravish me, you know what I thought about, Morgan? I wondered if you would ever want to touch me again."

"Always, Cat, always." He reached down a hand, stroking.

"Oh, Morgan!" She shuddered, closing her eyes tightly. "Make love to me, darling. Make me forget Maphis!"

Without further ado, he entered her. She shivered with joy. It felt good, it felt marvelous! No other man could ever make her feel this way.

She reached up and locked her arms around his neck, pulling his mouth down to hers; and they became one, moving in perfect harmony toward that mutual goal of fulfillment. And when it happened, Cat cried out, and her world seemed to go out of orbit, as wave after wave of pure sensation brought her to the final explosion of pleasure. Morgan shouted aloud, his body shuddering mightily.

When her world was finally sane again, Cat, strangely, thought of Anthony Mason, thought of him for the first time in days; she hoped that he was as happy as she was at this moment. She had not seen him since Morgan had come back into her life, but she had heard that he had followed her advice and employed Lotte Pryor as his nurse. . . .

Morgan interrupted her thoughts. "Cat, what are you thinking? You seem somewhere far off."

She smiled radiantly. "I'm thinking how happy I am. As Mick would say, by the saints, I am!"

He kissed her. "Speaking of which, we'd better be getting on."

"Now that you've had your way with me?"

He said gruffly, "It strikes me that it was rather the other way around."

In a short time they were on their way again. It was just after dawn when they finally saw the *Cat II*. The boat was pulled off into a side-cut, and there was no sign of activity.

"I wonder why they're just setting there," Cat said.

"I don't have the slightest idea, but I guess we'll soon find out."

As they stepped on board, Mick came out of the main cabin. His eyes lit up. "Catherine! By the saints, it's glad I am to see you safe and sound!"

He held out his arms, and she ran into them. Over her head Mick questioned Morgan with his eyes. Morgan said, "Yes, Mick, she's fine. I got to her in time."

Mick said fervently, "Thanks be to God for that, lad!"

Cat stood back, dashing tears from her eyes. "But why is the boat just setting here, Mick?"

"The horses plain gave out on us, girl. And I didn't know where to get any replacements," he said with a sigh.

"And Lars Anderson?" Morgan asked. "How is he taking to that?"

"Anderson left, lad, just before sundown yesterday," Mick said dolefully. "Someone came along in a buggy and gave him a ride. I tried to get him to wait until you two returned, but the bloody fool wouldn't listen. He said it was clear to him that we wouldn't be able to provide proper mail service, and that's what he's going to report to his superior in Washington City."

Chapter Twenty-Two

"OH, no!" Cat exclaimed in distress. "Now what are we going to do?"

Morgan ignored her question, staring at her father. He said slowly, "I suppose it'd do no good to try and fetch him back?"

"I'm thinking it would be a waste of time, lad. He had his mind set against us from the very beginning, you know that."

"Yes, I know. Damn!" Morgan struck his fist against the railing. "We were so close." He stared along the canal, his shoulders slumped.

"Morgan . . ." Cat took his hand. "Don't feel bad. We did our very best, God knows. If it hadn't been for what happened, we'd be in Buffalo now, or very close." Then she let her own distress show. "But what *are* we going to do?"

He turned his head, his eyes dull. "I don't know, Cat." He looked at Mick. "How are the passengers taking it? Are they all still on board?"

"Oh, yes, I made sure of that. I made free with the drink last night, and most took good advantage of it. They're still sleeping it off."

"Then, by God, we've got a load of passengers to deliver to their destination!" Morgan said energetically. "And there's still a good chance, if we get under way at once, that we can set a new speed record. We can use the horses we rode in on, Cat, until we get to the lock. There will be four fresh horses waiting for us there. This pair may not take to the traces very well, but they'll get us that far." He clapped his hands together.

Cat caught his enthusiasm. "Yes! We'll show them the caliber of the Carnahans *and* Morgan Kane."

Morgan asked, "Is Timmie still around?"

Mick nodded. "I sent the lad off to bed; he was plain worn out."

Morgan turned to Cat and quickly explained how Timmie had betrayed them.

Cat said pensively, "I guess I was wrong about him, Morgan."

"But the question is, do we give him a second chance? I'm for it, if for no other reason than the fact that he's a good hoggee and we need him."

"I suppose we must," she said with a sigh. She looked at Morgan with a slight smile. "Now that we've lost the mail contract, you don't have any ideas, Mr. Kane? You always seem to have one."

"Not this time," he said glumly. "I seem to be all out of fresh ideas. But give me time."

"We could use one." She faced Mick and said briskly, "Mick, you whip up a good breakfast for the passengers. Morgan, you roust Timmie out and hitch up the team, and I'll man the tiller. Let's get under way."

"Yes, sir, Captain!" Morgan saluted smartly. "Right away, Captain!"

"Well, I *am* the captain. That was your idea, remember?"

"I remember, but I'm not sure it was one of my better ones," he said gravely, but his eyes had a merry twinkle.

"Oh, get on with you," she said, and could no longer contain her laughter.

"That's my sweet Cat," he said; and cupping her face tenderly between his hands, he kissed her. As Mick went into the main cabin, Morgan whispered, "But we won't have any time to spare for a tryst under the trees, if we aim to set the record."

"I can wait until Buffalo. After all, I waited the whole winter long."

"Did you now? I wonder."

Before she could frame a retort, he was gone in search of Timmie.

The rest of the trip was uneventful, and they made good time to Buffalo. A large crowd awaited them there on the dock, and a great cheer went up as *Cat II* came in. Mick went ashore at once, while Morgan and Cat stood at the head of the gangplank, thanking the passengers for their patronage. As the last one disembarked, Mick came charging back along the gangplank.

"I just got the word, children! We set a new speed record!" He capered, performing an impromptu Irish jig.

Morgan let out a whoop, picked Cat up in his arms, and whirled her around. "We did it, Cat!"

She was out of breath when he set her down. "At least we accomplished something."

Mick said, "Something? Girl, I'm thinking 'tis a grand accomplishment, something no one else has ever done."

Morgan said abruptly, "I have some things to see to. I'll be back before dark."

As he strode toward the gangplank, Cat said, "Morgan? Where are you going?"

He continued on as if he had not heard her.

"Damn and blast that man!" she said explosively. "He has a habit of just taking off without a word of explanation."

"Morgan's not a lad a girl can be after keeping on a leash, Catherine."

"A leash? Since when have I tried to do that?"

"You know who I saw on the wharf?" Mick said slyly, gazing off. "Your doctoring fellow."

"Anthony?" she said in astonishment. "Anthony's here in Buffalo?"

"Yup. Several days, he said, waiting for us."

"Why didn't he come back with you?"

"Why don't you ask him? His boat is docked over there a ways." Mick indicated the direction with a nod.

Cat pondered for a moment. "I think I will. And if Mr. Kane comes back, asking where I am, tell him that I had some 'things to see to.' "

As Cat marched across the gangplank, her back stiff with indignation, Mick watched her with a fond smile. He knew what she would find on board the *Paracelsus*, and that pleased him mightily. He also knew the situation between Morgan and his daughter, and that pleased him even more.

As she approached the *Paracelsus*, Cat saw Anthony sitting alone under the strip of canvas at the tiller, his pipe going. He was sitting with his back to her, staring out at the canal traffic.

But when she started across the gangplank, he turned with a start, then rose to his feet with a smile. He met her at the end of the gangplank and helped her on board.

He stood with both her hands in his, his gaze searching her face. He said, "I'm delighted to see you, Cat. It's been a while, hasn't it?"

"Yes, it has, Anthony," she said, nodding. "And I'm happy to see you, too."

"Congratulations on your speed record. That must make you proud and happy."

"Yes, I'm quite pleased." She decided not to tell him that they had lost the mail contract.

"Come, come along up to the tiller, and tell me about your trip. It must have been exciting."

There was a faint air of reserve about him, but she could hardly expect him to greet her with open arms, after all that had happened.

They sat down together, and Anthony smoked quietly as Cat told him about their trip.

"This Maphis and Brawley seem a proper pair of blackguards," he commented.

"They were, a dastardly pair," she said heavily. "Thank God they'll no longer be around to plague us."

"You intend to stay in the passenger business?"

She nodded. "We hope to, yes."

"By 'we' I suppose you include Morgan Kane?" he said quizzically. "I heard that he was back."

"Yes, Morgan has been invaluable. Without him it would never have happened."

He looked at her intently. "Are you happy, Cat?"

She nodded, feeling color stain her cheeks. "And you, Anthony? Are you happy?"

Before he could answer, he looked past her and rose to his feet. Cat looked around and saw Lotte Pryor coming across the cabin toward them. She looked very pretty. Her step faltered as she recognized Cat, then she came on.

"There you are, Lotte." Anthony gave her a hand down from the cabin. "As you can see, Cat, I took your advice, and you were right. Lotte has become a skilled nurse. All she needed was a chance to do something worthwhile."

"Hello, Cat," Lotte said shyly. "I haven't seen you since I was ill, and I never did get a chance to thank you for nursing me back to health. I'm also grateful to you for suggesting that Anthony employ me."

A little taken aback, Cat murmured, "That's all right. I'm just happy that it worked out for you."

"I don't know what I would have done but for Anthony." Lotte flashed Anthony a stunning smile.

"How is your father, the reverend?"

Lotte shrugged. "He's gone."

"Gone?" Cat echoed.

"Yes, he left the Erie some weeks ago. He said that he couldn't bear the shame of it. First I sinned and caught the cholera, and now I'm living on a boat with a man, in an unmarried state. He's gone back to where we were before, to try and get a parish there."

Anthony took Lotte's hand and stared directly into Cat's eyes. "Lotte and I are to be married, Cat. That's why we were waiting here for you, hoping you'd be her bridesmaid."

Cat felt a tug of anger. The nerve of him, asking *her* to be a bridesmaid when he married another woman! Then she began to smile, both at herself and at them. It was obvious that they were in love and very happy.

"I would be glad to," she said simply, taking both their hands. "And I wish you both all the happiness in the world."

Walking back to her own boat a short while later, Cat was angry all over again, not at Anthony and Lotte, but at Morgan. Damn and blast him! He had told her he loved her, but he had not asked her to marry him; he had not even so much as mentioned marriage. Maybe he had no intention of marrying her. He had all the privileges of marriage now, without the responsibilities that went with it. . . .

She stopped short in her tracks.

What was she thinking? She was the independent one, the one who had refused to tell Morgan that she loved him, who had wanted no commitment, the one who had said that she was not ready for marriage. What had changed? She had changed, she must be honest with herself; it was foolish to pretend that she had not. She loved Morgan. If he was to leave her again, her life would never be quite the same, and the only sure way to keep him with her would be to marry him.

She determined to do something about it at once. Consequently, when she made it back to the *Cat II* and found that Morgan still had not returned, she was frustrated and upset. She paced, waiting impatiently for him to return.

It was almost dark when she saw him swinging along the dock, walking with a light step. As he got closer, she heard him whistling tunelessly. We lost the mail contract, we don't know if we can survive without it, she thought dourly, and he's behaving as if he hasn't a care in the world!

"Where have you been, Morgan?" she demanded the instant he stepped on board.

"You know, Cat, Buffalo is growing. There's a new restaurant just opened, rather elegant, I must say, for this part of the world. I thought we'd have supper there tonight. You even have to make a reservation. Can you imagine that?"

Cat gritted her teeth. "You didn't answer my question. Where have you been?"

"Oh, didn't I tell you?" he said with an innocent look.

"Damn and blast you, Morgan Kane! You know very well that you didn't!"

"Must have been an oversight," he said blithely. "There was someone I wanted to see in town."

"See about what?"

"Well, since we lost the mail contract, I figured it was up to me to get something to replace it."

Interested in spite of herself, Cat said, "Did you?"

"I did," he said somewhat smugly.

"Well, what?"

"Come on, let's get comfortable." Taking her hand, he led her across the cabin to the chairs by the tiller. "It has to do, partly, with this new restaurant I told you about. Some time ago I met a man in Syracuse by the name of Henry Wells. He works in Syracuse as a forwarder of freight and passengers both along the Erie and to points inland by stagecoach. The man is a visionary, with some grand ideas. He believes that express freight can become a reality along the Erie."

Morgan grinned faintly. "He even believes that the mail will eventually be carried by mail packet. That's how I fell into conversation with him. Most people laugh at his ideas, but then people have always laughed at a fellow with ideas before his time."

She said impatiently, "Will you please get to the point, Morgan?"

"I will, if you give me time," he said with his lazy grin. "The point of all this has to do with Henry Wells and the new restaurant here in Buffalo. He told me in Syracuse that he was coming here, and I had hoped that he would still be here when we arrived. Well, he was, and this is his idea. He talked the restaurant into buying the first shipment of fresh oysters ever to arrive in Buffalo!"

Cat was puzzled. "Fresh oysters? From the Atlantic Ocean?"

Morgan nodded. "That's it. They will be rushed up the Hudson by steamboat to Albany, where they will be shucked, packed in ice in containers, and hurried toward Buffalo by canal boat, with stops along the way for fresh ice, when the old melts."

"What does all this have to do with us?"

"What do you think, Cat?" He leaned forward. "He's agreed to let *Cat II* carry his oysters. He was quite excited when I told him about our speed record."

"He has! Oh, Morgan! You're a wonder!" She jumped to her feet and leaned down to kiss him. Then doubts set in. "But if we fail, it'll be worse than the mail run. If for some reason we're late, the oysters will spoil, and everybody will laugh at us."

"We won't fail, Cat. I have some ideas already. For instance, instead of using relay teams of two horses, why not teams of four, eight altogether?"

"Speaking of ideas . . ." She peered at him suspiciously. "You told me a few days ago that you were fresh out of ideas."

"At the time I was," he said with a shrug. "When I talked with Wells in Syracuse, we were only talking of the future, carrying perishable goods, fruits and vegetables, and express packages. I thought we might have a chance at that, if we won the mail contract. He made no mention of oysters then. By the way, we're having supper with Wells tonight, at the restaurant. He wants to meet you."

The mention of supper brought to mind what she was going to confront him with. "I saw Dr. Mason and Lotte

Pryor this afternoon, Morgan. They're to be married tomorrow, and they want me to be her bridesmaid."

"How about that? Lotte getting wed? Well, she might make the doctor a good wife. But instead of a bridesmaid, why not a bride?"

"And that's what I want to discuss with you, about us . . ." She stopped short, mouth agape as the import of his words sank in. "What did you just say?"

He had a twinkle in his eyes. "I said, why not make it a double wedding?"

She gave a shout of joy. "Oh, Morgan! Yes, yes!"

She flew at him, and he stood up quickly in time to catch her in his arms. She rained kisses on his face, then buried her face against his shoulder, tears of happiness burning her eyes.

Over her head Morgan saw Mick approaching along the cabin. The Irishman stopped short, and Morgan winked at him. Mick threw his hands high, performed a few jig steps, then turned and tiptoed away.

Morgan held Cat away and looked down into her eyes. "Cat, I've waited a long time for you to say something, and I think now is the time."

She looked at him in confusion. "Waited? For what, Morgan? I've just told you that I'd marry you."

He smiled, but there was still a question in his eyes. "Yes, but do you realize that you have never told me you love me?"

Cat felt herself flush. It was true. She had thought it, and this afternoon she had admitted it to herself, but she had never told him in so many words. The expression in his eyes told her that he needed to hear it, needed to know that he was loved, even as she did.

Rising on tiptoe, she put her arms around his neck and kissed him deeply. Then she took away her lips, moved them to his ear, and whispered, "I love you, Morgan Kane. I love you more than the Erie, more than *Carnahan's Cat*. I love you!"

She stepped back and looked again into his face. His

smile and the glow in his eyes told her that she was giving him as great a gift as he was giving her.

He hugged her close. "We'll be unbeatable together. We'll set the Erie on its ear!"

Cat smiled to herself and pressed even closer to him. She felt happier than she ever had, and at peace with herself and her world.

She and Morgan would have their fights, she knew, and their differences, for she was, as he had often said, a thorny wench, and he was a strong-minded man; but they would always work things out, because they loved each other, and that, after all, was the most important thing.